*The Longer
the Fall*

Praise for
Mortal Touch

Book 1 of the The Vampires of New England Series

"...a wonderful fictional treatment of the authentic vampire tradition in this region... has the honesty and local color that brings the characters and their towns to life and makes the plot palpably real."
Michael Bell, author of *Food for the Dead: On the Trail of New England's Vampires*

"I think you'll be genuinely surprised by some of the twists. Regan is a sympathetic heroine, and Arthen's variation on traditional vampire lore is fresh and well thought-out. The story riveted my attention throughout."
Margaret M. Carter, author of *Dark Changeling, Child of Twilight, Sealed in Blood,* and *Different Blood: The Vampire as Alien*

"*Mortal Touch* is an intriguing vampire adventure. Regan has worked hard to get her life back on track, but somehow trouble has found her once again. In this tension filled paranormal tale, Ms. Arthen develops a nicely detailed world with captivating characters and fascinating twists on vampirism. With a touch of mystery, suspense and passion, this is a wonderful escape from the ordinary."
Kimberly Swan, Darque Reviews

"The story comes alive, riddled with just enough creepiness to enjoy but not so much as to keep the reader awake at night...Inanna Arthen explores vampires in the modern world, attempting to account for both the mundane details and the supernatural, and she does so with relish. She makes vampires seem real, even approachable. That's what is so creepy about this book. You finish it and think—Oh, man! That is too real! I did not want to put *Mortal Touch* down until I had finished it."
Tonia R. Montgomery, Curled Up With a Good Book

"Having read so many vampire novels as I have, it is seldom that I find one that surprises me or that strays enough from the vampire conventions to appear original, and this is why I was pleasantly surprised to read *Mortal Touch*...this is a work that is well written and that at times gets quite suspenseful and horrific...*Mortal Touch* is definitely a novel vampire fiction aficionados will want to add to their collection."
Mayra Calvani, Dark Phantom Reviews

"*Mortal Touch* builds slowly to a swift and exciting end. The visceral violence of the story makes it feel quite personal and in some ways shocking. You can't help but feel the betrayal and powerlessness the characters experience. It's very well written. I also enjoyed that the New England area is like another character in the story."
Vicky London, Vampire Genre

The Vampires of New England Series

The Longer the Fall

Inanna Arthen

By Light Unseen Media
Pepperell, Massachusetts

The Longer the Fall
The Vampires of New England Series
http://vampiresofnewengland.com

Copyright © 2010 by Inanna Arthen and By Light Unseen Media. All rights reserved. No part of this publication may be reproduced, stored in a retrieval system or transmitted in any form or by any means, electronic, mechanical, photocopying, recording, or otherwise without the prior written permission of the copyright holder, except for brief quotations in reviews and for academic purposes in accordance with copyright law and principles of Fair Use.

Cover and interior design by Vyrdolak, By Light Unseen Media.

This is a work of fiction. Names, characters, places and incidents are either the products of the author's imagination or are used fictitiously, and any resemblance to actual persons, living or dead, business establishments, events or locales is entirely coincidental.

Perfect Paperback Edition
ISBN-10: 0-9793028-2-X
ISBN-13: 978-0-9793028-2-4
LCCN: 2010900623

Published by
By Light Unseen Media
PO Box 1233
Pepperell, Massachusetts 01463-3233

Our Mission:
By Light Unseen Media presents the best of quality fiction and non-fiction on the theme of vampires and vampirism. We offer fictional works with original imagination and style, as well as non-fiction of academic calibre.

For additional information, visit:
http://bylightunseenmedia.com/

Printed in the United States of America

0 9 8 7 6 5 4 3 2 1

❧ 1 ☙

Diana got on the road before sunrise that morning, taking US Route 1 up the coast from Boston. Although it was a weekday and school was still in session, the roads were already beginning to fill with vacationers. North of Brunswick the highway veered inland from the shoreline, passing through long expanses of deep fir forest interspersed with a bit of cleared farmland now and then. Occasionally the road crossed long wooden pile bridges that spanned tidal rivers on their way to the sea. The country seemed wild, empty and lonely.

She had been driving for six hours by the time Route 1 passed through Rockland and began working its way along the west side of Penobscot Bay. Caught up in the momentum of her adventure, Diana had stopped for fuel only once, and had snacked on an apple midmorning rather than take the time to sit down in a restaurant. Gas was running at a disgraceful $0.32 north of Portland, three cents more than the city. But at least it was plentiful. In the post-war economic boom, filling stations were appearing everywhere.

On the outskirts of Camden she spotted one of them on the south side of the road, two pumps in front of a small building with a single open bay and a faded Texaco sign over the peeling office door. A piece of plywood leaning against one of the pumps bore a cryptic "25.9" in runny red letters that looked like they'd been written with a blood-soaked finger. She pulled into the station next to the pumps, limestone gravel crunching loudly under the car's wheels. No one was in sight, and after a moment she tapped the horn and turned off the engine. The sudden quiet felt eerie—her ears were humming from the constant noise of the motor.

A young man in grimy blue coveralls emerged from the bay and hastened to her car, smoothing down his close-cropped red hair with one hand. He leaned his arms on the sill of the open driver's side window and peered in at her. "Fill it up, miss?"

Diana drew back an inch or two—his breath had a whiff of Wrigley's Spearmint that was almost obliterated by the intense fume of motor oil and sweat surrounding him like a cloud. "Yes, please. Just regular."

The young man brought the hose around to the side of the car and began pumping. The sharp smell of gas filled the air. "So, you on vacation?"

Diana glanced back at the young man and was amused to see him striking a pose, one hand on the pump, one tucked into a back pocket of his coveralls. "In a manner of speaking."

"You all by yourself?"

"No, my husband's in the trunk." Now there was a satisfying fantasy. The young man laughed, a little too loudly.

"Where you headed?"

"Pepperell."

"Oh, I know Pepp'rell. I got an aunt lives there. That's just the other side to Camden Hills State Park."

"I know."

He finished pumping and went briskly around to raise the engine hood, hissing at the cloud of hot air that stung his face. "You should be careful," he said, giving up on his attempts to open the oil cover. "Your radiator'll boil over. Lady stranded alone on the road, that's something to worry about." He shut the hood forcefully and produced a squirt bottle and long-handled squeegee from next to the pumps.

"In Maine?"

"Well..." he squirted copiously from the bottle. "You might have a long walk, getting help."

"This is a pretty reliable car. I've never had the radiator boil over."

"Ayeh, it's a Chevy. A forty-eight, isn't it? Good car. So, you staying in Pepp'rell?" The young man grunted as he stretched to squeegee the far side of the windshield.

"Yes, for a while, anyway. Anything I should be sure and take in while I'm here?"

"Well...not too many tourist attractions in Pepp'rell. They got summer people, but most of the doin's are in Camden. Nice place, Camden. We got a park down on the harbor, an outdoor theatre—Shakespeare, they do there, and concerts. And an opera house, all kinds of shopping, I know how you girls like to shop..."

"It sounds lovely. But I'll be staying in Pepperell."

"Lots of peace and quiet in Pepp'rell, if that's what you're after." He straightened up, absently wiping beaded sweat off his forehead. "But come to think of it, there is the Hermit of Pepp'rell Hills. Might be worth writing a postcard about, if you saw him."

Diana's mind and eyes had wandered off toward the woods across the road, but at the young man's words, she instantly snapped back to attention. "The Hermit of Pepperell Hills? Who, or what, is that?"

"No one knows, for sure. He owns this big piece of land back of the town, five hundred acres if it's a foot, with some old houses on it, and he lives in one of them. Comes into town sometimes, but mostly you never see him. Grows all his own food. Not an old guy, either. My aunt says he's real good looking, but he must be a vegetarian or something, 'cause he's dead pale and thin as a hoe handle. My aunt thinks he must be one of those...fairies, you know."

"He grows his own food?"

"He must, 'cause he never buys anything from Thornton's—that's the grocery in Pepp'rell. Mr. Thornton would deliver too, anything he wanted, so beats me where this guy gets his food if he doesn't grow it."

"Maybe he shops in Rockland or someplace."

"Sure, except he doesn't have a car. Can you figure that? But I guess he's got a big garden, herbs and everything. And he's got money, too. It's crazy. You want me to check your tires?"

"What?" She blinked, and shook herself. "No, I'm sure they're fine. They're brand new. Tell me, does this hermit have a name?"

"Yeah. Yeah, let me think." He peered off down the road, frowning. "Morris? Morton? Something like that..."

"You don't mean Morgan? Thomas Morgan?"

"Yeah! That's it." He looked down at her and his face suddenly fell. "Oh, gee...gee, I'm sorry, miss. He's not a friend of yours, is he? 'Cause I only know what my aunt says, and she can really get going, you know—"

"It's okay. I've just heard of him. What do I owe you?"

"Uhhh...that'll be two thirty two."

She rummaged in her handbag and gave him exact change, which he accepted with a look of regret.

"Thanks, miss. Stop by again, any time. I'm always here. You have any trouble with the car, you bring it here, nothing I can't fix. Brent Crothers, I'm in the book. Oh, and I do bodywork, too." He turned and gestured toward a car parked on the side of the station, its dark blue finish glistening in the sun. "Matt Taylor got himself rear-ended but good in April, I had to replace the trunk lid, both rear fenders, rocker panels, six coats of paint..."

"It looks brand new." Diana was sincerely impressed. "Well, Brent, if I have the bad luck to get rear-ended, I'll give you a call."

Brent's cheeks turned pink. "Wouldn't want that to happen, no," he said, stammering.

"Of *course* you wouldn't. Thanks, Brent. My name's Diana, I'll probably stop by again." Chuckling, she pulled back onto the road, her fatigue driven away by her growing elation.

Pepperell was one of those tiny New England towns you could easily miss if you sneezed at the wrong time on US 1. Like its sister town in Massachusetts, it had been named after Sir William Pepperell, the Kittery merchant who had won his baronetcy and his fortune by commanding the siege of Louisbourg in 1740. But no statue of Sir William posed on the town green—indeed, the community had no town green at all. The intersection of Main Street and School Street, which literally ran into Penobscot Bay with a pair of boat ramps, marked the center of town. Small businesses and commercial buildings lined Main Street for about a half mile, ending with the Schooner restaurant, which attracted diners from as far as Bangor year-round. From there, Route 1 hurried on to Lincolnville, which had an even more famous restaurant and a prettier beach, and on to Lincolnville was exactly where most vacationers went.

The Holliston House Inn, built in 1888 and boasting a full three stories of spacious suites, occupied the entire upper echelon of Pepperell's accommodations. Its dining room looked out over a rocky waterfront lined with commercial wharves, but along the horizon stretched the misty silhouette of Isleboro Island, like a bank of heather green fog.

The Inn's stateliness prompted Diana to take extra care in fixing her face and wind-snarled black hair before she peeled herself off the seat of her car and went inside. She tucked her black leather portfolio under her arm, unwilling to leave it in the car even for a few minutes. The front hallway was cool and dim, with carpeted oak floors and a wide curving staircase leading to the second story. Behind the desk stood a gray-haired man, suit coat on and buttoned despite the warm temperatures. "Excuse me...Mr. Wilkinson?" Diana said as he glanced up. "I'm Diana Chilton, I telephoned you yesterday."

"Oh, yes. I have a room all ready for you. Did you just arrive?"

"Just, from Boston. I hope you're still serving lunch, because I'm ravenous."

"Lunch is served until three. After that you'll have to settle for dinner," he said, smiling. "Why don't you register and I'll steer you straight for the dining room." He set the open guest book before her. "Are you traveling alone?"

"Yes," she said, thinking irritably, *why does everyone ask that? Do they think I'm hiding someone in my suitcase?* As she took the proffered pen, she added casually, "By the way, I'm supposed to be meeting someone here in town, and I'm not sure exactly where he lives. He wrote to me, but his return address is only a rural delivery number. I was hoping someone could give me directions."

"I'm sure that I can. Who are you looking for?"

"His name is Thomas Morgan."

Mr. Wilkinson pulled his head back, his eyes guarded. "Ah." He put a myriad meanings into that one syllable. "You mean our Hermit."

Diana paused for a moment as she considered the abrupt chill in Mr. Wilkinson's affable expression. "Yes, someone mentioned that you called him that."

"Um-hm. He's a little strange, that one. I'm not sure a young lady should be going out there all by herself."

"Why? Is he dangerous?"

"Who knows? But he's peculiar, no doubt about it. Lives back there all alone, never sees anyone except three or four times a year when he comes into town for something...keeps his hair long, too. He's got a tail right down in back, like he was one of the Founding Fathers. Very peculiar. And he's not too friendly to folks who go poking around up there."

"You mean he shoots at them?"

"Lord, no! We couldn't have that! But once or twice someone has needed to go up there and talk to him about town business, and he all but slammed the door in their face."

Diana signed her name in the guest book and handed back the pen. "I appreciate the information, but I really would like to see Mr. Morgan. Could you tell me how to find him? He is expecting me."

Mr. Wilkinson set the guest book back on its shelf and put both his hands on the desk, facing her squarely. "If he's expecting you, I'm surprised that he didn't give you the directions himself." His voice had a suspicious note.

Diana hesitated, caught, and Mr. Wilkinson raised his eyebrows in an infuriatingly smug way. "Look. I planned this trip at the last minute, and Mr. Morgan doesn't have a telephone. I didn't think it would be so hard to find his house, that I needed to have him draw me a map. He owns five hundred acres, doesn't he?" She rummaged in the leather portfolio and pulled out a small vellum envelope, hand-addressed in neat, angular script. "You see? Here's his letter to me. Note the postmark? And the return address?"

Mr. Wilkinson took the envelope and studied it long enough for Diana to become acutely aware of the soft tick of the antique clock hanging on the wall behind the desk. He had the look of someone who is reluctantly conceding a point, and Diana guessed that he recognized the handwriting. He returned the envelope to her with a shrug. "Take School Street straight back out of town for five miles. You'll come to a crossroads with a big chunk of gray granite by the side of the road and a wood fence to the other side. There's no sign, but everything on your right there is private property. Turn right and follow that road until the first turnoff on the left. There's a big stone house at the end of it. That's where he lives."

She smiled, to take the edge off her minor victory. "Thanks. I really appreciate it. I'm not just trying to annoy him, I promise."

Mr. Wilkinson only shook his head. "People do have a right to be left alone, if that's what they want. Every now and again some antiquarian comes in here wanting to take a look at that house, because it's the oldest one left in the county, built in 1715. I don't think many of them have gotten much of a look at it." He handed her room key to her, frowning.

Diana sighed. "We're both grown-ups, Mr. Wilkinson. If Mr. Morgan doesn't want to meet with me, I'm sure he'll tell me that. Now didn't you say something about lunch?"

She fortified herself with lobster salad and iced tea before testing Mr. Wilkinson's directions, which proved accurate. The lush green, thickly wooded countryside mixed second-growth forest with older patches of tall fir and pine. The air smelled richly of new foliage and there were more birds than Diana had ever seen. The bumpy, curving asphalt road dipped and swooped over the hilly terrain, growing steeper and higher as it wound up into a region unofficially known as Pepperell Hills.

At the granite boulder, Diana pulled up the car and hesitated, peering down the narrow graveled way on the right uncertainly. Finally she made the turn, the crunching stones under her tires sounding painfully loud. She almost missed the driveway Mr. Wilkinson had mentioned, little more than two ruts curving around through the tall grass. She guessed that the property had been cleared and farmed up to a more recent date than most of the surrounding area.

The drive came to an end in a broad open space directly before the house. Diana stopped the car, turned off the engine, and got out, being careful not to let the door slam. Shading her eyes, she gazed up at the building for several minutes. Lichen gave the tightly fitted granite walls a dusky marbling, but the masonry was in good repair. A broad central chimney rose above the hipped slate roof. The front door faced north, and the upper windows must have allowed a long view in all directions at one time. Long meadow grass nodded in the light breezes, mixed with rustling saplings of oak and maple, and the occasional squat little spruce.

She saw no external signs that the house was occupied—no car, no landscaping, no outbuilding, no artifacts or belongings anywhere in the vicinity, and not a scrap of rubbish or debris. The second floor windows appeared to be covered with heavy draperies. Under the mid-afternoon sun, the insects of early summer droned, and in the distance, she could faintly hear the trill of small amphibians in some unseen pond or brook. Behind the soft natural chorus yawned a profound silence, undisturbed by any human sound.

Yet the stillness was not empty. She could *feel* someone inside the house, with her inner senses tuned by years of training—there was a presence there. But as hard as she concentrated, she couldn't determine whether the person she felt was asleep or awake. The ambiguity of what she sensed puzzled her.

Finally she pocketed her car key and walked up to the front door of the house, where a flat wide stone set into the earth marked the threshold. A wrought iron knocker in the shape of a crescent moon was attached to the door. With a deep breath, she took hold of its hinged hammer and knocked smartly three times.

A whip-poor-will rose from the garden behind the house, keening its three-note cry. She detected no sound or movement within the house, and no change in the consciousness that she felt. She knocked harder, then impulsively grasped the door handle and depressed the old-fashioned thumb latch. There was no lock plate or keyhole, but the solid oak door didn't budge when she pushed, and seemed to be bolted or barred from the inside.

After a minute of indecision, Diana stepped back from the door and began to walk around the house. She paused to look furtively into one of the front windows. It belonged to a sort of parlor, with several pieces of nondescript furniture. A large braided rug hid the floor and a corner fireplace connected to the central chimney. She saw no lamps, papers or bric-a-brac, but no cobwebs or dust, either. A tabletop shone like glass where a long sunbeam touched it.

She continued on around the house. At the back of the house she paused, looking around in amazement. Almost two full acres remained entirely clear of saplings, and while meadow grass and tall weeds stood knee-deep, it was obvious that this area had only recently been neglected. Brent had mentioned a garden, but no food grew here. As her eye ranged over the clumps and lines of wild growth, she detected some sort of pattern, and fascinated, she walked forward. She felt one of her flats step on something loose and gritty, and looked down.

As far as she could tell, someone had used some sort of tool, like a garden hoe, to make precise ditches in the soil about four inches wide and deep, then filled the ditches in with gravel to create an outline. She followed this one, packed with locally quarried pink granite, and found that it made a great circle, encompassing an area almost three hundred feet in diameter. She paced it all the way around, more and more intrigued. Inside the large circle a series of progressively smaller concentric ones had been mapped out with a draftsman's precision and filled with different sorts of stone—black granite, gray granite, and white limestone. Mystical sigils, meticulously outlined in the same way, filled the spaces between the circles. Diana didn't recognize a few of them. The smallest circle, about one hundred feet across, contained a geometric design too complex for her to analyze. It seemed to be a seven-pointed star with an elaborate and irregular pattern laid over it. The entire garden was a vast mandala, traced out in chipped stone and solidly planted with herbs, what survived of them.

She got her bearings and slowly walked to the center point of the design. Here only a few wisps of grass struggled through a deep layer of pale green stone that she couldn't place at first. She knelt down and rubbed some between her hands, and gasped. He had filled the entire center space, some seven feet across, with crushed jade, a small fortune's worth. Jade symbolized longevity in some traditions, she knew. At the very midpoint of this sacred center, an unpruned wild rose bush erupted in a tangle of brambles, surrounded by yarrow, ginseng, and life-everlasting.

She knew instinctively that the geometric design had a deep meaning that she was failing to interpret. What was he trying to accomplish, and why had he given up? As she gazed around the open expanse, another puzzle arose. Where did Thomas Morgan get his food? She could see no sign or smell of livestock, no vegetables, not even a fruit tree. Most of the surrounding land appeared heavily overgrown with woods. *He has to eat—doesn't he?* Of course, he could have foodstuffs shipped from almost anywhere, if he wanted—but that begged the question of why he would bother.

A beaten track led to the back door of the house, and Diana intuited that Thomas Morgan used this entrance more than the front. It also was bolted, and her cautious knocking failed to evoke a response from inside. She squinted through one of the windows and saw a deep soapstone sink attached to one wall and a long table. For all the clues the room offered, the house might have been vacant and abandoned.

She returned to her car and stood by it for a few minutes, studying the curtained upstairs windows for a sign of movement. But nothing stirred, and the presence she felt remained as serene as a still pool. With a sense of disappointment, she got into the car and left. She decided not to return to Holliston House just yet, and drove instead to nearby Camden Hills State Park. She walked along the trails aimlessly, thinking—the black flies made it necessary to keep moving, but nevertheless the peace of the woods helped to clear her mind. The sun sank behind the steep hills, and in the twilight she saw several deer come to the shore of Lake Megunticook to drink. Finally exhaustion from her long day and a growling stomach prompted her to head back to Pepperell.

The Inn's windows glowed with warm yellow light, and a rich scent came from the dining room. Diana walked slowly around the wide veranda that completely encompassed the first floor, and stopped to lean against the railing and stare out at the Bay. Closely moored fishing boats now lined the docks. The Bay glistened softly in the moonlight, but a chilling breeze blew off of the water, and she turned to go inside. Then she realized that several men sat at the other end of the veranda, in heavy wooden Adirondack chairs set in pools of light from the first floor windows. She walked down to the men and their low conversation ceased, replaced by a chorus of "evenin', miss." Then she heard Mr. Wilkinson ask, "So, did you find your Hermit?"

All the men turned to look up at her with avidly curious expressions. "No," Diana said, feeling a bit self-conscious. "No one was home this afternoon."

One of the men, who wore a thick knitted vest over shirtsleeves, chuckled. "Fred, did you send this poor little girl all the way out there in the middle of the day?"

All the men except Mr. Wilkinson now laughed, and Diana glanced among them, perplexed and irritated. "Why?" she said, a bit too sharply. "Is there something I should know?"

"Well, now, missy, everyone knows that you can't raise the Hermit of Pepp'rell Hills in the daytime."

"You can't? Why not?"

"No one knows why not, but you can beat on the door and yell yourself hoarse and never get a stir. Don't know where he goes, but he won't answer the door." The speaker looked over at Fred Wilkinson, grinning. "Fred, don't you recollect when Alma Patton needed him to sign that paperwork for the lien he paid off when he bought the Schuller place? She must've traipsed up there six times altogether. Lord, I never seen Alma so mad. Then she went up 'bout suppertime one night, and there he was, cool as mackerel. Got a piece of her mind, he did, but he never apologized or even blinked, she said. Alma's got no use for him, you can bet on that."

"I remember that," said a man with receding sandy hair. "Then when the census man come in two years back, everyone told him, go up there after supper, but would he listen? He musta been from Boston, that feller, 'cause he made four trips before he figured it out. College boy, I betcha."

All the men were chuckling now, even Fred Wilkinson who looked at her with a shrug. "I'm sorry, Miss Chilton. I truly forgot. I've never had a reason to go see Mr. Morgan, and the daytime business just slipped my mind."

She couldn't stay angry before his sincerity, but she grumbled, "It would have been nice to know this before. Are you sure he's still there?"

"Oh, he's still there, no doubt about it. Someone's keeping the place up, and we see him around now and then."

"But what can he possibly do during the day?"

The man with the vest grunted. "Sleep, I s'pose."

"Sleep? When people like Alma are hammering his door down?"

The sandy-haired man leaned toward her. "Sister, let me tell you something. I know a man name of Tim Evereaux, likes to hunt nights up back of the hills there. He told me once that he used to cut down through your hermit fella's property, oh, two, three in the mornin' if he'd had a good night. He said no matter how late it was, he'd see lights on in that house. Just dim lights, mind, 'cause Morgan's never run the electricity in there, and he's still burnin' kerosene. But the lights are on all night, and when you burn kerosene, you don't go to bed and leave the lamps on, not in a house like that one, you don't."

The other men all assented, with nods, and Diana looked from one to another of them. "Okay, so he sleeps. He must be a deep sleeper."

"Or a deep drinker, maybe," said the man with the vest. "At least, that's one idea that's struck folks here."

"Now, I wouldn't be so quick to repeat that kind of thing, Walt. No one's got any reason to believe that," Fred Wilkinson said. But Diana considered this possibility. Much as she disliked the idea, it was a plausible explanation for the odd impression she'd picked up out at the house. "Thank you for the information, gentlemen. I think I'll go in now before it's too late to get dinner."

"Oh, you've got plenty of time," said Fred Wilkinson. "The special's roast lamb tonight."

"Yes, it smells wonderful. Good night."

As she walked on around the veranda to the front door, she decided she was far too tired to go back up to the stone house that night. *I'll go tomorrow night, right at dusk,* she thought. *I'll find out if this man has a drinking problem or not, whatever happens.*

❧ 2 ☙

As the high clouds trailing across the sunset had promised, the next day it rained. Diana slept in as late as she could, took a long bath, and spent the afternoon restlessly prowling around the Inn. She lingered over her dinner, and was startled to realize that it was full dark out. She went to her room, got her raincoat, and reviewed the contents of her portfolio. If no one answered the door this time, she decided, she would wait—all night if need be.

The drive seemed shorter than the day before. The rain beat so hard on her car's roof, it almost drowned out the thump of the windshield wipers. As she turned in by the granite boulder, her heart started pounding, and she consciously slowed her breathing, to keep her anticipation under some control. She followed the drive around its long curve and pulled up in front of the house. She could barely see the stone façade in the dark. As the downpour reduced to a light sprinkle, she started to get out of the car and froze, catching her breath. A faint light showed in one of the front windows of the house. Moreover, the presence she had felt the day before was now quietly alert. He knew someone had come.

Hugging her portfolio tightly under her arm, she felt her way to the door and knocked. Seconds ticked by, and she heard no approaching footsteps. Just as she was wondering if she should knock again, she started at the sound of a heavy bolt being shot back. The latch clicked, and the door opened.

A figure stood silhouetted against the dim light that spilled into the other end of the tiny entrance hall. She could make out nothing of his face or clothing, only that he was medium height and lean. She waited for him to ask her what she wanted, but he didn't speak, and finally she cleared her throat awkwardly. "Excuse me...are you Mr. Thomas Morgan?"

In the pause that followed she felt that he was taking in every detail of her appearance, although she couldn't imagine how he could see her. "Yes, I am. May I know your name, and your business here?" He spoke in the melodic baritone voice of a trained singer or actor, with the faintest trace of an accent.

"I'm Diana Chilton, I wrote to you, and you replied that you'd be willing to speak with me..." She fumbled in her coat pocket for the small envelope, but he stepped back, opening the door wide.

"Yes, of course. You'd better come inside, before you catch your death."

Somewhat incredulous, Diana walked past him into the house. He shut the door and shot the thick iron bolt, while gesturing toward the wall behind her. "You can hang your wet coat on one of those pegs." She took off her dripping coat and groped for a peg in the dimness, surreptitiously wiping moisture off her face with her sleeve.

"Come back into my study, I have a fire going there."

She followed him through the doorway on the left, which led to the twin of the front room she had spied into the day before, appearing just as unused. Her host ushered her through a door in the back wall of this room into a space that seemed cluttered and crowded. Two armchairs stood before the corner fireplace, and a sweet fragrance seemed to radiate from the fire itself. Shelves lined three of the walls, mostly filled with books, along with glass and ceramic jars, ledgers, and some unidentifiable items. An immense old desk of carved oak occupied the corner opposite the fire, with two kerosene lamps illuminating a jumble of papers, writing implements and books. As the light came entirely from the lamps and the fire, she couldn't make out a lot of detail.

Thomas straightened up from removing something from one of the desk drawers, and as she finally saw him in the full light of the two lamps, Diana caught her breath. She knew that face better than her own by now—pale, high-boned, with large dark eyes and heavy brows. His dark hair was pulled straight back from his forehead, and just as Fred Wilkinson had told her, he did have a ponytail, tied back with a narrow black ribbon. He obviously selected his clothing, dark trousers and a heavy fisherman's sweater, for comfort rather than appearances.

She realized that he was returning her appraisal with a lifted eyebrow, and she blinked, embarrassed to have been caught staring so rudely. "I hope I'm not being too forward, just dropping in on you like this. You did say...oh, thank you." She accepted the folded handkerchief he handed to her.

"Not at all—I don't think you're forward, that is, merely a bit precipitous. Did you pack your bags as soon as you received my letter, or before you mailed yours?"

Diana looked at him sharply, but his expression was almost solemn. "Well, I...there wasn't much point in passing more letters back and forth. Some things have to be discussed face-to-face."

"Very urgently, it seems, if you didn't even have time to send me a telegram with advance notice of your arrival."

His tone was so deadpan, Diana wasn't sure if he was teasing her or not, but he didn't sound irritated. "It's not that, really. Some personal...things...just made this a good time for me to get away." She daubed at the water that was still dripping from her hair down her forehead. The threadbare handkerchief was stiff linen, coarse and knotty with faded embroidery in one corner. She had a guilty sensation that she was wiping her face with something that belonged in a museum.

"If you piqued my curiosity before, you're certainly intriguing me now." To Diana's confusion, Thomas leaned toward her and sniffed. "It was you who walked around the house yesterday afternoon, wasn't it?"

"Yes, I...I didn't mean to pry, I just thought..." She could feel her cheeks flush. Had he really *smelled* her, or had he seen her wandering around on his property? She hoped he hadn't sensed her psychic attempts to detect his presence, since some people took a very dim view of such things.

"I'm sorry that I missed you. In point of fact, Fred Wilkinson told me today that you were here and looking for me. I thought you might try again tonight."

"He did?" For a moment, Diana felt a surge of anger, but then she recalled her first conversation with the Inn's proprietor. "Oh. I guess I shouldn't be surprised. Of course, he neglected to tell me that you're best contacted in the evenings."

"Yes, I'm well known to keep odd hours. But why don't we sit down?" He gestured at the armchairs, and she sat in the one nearest her, carefully putting her leather portfolio by the side of the chair. She noticed his eyes following it as she did so. The warmth of the fire felt delicious, and she sighed, relaxing in spite of herself. Thomas sat in the chair opposite her, crossing his legs in limber European fashion. "It's been quite a few years since I've had an opportunity to speak with a fellow initiate of the Order. But perhaps we should test each other before we say anything more along that line?"

"By all means, let's go by the book." Diana couldn't keep a bitter edge out of her voice, and she smiled weakly when Thomas gave her a quizzical look. "You're right, that's what we're supposed to do. Shall I start?"

"I'd like to hear you speak the words you wrote in your letter. Can you?"

"You mean, do I really speak Welsh?" She paused a moment to collect her thoughts and make sure she had the consonants at the right angles, then slowly repeated her own translation of one of the Order's password phrases. *"Y golau arian yw'r golau byd a'r golau gwir a'r golau bywyd."*

A somewhat distant expression crossed Thomas' face. *"Rydyn ni'n sefyll llaw yn law yn y golau bywyd, y golau gwir, y golau byd, ac uwch pob, yn y golau arian."* The words of the response curled from his tongue with the natural grace of a native speaker. He was silent for a moment afterwards, as though savoring a delicate flavor. "I hate to think how long it's been since I heard that language spoken. Why on earth did you learn it?"

"It wasn't actually my idea, but I like it, it's different. I've got some Welsh in the family tree, and I was interested in the myth cycles."

"So the Order is still full of Celtic romanticists, trying to re-invent the Druids?"

She grinned for a moment. "Yes, I think there are just a *few* of those left."

"And still holding the Beltene revels, in this day and age?"

"As enthusiastically as ever. Dr. Kinsey would have a coronary." Her smile faded. "Not that I've been to one for a couple of years." At his inquisitive look, she said apologetically, "I've been going through a pretty nasty divorce."

"I'm very sorry."

"Yes, well, probably for the best. It was all over in March, anyway. But I wasn't about to go to Beltene and run into my ex-, that's for sure. So much for the best thirteen years of my life."

"You can't be serious. Your husband must have taken a child bride."

"Don't be silly. I'm thirty-one—yes, I don't look it, I know. But I'm over the hill. Pointless to lie about it."

"That's a very young age to be so cynical. You must have divorced your husband for mayhem and cruelty."

She laughed out loud at that. "Oh, no. Stephen wouldn't have the guts to raise his hand to me—just his voice, early and often. Besides, I'd hit him back, and he knows it."

"I'll certainly keep that in mind." This time he did show a hint of a smile. "But I don't think this is the personal thing that put you on the highway to Maine, is it? Let's talk about why you are here. I'm rather eager for an explanation of all those mysterious allusions and hints in your letters to me—as I'm sure you intended. You said you'd learned a great deal about me that made you believe we could be of help to each other. Now that we're face to face, could you elucidate on those statements?"

"Yes, of course." But despite her crisp reply, Diana hesitated, frowning down at the hearthrug between them. "I'd like to fill in some of the back story, though."

"By all means."

She drew in a deep breath before she started speaking, fighting down a sudden attack of what could only be called stage fright. Moving from casual banter to the meat of the issues was a bigger step than she'd expected. "I've had a pretty...unconventional life, even by the standards of the Order of the Silver Light. I was raised in the Order, to begin with, and my parents are...wealthy Bohemians, I guess is the simplest way to describe it. I never even went to school, I was educated at home, and in the Order. I came into a lot of money when I turned twenty-one, and I started up a charitable organization to help the working man and the poor, it's named Bread and Roses. Maybe you've heard of us?"

Thomas only nodded. He was concentrating so intently on her words that Diana had to restrain herself from fidgeting in the slightly lumpy chair.

"We had our tenth anniversary this year, and we're doing very well. We run boarding houses, a soup kitchen, job training programs, we help in emergencies—Bread and Roses employs twenty-two full-time staff now, and we've got about eighty dedicated volunteers."

"And you manage all that yourself?" He looked amazed.

"Oh, no, the Director runs the day to day operations. I was Chairwoman of the Board, but...I've stepped down, temporarily. Oh, they'll chug along just fine without me—better than fine, I suspect. The staff runs the programs, the volunteers do the work, all they need from me is the signature on the checks, and I've turned that over to the trust now. I'm completely superfluous. I was just underfoot hanging around all the time."

"Hanging around? You mean you actually worked in the kitchens?"

"Among other areas, yes, about thirty hours a week until recently. To tell you the truth, I was just keeping myself busy, not that it *helped* my marriage, but...Mr. Morgan, don't mistake me for some Boston Brahmin dilettante. Some of my funds are in long-term investments, but most of my money goes to various causes, and so does a lot of my time. I'm not suited to a life of leisure, and frivolous luxury bores me. I don't believe that my social responsibilities begin and end with throwing money, just because I have a lot of it."

"That sounds most commendable. But why have you stepped down from your own Board of Directors?"

She sighed heavily. "I guess I feel like I've come to a kind of crossroads in my life. It's 1952, we're more than half way through the century. In a couple of years I'll be officially middle-aged, and I have nothing to show for it but a failed marriage and a Sisyphean vocation. No matter how much we do, it seems like things just keep getting worse and worse. There are scores of organizations like Bread and Roses, and we might as well be fighting the Chicago fire with teaspoons and atomizers. Look at the twentieth century so far. We've already had a global depression, epidemics, two world wars—how many people have been killed in this century alone? And there's going to be another big war. This thing in Korea...I can feel it. Truman as much as said so."

"And many thoughtful people agree with him. I'm not sure I do. After all, if you take a long view of history—"

"A long view of history consists of an unbroken landscape of wars, Mr. Morgan, everywhere in the world except Antarctica."

"If that's all that you choose to look at."

Diana stiffened. "Oh, yes, it's all how I look at things, isn't it? I shouldn't be such a doomsayer, see the glass half-full instead of half-empty—" she stopped when he raised a conciliating hand.—"

"Miss Chilton, I'm very impressed by your dedication, but working whole heartedly on solving the world's problems does tend to be overwhelming. I can see why you'd need a sabbatical. Trust me, I speak from long experience on this, and I don't mean to sound unsympathetic."

Diana's shoulders sagged. "I'm sorry."

"No need to apologize. But I am wondering how this relates to your needing my help."

"I'm getting to that. You see, despite the fact that I'm a third generation member and was practically born in a ritual room, I'm not exactly the golden girl of the OSL. In fact, six years ago, I managed to get myself into a lot of hot water."

"What on earth for?"

"Insubordination. I wound up formally censured for being such an agitator."

"Ah." From the look on Thomas' face, Diana thought he was favorably impressed rather than otherwise. "What were you agitating for?"

"I was convinced, at the time, that the Order had a hidden element, an upper level that was working to influence change in the world politically. I wanted in on it."

He looked sincerely perplexed. "A hidden element...are you talking about a sort of Illuminati, or White Brotherhood?"

"Something like that, but in a benevolent sense, not just some kind of power cabal or secret conspiracy. I thought, you see, that this was the rationale for the rank of Magus being restricted to men—because it was involved with all those gritty realities like finances, and war, and government, that women are considered too delicate and irrational to be trusted with."

"But you don't think that now."

"No. I reluctantly concluded that there is no such shadowy upper group within the OSL. I was an idealistic idiot. The Council is made up of the same fallible human beings as every government on earth. The only difference between us and the Vatican is our ideology, and they ran the Inquisition. We probably would, if we could afford it. We just have a different definition of heresy. The Order doesn't involve itself with the world, at all. We learn how to be magicians and transform ourselves, but not how to use the magic for anything practical."

Thomas frowned. "Doesn't the Order still teach that the essence of magic is to change the universe by changing yourself?"

"As a theoretical doctrine, yes. Do you believe it?" He hesitated, as if he wanted to say yes but couldn't quite do so. "I'm not saying that I don't accept that in principle, Mr. Morgan, but I've come to feel that individual accomplishments aren't enough. What we need is something that combines true power with real continuity, the kind of focused Intention that doesn't change with every new Director or Board or Council. Left to itself, the world is trapped in this insane repetitive cycle—a dark age, a period of enlightenment and then a fall back into barbarism or fascism, over and over. People today talk as though scientific knowledge and modern medicine are equivalent to progress, but progress is an illusion. We spend more money and ingenuity on building bigger armies and more powerful bombs than anything else."

Thomas was starting to smile. "I can't argue with your description of human history—or your opinion of its futility. But you've just given incontrovertible evidence that there are no hidden influences pulling the strings, for humanitarian reasons or otherwise."

"Maybe not. Or maybe there are and we simply can't imagine how much worse it would be without them."

"That sort of argument could be offered in defense of almost anything. If the Order of the Silver Light did have such a politically active wing, just what do you think it would be doing? Contrary to all the paranoid fantasies about secret conspiracies, working entirely behind the scenes has severe limitations. You can't effect real change in the world without being fully involved in it. How could the Order, or any such organization, be invisible and still make a difference?"

Diana was quiet for a moment, looking down at the shadows beyond the firelight. Then she straightened up in the chair and very deliberately met Thomas' eyes with such an intense look, he blinked. "That's one of the things that I was hoping you could tell me."

"I?"

"You see, Mr. Morgan, I realized that the only way any such organization could achieve real continuity is if its members are able to maintain that continuity as individuals. By-laws and traditions and histories only go so far. Each new generation brings in its own perspectives and concerns, so you get the same cycles on a local scale. The only way to transcend the cycles is to outlive them. I'm talking about physical immortality, Mr. Morgan, something I've been researching for the last five years. That's what I'm here to talk to you about."

There was a long silence. Thomas didn't look away from her steady gaze, but his expression had become wary and guarded. "I see."

"I fully expected you to be discreet, but please don't be disingenuous with me. I'm an Adeptus in the Order of the Silver Light, Mr. Morgan, and so are you. I'm convinced that we have a great deal more in common besides that. You can trust me, I swear. You wanted to know what I was talking about, when I said I'd learned things about you. Let me show you."

For a few moments, Thomas appeared ambivalent as to how he would answer. At last he shrugged. "All right."

"May we use your desk? I need a little bit of space." He nodded, and they both got up and went over to the oak desk. Thomas scooped his papers and paraphernalia into a loose pile and set it on one of the bookshelves, while Diana moved the kerosene lanterns to each upper corner of the broad surface. She opened her portfolio and removed a sheaf of photographs, which she lined up in neat rows. The eight by ten black and white photographs included enlarged details of old paintings, engravings, and one drawing, and then copies of old photos, a few of them rather blurry. In each one was a distinctly similar face, sometimes appearing as the main subject of the picture and sometimes merely a figure in the background. Diana glanced at Thomas, who was studying the photos with a stunned expression. "I'm assuming that you recognize most of these? You may not have known they still existed."

He opened his mouth as if to reply, but closed it without saying anything.

"I was initiated to Adeptus rank seven years ago—"

"When you were twenty-four?" She wasn't sure if Thomas was disbelieving or just startled.

"I'm not bragging. I had a very early start, remember. As you know, that's the highest grade that women can attain. After I was censured, I started working with a mentor within the Order, and at that time, I encountered something that proved there were certain, possibilities, that I hadn't previously understood.

My investigations began mostly from curiosity but I'll admit that I became somewhat obsessed by what I was learning." Thomas frowned slightly but only nodded at her to continue.

Clearing her throat, she went on, "At first, most of the information I found wasn't really verifiable. It consisted largely of anecdotes and second hand reports and somewhat dubious accounts of sightings, that sort of thing. But then I found a body of historical information deep in the OSL archives. That gave me a number of leads to a handful of specific individuals. With those clues to go on, I was able to trace most of them in conventional records, through a series of identities. Some of them had been members of the Order and some had not. All of them eventually disappeared from the public record, which only means that the paper trail dead-ended, or picked up someplace that I couldn't find it. But there was one that I managed to trace right up to the present day." She glanced at him again. "Shall I tell you the specifics?"

"You can't just leave me in suspense after all this." Thomas' tone didn't have a trace of flippancy.

Diana pointed to the first photograph, a close-up of an old painting. Unlike the others, its subject was a boy about twelve years old. "Dafydd Morgynne, born in Cardiff, Wales in 1723, as far as I've been able to confirm. He seems to have been something of a prodigy. His parents were fairly well-to-do, although they died young and left no other living children. They had him educated, however, which wasn't common in Wales at that time. Dafydd went to Oxford at the age of fourteen and read the law, and became a barrister in London. He then used a lot of his time and money to campaign for the civil rights of British subjects in Wales, Ireland and Scotland. After a while, his nationalist views attracted so much negative attention from the Crown that he had to go live in France for over a decade. By that time, he already seems to have been involved with the OSL. He came back to London and resumed a law practice, but reportedly was suffering from some kind of illness that limited his activity. In 1765 he abruptly left the Order and Britain. But whatever his illness was, he didn't die from it."

"How can you be so sure that he didn't die?"

"There's no record of it. Dafydd Morgynne, Esquire was wealthy enough that his death and funeral would never have gone unnoted, but he wasn't so wealthy or well-connected that it could have been completely covered up. He had to leave his estate to somebody. The laws at that time were absolutely rigid about inheritance."

"Granted." Thomas heaved an almost imperceptible sigh. "Please continue."

"From then on, he seems to have moved his money, and himself, from place to place assuming new identities—very skillfully, I might add." She pointed to more of the photos as she went down the list she had memorized so carefully. "I found him back in Paris in 1784 under the name of Michel Bouchard, in Cardiff in 1820 as Michael Davies, Inverness in 1862 as John David Morse and Nottingham in 1888 as Morgan Bruneaux. He first appears in New York City in 1916 as David Michael Brown, where he has a somewhat more prominent career thanks to the attention he attracts from the tabloids. There are numerous photographs of him from that time, as you see. David Michael Brown simply drops off the face of the earth in 1929, and in 1937 he turns up again in Philadelphia." She paused a moment, but Thomas gave no hint that he was prepared to verify her theories. He reached out and touched one of the photos gently, as though testing to see if it was real.

"How can you be so sure that all of these names belong to the same man? Physical resemblance only implies a family relationship, if that."

"Well, there's no way to be absolutely sure. But there is some fairly persuasive evidence—with plenty of gaps, but it all tends to add together. There are some surviving financial records, transfers from one bank to another. There is similarity of handwriting and signatures, and of writing styles. All of them were lawyers, or worked in legal fields in some way, usually for some kind of leftist social or political cause. Also, each one of them sought help from the OSL at some point—that was a major factor tying them together, bits of information in the OSL archives. Belonging to an underground organization definitely oils the wheels when it comes to transferring funds and getting out of difficult situations—like France in 1789." She saw him wince at those words, but so subtly, she wouldn't have noticed it if she hadn't been watching for it. "I don't think anyone without access to the OSL archives could have found the critical links. And finally, there are...fingerprints."

"Fingerprints?"

"In at least three cases, as I examined some of the original documents, I realized there were partial fingerprints. They wouldn't hold up in court, they don't have enough, I think they call them points, to be considered a one hundred percent match, but what there is of them, do correspond."

"Good Lord. So, you're not only a crack detective, you analyze fingerprints?"

"Of course not. But I can afford to pay people who do. Along with graphologists and textual analysts, all of whom are firmly convinced that I'm nuts."

"What did you say when they asked why you wanted the analyses done?"

"That it was none of their business. The graphologist decided that I'm trying to establish inheritance rights to some abandoned Swiss bank account. He asked me rather rudely whether I didn't think I had enough money already. But the others just cashed their checks. That's what people do, mostly."

"You might be surprised...what can take hold of someone's curiosity, that is." Thomas glanced down at the palm of one hand with a perplexed frown for a moment, then sharply closed his hand and looked back up at Diana. "So, in 1937..."

"In 1937...you, Thomas Morgan, appear in Philadelphia. Before that, there isn't any record that you ever existed."

There was a long pause then, as Thomas studied Diana soberly. "With all of that sleuthing, I'm surprised that you didn't turn up my birth certificate."

"Oh, of course I did—the copy on file, that is. March third, 1912, Laurel, Maryland. But it's a forgery. Your parents' names are listed as Gwyneth and Robert Morgan, but their names can't be traced further back, there's no record of their owning or renting a home, paying taxes, or holding a job in Laurel, and no Gwyneth Morgan was a patient at any lying-in hospital around that date. They don't seem to have any relatives, and no friends recall the Morgans, or their son, who was never enrolled in school."

She reached into the portfolio again and took out several more photographs, each one a close-up of a document. "Birth certificate, and baptismal record, although your baptism is not noted in the parish record of any church in the district. Your passport lists your religion as Methodist, but then, your passport itself is a phony. Oh, and this one is truly brilliant—your current law degree. 1936, Quincy College in Maryland, but Quincy College's administrative offices burned to the ground in 1937, destroying all records and therefore all chances of verifying your degree—except through the memories of faculty or staff, and no one formerly associated with Quincy College has ever heard of you. You never tried to pass the bar in Pennsylvania, either. The only bona fide documents I found for you there are related to your buying this property, from Philadelphia. Then you moved up here, and you've been here ever since."

His expression was now darkly thoughtful, and he gazed down at the photos lined up before him as if he wasn't really seeing them. "I'm amazed that you were able to find such a clear trail," he said slowly. "Many a genealogist would be seething with envy at all this documentation—five countries, and more than two hundred years."

"I don't think you have to worry that anyone will duplicate my research, if that's your concern. The most crucial pieces of information are only available in the OSL archives. Without them, I wouldn't have had a starting point. And the archives are only accessible to initiates above Adeptus grade."

He nodded, pursing his lips, and Diana suddenly found herself wondering what he was thinking. He wasn't reacting as she had expected and prepared for, but she couldn't read his expression. Finally he straightened his shoulders. "Would you like a brandy? Because I definitely would."

It took a moment for her to answer. For just an instant, as he raised his face toward the ceiling and the amber lamplight limned his profile, his image seemed to shimmer, and she saw him dressed in the garb Dafydd Morgynne might have worn on the streets of London. The illusion was gone in an eyeblink, but Diana felt disoriented, as if she'd been looking down a portal through time itself. She gave her head a small shake. It was his long hair, and the photos they'd been staring at, and the dim flickering light. "I'd love a brandy."

He got a decanter and snifters from one of the shelves and poured two generous shots. They returned to the armchairs by the fire, and Diana watched Thomas as he downed half his glass in one swallow, then sat utterly motionless, eyes closed, for quite a long time. She might have worried about an ordinary man, but he simply appeared to be entirely concentrated on the taste and sensation of the brandy. She took a sip of her own drink and it was extraordinarily good cognac, but it didn't rivet her to the spot.

At last he drew in a deep breath and opened his eyes. "Who was your mentor in the Order?" he asked, almost absently, as he watched the light playing on the balloon snifter.

"I'm sorry, I—I'm not allowed to reveal that."

"I understand. Wasn't your married name Winthrop?"

She gaped at him. "Yes, but how…?"

"I still have contacts in the Order, Miss Chilton."

"Contacts? And they've been talking to you about me?"

"Not to any great extent, and not just idle gossip, I assure you. By the way, I was initiated into the Order while I was still at Oxford, and I never formally left."

She was still so flummoxed by his question about her married name that it took a moment for his last statement to register. When it did, she felt as though a lump had been dropped into the pit of her stomach. "You mean…you're admitting that it's true? You're not just going to deny it all and laugh at me?"

"If I wanted to do that, I should have done so long before this. Denials now would be, as you so rightly put it, disingenuous. Yes, I admit it. I was born in 1723. Your names and dates are accurate, although you've missed a few here and there. But does my admission really prove anything? I might just be humoring you, after all."

She sat back and looked at him, too overwhelmed to speak. He had just confessed to being over two hundred years old, and there he sat in his sweater and scuffed shoes like a slumming college student. But the illusion she'd seen a few minutes ago suddenly clicked into place, and she had no doubt at all. His features, his slight build, his inflection and words, the odd grace of his movements, all supported the truth. He didn't belong to the twentieth century. He was as much an image of the long-vanished past as the portraits and photographs spread on his desk. "No, you're not humoring me, Mr. Morgan. Your admission is self-evident. All I have to do is look at you to know that."

She saw a shadow of something like surprise in his expression for a moment. "And what is that to you, Miss Chilton? If you've spent most of your life in the Order, and attained the rank of Adeptus at such a young age, I have no doubt that you've confronted many things at least as remarkable as I am. Just what do you hope to accomplish by proving your case?"

"Not what you're assuming, Mr. Morgan. You're probably right about what I've witnessed, although I'm not convinced that I really know just how remarkable you are. But I didn't come here to blackmail you or make demands, or even to crow about figuring out your secret. As fascinating as I'm sure your story is, I don't have to know what you are, and why. I'm here to ask you—no, to implore you—to share your knowledge, to put me in touch with people who are really doing something meaningful with their power. I've learned enough about how things work to understand that I need an entree, someone who can vouch for me. Whatever I need to do to prove myself, to you or to them, I'll do it."

He looked down at the snifter in his cupped hands for a moment. "Miss Chilton...you must believe me in this. If I knew of something, and was forbidden by oath to reveal it, out of courtesy to you as a fellow Adeptus, I would say that much. But your conclusions about the Order of the Silver Light are correct. They have no politically active secret wing manipulating governments or influencing the course of history, and I'm aware of no other lodges or secret societies that do."

As Diana slumped back in her chair with a heavy sigh, Thomas said curiously, "Did you really believe that I was part of some such mysterious inner circle? You never found a hint of such a thing in all your research, did you? If it had been true, why would I have gone to the OSL every time I was in dire straits? For that matter, why would I have been in dire straits so often?"

She smiled weakly, because his tone was humorous. "Oh, I don't know. I suppose I thought that if any groups like that existed, you at least would have encountered one, or heard of one. Not just because of how long you've lived—because of the work you've done throughout your life, and the causes you supported."

He shook his head slowly, his eyes somber. "I've never heard of one that didn't prove to be a fraud, or that actually achieved anything. I entirely sympathize with your quest, don't mistake me. It's easy, and so tempting, to convince ourselves that someone, somewhere, must have control over the chaos that is human history. I searched for such shadow organizations myself, for much of my existence. That was how I encountered the Order in the first place. But I've come to accept that we must trust to God's hand for guidance, and for what you call continuity."

"Too bad God couldn't save the Jews in Germany."

Thomas frowned unhappily. "God's influence in this world is often obscure to us, I admit."

"To say the least. But I think that we're here as emissaries, that we're meant to be doing divine work for the gods, not passively sitting back and submitting to the will of a higher power."

"You're preaching to the choir, Miss Chilton. But look at your own dilemma. It's obvious that you're doing as much with your resources as any single human being could, yet you're still frustrated to the point of despair. I understand completely. I also have a sense of obligation to the oppressed. I've always fought for their causes, in any way I could."

"I know. You even have an FBI file for it."

"I do?"

"From the 1920s, all that pro bono work you were doing in the New York ghettos for the Russian Jews—and other immigrants, but it was the Russian ones that had J. Edgar worried."

"Yes, and the Negroes. I knew the authorities were worried—that's why David Michael Brown had to disappear in 1929. You see, that's precisely why immortality is no advantage. You end up with less continuity, not more. How can you stay in one place for more than two decades and not age? I had difficulty staying for as long as one."

Neither of them spoke for a few moments. Diana took a sip of cognac and savored it slowly, considering what Thomas had said. "If there are no such groups...have you ever thought about starting one?"

She flushed when he laughed out loud, but he wasn't mocking her. "Yes, I have," he said when he recovered himself. "But an organization with one member is rather pointless."

"But surely you—I'm sorry, but it's hard to believe that you couldn't find anyone who would have been willing to join you. Bread and Roses has volunteers who make me look jaded."

"Their willingness was not the fundamental issue," Thomas said quietly.

Diana puzzled over this reply for a moment, then she realized what he meant. "Your immortality was the fundamental issue." She looked at his dark expression, and he simply inclined his head once. "You didn't want to pass on the secret of how it's done? So how *did* you accomplish it?" He looked down, and Diana suddenly felt abashed, as though she'd accidentally said something offensive. "I'm sorry, I didn't mean to just blurt it out like that—"

"I was wondering when we'd get here, actually."

"Mr. Morgan, I didn't come here looking for the secret of immortality. At least, not for its own sake."

He studied her soberly. "I'm inclined to believe you, Miss Chilton. If you were only interested in pursuing immortality as an end, you would have asked me very different questions. I know, because I've heard them all before. You're after something else. But you wouldn't be human if you weren't tantalized by the potential. I would have been."

Diana only shook her head. "It is tantalizing, but this isn't my first bite of the apple. I said earlier that I began my researches because I became aware of certain possibilities. I can't say more than that, but trust me, I've had several years to consider the pros and cons of an extended lifespan, on a very practical level. I'm still not sure what I think."

"Then you wouldn't accept immortality, on any terms, if it was offered to you?"

"On *any* terms? No. On the right terms..." She was silent a moment, brooding. "I'm still not sure. But I do know I wouldn't want to be immortal and alone. That's partly why I'm trying to find some kind of organization, or group. The hints have been maddening, but obviously they're all just false leads and misdirection."

"Suppose you did find exactly what you're looking for, and the offer was made? What then?"

She couldn't meet his hard unwavering stare. "I can't answer that hypothetically. I guess it would depend on a lot of things."

He relaxed slightly and leaned back in his chair. "A wise answer."

She stiffened a little. "But you accepted it, obviously. What terms did you find persuasive?"

"I wish I'd been offered some. I did nothing to attain immortality, Miss Chilton. This was done to me. I never chose it."

"Then...your state is involuntary, not something you consciously maintain?"

"Oh, it has its maintenance. And I have reason to believe that the state can be passed on. But I will not do that."

"Why?"

He was quiet for a moment. "For one thing, it's a rare aspiration. It's often said that everyone would like to be immortal. But few humans have the stamina to survive even one lifetime of grief and labor without becoming exhausted and cynical. Very few of those would choose to continue outliving everything and everyone around them."

"I'd agree with that. Is that how you'd describe yourself—exhausted and cynical?"

He looked startled. "Why would you think that?"

"I could never understand why you went into complete seclusion here. After so many years of public service and civic engagement, and all your passion for social justice, you didn't even try to pass the bar in Maine. What happened?"

He looked down at his snifter pensively. "I suppose I was tired. I'm no reactionary about change, and novelty, and progress, indeed, I relish them. But every innovation means losing something comfortable and familiar. Eventually the sheer weight of it begins to bear down. I meant to continue my profession, or I wouldn't have bothered to"—he almost smiled—"forge yet another law degree. But when I got here...I decided to pursue other things."

Diana felt that he was evading the real answer, but she wasn't sure she had the right to press him. "I am curious, though. What do you mean by saying you have reason to believe your state could be passed on? If it isn't something another person could attain through a magical discipline, then, hypothetically, what would be involved?" When he paused, looking down again, she said, "I understand if you don't want to reveal that—"

"I do want to," he broke in. "But it would be impossible to convey it to you with mere explanations. This is beyond your experience—the words would mean nothing to you."

She felt a surge of irritation, although she knew she was overreacting. "I'm not stupid, Mr. Morgan. If I'm stepping over any lines, you can slap me down any way you like. But don't condescend to me."

"That's not my intention, believe me." He rose and walked over to his desk, and stood there for a few minutes, leaning with both hands on the desktop, apparently lost in deep thought. Rivulets of rain water cascaded down the windowpanes, catching golden threads of light from the kerosene lamps. She wondered what he was thinking about—his expression made her a little uneasy. Finally he straightened up, sighing, and looked at her.

"Do you believe in destiny, Miss Chilton?"

She frowned, wondering what this change of subject meant. "Up to a point. I think we make our own destiny."

"Then you don't see the guiding hand of the Almighty in unforeseen events?"

"Sometimes, but Aesop said the gods help those who help themselves, and it's still true."

He came back to the fire and sat in his chair, but on the edge of it, leaning toward her. "I agree. God gives us opportunities, and it's our part to act on them. But surely you can see a guiding hand in the very fact that we're speaking tonight? Think about this: for five years, you've been searching for me. And for those same five years, I've wondered how to approach you to ask for your help."

"My help? But why—" she broke off as he indicated he had more to say.

"And now you've appeared on my doorstep, moved by impulse and fate, on the night of a full moon...is there not at least a shade of destiny in that?"

"Well, I..." She could see the truth in what he was saying. The significance of the date had not even occurred to her, but then, she'd had no idea that he knew she existed, let alone wanted to get in touch with her. "You speak of my helping you, but I don't understand. If destiny has brought me here to help you, then what is it that I can do to help you? Or is this something else that there's just no point in trying to explain?"

"I can't explain, because it must be shown." He got up from his chair, took her empty glass from her and set it aside. Then he grasped both her hands and pulled her to her feet. She was startled to realize how strong he was. "Don't think I underestimate you, Miss Chilton. I know the level of endurance and fortitude it takes to achieve Adeptus rank, even in the twentieth century. This won't be easy, but it's necessary. You've journeyed five years and hundreds of miles to find me. This is your choice. Do you want to see what you really came here to find?"

Diana stared up at him, her mind too flooded with questions to voice any one of them. She had no idea what this demonstration involved or why endurance and fortitude might be required, but her confusion and apprehension were overwhelmed by devouring curiosity. "Yes," she whispered, abandoning caution and sense. "Show me."

He let go of her hands and deftly untied the loose silk scarf she wore around her neck. Startled, she reached up and took the scarf from him. Before she could speak, he caught her shoulder with one hand and her jaw with the other, pulling her close against his body. "Hold still," he said softly. "This will hurt a little, but don't move." Before she could think he had tipped her head back and bent down to put his open mouth against her throat, where the vein pulsed close to the skin. She felt the wet sucking pressure of his mouth, and squeezed her eyes shut, her heart pounding. She gasped at a sudden jabbing pain and a sensation as though her skin had simply broken open, and a wave of vertigo made her stomach turn over. Thomas let go of her jaw and wrapped his arms around her, pulling her tightly against him. She could feel his mouth moving against her throat, a sense of slippery warmth, and a small trickle soaking into the edge of her sweater and making it stick to her skin. *He's drinking my blood*, she thought incredulously, for she could feel him drinking in rhythmic swallows. Her only emotion was sheer awe at the surreality of what was happening.

After a few moments, she wanted to push him away, or at least protest, but she couldn't. The tension in her muscles dissolved, as though she had been injected with some kind of drug, and her body sagged loosely against his. Seconds became minutes, and she began to feel dizzy and lightheaded. Her stomach started to turn over and lurch with nausea. He went down on his knees, still holding her and still drinking, allowing her to fold up beneath him as though she were a garment he was wearing. She couldn't get enough breath, and her heartbeat felt strange—now rapid and shallow, like the running footsteps of a small animal, then pounding, then almost imperceptible. Her eyes were open, but she couldn't see anything, and her hands and feet were so numb she couldn't feel them at all.

She could sense something portentous surrounding them on all sides. It was as though they were kneeling on the back of some great beast, so huge and so ancient that they had climbed up on it thinking it a mountain, and now it was coming to life, heaving and thrusting upward to throw them off. Suddenly it cracked open and caught fire. Raw power seethed beneath and around her. A great, coiling vortex of energy, powerful enough to reshape the world with no more effort than thought, tensed and focused into a point above her. She recoiled desperately as it poised itself to lance through the center of her being and transform her—body, soul and mind—into something alien and inhuman. She realized that Thomas somehow had control of this power and was holding it back with all of his will. Fervently she prayed to him, as she had never prayed to anything, not to release that vortex into her. It began to withdraw, slowly, and she thought she must be dying, because she couldn't breathe at all. Smothering black tendrils covered her face and tightened. Then something ice cold touched her neck, and that was the last thing she remembered.

❧ 3 ☙

The chickadees awoke her—a pair of them, singing their two note call and response from some distance away. The long notes seemed to cry sadly, "love me...love you..." over and over. She lay quietly in bed for a time listening to them, feeling a soft breeze on her face, full of the smell of warm wet grass. She wasn't sure she was truly awake, since she felt so insubstantial.

She opened her eyes, finally, blinking at the uncomfortably bright light. She was lying on a four poster bed in a room she had never seen before, coarse linen sheets and a piecework quilt smoothed tidily over her. A bureau stood against one whitewashed wall on a worn braided rug. The light breeze billowed frayed calico curtains and a dazzling square of sunlight gleamed on the broad plank floor. Puzzled by this, she turned her head to look for a bedside table that might contain a clock. A sharp twinge of pain in the side of her neck made her wince. As she reached up to touch the spot in puzzlement, she remembered. Like a blurry slide snapping into focus, everything that had happened the night before came back to her.

She lay very still, her heart beating quickly. She realized that she was in bed fully dressed, except for shoes. That was somewhat reassuring, although she thought she would have forgiven his being bold enough to take off her stockings. She felt very weak. Even attempting to reach her hand out made her breathless and dizzy. After a moment she pushed the covers down to her waist, braced her hands on either side, and tried to sit up. She barely raised her head from the pillow before her heart was laboring so heavily it frightened her, and she sank back down, gasping for breath. She closed her eyes, fighting down panic at her helplessness.

She tugged the quilt back up to her chin and huddled down under it. In her wildest imaginings she had never anticipated this. Her principal associations with vampires were folklore compendia and blood fetishists, or the likes of Aleister Crowley and his Serpent's Kiss. As a novice, she had studied Dion Fortune's chapter on psychic vampirism, and of course, she had read *Dracula*, but...the memory of Thomas' mouth against her throat came to her, and she shuddered, although the memory evoked ambiguous feelings. It seemed that the venerable Auntie Dion had omitted some critical details.

With nothing else to do except lie there and wait, she tried to keep her thoughts from running out of control. *What does he want with me?* kept pushing itself to the front of her mind, and she kept pushing it back, because there was no way to answer that question, and she didn't want to speculate. She thought now of every vampire legend or story she had ever heard, trying to compare them with the man she had met, wondering what, if anything, might be factual. Where was Thomas now? Was he sleeping in the next room, or did he go someplace hidden during the day? Would he awaken at the moment of sunset? Was he awake now, somewhere around the house? Was he going to keep her here?

Was he going to kill her?

Stop it, she thought, angry with herself. *Stop it.* She closed her eyes and began breathing in the five-two-five pattern of the Annwfn meditation, carefully, so she wouldn't hyperventilate. She induced a light trance and went through the figures of the pathworking, methodically and painstakingly visualizing each detail, each movement, as vividly as possible. Her trance deepened, and she walked through a great shadowed room, with fan vaulted arches high overhead, and torches flickering in sconces on the walls. Ahead of her was a golden throne raised on a high dais, and sitting on the throne was a woman, her face shining with light so brilliant Diana couldn't make out her features. The woman extended a hand in a slow gesture, indicating a crystal globe that stood at her feet. Diana walked to the globe and knelt at the woman's feet, peering into the rippling center of the crystal. She saw a small building explode into a ball of flame, drops of blood soak into a hard dirt floor, blinding snow that seemed to fly from every direction at once, a field full of dandelions going to lacy balls of seed. The crystal went black, and from its depths a coiling vortex of energy suddenly appeared and began twisting up toward her with incredible speed, contracting and focusing into a point like a lightning bolt. She flung herself backward, falling, and opened her eyes with a gasp, her fingers clutching at handfuls of linen sheet.

I was dreaming. She had fallen asleep during the meditation, which was rather sloppy of her—novices got the soles of their feet switched for that. Her physical state explained that lapse, but if anything, she felt even worse now. The room had grown far dimmer, and flat black night pressed against the panes of the windows. She turned her head to find the source of the room's light and a shock ran over her. There sat Thomas by the bed, so still that the old wooden chair had not given the slightest creak to reveal his presence. He looked down at her with an expression that was thoughtful and a little sad, and she slowly recovered her equilibrium.

"I didn't know you were there," she said, because she had to say something to break the silence, or she might have to just scream. "Have you been sitting there long?"

He shrugged. "A little while. I didn't want to wake you." He leaned over and touched her forehead and cheek with the backs of his fingers, like a mother with a feverish child. He didn't seem to like what the touch told him. "How do you feel?"

"How do I feel? How do I *feel*?" She turned her face back up to the ceiling. "I can't even sit up. And I'm so thirsty..."

"Yes, you need to drink." He got up and went to the bureau, where Diana saw a tray with a pitcher and crockery, and several lighted candles. Thomas filled a glass with water and sat on the bed next to her. He put his arm around her shoulders and raised her to a half sitting position. She expected to flinch from his touch, but instead she felt his arm around her indefinably comforting. He held the first glass for her as she drank—cold well water, with a sweet earthy taste. She drained the glass and he poured another for her, then another, until the pitcher was empty. By then, she could sit up by herself, and with great effort, she pushed herself back so she could lean against the headboard of the bed.

She touched her throat, where she could feel an odd puckered bump, hot and painful under her fingertips. "You almost killed me, didn't you?"

"Yes."

"Was that your intention?"

"It was the only way to show you what you needed to see. I would had to have done so, sooner or later. I saw no reason to let you go on feeling...condescended to."

Reminded of her irritable remark the night before, Diana looked away from him. "You might have given me some warning."

"You wouldn't have—"

"—understood, I know. Well, I have to confess something, Mr. Morgan. I still don't. Last night, you said you had been wishing you could meet me, that you wanted me to help you. And now you talk about showing me what I needed to see. Can you possibly clarify any of this in some way that doesn't render me unconscious?" She struggled to keep emotions of fear and outrage in check. Both were alleviated by the expression of shame that shadowed his face.

"Perhaps I was a bit too...hasty. But I feared that if you decided I had nothing more to offer you, you'd simply leave, and I wouldn't be able to find you again."

"So much for destiny? Believe me when I say I'm a hell of a lot easier to find than you are."

He smiled faintly. "That depends on one's resources. I'm not the only one of us who has changed names."

Diana let her head fall back against the headboard. "I'm not planning to rush off anywhere. I've burned too many bridges behind me for that. But Mr. Morgan, right now I've got to get back to the Inn. They're going to think I've skipped town."

"Oh, no, you don't have to worry. I've taken care of all that for you."

"What do you mean?"

"I stopped by the Inn a short time ago and spoke to Fred Wilkinson. He was quite concerned about you, but I assured him that you were fine."

"But how did you explain why I didn't come back last night?"

"I simply said that we had gotten to talking so late into the evening, you decided to stay overnight here rather than risk disturbing the other guests."

"And they believed that?" The idea that such a facile explanation would be accepted without question disturbed her.

"I've lived here for quite some time, you know. I have some credibility. And it's well known that I have no telephone, so you couldn't have called." He paused for a moment as Diana thought about this, recalling Mr. Wilkinson's protective attitude toward the Hermit the day she arrived. "I also informed Mr. Wilkinson that you'll be staying with me for the next few days."

"You what? I will? Wait a minute—"

"You'll need your things, so I picked them up for you." He nodded toward the doorway, where Diana recognized her own suitcases set neatly against the wall.

She stared at Thomas, aghast. "So...what's the story here?" she said, trying to keep her voice steady. "Are you keeping me a prisoner? A private blood bank, perhaps, and you'll make sure I'm never quite strong enough to get out the door?"

He looked genuinely shocked. "Good God! What an appalling idea!"

"Then what am I supposed to think?"

"It should be obvious that you can't go back to the Inn until you've fully recovered, in any case. I had to say something to the Wilkinsons, immediately, or they'd have sent the authorities to look for you. Miss Chilton, you have absolutely nothing to fear from me. I want you to regain your strength as soon as possible."

"Why? What do you want from me?"

He sat back, rubbing his face with his hands wearily. "I'm afraid I've made a dreadful mess of this."

"Non-responsive answer, counselor."

He blinked, then half smiled. "Sustained. Miss Chilton, what I am proposing is a magical collaboration—a working of such magnitude that...well, I couldn't think of any way to describe it unless you first saw for yourself what we'll be up against. I tried, believe me. But I could find no words that even approached the reality, and I couldn't possibly ask you to make a decision on second hand information—not about something like this."

"Well..." her curiosity was piqued, but she hated to let him off too easily. "You still might have prefaced your demonstration by saying that."

He looked down. "I concede that. But..."

"It's a moot point now, isn't it?" He didn't answer, and Diana sighed heavily. "Can you explain your proposal, or do I have to go through something else? I'm sorry, but I don't have any idea what I was supposed to have seen."

His head jerked up. "But you must have seen it. That's why I went so far, to make sure. That's the only way it can be seen—*I* saw it."

She could only shake her head. "I didn't see anything. I couldn't feel anything,

I couldn't breathe..." but even as she spoke, a memory was returning, and with it a fear so deep that her hands started to shake.

"Think back to last night. Think back to the last moment you can remember."

She closed her eyes, and it came to her, as it had a few moments ago in her dream: the coiling, fiery vortex, bearing down on her. She shuddered and opened her eyes with a gasp. "I remember...it was like something alive, but made of such power..."

"Yes," he whispered.

"You mean that thing is real? Not just...not just some kind of deathbed hallucination?"

"It is the most real thing that you will ever encounter."

"What is it?"

"I call it the dragon, because that's what it resembles. I don't know if it has a name of its own."

She remembered the terrifying feeling from last night, that the thing, whatever it was, contained the ability to utterly and effortlessly transform whatever it touched. "That power...is what makes you immortal."

"Yes."

"And what does your proposed magical collaboration have to do with *that?*"

His face twisted, as though he was struggling with a profound emotion, although Diana couldn't interpret it. "I am its slave, and I want that partnership ended. I want to master the dragon—or break free of it. That is why I need your help."

"You must be joking, Mr. Morgan."

"I most definitely am not joking."

"But I wouldn't know how to challenge something like..." she fumbled into silence, cold fear gripping her body. The thought of encountering, let alone combating, what she had perceived last night was enough to make her break into an icy sweat. "I'm not invincible, or omnipotent. Nobody anointed me God, Mr. Morgan—I know when I'm outclassed. I could no more face that thing down than I could wave a wand and stop a hurricane in its tracks."

He took her shaking hands and squeezed them tightly. "I understand your apprehension—more than you know. But don't allow your fear to magnify your adversary. I believe this thing can be defeated. I can't do it alone. I have not the skill or the native ability. But you do. I was told..." he paused, as if catching himself just in time. "I understand that your native ability is unprecedented, and your skill almost its equal."

She stared at him, caught between her emotions and the flattering content of his words. "Don't believe everything you hear."

"My source is unimpeachable."

"Who?"

He only smiled, shaking his head. Frustrated, Diana looked down at the colorful quilt. "If you're its slave, how can you act against it? Doesn't that mean that it controls you?"

"It does not control me. It tries. It wants me to..." he glanced at her uneasily. "Don't get angry again, but...explaining what it wants will require a long story. Which you will hear," he added firmly as Diana opened her mouth to speak.

"But, Mr. Morgan—if, beyond all probability, we succeed in this...doesn't that mean you'll die?"

His gaze didn't waver. "Quite possibly. I have no idea. But I'm prepared for that."

"Is that what you want?"

"No. I'm not seeking death, or simple release from my immortal state. I don't know if our success would achieve either one. But death would be preferable to the alternative—and the alternative is becoming harder and harder to resist."

Diana drew back against the headboard, thinking about her arrival the evening before, their conversation, Thomas' admission, and finally what had happened after she so recklessly looked into his face and said, "show me." In her imagination she saw again that blinding coil of pure power, and she hugged herself tightly. "Mr. Morgan...I'm sorry, but...I just don't know. This is all so...I didn't come here for this."

"Yes, you did," he said softly. She looked up at him, startled, but he went on before she could speak. "This is exactly what you came here for. Miss Chilton—I'm asking you to attempt a great working with me, something that transcends the boundaries of this world. In all your years with the Order, have you ever been offered such an opportunity? Haven't you always longed for a challenge that would truly test your skills, push every limitation you've ever met? Isn't that why you've left the Order's circle now, your frustration with them for holding you back, for refusing to allow you access to their deepest Mysteries? Don't you welcome a chance to prove what you're capable of, to yourself if not to the Order?"

She stared at him, suddenly feeling self-conscious and exposed. "How do you know—"

"I've seen it. I told you last night that I knew what you were looking for. For five years, you've been seeking this. Are you just going to walk away from this chance now? The woman who was brave enough to come alone to my door, to enter my home, not knowing what manner of creature she was trusting her life to...that woman could not be afraid."

"Stop. Stop talking for a moment." He sat back, looking down at the floor, as if to give her privacy to think without being watched. Diana felt so shaken, she wasn't sure how to react. *They say that knowing someone's true name gives you power over them,* she thought bleakly, *but it's not so. It's knowing their deepest, most secret desire...that's how you conquer them.* He was right. The very idea of approaching a work so ambitious, of attaining such power, awakened a temptation in her so intense it was almost a raw lust. All of her years of training warned her that such a temptation was the greatest of magical traps. Yet she felt it gripping the very core of her soul so deeply that she knew she could not refuse this chance without regretting it for the rest of her life. The seven years since her final initiation, her formal censure, her most recent humiliation, the despair that she was forever excluded from advancement in the Order because she was a woman...all of these suppressed resentments and yearnings suddenly welled up uncontrollably. Her feelings of anger and violation at Thomas' actions faded into hazy inconsequence before this desire. After all, hadn't she walked right into this situation, almost as presumptuously? And now her reward was a chance to work with a magical equal, with no rules, no hierarchy monitoring them, no limitations...

"Mr. Morgan," she said, and he looked up, almost startled, as though he had been lost in thought as well. "I'm going to need a great deal more information before I can make a decision like this."

"I know, and I'm ready to answer your questions. You need only ask."

We'll see about that, she thought. "But first, there's one thing I need to know now. *If* I consider your proposal, carefully and thoroughly, and if I decide that I cannot, or will not, help you—will you accept that, and let me go?"

He stared at her, struck, for a long moment, and she saw him swallow. "Yes," he finally said, almost inaudibly, and then looked down. "I don't know."

"Good. You're being honest."

He looked back up sharply. "I wouldn't keep you here in this house against your will. You are not a prisoner, Miss Chilton..."

"But...?" When he didn't answer, she said, "You won't give up trying to persuade me to reconsider, will you?"

He closed his eyes for a moment. "Don't think so ill of me. You're my only hope now. I've tried everything I could do on my own. If this fails, there is no hope. I know that."

She knew that he touched her pride by calling her his only hope, and tried to stifle that additional weakness. "All right. No promises, but I am considering. Are you willing to tell me the truth—the whole truth? With no more you-couldn't-understand nonsense? And fair warning before any practical demonstrations of the indescribable?"

"I swear." He stood up, reaching for the empty pitcher. "This is likely to be a long conversation. Are you hungry?"

She hadn't eaten since dinner at the Inn the night before. At the mere thought of that meal, which she'd scarcely tasted, her stomach rumbled. "Starving."

"I have some food for you, and I'll get some more water. You can eat while we talk." Diana listened carefully after he left the room, wondering where in the house she was, but his footsteps were so quiet, she couldn't even tell when he went down the stairs.

He returned with a tray containing a fresh pitcher of water and a variety of food—bread, butter and cheese, fruit, and a paper plate of homemade cookies covered with waxed paper. He set the pitcher on the bureau and put the tray on the bed. "You needn't stand on ceremony," he said, filling up the water glass.

"Bon appetit."

"What a charming little picnic," Diana said with amusement as she spread a piece of bread with butter and added slices of cheese. "But I guess you wouldn't have a lot of food around if you never eat it, would you?"

"Oh, I eat ordinary food sometimes. It doesn't taste the same as it once did, but I even get cravings occasionally, especially for sweets. Unfortunately, I can't cook—I can barely boil a kettle of water. All of this is from a little farm stand I sometimes visit."

"It's delicious." She chewed a bite of sandwich thoughtfully. "But...you're a vampire, that's the right word, isn't it?"

He shifted uneasily in the chair. "Yes."

"That means you have to drink blood to, to sustain yourself, to continue existing?"

"I assume that's true. I only need a comparatively small amount of blood every few days, and it needn't be human. But food doesn't nourish me. What the blood actually does for me, I don't really know."

"What happens if you don't get blood? Can you starve?"

"If I try to abstain for too long, I...lose possession of my faculties. That is not something I dare to risk. But theoretically, I don't think I can starve."

"Why not?"

"Because in order to starve, I would have to be able to die. I can't. I'm bound to this world. I heal from any injury, although it is rare for me to incur one. I'm immune to illness. I'm not affected by heat or cold. In the strictest sense, my body isn't physical."

"Now what does that mean? You felt pretty physical to me."

"Well, among other things, I can...dematerialize."

She stared at him. "You're kidding. Just like that?"

He nodded.

"Oh, come on, I have to see this."

He looked embarrassed. "I feel like a fool doing it."

"Don't be silly! You can't make a claim like that and—" she stopped, open mouthed. He was gone, just like that. "Wow." There was a shimmer in the air, and he was back. "Clothes and all. That's quite a trick."

"I seldom use it. I dislike feeling so...ephemeral."

It took Diana a few moments to recover from her amazement. "So does this mean," she finally said, trying to think what else fell among the parameters she'd reviewed that afternoon, "you can't be killed by anything? So much for all the folklore about stakes and beheadings and whatnot?"

"That's more or less correct. Even if I'm faced with something very destructive, my body will simply dematerialize to avoid it. It seems to be a sort of reflex."

She tried to imagine this, and couldn't evoke anything that didn't belong on the pages of a comic book. Still..."That sounds somewhat enviable."

"Do you think so? It has its disadvantages."

"Such as?"

"Sometimes I can't control it."

She decided to let that one go for now. "Last night, you seemed to be looking at me when you answered the door, even though it was pitch dark. I gather that your night vision is rather extraordinary."

His smile was bitter. "That's something of an understatement. It's never dark to me anymore. There are times when I miss darkness, as strange as it seems. It lends an illusion of privacy."

"In town, people told me that you're never around during the day, and won't answer the door. Do you sleep all day?"

"My fellow citizens have selective memories. I don't see well in sunlight, but I'm often awake on dark days. Sometimes I don't answer the door because I just don't want to be bothered." He gave her a quick glance. "That was not the case when you were here, though. I think you must have been nervous about disturbing me."

Recalling how gingerly she'd padded around his house, Diana smiled sheepishly. "Yes, I was, silly me. So, Bram Stoker got it all wrong—you don't spend your days lying like a corpse in a coffin somewhere."

He stiffened his shoulders. "Certainly not. I sleep anywhere you might—usually in bed in the room next to this one, in fact. I'm no revenant, Miss Chilton."

"But even so...you're not really *alive* anymore, are you? You don't need to eat food. You vanish and reappear like a ghost. You don't really breathe. I don't think you have a heartbeat, either." Her voice fell to a hush. "Did you die?"

"Yes, I died." The bitterness in his voice was not directed at her. "But I'm not some reanimated cadaver. I detest graveyards, and I can't bear being in the same house as the dead—I never could."

She offered no argument, since he didn't seem corpse-like to her, either. Unearthly, yes, but nothing like the descriptions in nineteenth century Gothic literature, or the folklore collected by Summers or Wright. In the silence that followed, she thought over what he'd told her, trying to fit it together into a coherent picture.

Thomas eventually relaxed in the chair and looked slightly abashed. "Forgive me. I'm not used to talking about myself so frankly."

"I seem to have hit a nerve, of some sort. But Mr. Morgan—you say you died, but you're not dead. You say you're not physical, but you're solid and you need solid sustenance. Just what, exactly, are you?"

"I don't know. I wish I did. I never had anyone to explain it to me."

"Are there others like you?"

"Exactly like me?" He shook his head. "Not a one, of which I have ever been aware."

The way he phrased his answer sparked her curiosity. "Other vampires, then?"

He hesitated before he spoke. "They're very rare, and they're not our concern. I feel that I should respect their confidentiality, beyond that."

How tantalizing...and how frustrating, she thought, but immediately shelved her regret. She had plenty to occupy her with just one vampire for now.

"So...you said last night that this was done to you, and you didn't choose it. But now you say you've never met another vampire like you. What happened to you? How did you meet...that thing?" She felt uncomfortable naming the dragon aloud even by Thomas' invented term, it seemed so formidable.

He looked down, smiling slightly. "It's a long story—and something of a confession. You could say that I got exactly what I deserved. But I'll let you decide that." He got up and went to lower the window sash a few inches, since the evening air was becoming quite cool. He stood looking out of the window for a minute, apparently collecting his thoughts. Then he came back to the chair and sat down.

"I'd like to begin with a caveat. I don't know if everything in this story actually happened the way it seemed to. In all the times I've relived it in my mind, I've never found a single thing out of place, or the most trivial missing detail, to suggest that my memory was a vision, or a dream, or a delusion. But I scarcely believe it myself, and I would never credit this account if I heard it from another person. I want you to know that I realize how incredible some of this is going to sound to you."

"I'll consider myself duly warned. But the boundaries of what I'd hold to be possible have pretty much been eliminated in the last twenty-four hours."

He nodded. "Then I'll begin by asking you a question you probably will find odd. Would you consider me a handsome man?"

She was taken off guard by this query. "Well, yes. You're a bit pretty for my tastes, but you're certainly good looking. Why?"

His smile was grim. "When I was twenty, I would have called that response damning with faint praise. God, I cringe now just to think what a vain little monster I was. You see, it was no advantage to be *Cymro*, a Welshman, in London in those days. As far as the English were concerned, the Welsh were dwarfish, homely, stupid, primitive, dishonest, shiftless, cruel, and illiterate. Do you know that on March first, Saint David's Day, it was considered great sport to hang effigies of Welshmen from makeshift gibbets in London?"

"I never heard that one, no."

"Since I had a handsome appearance, education, and wealth, I wasn't satisfied to defy the English bigotries. I set out to avenge them, and not only in Parliament and the courts. I dressed in the costliest and most fashionable clothing I could find, just so I would outshine any Englishman I met. And I was a ruthless rake when it came to women—especially the *Saesnesau*, the fair-haired, blue-eyed darlings of the peerage. Virgins, wives, or widows, it didn't matter to me. I could get any of them into bed, and once I had them, I treated them worse than any procurer treated his whores. It wasn't just for political reasons that I had to flee to France.

"But God was paying closer attention to me than I supposed. As I grew older my face stayed youthful, which only made me vainer than ever. But one day when I was in my late thirties, I noticed a small sore on my cheek. I thought little of it, but it didn't fade as such blemishes normally do. It stayed there, month after month, then turned angry red, and then black. It began to spread."

Diana let out a long soft breath. "Cancer."

"Cancer it was, and despite all the physics and medicines I was offered, within three years I had but half a face. The sore grew until it ate away my cheek and left a gaping hole, so you could see my teeth grinning out at you, what teeth were still left. My eyelid developed a great wen which closed the eye, and the disease was getting into the bone and misshaping my jaw. Yet the damnable thing refused to kill me, and I imagined the day would come when I would look in the glass and see nothing but a fleshless skull looking back at me, and yet I would still be alive. And I knew this was God's punishment on me for the manner in which I'd used my looks to debauch and deceive, and the worth I'd placed on them."

"So, what happened? There's not even a scar on your face now."

"Yes, and you see the price I was willing to pay for it. I finally returned to England. By then, resuming my law practice was out of the question. I wore a tight leather mask over my face, which supported my rotting flesh and hid the ravages of the disease. Of course, I could only eat in private, since half of what I tried to swallow ended up running down my neck. I went back to the Order then, seeking desperately for some resolution. I thought I would have welcomed either death or healing, but I was far too craven to just take my pistol and finish the matter. No one would have cared. My parents were long dead, and I had never married. But I said, as often as I could and to everyone I could, that I would do anything for a cure, would pay any price to have a face again. I wish someone had warned me. Never, never say that you will pay any price. There will always be someone listening to take up your bluff."

He paused, his eyes distant. Diana said softly, "And who was listening to you?"

"I never knew who she was. I thought at the time that she was a high-ranking member of the Order. She visited my chambers late one night and told me that she'd heard of my promise and could help me. She was tall, a head taller than I was, exquisitely dressed, but she veiled her face, and she was not a young woman. Nonetheless she was beautiful, even seen through her veil. When I asked for her name, she only smiled and said, 'You may call me Your Ladyship.' At one time I would have laughed her out of the room to hear that. Now I didn't care. I called her Your Ladyship—as well as I could pronounce it with half of a mouth.

"She didn't name a price. She gave me a time and a place to meet her, and I did everything she instructed. It was a great house on an estate in Windsor. I was told to come alone, so I traveled there on horseback. When I arrived, there were no servants, no dogs, no signs of life anywhere. I tied my horse by the front door with my own hands. The door was standing open, and I went inside. The house was completely dark and silent, and I had no idea what to think. But I could see a glimmer of light and smell burning tallow, so I walked up the stairs and down a corridor until I reached a ballroom. Every chandelier was ablaze with new candles, freshly lit, but the room was completely empty except for one figure—Her Ladyship, dressed all in white, standing in the center of the room.

"I walked forward to face her. She was smiling, and her long fair hair flowed loose down her back. She looked to me like an angel. 'Do you come of your own free will to pay any price in exchange for your face?' she asked me, and I said, 'Yes, I do.' She told me to remove my mask, and I undid the straps and peeled it away. She reached out and laid her hand over the gaping hole that had been my cheek, and she said, 'Then, Dafydd Morgynne, I grant your request. I give you a pretty face, one which neither age nor scar nor illness shall ever touch, and you will grace Middle-earth with your beauty until the end of time.' Before I could think about what this meant, she said, 'Look above you,' and I looked up, and I saw..."

He broke off, his eyes haunted. "How can I describe it? But then, you saw for yourself. I thought it was a dragon, the way it writhed and twisted. It was alive, yet made of fire. It shot down at me and penetrated my body, and instantly I was aflame, every part of me, and never had I felt such agony. I lay on the floor, screaming, suffused with this pain that would ebb a little, then return with greater strength, like the incoming tide. I have no idea how long this went on, but it seemed unending. I found myself at Her Ladyship's feet, and I kissed her slippers and begged her to kill me. That's all I wanted then—not beauty, not healing, only death to deliver me from that terrible flame. She knelt down and said..."

He paused, and Diana whispered, "'As you wish.'"

He looked up, startled. "How did you know?"

"This is so familiar...I don't know why, it's like a fairytale."

"Yes, it is. Because you see—but I'm getting ahead of myself."

"Did she kill you?"

He shook his head. "The pain was ebbing then...I think it had come three times, and I could feel it gathering for a fourth assault. She was wearing a dagger at her waist, and she took it from its sheath and handed it to me. I cut my own throat with it."

There was a long silence, and finally Diana let out her breath explosively. "My *God*. So what happened then?"

"I awoke in my own chambers."

"But..."

"My face was whole...indeed, there was not a scar left anywhere on my body, save one. I looked as you see me now—as if twenty years had been taken away. Even my hair was raven black once more. But I never saw Her Ladyship again. And I quickly discovered that there were a great many conditions in the compact I'd made which I had not bothered to ascertain beforehand."

"Did you ever go back to the house and try to find her?"

"Oh, yes. The house belonged to a duke, and when I passed by there only a night or so later, it was filled with serving staff, horses, dogs, guests, the duke and his family, and none of them behaving as though anything untoward, such as a lake of blood on the ballroom floor, had ever been discovered."

Diana shook her head slowly, her imagination forming a vivid picture of the candlelit ballroom, of Thomas putting the knife to his throat and...she shuddered. "Were you taking opiates? Laudanum?"

He nodded. "But I've thought of that. I didn't take any physic at all for three days before this occurred. Her Ladyship so instructed me. My mind was clearer than it had been in some time, although I was in quite a bit of pain." He smiled bitterly. "I told you that I would find your skepticism wholly forgivable. Notwithstanding my involvement with the Order, I never thought of myself as a fanciful man. I was schooled in Aristotelian reasoning, law and rhetoric. I would have thought the entire incident was a dream, or a vision, myself—except that there were several substantial pieces of evidence to the contrary."

"You had your face back, to start with."

"To start with, yes. And then there was the complete transformation of my essential nature into something...inhuman. Realizing that I had to drink blood for sustenance, that simple sunlight would sear my skin to blisters in a matter of hours, that wounds closed themselves in seconds...my existence was about to become a series of shocking discoveries. But before I knew any of this, I awoke in clothing stiff with blood, and still holding Her Ladyship's dagger. My hand was clenched around it so hard I had difficulty loosening my fingers."

"Do you still have it? I'd like to see it."

"I'll show it to you. Perhaps you'll find some meaning in it. It's quite curious."

She suddenly recalled another detail from Thomas' story. "What about your horse? If you awoke in your chambers, what happened to your transportation?"

"Ah, yes..." his face darkened. "I'd hired him, as men without households usually did at the time. He was in the stables behind the building where I was living. When I finally remembered the poor beast and went down to see to him, I discovered for the first time how overwhelming my new thirst was. I had known I wanted *something*. Until I smelled living blood, I wasn't conscious of *what* I wanted."

Diana swallowed uncomfortably. "You drank your horse's blood?"

"I couldn't stop myself. I'd seen horses bled, there are veins close to their skin, very easy to find. I'd been given a steady, patient chestnut gelding, and he'd been standing saddled and bridled all day, unnoticed by anyone. He nickered to me when he heard me approach. I walked up to him blindly, carried along by the smell of him, and I simply..." He fell silent for a moment. "That's when I knew exactly what kind of a bargain I'd made—when I came to myself and realized that I was standing beside a trembling animal slaking a thirst for blood. Then I finally comprehended the depths of my own stupidity, not merely the night before, but through all of my life...and it was too late."

Diana reflected that drinking blood didn't seem like an unfair price to pay for immortality, although she decided to keep this opinion private. "You said all your scars had disappeared, except one?" Her guess was confirmed when he pulled down the collar of his sweater so she could see the thin ragged line running from below his ear to his collar bone. It hadn't been a clean cut.

"The last one," he said very quietly, and Diana had to swallow hard.

"Who do you think that woman was? Do you have any idea?"

"Oh, I have an idea, think of it what you like. In *Cymru* I had heard of a people that lived under the earth—a people perilous and beautiful, with the power to grant wishes to those fool enough to ask for them. They are the people who listen when we speak those words best left unsaid. They are the ones who hold the glass up to our own follies. The Tylwyth Teg, they are called."

"The Fair Folk."

"Yes. Because who else would have damned me to Middle-earth? It was a strange phrase to use. In Medieval times, Middle-earth was the name for this world, the land between Heaven and the underworld, the realm of the faery folk. That's where I think she was from."

Diana pondered this darkly. A few days ago, she would have had a more dubious response. She'd thought the myths of the faery realm were archetypes and psychological symbols, possibly inspired by some kind of truth, but not to be taken literally. But after last night, and seeing Thomas dematerialize before her eyes, she was far less confident about her interpretation of myth.

"I guess there's just one major question left to ask," she said finally. He waited expectantly, and she met his eyes. "Just what, exactly, does...the dragon...want you to do, that is so terrible, you're going to such lengths to avoid it?"

He looked away from her uneasily, but by now he knew better than to evade the question. "It wants me to...pass it on, to release it into other human beings."

"And make them vampires like you?"

"Presumably. As I've never succumbed to the temptation, I don't know for sure what would happen. I don't want to know."

"Why? Is your existence so unbearable, that you'd rather be dead than share it?"

"It's not that, although..." he was quiet for a moment. "You can't imagine the agony of that experience. There are no words strong enough to describe it. Saying that it's like being burned alive only conveys a dim shadow of the reality. I couldn't possibly inflict that much pain on another, especially someone who I cared for, or respected, enough to want them to share my immortality. You see the dilemma, don't you?"

Diana reluctantly thought back to last night, when she had realized that Thomas was restraining the dragon from reaching her, and how desperately she'd prayed to him not to let it go. "I think so...as you say, I can't really understand it the way you do."

"That's part of it. The other part...that ordeal is fatal. Anyone who is devoured by the dragon dies, and dies horribly. I've never caused the death of another human being—not once."

"Never? Not even in your law work?"

"I was never a prosecutor. I lost cases, and that was bad enough." He smiled wryly. "I've been a fugitive from more than one death sentence, myself. I long ago wearied of seeing death inflicted for any reason. I don't want to be responsible for that."

"But...all initiations follow a death and rebirth pattern, and you're never prepared for what it's really going to be like. If you were, it wouldn't be a true initiation. If someone sincerely wanted it..."

He gave her a keen look. "Do you?"

"Well, no, I'm not saying that, I'm just trying to get a clear picture, that's all."

He smiled but didn't argue. "Initiations are metaphorical. Really, Miss Chilton, think about it. Imagine saying to someone, 'I love you and want to be with you forever, so pardon me while I let you be raped and tortured to death.' That's the analogy. It doesn't seem like an auspicious beginning for a partnership, does it? Especially when I can't even offer certainty of the outcome."

"But what other outcome could there be?"

He shrugged. "Who knows? What do you think that power would *not* be capable of? But I can never forget that the Good People are renowned for their tricks."

"But...if you don't want to pass your condition on—why go to such lengths? Why not simply refuse to do it?"

"The dragon isn't a passive force, content to have done its work on me and let be. It has been pressuring me for many decades now to continue what it started."

"Pressuring, how?"

"Every time I drink from a human being—and I do so infrequently—I perceive the dragon, tempting me, pushing at me to continue past the point of no return. At first, that wasn't the case. But once it started reappearing, it became more and more insistent. Now...I dream of it. I find myself falling into long brooding spells, thinking about it. Last night...it required every shred of will that I possessed not to release it into you. For a moment, I thought I would lose control of it."

"I was...aware of that, believe it or not."

"It has long been a maddening obsession, Miss Chilton, and I can't risk madness. My capacity for doing harm is much too great for that. This is why I'll do anything to break the dragon's hold over me. I can't choose death by any other means, no matter how noble my reasons." He glanced at her sharply. "Not that I wish for death. You asked if my existence was unbearable. I would never say that. But...there is an intensity to it that is wearying. Every sense is acutely tuned, every experience is heightened, my awareness of the emotions and reactions of other living things is nearly preternatural. I'd always lived in cities, I loved being in the midst of humanity. But the twentieth century has brought a cacophony of industrial noise and stink that modern man no longer even notices. Unlike mortals, I can't shut it out."

"That's why you moved up here."

"I had to, to keep my sanity. You can see my dilemma. I have peace here, but I'm no longer able to do the work I pursued so passionately for my entire existence. Without that, what is the point of continuing?"

"There must be some solution, Mr. Morgan—there must be."

"Perhaps there is. There's much about this world that I would miss, but I've had more than my share of life. After all, death is part of the natural order of things. How long can I expect to cheat it?"

After that, Diana could think of nothing more to ask, and Thomas seemed to feel no need to fill the silence. The room was very still. The moon had risen, lightening the night sky outside. Earlier there had been crickets and other insects singing in the fields around the house, but now Diana couldn't hear them. The candle flames burned straight and steadily. She could feel her heart beating rapidly, and a chill of fear tightening her stomach. But it was her own decision that frightened her—the decision that had already been made by some part of her Will above her rational mind and ego.

"Thomas," she said softly, and he looked up at her. "I'll do it."

He blinked, looking not so much surprised as incredulous. "Are you sure?"

She closed her eyes for a moment, gathering her thoughts. Thomas, sensing what she was about to do, waited motionless. Finally she opened her eyes, and took Thomas' right hand in her own. "I will help you, Thomas Morgan. I will join you in this work and see it through to its conclusion. I swear by the silver light."

He must have been holding a breath by habit, because he suddenly released it in a long sigh, as his grip on her hand tightened. "And I swear by the silver light to complete this work with you, regardless of its end."

As he spoke, Diana felt a vertiginous sense that time had stopped, like a movie when the projector is halted. For one moment, it seemed as though the very walls of the room were paying attention, and even inanimate objects paused with bated breath. *And who was listening to you?...They are the people who listen when we speak those words best left...* but suddenly the surreal feeling had vanished. The candle flames flared in a breeze from the window, and the trilling of crickets filled the night outside. Diana sighed, her shoulders sagging. "I think it's time we got onto a first-name basis, as fellow initiates and peers, if nothing else."

"I am not sure," Thomas said with an uneasy smile, "that I would quite consider myself your magical peer...Diana."

She gave his hand a comradely squeeze and let it go. "I'll give you credit for seniority, at the very least." Her humorous tone was slightly forced—the full import of the oath she had just made was slowly sinking in, and she felt a bit stunned. *Ah, Mother Goddess, what have I done?* But it was too late for doubts now. She had stepped through the door and there was no going back. She felt exhausted, and she sensed that Thomas, as well, was only beginning to appreciate the meaning of the agreement they had just made.

He rose and gathered up the food, refilled the water glass and placed it next to the bed. "You should get some sleep now," he said, and she didn't argue, because she could barely keep her eyes open. "If you need anything, call for me. I promise, I will hear you. You'll be recovered in two days. Then we can begin our work."

4

"We're definitely going to need an athanor." Diana sat back and flexed her stiff shoulders. Thomas, who was feeding kindling into the massive iron cook stove, glanced up with a look of brief surprise. It was the first time Diana had spoken all evening, and he had become accustomed to her studious silence.

A week had passed since the rainy night when Diana knocked on Thomas' door. For the past three nights, she had spent most of her time in the large brick-paved kitchen at the back of the ground floor. She had covered the entire surface of the long trestle table with papers and ledger books filled with the notes and records Thomas had made of over a century of magical workings. For days, she had been poring over one failure after another, until she felt somewhat depressed by the sheer cumulative effect. Thomas had explained the garden out back, his most recent effort, as an attempt to create an earth grid that would contain the dragon's energy and possibly send it to ground. That scheme, five years in the planning and building, had proven just as fruitless as all the rest. Since then he had been evolving a completely new approach, a direct confrontation with the dragon itself.

Thomas left the cold stove and came over to join her at the table, leaning over to study her own pages of notes and diagrams. "Do you really think it will succeed?"

"I think it *could* succeed. Only the completion of the working will unequivocally answer that question. But the concept is sound and your outline seems like a very good one. What it needs is a focal point, something that can contain the level of power we'll build up over time. That's what the athanor will do for us."

His brow furrowed in slight puzzlement. "I thought that an athanor was simply a small furnace, or oven of sorts, a laboratory tool."

"That's exactly what it is. But there are other ways to use one than processing alchemical compounds. You might not be familiar with this technique, I was taught it by Le—by my mentor. The athanor maintains a steady heat and pressure for the duration of the working. This mirrors on the material plane what the magical energy is doing on the etheric one. Do you follow me?"

"I believe so."

She rummaged for an unmarked sheet of paper and a pencil. "Look, this is how it's built," she said, sketching quickly. "Two walls of thermal brick, sealed, with a layer of silicon sand in the middle. The furnace underneath works like this, very simple, it's a closed firebox like the stove there...and it's vented so... and that will burn as long as forty-eight hours at a time, not that you want to let it go longer than twenty-four or the temperature won't stay level. Then inside you have a sealed chamber made of three layers of metal—copper, brass and iron—like so, and inside that there is a glass vessel. The vessel contains the energy, and *that* is the focus of the working."

He tugged the paper toward himself and traced the pencil marks with a finger. "I see...it just burns wood, not coal?"

"Yes, hardwood, like oak or maple. We don't want it getting too hot, you see. I assume we'll have no trouble getting seasoned firewood around here."

"None at all. I own four hundred acres of woodlot. But I'm curious—what is inside the glass vessel?"

"Well...we may have a slight challenge with that. Can we shelve that detail for a moment?"

He hesitated, then gestured that she continue.

"Now, I like your ideas for the structure of the working itself. Structure is always arbitrary, anyway, since it's only a focusing device. I agree that the charge and incantation can be in Welsh, because of its being your native language and all, but that means you'll have to write them. My Welsh is shaky, and besides, ritual script is best composed solo."

"But you know the cadences," he said urgently. "That was one of the reasons I needed your help to even plan the working. I was never trained in using the cadences."

"Yes, I know the cadences." She rested her forehead on her hand, suddenly tired. Even after a week, her levels of endurance were not quite up to their usual vigor. "Look, I'll give you the syncopation patterns and the syllable counts for the lines. The rest of it is all in the melody and inflection, and it won't hurt if the word emphasis is a bit odd here and there. We could sing nursery rhymes as long as the cadences are correct. Can you work with that?"

"I'm sure I can." He bent back over the notes. "So, we build the athanor and begin the working. Every day?"

"Without fail. I wanted to suggest that we time the daily working to correspond with the season. That would mean we work at midday during the summer. Will you be able to function, staying up all day when it's hot and sunny?"

"I'll see to it that I do. You might be wise to avoid annoying me, however. I can be a bit prickly during the daytime."

"I'll remember that." She got up from the table and went to the deep soapstone sink attached to the kitchen's west wall. The house had running water as long as the five hundred gallon cistern was hand-pumped at intervals to keep it full. She drew a glass of cold well water and drained it. The weather had been hot and clear, and she was thirsty almost all of the time. She leaned back against the sink and watched Thomas as he read over her notes again, her eyes following the lines of his lean body, thrown into contrasts of light and shadow by the dim kerosene lamps. Until she was on her feet, he had cared for her as solicitously as a parent, but her feelings toward him, as ambiguous and complicated as they were, included nothing in the least filial. She shook herself before he could notice what she was doing and returned to the table.

"How long do you estimate this is going to take, all told?" he asked as she sat back down. "I gather you were doing quite a bit of calculating."

She picked up her pencil and tapped the tabletop nervously with it for a moment. "Based on planetary cycles, and what I'm estimating for the tipping point...about eighteen months."

Thomas sank slowly down onto the bench, blinking. "A year and a half. And working every day."

"And feeding the athanor and monitoring it. That won't take a lot of time, but it will have to be done every day." He was so quiet for so long that she finally said, "You're not really surprised, are you? That seems short to me, but one mistake we really can't make on this one is timing the ending. It will peak when it peaks, and we can adjust as we go along, but I'm estimating at least eighteen months."

He shook his head finally. "It's just that...you'll be here all that time."

"Well...that would be the most practical arrangement. There's already enough curiosity about us to make things awkward if I live in town and constantly travel back and forth. With the scope of this project, I really need to be right here."

He finally gave a dismissive shrug. "I've never lived with anyone for so long, especially not since...but you understand why."

"I understand what you told me, but...Thomas, you were able to hold back the dragon that first night. I have trouble imagining a more extreme situation arising than that." He only frowned without answering. "If I'm going to trust you, you have to trust yourself." Finally he sighed and nodded. Diana turned briskly back to her notes. "We do have a pretty tight squeeze around the exact time we commence the working. We need to begin on the Winter Solstice. That means everything constructed and ready to go—everything. If we can't do it by this Solstice, we'll have to wait at least six months, possibly a year."

"*Can* we finish by then?"

"It depends on how quickly we can assemble the materials. With all the lime burning kilns here on the Bay, we shouldn't have trouble getting the materials for the athanor. I know a place where we can have the metal parts for the chamber forged for us. They've done it before. We'll need to have them welded together, but that can't happen before the glass vessel is ready. And the athanor can only be built so far before we'll need to have the metal chamber. The hardest work will be constructing the athanor itself."

"I presume this is a formal construction?"

"For this? Are you serious?" She laughed. "Every brick consecrated individually. Each one set in ritually. Every component of this entire device will have to be consecrated, re-consecrated, ritually sealed, ritually set into place, ritually sealed again. And it all has to be done by Winter Solstice. Are you still game?"

He smiled. "It will be quite an adventure. I've lost the knack of racing against time. What were you saying about the glass vessel? Maybe we could get back to that."

"Oh, that." She sighed. "It needs to contain a compound, which has a particular combination of magical and chemical properties—something that has been made by an alchemical working. I could create a compound that would have the qualities we need—maybe. But it would take time, and chemicals I don't have, and another, ordinary athanor which I don't have access to easily. And alchemy is not my forte. But I know someone who…well, he used to be a member of the Order."

She paused, as Thomas studied her expression. "Not your former husband, I hope?"

"Oh, no! Goodness…Stephen could never do anything like that. He'd push his alchemical skills sugaring his coffee. No, I'm talking about Gregory Fitzhughes. He's brilliant, a genius in some ways, but…I feel honor-bound to warn you. He earned a rather cruel nickname in his last years with the Order. Some people called him the Mad Hatter."

"Because he made hats, or he was just mad?"

"Because he went mad for the same reason the hatters did—he got careless with his mercury, and several other highly toxic materials. He's not really mad, of course, that was just a nasty jibe. He was always eccentric, and he had radical political views, so he struck people as being pretty far out all along. Then after he poisoned himself, his mind sort of…splintered, I guess. It was like he had three trains of thought going on all the time. If you knew him well, you could keep up, but for newcomers, and casual acquaintances, he could be a bit off-putting, I'm afraid."

"I'm surprised that someone so skilled would have made that kind of mistake, especially when it led to such severe consequences."

"He was pushing it. He always did. He said it was impossible to achieve the results he wanted without directly contacting the chemicals. People stopped kidding about it when it became apparent how serious it really was."

"But he's still able to make his compounds."

"I trust his compounds, absolutely. I'd trust him with my life. The main problem is negotiating with him. He was never the sort of person who would work for hire, as it were, and he was much too iconoclastic to play well as part of team."

"I'm willing to pay any amount he asks."

"Money was never something that Gregory considered a priority. You know how they say that everyone has a price, if they're offered enough? I think Gregory is the only person I've ever met for whom that isn't true. But that doesn't mean we can't strike some kind of a deal. I'll just have to try to get in touch with him. I'm afraid he didn't leave the Order voluntarily, and I haven't talked to him since then."

Thomas sat for a moment mulling this over. "You also mentioned welding."

She shifted uncomfortably. "Yes, and that's going to be the trickiest part. We'll have to be working ritually as the pieces are welded, and it will take at least a few nights to finish. It will have to be done here, in our magical working space, and whoever does the welding will need to know something about what's going on, so we can coordinate the practical aspect with the magical one. The welder doesn't have to be a magician, but…it might be hard to find anyone around here that wouldn't be spinning tales all over the place, and that's if they didn't run for their life the first night and refuse to come back. We'll have to pay someone a lot of money, and even then we could have confidentiality problems."

"I may be able to solve the confidentiality question, at the very least."

"Really? How?"

"I have some ability…a very minor ability…to influence."

"You mean, like hypnosis? That can be unreliable." She had seen members of the Order pull off some amazing feats, on completely unaware subjects, but sometimes the subject rejected the suggestions, or the conditioning wore off.

"It's not as simple as that. It's definitely reliable."

Diana put down her pencil and crossed her arms. "Thomas—this is important. Don't be so damnably vague."

"All right! I can blot out memories, when I am…when I am deeply connected to other people."

"You mean, when you're drinking their blood."

"Yes. It's very crude—I'd get about the same effect by bashing in the poor soul's head with a hammer. The person almost always faints dead away on the spot. And it's very limited. I can only make an individual forget the most immediate events and experiences. But I can sometimes use the same connection to exert a sort of enhanced persuasion—arrange his thoughts so that he will cooperate, and won't reveal anything we ask him not to."

"What if that doesn't work?"

"Then I can blot out his memory, and we may have to try someone different, someone more receptive to being influenced."

"You can't influence them and also blot out their memory at the same time?"

"Unfortunately not. It's one or the other."

She stood up abruptly and went over to the stove. "I'm just not sure about this, Thomas. It seems awfully risky, and…" she touched the spot on her throat where there was still a contusion, almost faded by now. "You have to be taking their blood to do it?"

"Yes, I do. Why? Do you have someone in mind?"

She wavered, angry with herself for judging Thomas, but struggling with both guilt and discomfort. The thought that she was helping to trick an unsuspecting person into a coercive arrangement made her squirm. Finally she sat back down on the bench. "I think I met someone who can do it, on my way here."

"Who might that be?"

"There's a little Texaco station just below Camden—a young man runs it, alone as far as I can tell. I got the feeling that he'd appreciate the extra income. I think he could do it, if he'll take the job."

"He sounds like a likely candidate. I know that little filling station. Young people are usually more open to influence."

"It would be easier to hire someone local. He seemed rather fascinated by you, he told me all about the Hermit of Pepperell Hills when he heard I was coming here."

Thomas chuckled. "My notoriety reaches as far as Camden."

"I just hate to actually…I mean, he's only a kid, I don't even think he's old enough to vote."

Thomas shook his head. "It's the only solution that really makes sense. Diana, we can't proceed if we're going to shrink away from every hard exigency. No one will be harmed—not substantially. But as you yourself just said—what would happen if our plans did become public knowledge?" He moved closer to her and put a hand on her shoulder, making her straighten up suddenly. "Imagine how much trouble could be caused just by curiosity seekers, let alone those with hostile motives. We can't possibly take such a risk."

"You're right." She shifted away from him, because his touch was distracting, and gave him a resentful scowl. "You must have been one *hell* of a lawyer."

He stifled a laugh. "So I was told. Offer him whatever payment you wish—be exorbitant, if that makes you feel better. When can you speak to him?"

"Any time, but before I do that, I need to go to Boston for a few days. I need to close up my apartment there, and meet with the trustees and Board of Bread and Roses. I need to order the parts for the metal chamber, and I'd prefer to do that in person. And I need to find out where Gregory is—I'm not sure where he's living now. I know he's not in the city anymore."

Thomas nodded. "Perhaps I could arrange for the bricks and other materials for the athanor."

"Well, one of the things I'll be getting is the plans for that, but I can write out what you'll need. That's a good idea, actually." A sudden thought occurred to her. "You know, I haven't even considered where we'll build this thing. Is there enough headroom in the cellar for an athanor? It's going to need a chimney of some kind, too. We might have to cut through the floor."

"We won't build it here. But we do have a perfect place for it." He got up and went to the wide workbench that ran along one wall of the kitchen, and took up one of the kerosene lamps that stood there. "Come on and I'll show you."

They went out the kitchen door and around the house, Diana carrying the lantern because only she needed it to see. Thomas walked quickly ahead of her, never once stumbling on the rough ground, despite the darkness. The waning half moon had not yet risen and stars glittered coldly overhead, the Milky Way arching across the sky like a veil. A few hundred yards down the gravel intake road, Thomas turned onto a narrow path that cut through the woods. He moved almost silently between the high bush blueberries and thick saplings. After some ways the path widened and then emptied out, like a river delta, into a large clear area. Dimly visible in the starlight loomed a white farmhouse, its windows boarded with plywood. Thomas walked halfway across the clearing and stopped, gazing at the house in silence. Diana caught up with him, slightly out of breath.

"You own this?"

"Yes, this is the Schuller house. It came with the last parcel of land I purchased. It dates back to 1895."

"It's..." she tried to think of something complimentary, but the boxy house was small, unremarkable and in poor condition. Trash and debris was scattered around the back dooryard, including an ancient washing machine and a number of old tires.

"It's a wreck," Thomas said cheerfully. "But it's structurally sound, and has a very useful feature. Follow me and watch your step."

They picked their way across the lumpy, littered yard to the back stoop, where a screen door hung from one hinge, rough holes punched in the screening. Thomas pushed the screen door aside and produced a small key from his pocket, which he used to unlock a steel padlock securing the back door. The door swung inward with a long squealing moan, stopping when it scraped into a curving track worn into the floorboards. Thomas stepped inside, turning back to beckon Diana in with the enthusiasm of a welcoming cocktail party host. Gingerly, she stepped over the threshold.

The lantern's wavering flame made more shadows than light. Stray litter and dead leaves stuck to the creaking and badly warped floors, and Diana's footsteps echoed off the bare walls. Smells of damp plaster, rotting wood, and wet soot from the chimney filled the stale air. Flat graying plywood pressed against the cracked glass of the windows. Diana could feel her skin crawling, and kept as close to Thomas as possible without risking an accident to the lantern. They went into the kitchen, where empty cabinets gaped and an old bottled gas stove stood with one oven door fallen permanently ajar. Thomas went to a door in the kitchen's interior wall and quickly opened it. Cold, clammy air poured out and swirled around them like fog, heavy with the odor of stone and damp earth, and Diana took a step backwards.

"Thomas, you've got to be kidding."

"Don't be so squeamish! What's a cellar after everything you've been through? Come on!"

She followed him down the cellar steps, holding onto the iron pipe railing fixed into the lath-and-plaster walls. The steps, at least, seemed sound, and she was surprised at how long they were. At the bottom of the steps she held up the lantern and looked around. "Amazing."

The cellar had a clearance of at least eight feet and seemed larger than the exterior of the house. The foundation walls were tight mortared granite fieldstone and despite the damp smell, appeared dry. But Diana immediately saw the feature that most interested Thomas.

"Why on earth did they put a huge fireplace like that in a cellar?"

"Soap."

"Soap?"

"For decades, the Schullers made soap and sold it. They built the house with this cellar so they could keep up their business during the wintertime. There was a lot of soap making paraphernalia here, but it all got sold to collectors when the house was closed ten years ago."

"Soap…no wonder the floorboards are so warped."

"And doubtless replaced entirely more than once. Still, it was a going concern, while it lasted."

"Is there a bulkhead to the outside?"

"Over there."

She walked over to it, examining the stone steps leading up to the slanting wooden doors. Then she took a closer look at the fireplace, her jitters of a few minutes ago completely forgotten. She peered up the wide flue, and saw stars winking back at her from the night sky overhead. "You're right. It's perfect. There's more than enough space, and we can vent the athanor up this flue. There's plenty of leeway for the dampers."

"So I should have the bricks delivered here?"

She looked at him, suddenly realizing that as of this moment, they were committing themselves to the plan she had so roughly sketched out over the last three days. *Maybe we should think about this…do a divination, take some dreamtime…* but no. *If this fails, there is no hope,* and she knew, instinctively, that Thomas was right. Perhaps they shouldn't even acknowledge failure as a possibility. Perhaps that was the only way to even approach a working of this magnitude.

"Yes, do that, as soon as possible. I'll leave for Boston in the morning."

∞ 5 ∞

At sunset of the Wednesday after Independence Day, Diana lay on top of the granite boulder by the turnoff, listening to the crickets chirping in the long grass beside the road. The day had been hot and humid, and the evening coolness was a relief. She knew Thomas was probably awake by now, and she was hungry, not having eaten since morning. But she was exhausted, and discouraged by the contents of the letter she had taken from the weather-beaten rural mailbox a few minutes ago. Although she and Thomas had certainly been making progress in the past three weeks, not everything was going as smoothly as she would have liked.

She'd had no difficulties negotiating an early termination of her Back Bay apartment lease, given the acute housing shortage in the city. The landlord had actually seemed rather delighted for the chance to raise the rent when he listed the property. She'd put most of her things in storage and hired a moving service to drop off several dozen cartons of books, magical supplies, and clothes at Holliston House Inn to be picked up when she got back.

Maurice, who co-owned the South End artists' foundry with his long-time partner Conor, had asked no questions when Diana presented him with the plans for the metal core components. The foundry had done projects for the OSL before. He did mutter unhappily about the price of copper since the war. By that time, Diana had been out of sorts and irritable. Her morning had been spent in a lengthy meeting with the Board of Directors of Bread and Roses. The Board and trustees had all been so cheerful in their confident assurances that they would keep the foundation thriving in her absence that Diana almost expected to be presented with a gold watch and ushered out the door. Still stinging from a sense of feminine uselessness, she'd pulled out a fifty dollar bill and handed it to Maurice without another word. He stared at the bill blankly as though it was an encrypted message. "I didn't mean I couldn't get it," he finally said, sounding hurt.

"This is a rush job, and I know you can always use cash," she'd told him, and he'd pocketed the bill without thanks or further comment, as befitted the recipient of a good old-fashioned Boston bribe.

"Bronze is high too, it's all going for war monuments."

"Well, you just bill me for whatever's fair, Maurice. Four weeks?"

"That's awfully fast. Make it six. You don't want me to cut corners, right?"

"As if you would."

"Umm, flattery. I'll try for five."

Diana couldn't help laughing. "I'll call you to check how it's going."

It was only after every other errand had been taken care of and every possible loose end tied that Diana made the final stop on her itinerary.

Like the organization it sheltered, the Motherhouse of the Order of the Silver Light presented a deceptive appearance to the outside world. From the sidewalks of Beacon Street, passers-by saw the well-kept façades of two four-story Boston brownstones, their high granite steps flanked by tiny trim gardens behind wrought iron fences. But one entrance was a false door, and what appeared to be two buildings was in fact one. The walls it shared with neighboring houses on either side were heavily soundproofed, and along with its other architectural oddities, the OSL's HQ sat atop a three-level-deep basement.

There was no one on the first floor when Diana let herself in with her private key. Grateful for that, she took the somewhat rickety manual-control elevator down to the lowest basement level. The archives were warm and a little stuffy, since the air conditioning was only turned on while ceremonies or meetings took place. The OSL adhered to a Naturist and somewhat Luddite philosophy, like that of Thomas Jefferson or William Morris, both of whom had been initiates in their time. The file cabinets containing records of inactive and former members stood in a row near the archive entrance.

The most recent of several address changes on Gregory's record sheet listed an apartment in Brighton. Diana knew that was five years out of date, because she had gone there to investigate why her letters were being returned undeliverable. Stephen had found out, somehow, and this had led to one of their biggest fights ever.

She thumbed through the folder without finding any other notations that postdated Gregory's departure from the Order. As she started to return the folder to the drawer, she noticed a small card almost slip out of the side. She pulled it out and saw a jotted note: "Box 62, Manchester, New Hamp." There was no clue as to when the card had been added to the file or even whose address the box number was, but she made a note of it, intending to mail a short letter that very day. As she locked up the archives, she felt her shoulders tensing. She had an appointment to keep before she could leave, and she wasn't looking forward to it.

Roderick's fourth floor study door hung slightly ajar and there were no lights on inside, but Diana knocked anyway, just as a courtesy. When she heard no response, she went in and closed the door behind her. She walked behind the desk and stood looking down out of the handsome oriel window at the evening traffic creeping along Beacon Street. The gaslight street lamps of an earlier age glowed weakly in the stronger glare of their taller electric descendents. Their light glittered in the protective sigil that had been cut into the glass of the center window, supposedly by L. MacGregor Mathers. Diana had always wondered what Mathers thought would try to get in.

When the door behind her opened, Diana didn't turn around. Reflected in the window, she could see Roderick's tall form hesitate in the doorway, backlit by the crystal globed sconce in the hall. Then he pushed the button on the wall switch and the twin lamps on his desk came on. Diana squinted a little at the flush of warm light, but kept her gaze on the window. "Magus Vale. How good of you to come."

Roderick Lowell Vale, Presiding Magus of the Order of the Silver Light, closed his study door and walked over to sit wearily in his expensive executive desk chair. Lean and raw-boned, he was sometimes mistaken for Michael Rennie, the film actor, but his voice was deeper and had the low soothing tones of a practiced hypnotist. "I'm sorry, I didn't expect to be so long. Daniel Cobert caught me just as I was leaving, and I had some difficulty getting away from him."

Still studying the traffic below, Diana said dryly, "I can just imagine. That little windbag is going to be the next P.M."

"He's welcome to the post."

Diana turned to look at him. "Really? You know, some people say that making others wait for them is a way of expressing power and dominance. The longer you make others wait, the more you enjoy the control you have over them. Or so I've heard."

Roderick's smile was thin. "Are we going to talk about you, Diana, or are we going to have another argument about politics?"

She shrugged. "What's the difference?"

Roderick extended a hand toward the chair facing his desk. "Please."

With a sigh, Diana left the window and sat in the deep upholstered armchair, which doubtless would have given another man a feeling of clubbish camaraderie. She felt like a little girl sinking into it, and shifted a bit to keep her feet firmly on the floor. "I'm here because you asked me to meet with you. I'm not sure just what it is that you want to discuss. The Council accepts my reasons for taking a leave of absence. My affairs are in order. I'm a free woman now, in every sense. Are you going to try to talk me into staying, Roderick—or are you speaking for your cousin Stephen here?"

"I am certainly not taking Stephen's side, any more now than I have done for the past several years," Roderick said stiffly. "And as for talking you into anything...I do want to make sure that there's nothing more I could say, Diana. If you need any reassurances as to how highly we value you as an active member of the Order...if, perhaps, I've assumed that you realize that you're..." he hesitated, appearing uncertain at her reaction to his words.

"Realized what? You're not implying that I've distinguished myself somehow, are you, Roderick? In what way?"

"In what way? Diana—let's begin with your level of dedication, the hours you put in, the amount of time you've spent working with apprentices—"

"All very easy for me, considering that I don't have to support myself and I don't have children." She snapped off the last words more sharply than she intended.

"You founded and oversee a philanthropic organization that serves three states and employs more than twenty full-time staff."

"And I spent so much time on it that my marriage went to hell."

"Your marriage would—" Roderick stopped, obviously not prepared to go further in that direction. Diana had always suspected that Roderick would like to have proposed to her himself, and was glad she'd never been forced to turn him down. "It's perfectly understandable that you're feeling bitter, but it's only been three months. These things take time."

"They take less time with more distance. I'm sure you can appreciate that. Meanwhile, the Order will chug along perfectly well without me, just like Bread and Roses will. They both have plenty of fine, upstanding *men* at the helm."

Roderick leaned back in his chair, frowning unhappily at the glossy oak surface of his desk. This was ground that had been well-churned between them. "I hope that you don't seriously doubt that your abilities are recognized and acknowledged, Diana. You were the youngest initiate to attain Adeptus grade in history, I believe."

"But that was seven years ago, Roderick. And fifty years from now, I will still be just an Adeptus. I will never be a Magus. I can't hold office, I can't preside in ritual, I can't initiate, I can't even serve on the Council. All the dedication, talent and precocity in the world can't outweigh the fact that I'm female."

"I know you hate hearing this, Diana, but there are reasons for these rules."

Diana made a rude sound. "Of course there are, there are *reasons* for everything. But they're lousy reasons, and they've been obsolete for centuries, if they were ever valid at all. But I can't challenge the rules, Roderick. Only a Magus can do that."

After a pause, Roderick said, "You know—you're not the only one with cause to be envious. I was certainly never offered a chance to work with Levoissier. Maybe you don't fully appreciate how far above the rank and file that places you. Grades above Adeptus are chiefly administrative, there's not much more training. But what you've been doing for the past five years—what does Levoissier think about your leave of absence?"

Diana abruptly got up from the chair and walked across the small room to stare unseeing at the bookcases that lined the wall from floor to ceiling. Watching her, Roderick's brow creased. "Have you even discussed your plans with him?" he finally said after the silence had stretched for nearly a minute.

Diana slowly turned to face him. "I'm not working with Levoissier any more." It was the first time she had spoken the words out loud to anyone. It wasn't merely the humiliation of admitting it. As long as she didn't say it out loud, she could almost pretend that it wasn't true. "From the look on your face, I'm inferring that you didn't hear about this from Levoissier."

"I—no, I had no idea that—when did this happen?"

"Just before I went to Maine." It almost soothed the sting, at least for a few minutes, to see Roderick rendered so speechless.

"But...did you...did he...was there any explanation?"

"How nice of you not to immediately ask, 'what did you do wrong?'" Diana walked back to the armchair and dropped heavily into it. "That's the first thing I asked."

"What did he say?"

She forced a smile and raised her hands in an exaggerated shrug. "You know Levoissier."

"I *don't* know Levoissier—certainly not the way you do."

"All he would say was something vague about our having gone as far as we could go at my present stage of development. Made me feel like something he was growing in a jar in his laboratory."

Roderick shook his head, still appearing stunned. "But the two of you were—it doesn't make any sense."

"I'm sure it makes sense to him. I'm not as surprised as you are, Roderick. After all, Levoissier isn't exactly a normal man, is he? He doesn't operate by the same rules as the rest of us. Time means nothing to him—and neither do feelings and loyalty. Look what he did to Gregory Fitzhughes."

Roderick winced at the name. "That was a completely different situation, Diana. I know you were angry about that, but..."

"There were good reasons. Naturally. But he was working with Levoissier, too. And Levoissier never came to his defense, not a single word." She looked at Roderick soberly. "I'd appreciate it if no one else knew about this."

"Of course." After a moment, Roderick said quietly, "Are you coming back?"

Diana's gaze wandered around the shadowy room. For the first time, she imagined never seeing the OSL's Motherhouse again, and a cold pang went through her, as if she had been stabbed by a ghostly icicle. "How could I not? The Order is all I know, it's my life. I'm not leaving forever, Roderick. I just don't know how long this will take."

Thinking back to this conversation as she turned the letter over in her hands, Diana sighed heavily. Bats flitted overhead in the deepening twilight sky, and the mosquitoes were starting to bite right through her denim jeans. After a few swats, she sat up, jumped to the ground and began walking up the gravel roadway.

The whip-poor-will rose, keening, from the garden as she came around the back corner of the house. The lamps had been lit in the kitchen, so Thomas was awake. He had no need of the light himself unless he was doing close work, but he always lit the lamps for her if she was out. She pushed open the heavy door and entered the kitchen.

"There you are." Thomas looked up from feeding the fresh fire in the cook stove. "Where have you been?"

"Out getting the mail."

"Anything interesting?"

"Well, yes and no." She perched on the edge of the table, her feet propped on a bench. "I called Maurice today, and they've finished casting the copper and iron. The bronze has just been shipped by his supplier, but he thinks they'll have it in a week, and as soon as they cast it, they'll ship everything to us."

"Can't they ship what they've got?"

"They want to make certain everything fits together properly. We can't do anything until we have all the pieces, anyway."

He nodded. "Is there any more information about the compound?"

"Well…" she removed the letter from her pocket. "This came today." She handed it to Thomas without further explanation.

"From Mr. Fitzhughes." He unfolded the letter. The scrawling penciled handwriting evoked no comment—this was the third letter they'd received. Thomas read aloud, "'Sorry cannot negotiate by mail, will only deal in person. Cannot confirm availability of compound or discuss price by mail due to security concerns. Please make arrangements to meet in safe location for further details.' Well. He's obviously not budging from his position. Are you sure we want to deal with this fellow? He certainly doesn't seem very…trusting."

"I think the word you're avoiding is paranoid." Diana smiled weakly. "Yes, that had something to do with the problems he had in the Order. But—" She shrugged. "You want my honest opinion? I don't think he's mistrustful of us, and I'm not convinced he's that suspicious of the United States Mail. He just wants us to meet with him in person before he'll commit to anything, which isn't unreasonable. But he's not going to come right out and say that, because it just sounds too, well, businesslike for him. I did find out where he lives."

"How did you do that?" The Manchester Post Office had refused to disclose a box holder's street address.

"Oh, his name reverberates through the Manchester City Hall. He hasn't paid his property taxes in four years. There's a lien on his place."

"You'd think he'd welcome a chance to earn some money, then. He can't have many buyers for his alchemical concoctions."

"He might not pay his taxes, anyway. He always used to rant away about the evils of government and the criminality of taxation. And that was before he got too much quicksilver under his nails."

Thomas leaned against the table, folding his arms. "Well…what do you want to do? Time is passing, and we need to make a decision. Can you create a compound yourself?"

"Not without going to the Order for assistance, and I would rather not do that until I know I have no alternative. I guess I'm going to drive to Manchester and see Gregory in person."

Thomas looked at her thoughtfully. "What is your history with him, if I might ask?"

"History? What makes you think there is one?"

Thomas chuckled. "I hope you don't mean that question seriously. Every time we discuss Mr. Fitzhughes, you get this certain *look*—and that's only half of it."

"You don't really need to ask, then, do you?"

"Don't snap at me. A lawyer who can't read below the surface doesn't last very long, in or out of court. I have the sense that there's more between you and this alchemist than fellowship—or even a few OSL Beltenes." He handed Gregory's letter back to her, and as she was replacing it in the envelope, added, "I've noticed, for example, how carefully you've put away each one of his letters. And don't get angry at *that*." Diana, who had opened her mouth to spit out a retort, closed it. "You really are a most volatile woman."

After struggling with her reactions for a moment, Diana finally sagged with a resigned sigh. "It's very complicated. Yes, there's a history. Yes, it went beyond the accepted parameters of the Order's circle of free love, at least the parameters that Stephen was willing to accept. He could handle Beltene, but..." She was silent for a moment. "That was one of the things that finally broke up my marriage."

"Your relationship with Mr. Fitzhughes?"

"Oh, Stephen was in no position to be jealous or judgmental about that. No, it was..." she glanced sidelong at Thomas' quizzical expression. "Stephen always wanted children, and I just couldn't seem to have any. I had four miscarriages and a therapeutic abortion, and after that...I never got pregnant again."

"I'm very sorry." Thomas' voice was genuinely sympathetic.

"Thank you. But the real issue was...after Gregory was forced to leave the Order, Stephen convinced himself that the reason I lost the babies was that... they weren't really his."

"Ah, I see," Thomas said wisely.

"It wasn't. True." Diana snapped the words off like she was cutting glass, suddenly angry beyond reason.

"I'm sure that doesn't even come to close to being any of my business."

"Yes, well...I guess you didn't ask, did you? Sorry." She paused and took a deep breath to regain her composure. "You see, Gregory just dropped out of sight after he left the Order. I'm sure he was very bitter. These are the first communications I've had with him in five years."

"What actually happened? I haven't heard about anyone being drummed out of the Order for nearly a century."

"I wasn't privy to everything, but the Council apparently felt...well, they *said*, that if Gregory's mind continued to deteriorate, he might blab about the Order to outsiders, or invite strangers to ceremonies, or...who knows what kind of nonsense."

"You didn't agree."

"That's putting it much more politely than I did. I probably should have..." She broke off, her mouth tightening. "I don't think I did Gregory any good. I went running around collecting medical documentation and making a case. I was sure his symptoms were reversible and he'd improve, not get worse, but I just got informed that I wasn't a doctor. Poor Roderick, the Council had just appointed him Presiding Magus and the first thing they did was drop this into his lap. He finally told me to shut up before he had to discipline me, on top of everything else. I'd just been formally censured, so...I shut up."

Thomas considered all this, looking thoughtful. "Was Mr. Fitzhughes raised in the Order, like you?"

"He was brought in as a teenager, by...by a mentor. I'd known him a long time. But you see, the worst of it is, I never got to talk to him about what happened. I didn't know how he felt about his friends who were still in the Order, or me...I even wondered if he counted me among the enemy. I'm still not sure."

"Is that why you suggested him for the compound—so you'd have an excuse to find out?"

"I suggested him because he's the best, if we can get him. But...yes, you're right. It does give me a plausible excuse. It's not personal and...it's not just me." She looked up. "You know—you could come down to Manchester with me. I think you'd find Gregory very interesting. And likewise."

"Oh, no, I don't think so. You're the one who knows him, and I suspect this tangle will take some sorting. I'd just be an additional complication. You'd better go right away—it's getting late in the game for us to make other arrangements."

She went to the stone cooler where they stored perishables, and took out a covered saucepan of soup. "I know. Especially because the bricks were delivered today."

"That's a week early!"

"Well, he said they had a load going to Bangor so they put ours in with it. Whatever, they're here, all stacked in front of the Schuller house on flats. I put the invoice on your desk."

"So we can begin building the athanor any time now."

"We can lay the bottom and the firebox and bring the walls up about a foot or so. I'd rather wait until we can fit the chamber into it, but we can adjust the inner wall before we seal it."

"But we'll need to consecrate the bricks first."

She set the soup pan on a burner and went to find a spoon. "Yes, but we can do those in batches. I mean, each brick individually, but we can consecrate a batch and then set them in."

"Ritually."

"Yes, but don't worry. I've done this before, and it takes on a kind of rhythm of its own. Before long you'll be putting on your shoes and socks ritually. It's somewhat habit-forming." She paused in stirring the soup to look over at him. "You do realize what kind of state this is going to leave you in psychologically, don't you? We really haven't discussed that."

"I hadn't thought much about it, but it doesn't matter."

"Thomas, I think it matters a great deal. You're assuming a hell of a lot here. You've never done anything like this before, and it's going to demand energy and concentration in a way you've never experienced. You need—we both need—to be completely honest with ourselves about how we're being affected, at every moment."

"But you're my partner," Thomas said reasonably. "Isn't that part of a joint working, to be aware of one another's possible missteps and forestall them? Working alone, one doesn't have the same perspective, but partners look out for each other in a working." When she didn't answer him, he added, "isn't that so?"

"It can be, but...in this case, I'm not sure either of us will have the perspective to keep an eye on the other, especially as we progress. And there are still things you're keeping from me, critical things, about your needs, your habits, your nature—don't look like that, I'm not stupid. There are."

"Nothing that directly affects the working. I've told you what you need to know. I haven't demanded to know every detail about you, have I?"

Fine, whatever you say, she thought, turning back to her soup. She stirred for a few minutes as the fire crackled in the firebox.

"Do you think it may be time to talk to our welder now?"

She looked up at the soot-darkened oak beam above the stove, pursing her lips unhappily. "I'd rather wait until we have the parts to show him."

"Do I detect a hint of procrastination here, Diana?"

She was silent. Steam suddenly engulfed her hand and she jerked the spoon from the bubbling pan and reached for a kitchen towel to remove the pot from the burner.

"Diana? If you prefer, I'll talk to him. From what you've told me, I should make quite an impression on him."

"No, that's...that's all right. I'll do it." She took a deep breath. "As soon as I get back from Manchester."

ꙮ 6 ꙮ

Old Goffstown Road wound out of the outskirts of northwest Manchester, lined with postwar wood frame bungalows. Potholes and frost heaves pitted and bumped the asphalt surface. Children played in knots and clusters in the small front yards, their sneakers scarring grass baked to a yellow mat by New Hampshire's summer heat. After a mile or so, Diana drew up before a lumpy two-story farmhouse with the tarnished brass numbers "904" barely visible on one of the front porch posts. It certainly looked like a mad scientist's lair. Paint peeled from the cracked and rotting clapboards, numerous shingles had shed from the roof and taped cardboard rectangles patched many of the windows. Aloud, she murmured, "This must be the place."

She pulled into the dirt driveway and got out of the car, regarding the sagging front porch with deep suspicion. Looking around, she noticed a sort of footpath beaten through the tall weeds from the driveway toward the back of the house. She followed it and came to a ground-level door that appeared to lead directly into the basement. Pausing a moment to collect herself, she knocked.

The door opened so suddenly that she took a startled step back, a hand over her mouth. For a moment, she was too overcome with emotion to speak. Gregory looked a little older and even thinner than she remembered, and he had let his hair grow. The silvery blond curls almost touched his shoulders in masses of ringlets. For a moment he only stared at her, as if he was unsure not only who she was but what she was. Then he broke into a slow smile.

"Hello, Gregory." Diana winced inwardly as her voice caught on his name.

"Diana," he finally said—perhaps she wasn't the only one who'd had trouble speaking. "It's good to see you."

"I would have written or cabled first, but we got your last letter, and I thought I might just as well drive down here." She gestured in the direction of her car.

"I knew someone was coming today, that's why I put on my best shirt." He brushed once at his shoulders, as though dusting off crumbs. The stained, threadbare dungarees and plaid flannel shirt did appear surprisingly clean. He peered behind her quizzically. "Is it just you?"

"Just me."

His smile broadened. "That's even better, then. I was sure there'd be someone else. But don't stand there on the doorstep, come in! There's not much on the outside worth more of a look than you've just had, but I'll show you my shop, watch the steps now…" As she took his outstretched hand, she could feel that his long fingers were knotted and criss-crossed with small scars. He put his other arm above her head protectively, even though she was inches from needing to duck under the low door lintel the way he did.

The steps led down into a cellar-cum-laboratory. Gregory had shoehorned a small athanor, vented to the brick chimney, into the space by the hulking furnace. He led Diana around the spacious low-ceilinged room, pointing out and explaining each feature of his rather impressive workshop. A comparison of this meticulously kept area with the exterior of the house made it clear where his financial priorities were. But Gregory would always have gone without food and heat if he had to choose between those and alchemical supplies, and he'd never had much money to allocate.

Listening to him, and asking questions, Diana observed with a private sense of vindication that the obvious effects of the damage he'd suffered from his chemical recklessness were much alleviated. They ended up by the athanor, which was emitting soft ticking noises as it cooled, and Diana asked a number of questions about how he had constructed it and what its capabilities were. Finally, Gregory fell silent and looked at her for a few moments. "But this isn't a social call, I know that much. You've come about your compound, have you?"

"That is the main reason I tracked you down now, Gregory, I admit it. But I don't think a day has gone by these past five years that I didn't think about you, and wonder how you were doing. I tried to get in touch with you after you left, but my letters were returned by the post office. You didn't leave a forwarding address when you moved from Brighton, and no one seemed to know where you were. It wasn't easy to find out where you're living now."

He only nodded, his expression resigned. "That was a bad time for me. For a long while I didn't want to hear from anyone in the Order, or almost anyone. Banished to the outside like a cowan, after all those years, and no one speaking for me, not my best friend Jack, nor even *him*—I was too ashamed by it. I wanted to talk to you, Di, but—I was afraid I'd get you into trouble. More trouble that is than you already were."

"I understand," she said, inadequately. She tried to imagine what it would be like to be banished from the Order, and couldn't. "Gregory, I'm so, so sorry, for all of it. I should have kept on looking for you, I shouldn't have worried about trouble, but…I was trying so damn hard to make my marriage work."

"I don't blame you for that, Di. I'd expect no less of you, you never give up on anything."

She had to look away from him. "Jack quit the Order, and he left the state right after that, as far as I know."

"He's in Colorado, I heard, that's where his family lives."

She reached out and touched his arm, and he caught his breath. "You seem better, though, Gregory, than you were six years ago—much better. Especially your speech, and you're not—" she broke off, suddenly feeling tactless.

But Gregory didn't seem offended. "You're right, some things are better. I don't shake nearly as much, and I hardly ever take a fall now. But I'm not always as well as this, Di. There are good days, and bad ones, and I don't see so well, or hear so well, as people think I should. Bright light hurts my eyes, and my ears hum all the time. Too many bad days, too many mistakes, and the jobs I can get—they say thank you, good bye. I've had no luck since I left Boston, seven jobs I've taken and lost them all. I should have stayed in school, after all. All my time spent in the Order—and what did I get from that, when it was all over? Thank you and good-bye. I wasn't good enough for them, all those Vales and Lowells and Winthrops, that was the truth of it. They wouldn't have been so quick to show one of their own the door."

"I know."

Gregory looked surprised at the bitterness in her voice. After a moment, he said, "So...I heard that after I was gone, *he* took you on, is that right?"

"He...you mean Levoissier?" She drew in a long breath, feeling her cheeks reddening. "That shouldn't have been repeated, Gregory."

"I never repeated it. Not to a soul."

"Gregory, I—what would you have done? It was two years since I'd reached Adeptus, I was going nowhere. I don't know why Levoissier didn't say anything in your defense, but..."

"I'm not accusing you, Di. I just wondered if it was true, that's all."

"Yes, it's true."

"I just thought that the next time you see him, you could ask him something for me." He was watching her face intently, and he frowned at her expression, although she wasn't looking at him.

"I'm afraid I can't ask Levoissier anything, Gregory. He's shown me the door. And I don't know why."

There was such a long silence that Diana finally looked up at Gregory in puzzlement, and was even more bewildered by what she saw. He stood motionless, gazing into the distance, his brow furrowed, as though he had just been presented with a clue to a dark mystery and was pondering its significance. "Five years and five years," he almost whispered, as though he was talking to himself. "What can that mean?"

"Five years and...I don't understand."

He looked down at her, blinking, as though he'd forgotten for a moment that she was there. "Nor do I. He doesn't see things the way the rest of us do, Di, all those centuries behind him. He's always spinning patterns, and the rest of us are just the threads he uses."

"It's not like he's God, Gregory."

He shook his head slowly. "Now that is a true statement. God is merciful." She didn't know how to respond to this, and after a few moments, Gregory half smiled. "But this is a poor reunion, isn't it? We should be celebrating, Di, like old friends. But first, we have business to talk about, don't we?"

Diana cleared her throat. "It really is very important, and we're working against a deadline. Can you make a compound for us? We're willing to discuss any terms you ask."

He simply looked at her in silence, his expression enigmatic. But when Diana started to speak again, he reached out and put a finger on her lips.

"I have one more thing to show you, come over here." He walked toward the far wall of the cellar, beckoning. She followed, taken by surprise, to where a heavy wooden chest she had assumed was a tool box stood against the wall. He knelt down beside it, undid its complicated encoded latch and lifted the lid. Inside the chest, carefully nestled into a deep bed of gray fluff made from cattail rushes, was a heavy glass bottle filled to the brim with an iridescent liquid that appeared to glow with its own nacreous light.

"You made it already?" Her voice was hushed, partly from incredulity, partly from awe. She extended a hand over the bottle, feeling tiny prickles in her palm. The purity of the compound's magical nature was as close to perfection, she thought, as a mortal could have achieved—certainly closer than she ever could have accomplished on her own, if she had taken a year in seclusion to make it.

"Ay, after your first letter came, that's when I started it." He stared raptly at the bottle as well—as anyone would have who glimpsed it. The soft shimmering colors played like light on water. "This is what you wanted, then?"

For a moment she couldn't speak. "It's...it's perfect, Gregory. But—how did you *know*?"

"From what you said in your letter—and I *see* things now, Di. More than before, even, I can't explain it. But this..." he stroked the surface of the glass with one finger, and the colors moved and changed where the shadow of his hand fell. "It's the best I've made, or ever will. And it had to be, since it was you asking for it." He reached over and gently closed the lid of the chest, since the compound could not be exposed to ordinary light for long. Diana knelt silently before the chest, her hands folded on her knees, too overwhelmed to collect her thoughts.

Finally she said, "Your letters said...you would only negotiate in person. We should talk about a fair price, Gregory." She couldn't imagine attaching a dollar amount to what she had just seen, but a token exchange, at least, was required. "It's a basic magical principle, you know that."

"Ay, I know that. Can you stay for a bit, Di?"

"Of *course*."

"Let's go upstairs, then, and talk about it. I've some wine I've saved, would you like some of that?" He rose, extending his hand to help her up.

He led her up the inside cellar stairs to the first floor. The rooms were mostly empty of furniture and dim with a greenish light from the shaded windows, as though they were at the bottom of a pond. Gregory's hand trembled slightly holding hers, and Diana remembered that this, like the occasional twitching in his face, was part of his illness that was unlikely to ever fully go away. An unexpected anger began to well up inside her. Did Roderick know what Gregory had been reduced to? Did Levoissier? Would anyone care?

They went into the kitchen, where cracked dishes lay drying on frayed towels. "I cleaned up a bit, for company," Gregory said, and the premises did indeed appear tidy, although the general impression suggested disuse rather than maintenance. Gregory took a dusty bottle of wine and two small wineglasses from a cupboard that contained very little else. She sat down at the table and watched him concentrate fixedly on removing the bottle's cork. When it was out, he set the bottle on the table between them, shifting it carefully this way and that until it was precisely centered. "Let that breathe a bit," he said, and leaned back in his chair studying her with the frank and somber gaze of a cat.

"You haven't changed, Di," he said softly. "and that's not the way of things. My sister now, she doesn't look the same as she once did. You watch women, you watch them get old. But not you. Why is that?"

She shrugged. "You haven't been watching me long enough, I guess. I'll get old, never fear."

"No, you won't. I can see it in you, you're one of the ones the Sidhe will touch..." She looked up sharply, feeling a sudden alarm. Whom the Irish called the Sidhe, the Welsh named the Tylwyth Teg...

"I hope not."

"Ah, be careful what you wish for, Di. Don't wish to get old. Tricky, the Sidhe are. They always know what you really want." He reached out and stroked her cheek with his hand. She closed her eyes for a moment, enjoying the sensation.

"Aren't you lonely here, Gregory? It doesn't seem to suit you, an old house out in the middle of nowhere. You always liked the city, or so you said."

"I didn't have much choice, after all. I inherited this place."

"Inherited?" She looked around the room bleakly, and Gregory chuckled.

"It wasn't me who let it run into the ground like this, and the tax lien was on it before I got here. But with any luck, the City of Manchester will throw me out on the street before the roof comes down on my head."

"Oh, Gregory..."

"It's the least of my problems, Di."

"Then what's the worst of your problems?" She retorted without thinking, but the anger in her voice wasn't meant for him. He seemed to realize that, because he smiled.

"There'd be places for me to go. I lived with my sister and her family after I left Brighton, till all the screaming children drove me out into the streets looking for my wits. I was welcome enough there, my sister's broad minded and she's fierce about family. But our aunt died, or great-aunt it was, and left me this house. I offered a share in it, but my brother-in-law doesn't want to move up here, so I did, because it was better not left empty. It's lonely, yes, but anyplace would be lonely, Di, with all my old friends ashamed of me."

She caught his hand. "Gregory, that's not true. I was never ashamed of knowing you."

"Maybe not, but others were. I'm not so easy to talk to, strange Gregory, the Mad Hatter. That's what they say, isn't it?"

She looked down, suddenly remembering what she'd told Thomas about Gregory, and flushed at the memory of her own words. She forced herself to meet his eyes. "That's what they say."

He nodded. "Sometimes I can hear how I must sound, but sometimes I don't, so well. And that's my own fault, I never tried to say it wasn't. But I'd never have forgotten myself so much as to betray the Order, or my friends. They lied about that."

"I know." She was still clasping his hand, and she realized she didn't want to let go.

"That's what hurt so much, you know. Say I was a fool, say I was a poor example for the apprentices, say I brought my failure on myself...I couldn't argue with any of that. But to say I couldn't be trusted...that was a hard thing to hear. The quicksilver didn't twist me inside as badly as that."

She reached out and took his other hand, as well. "I was so angry about that," she said fervently, surprised at how emotional she suddenly felt now. "Roderick finally told me he'd have to discipline me if I didn't...ease up on what I was saying. And then there were fights at home, so...I just put my feelings aside. There was nothing I could do."

"Nothing I'd have wanted you to do," he said quietly. He made no effort to withdraw his hands from hers. "Do you remember Beltene, Di?"

She had to smile. "Which one?"

"Any one." His fingers curled around her hands, caressing the skin. "I miss that, I do, more than anything. Not once, you see, in all this time...did you go this year?"

"No. No, I didn't go."

"Mr. Tight-Ass-Folderoll Stephen Lowell Winthrop finally lock you up, did he?"

She smiled bitterly. "Not even Stephen could be that hypocritical. But neither of us went this year." She took in a deep breath and met Gregory's eyes. "I'm divorced from him, Gregory. So you see, I did give up, finally."

His blue eyes widened. "When?"

"This March. It's been a long time for me, too. Stephen and I hardly spoke for months and...there hasn't been anyone else. No matter what he thought."

"Ahhh..." he breathed, and he drew her hand to his lips and kissed the backs of her fingers, almost not touching them. She could feel a shiver run all the way down her arm until it coiled in her loins and poised trembling there. "We should celebrate then, Di. Our own Beltene, just ourselves, and then you take your compound and go, and that will be payment enough for me. There's nothing else I could ask for."

"Oh, no, Gregory—you deserve more than that, really."

"Ay, but if I'm lucky I'll be spared what I truly deserve. Will you say yes, Di? I want to feel you, inside and out, like I have in my dreams…" he kissed her hand once more and she closed her eyes, her mouth dry.

"Yes," she whispered, "yes, I want to. But not for payment, Gregory, I won't think of it that way, not ever…" and he rose and pulled her out of her chair into his arms and kissed her. She pressed her body up against his, opening her mouth to his probing tongue, meeting it with her own, caught up in his sudden urgency, as if a dam had broken and released a flood that could not be tempered or stopped.

Finally he broke away, leaving her gasping, and tugged her toward a doorway, saying, "this way then, we've a place to lie down." She followed him into what evidently served as his bedroom. Rumpled sheets half-covered a mattress on the floor and piles of clothing filled every corner. They tumbled down together on the mattress, which settled the problem of their disparate heights.

"Just leave the work to me, then." Gregory began unbuttoning her shirt from the bottom up, kissing her bare stomach, so that she doubled up in giggles.

"Straighten out now, you're flopping like a fish on the bank."

"You're tickling me—oh! stop it!" He did, and she wiped tears from her eyes, gasping. She realized, dimly, that she hadn't laughed like that for months.

"I'll have to give you more than a tickle, if you're going to act like that."

They pulled her shirt off as a mutual effort and she tossed it aside. She sat up and unbuttoned his shirt down to his waist and buried her face in the warm blond curls that covered his chest, and he sighed, letting his head fall back. She kissed his chest, working along the curves of the muscles, noticing that she could feel the bones too easily, then her lips sought out his nipples and she traced them delicately with her tongue. He said something unintelligible and unhooked her bra, quite neatly considering how she was distracting him.

She shrugged off the bra and tossed it after the shirt, and then arched backward as Gregory cupped her breasts in his hands, his thumbs brushing the nipples until they perked up tauter than they already were. She fell back on the mattress and wrapped her legs around him as he stretched out his body on top of her without pausing his slow, deep kisses.

They finally broke off in wordless agreement that their remaining garments had become a severe hindrance. Diana kicked off her sandals, and Gregory undid the zipper of her slacks and pulled off all the rest of her clothing in one move, then slid out of his own dungarees with an undulating motion that resembled a caterpillar leaving its cocoon. He tossed off his shirt as an afterthought. They wound together, kissing more and longer, hands roving everywhere they could reach.

She'd refused to acknowledge how much she missed this, Diana realized, how much she'd ached just for the touch of Gregory's long boned body, all hard knobs and sinews and taut muscle. She couldn't get enough of the feel of it, every bit of him, from the calluses on his feet to his pale curling hair, lighter than ever with a lacing of early gray. A scrawny scarecrow, he'd once called himself, but she'd never seen him that way. Besides, it would be a rare scarecrow that could boast of an endowment that had won locker room contests. But even as her hands found that feature now and affectionately fondled its length, making Gregory break off his kiss with a gasp, she had to push away the distracting thought, *but he's so thin now...*

They had to pause to catch their breath. "I can't wait, then," he said huskily. He gathered her in, cautiously, and sank against her, his long sinewy legs stretching off the mattress. It took him a moment to find his set, and when he felt it he pushed once or twice then quite suddenly braced both arms and thrust all the way in at once. She gasped and clutched at him, for it had been so long she was too tight, and he hurt her a little. After a few breaths she let herself relax around him, and followed the long waves of his motion against her, feeling the muscles of his back under her hands as they rippled from his shoulders down to his waist over and over again. The sensation of his skin flat against her, belly against belly, his sharp-boned hips rubbing her inner thighs, the hardness of him filling her, was intoxicating. But it was over too soon; after just a few minutes he shuddered and made a sound that was almost one of pain, and fell against her, his face buried in her neck and his hands twining in her hair. After a time he pushed himself up on his elbows and looked down at her, stroking her face with his hand.

"Did I hurt you then?" he asked, and she smiled sheepishly, embarrassed that he'd noticed.

"Not really. That was just the ice breaking."

His mouth curved into a slow smile. "Oh, I like that," he said softly and shifted off her to one side, where he lay for a time stroking her body with his fingertips.

"You have the softest skin, Di." She turned on her side to face him, and touched his belly, weaving small circles and figure-eights teasingly over the bare skin.

"So do you." He closed his eyes, occasionally catching his breath as her light hand trailed through the thatch of curly dark blond hair at the base of his belly. He gasped suddenly and half sat up, and she pulled back and sat up herself, laughing. "Now who's flopping like a fish? I'm going to have to hold you down, aren't I?"

"Oh, I'd like to see you—" he broke off as she sprawled luxuriously on top of him. He wrapped his arms around her and they kissed for a while. He became more purposeful, his hands cupping her buttocks and sliding down between her legs, and she kept breaking off her kiss to catch her breath. Abruptly, he sat up and shifted her off onto the mattress, chuckling.

"Now then, enough of lying flat as a cat, turn yourself around and put your head down..." and he reached an arm under her hips and pulled her behind up in the air in a most undignified fashion. She grabbed at the sheets to keep her balance, remembering that Gregory had always had a taste for intercourse from this awkward angle. But he was good at it, unquestionably, for he was already sliding into her, pulling her hips up tightly against his stomach and thrusting so rapidly and forcefully that the side of her face was almost ground into the sheet. Taken somewhat off-guard by how fast he'd launched into this, she put her hands out onto the floor to brace herself and finally let out a squawk of mild protest.

"Slow *down*, you're pushing me right off the bed here, Gregory."

He chuckled, but shifted his grip a bit and slowed his attack significantly, saying, "sorry then darlin', I'm just forgetting myself..." He found a long leisurely stroke that seemed to match breath and heartbeat at once, and Diana gave way to it, almost hypnotized by its pulse, even though he paused now and then to get his wind, and she felt herself relaxing more deeply than she had in months. But when he finished and sank back with a groaning sigh, she disengaged herself with a slight sense of disappointment.

Wearied for the moment, they curled up on the mattress, nestled together as comfortably as the old bowls in the kitchen cupboard. The sheets were twisted into a tangled ball at their feet, leaving the striped ticking bare. Late afternoon sun angled underneath the bottom edges of the drawn shades. Diana lay still, caressing Gregory's arm and hand which draped over her to rest on her shoulder. She thought he might have fallen asleep. *I need to get back*, she thought reluctantly. Thomas would be eager to hear how negotiations had gone and whether Gregory would make the compound for them, and she certainly had good news as far as that went. But if she left now, she would be driving until nearly midnight. And she didn't want to leave, at least not yet. She'd promised to go talk to Brent when she returned to Maine. When Brent came to the Schuller house, to see where he was to work, to hear all the details, to meet Thomas...a cold chill squirmed in her stomach. *It's not the blood*, she thought. *It's the rest of it...*

She must have shuddered, because Gregory stirred against her. "What is it, love?" His voice was clear, with no trace of drowsiness. She wondered what he had been thinking about, lying so still. It reminded her of Thomas' unearthly stillness when he rested, and she shuddered again, not knowing why, and sat up. He sat up as well, pushing tangled hair away from his face. "What?"

She shook her head. "Nothing...I mean, it's nothing to do with you, Gregory. I just...I have to get back. I can't stay."

She moved to stand up, but he reached out and caught hold of her thigh, so that she couldn't move further without tearing out of his grasp. "You haven't worn me out yet, Di." He was smiling, but his eyes were serious. "I've been wondering. Why do you need my compound so badly, and what are you doing with it tucked away into that little mouse hole up in Maine? You should tell me, as I'll be in the center of it all, in a way. This is a Great Work, then?"

"Yes. But I can't tell you more, Gregory, I'm sorry. I really can't."

"Is it a good thing you do?"

"I hope so." She gently pulled away from him and got up, feeling slightly dizzy. "I need some water, Gregory, I'm really thirsty. I'll be back."

She went into the kitchen and drank water straight from the tap. The wine bottle and glasses were still on the table. She sat down on the edge of a chair, her sweaty skin sticking to the scarred wood, and poured a glass of wine. Gregory emerged from the bedroom and came to the table to sit down opposite her. "Want some?" she asked, and he nodded.

It was very good wine, and she sipped slowly, savoring it. Shadows were slowly blooming from the room's corners, and Gregory lit a candle that stood on the table in a holder made from a catsup bottle. It must be sunset. *Thomas will be waking up...*Abruptly, she drained her glass and poured another.

"What is it?" Gregory had only half-finished his own first glass. "I've seen you do this before, Di. Tell me." He reached out and covered her hand with his own. "What's happening to you up there? There's something fey going on with you, I can see that for myself. Something's touched you that ought not to be walking in the world. Tell me what it is. A secret will eat you out from the inside, till there's nothing left of you but the skin...look, you're trembling now. What is it?"

She covered her face with her hands for a moment. "Oh, Gregory. I can't tell you. I just can't. The working is set now, it has to be held. You understand that. Besides, it involves another person's private business. I'm not free to discuss it."

He sat back in his chair, taking a pensive sip of his wine and studying her. In the candlelight, she could see the wineglass trembling in his hand, and wondered how long it had been since he'd eaten. Under his sober gaze, she fidgeted a little, recalling what he'd said about *seeing*. "I'm wondering," he said slowly, "whether you should go on with this, love."

"I don't have a choice now. I've made a vow—we both did."

"You could ground it, then, the two of you."

She shook her head. "No. No, it's not possible. It's too late." *And nothing could persuade Thomas to consider that now...*

"And what if it turns on you, love? What if the working turns inside out? Such power as you must plan to raise, imagine what that could do."

She stared at him for a moment, and then laughed. "Oh, Gregory—you mean like those old scare stories we used to tell the apprentices? Intention like this can't turn, there's too much Will behind it. It might fail. I accept that. That would be disastrous enough. But I'm an Adeptus, Gregory, I'm not setting off magical firecrackers that might blow out the wrong end. That's kid stuff. Tell me the truth, have you ever heard of a Great Work turning?"

He took another drink of his wine and nodded soberly, without speaking. "When?"

"It happened to him...Levoissier...or so he said, once."

Taken aback, Diana stared at Gregory for a moment. He didn't look as though he was joking. "Are you sure he was serious?"

"It was a very serious conversation we were having, is all I can say about that."

"Well—what else did he tell you about it? What was he attempting to do, and why did it turn?"

"That, he wouldn't explain. But he said it was the best magical lesson he ever learned. I got the feeling that it was the hardest, as well."

"They're often the same thing, aren't they?"

"That is a fine and true statement, love."

Diana frowned down at the table top. "Did he say anything about the effects of the work turning—what actually happened?"

"He said it was like everything went into reverse, and then snapped back the right way again—those are his words. It sounded like it wasn't something he would hurry to do a second time."

They sat in pensive silence. Finally Diana asked soberly, "Is that what you *see* happening, Gregory? Did you tune into something while you were making the compound, are you trying to warn me?"

"No, I didn't see that, Di," Gregory said without hesitation. "I wouldn't want you to think that. I'd have told you before, if I had. But there's this feeling I have—that there are more hands stirring the broth of this working than you know about. And I don't know what might happen, if you're not taking that into account. Does this mean anything to you, Di, *are* you taking that into account?"

"I think so," she said after a moment. "I think I know what you're feeling, yes."

He smiled, although his eyes still looked doubtful. "Then I'll trust your judgment, Di—which I do, anyway, or I wouldn't have made the compound to start with."

Diana got up and walked over to the shaded window, peering out along the edge of the blind into the empty backyard, where a line of tall old lilac bushes were shadowed by dusk. Gregory's eyes followed her hungrily and she turned back to see him watching her with a dreamy expression. But she felt oddly chilled, despite the oppressive warmth of the room. "I should leave, Gregory. It's a long drive back."

"Stay the night, love, you're welcome. Don't drive when you're worn out. You can leave in the morning, surely your partner up there will understand. Or is he such a taskmaster as all that?"

She tried to laugh, without much success. "No, no, I'm sure he's in suspense, but he's not trying to boss me around, really. I'd like to stay, but—" suddenly she shivered and hugged herself tightly.

"You can do what you want. But it pains me to see you like this. You can't leave in this state." He got up and came over to her, putting his arms around her. "I know what you need, you've not had your own satisfaction from me, I've been so quick..." and he was kissing her face lightly, stroking her hair back from her temples and forehead.

"Gregory, that's not your fault, really. It's just been too long, I've lost the knack for it."

"Nonsense, you can't. I still have a trick or two left in me."

"Really, Gregory, you don't have to..." but his mouth stopped her before she could finish and she gave up, finding something better to do with her tongue than talk.

"Now watch this," he said, "put your legs around me..." and he took hold of her waist with both hands and lifted her up, pressing her against the wall with his body. Startled, she reflexively clutched at him with legs and arms, and he caught hold of her buttocks with his hands, saying, "don't pinch me now with those strong legs of yours. I'm not a horse, I won't let you fall." Feeling strange to be looking slightly down on him, she bent down and met him in a long kiss, and as she did he pushed up more tightly against the wall and let her slowly slide down onto him, with a few stops and starts as she had to let her own grip release slightly on the way. He crushed her against the wall, so hard that the pressure on her bones was almost painful, but the resulting effect was unexpected. As he thrust upward into her, the sensation nearly overwhelmed her with its intensity, and she pushed her head back against the peeling wallpaper, her toes curling, caught up in the rough, repetitive stimulus that blotted everything else from her mind. This went on far longer than before, Gregory being on his last wind now, and she began to feel dizzy from hyperventilating. Suddenly she climaxed so violently that her body shuddered in waves from head to foot, and she cried out over and over again, not even certain if she was feeling pleasure or pain. He sank down to a kneeling position, spent finally, and they clung to each other as Diana started to laugh helplessly, not even knowing why.

"I do feel better now," she managed to say at last, wiping tears from her eyes. "But no more, Gregory, or I'll be too sore to drive the car tomorrow. Look at you, you're shaking all over."

He rested his forehead against her shoulder, still breathing hard. "I'll be all right, love."

Their skin was slicked with sweat, and Diana pushed her soaking wet hair away from her forehead. "Do you have a bathtub big enough for two in this place?"

"Surely, for two and their four children, at least. You feel like a swim, Di?"

"I think I do. Let's take the wine, and the candle, and go fill the tub, and we can get in, and I'll tell you some of the news you've been missing all these years, and you can tell me..." she paused, looking sadly around the barren kitchen, "you can tell me what you've been living on here all this time, Gregory."

"That won't be a long tale. My sister has been helping me some, sending food, mostly. She's a bit late with it this month, that's all. And there are a few people who give me odd jobs, when they have them, and I'm able to do them. But it's not much."

"Are you content with that, your sister helping you?"

"No," he said softly. "But let's go then, and we'll spend the night getting all wrinkled if it pleases you, Di. You've picked fine weather for it."

They talked late into the night, as the crickets sang from the overgrown front yard, about gossip and magic and alchemy, her divorce from Stephen, old friends, how she had found his address, the problems he had with the City of Manchester. Finally they fell asleep on the mattress, and Diana awoke to the first bird sounds of early morning and lay listening to Gregory's quiet breathing. *I married the wrong man*, she thought with bitter amusement. *Marry one who sleeps like a baby, that will be my new rule.* Stephen snored.

When Gregory awoke, they dressed and went to the basement, and he helped Diana carefully pack the chest containing the bottle of compound into the back seat of the car, where it would be cooler than the trunk. She was ravenously hungry, and she still hadn't seen Gregory eat anything. When his stomach growled, she said, "would you like to go into town with me and get some breakfast?" He hesitated, but his face had a wistful expression. Diana braced herself.

"Gregory," she said firmly, "I told you that last night was not compensation for the compound, and I meant it. You're not in any position to refuse a reasonable offer. Now come on, we're going into town."

"So you think my compound is worth the blue plate special?"

"No! The blue plate special is for last night—okay, it's for the third time last night. That was above and beyond the call of duty." He'd started to laugh, which was a good sign. "After breakfast, we're going to City Hall."

"You're going to marry me, love?

"You haven't asked me yet. No, we're going to pay off the lien on this house."

His face fell. "Oh no—I couldn't let you do that. That's too much."

"It's only money, Gregory. You deserve it at least as much the poor sad sacks who live at Bread and Roses. I don't want you to be evicted. I might need you for something, and how I would find you again? And your poor old great-auntie would haunt you, if you let the city take her house. She left it to you for a reason."

She watched Gregory patiently as he wrestled with his principles. The fact that his stomach was audibly cramping so badly was in her favor. "All right," he said finally. "But only for you, love, and for my great-auntie Rose, may she rest in peace."

She waved to him impatiently. "Come on, get into the car. I'll buy you a box of groceries, too." As she started the engine, she said, "This is the tip of the iceberg of what I owe you, Gregory. For the compound, and for last night, and for the last five years. It doesn't matter how you feel about it. I'll never repay you for all that."

He gave her a strange smile. "Oh, don't be so sure, love. I might come up with something, at that."

7

Déjà vu, Diana thought as her car slowed on Route 1 just south of Camden. It was about five in the afternoon, and the road glittered under the fierce July sun. The traffic had been far heavier on the way up from Manchester than it had been on her drives from Boston, before the end of school and the start of vacation season proper. Small town Main Streets now bustled with pedestrians, cars crawling along them in tight lines like linked carnival rides. Small pleasure craft speckled Penobscot Bay wherever she glimpsed the water, their triangular white sails gleaming in the sun. Scarcely any motel or cottage she passed, from Portsmouth to Camden, displayed a vacancy sign. Brent must be doing a land office business.

Indeed, he was deftly servicing two cars at once as she turned into the station's graveled yard. Diana pulled over to the side of the building and parked, then got out and stretched, grateful to be standing up. She waited until the second customer had paid and pulled back onto the road before she walked over to the pumps. Brent, unaware of her approach, carefully smoothed out his thick fold of bills before tucking it back into his overalls pocket. Dust still hung in the heavy air.

"Looks like you need to lay some oil down on this yard."

"Ayeh, it's been dry," Brent said absently. "What can I do ya for, miss?" He turned around as he said this, and his expression dropped. "Omigosh! It's you!"

She laughed, partly at the look on his face and partly from real surprise. "So I've been told. Am I some kind of celebrity?"

His sunburned cheeks turned even pinker. "Well…you know, I remember you comin' through and all, that day, and we talked about Mr. Morgan, and then hearin'…well…"

"Yes, I can just imagine what my reputation around here must be. Believe it or not, it's strictly business, Brent. I'll tell you all about it. Look, is this a busy time of day for you?"

He looked up and down the road appraisingly for a moment. "Depends. It's 'bout suppertime now, and things slow down a bit then, least on weekdays. I got a fan belt to replace on that Ford in there," he gestured economically toward the station's bay, "but it's hard with people pullin' in all the time."

"When do you close?"

"Well, we're open 'til eight during the summer. Open at six, close at eight."

She stared at him. "Holy *cat*. That's fourteen hours, Brent! You're here alone all that time?"

"I got a cousin comes in sometimes, but he's just fifteen, so I got to watch him pretty close. Can't afford to pay anyone. This is my dad's station, and it's all we got. Got to stay open during the season, 'cause that's when we make the most. Not much business after the summer people go."

"You're not open on Sunday, are you?"

"Half the day, but just in the summer. I come down after church."

He's not going to have time to take on an extra project... she thought, dismayed. She shaded her eyes against the glare from the western sky. "Can we get out of the sun for a minute?"

"Oh, sure! Come on, I got a couple chairs in the office."

They walked across the crunching gravel and entered the tiny office. A small fan with a badly bent wire casing did little to move the stifling air, which smelled overpoweringly of motor oil. A bulletin board jammed with thumb tacked work orders, fuel invoices and, she noticed, unpaid customer bills hung over a two-drawer wooden desk. Stacked boxes of motor oil, engine parts and antifreeze left barely enough room for a wobbly straight back chair and Brent's rolling office chair with its broken back.

"So," Brent said, leaning forward awkwardly because of the broken chair back, hands clasped between his splayed knees. "You got something to talk about?"

She wiped sweat off her forehead with the back of her hand—*gods, it's hot.* "Yes, it's kind of a...business proposition." He nodded, frowning slightly. "Mr. Morgan and I are working together on a project. We need someone to do some welding for us up at his place. Could you take on something like that?"

He rubbed the side of his nose thoughtfully. "Welding...This would be what, a boiler or something like that?"

"Not exactly. It's something like a, well, an art project. There will be six pieces, of different kinds of metal, and—it's hard to explain, you'll just have to see it. It's very simple, really. It's just very meticulous work. But if you can weld a car body, you can do this."

"I could do it in a couple of days, maybe? Simple like that?"

"I'm not sure how long it will all take. It has to be done in sections, you see, and allowed to cool."

Brent studied his clasped hands, his forehead creasing. "I don't know," he finally said. "I can't really leave the station, you know..."

"This would be after hours."

He shook his head. "After hours, I'm usually here, doin' jobs like that Ford."

She closed her eyes a minute, thinking rapidly. "It can wait until after Labor Day," she said, praying that she wasn't making a serious mistake.

He looked down at the concrete floor, pursing his lips.

"We're prepared to pay you a lot of money."

He looked up. "Nothin' illegal, is it?"

"Absolutely not," she said, thinking wryly, *At least not in the 20th century.*

He was silent for another minute, calculating. "Well, if it can wait till Labor Day...I wouldn't say no to some extra money, not then. Station closes at six after that. You say I got to come all the way up there for this?"

"I'm afraid so. It all fits into something we're building, so the work has to be done in place."

"Okay," he said, although his tone indicated understanding, not agreement.

"Do you think you can take it on? We'll have to find someone else, if not, and I'll need to do it soon."

He shrugged. "No reason why not. I'll just need to schedule it in and all. Could you tell me more about this job? What'll I be doing, exactly?"

She took a deep breath. "Well, like I said, it's a little hard to explain, Brent. We're having the parts made up, and they haven't been delivered yet. When they are, we'd like you to come out and see them, and see where you'll be working. It won't make a lot of sense until everything's in front of you. Does that sound okay?"

"Sure. But 'we'—you mean Mr. Morgan?"

"That's right."

"You mean I'm going to get to meet him?"

She swallowed uncomfortably. "In person. You're going to get to know him pretty well, in fact."

"Gosh. He's practically a legend around here."

"You're probably going to be disappointed."

"I don't think so." Brent's face pulled into that irrepressible grin. "Not from what my aunt says...jeez!"

"Something to look forward to. Look, when the parts arrive, I'll give you a call and we can set up a time, okay? It should be just another couple of weeks. I know you're real busy now, but I hope you can manage to fit us in."

"Oh yeah...I wouldn't miss this. Look, shake on it, okay?" He extended his grimy hand, and Diana shook hands briefly. "That'll hold us till we get a job contract in writin'."

"Thanks, Brent. We'll be in touch."

Two weeks after her conversation with Brent, Diana sat in the front room of the Schuller house, carefully cutting a bolt of white silk into precise squares. She had cleansed and consecrated the bolt that afternoon, a working which had taken three hours to complete. Once the squares were cut, they could be charged, and then they would be ready to wrap each brick as it was consecrated. The simple work of measuring the cloth, squaring the line and cutting seemed like rest and relaxation compared to the intense concentration required by the magical procedures. Diana felt as though she had been in an unremitting state of exhaustion for weeks.

After returning from Manchester, she had prepared for the elaborate task of sealing Gregory's compound into the glass vessel. It had taken two days to create the vessel itself, and she had burned her hands twice. When the vessel was ready, she had gone into seclusion, fasting for three days while she meditated and performed self-purifying rituals. The physical act of filling, siphoning and sealing the vessel took only minutes—the enclosing ritual required another three days. By the time she emerged from the house where she had retired for the working—yet another of the four houses on Thomas' land—she was weak, shaking and ravenous. Yet she had experienced no visions or dreams during the procedure, and her divinations had been ambiguous. Perhaps she was just allowing herself to become too tired.

She folded the square of silk and placed it with the others in a wooden box lined with the same softly glistening material. She reached for the bolt to unwrap another length of cloth, but suddenly extending her arms seemed like too much effort. She let the end of the bolt drop and sank into her chair, putting her head down on her crossed forearms. Her eyes were strained and burning from the dim light of the kerosene lamps, and she closed them, listening to the muffled trilling of insects from the woods outside.

"Are you all right?"

She started and raised her head. Thomas stood in the doorway, two of the fine-textured yellowish bricks cradled in one arm. She blinked at him, wondering how long he'd been there. She hadn't heard a sound, and the warped floors creaked even under Thomas' footsteps. To get to the inner door silently, he would have to have dematerialized. *But why would he do that?*

"Sunset already?"

"It's past eight o'clock."

"I had no idea." She'd been cutting cloth for over two hours.

Thomas turned away and took the bricks into the small room next to the kitchen which they had consecrated as a ritual room for preparing the athanor materials. The floorboards creaked loudly and variously under his feet, and Diana frowned. When he emerged from the room, she said, "Strange that I didn't hear you come in."

Thomas paused in the doorway and looked at her silently for a moment. "I'm sorry if I startled you."

"Did you not want me to know you were there?"

He looked away from her and went into the kitchen. She sat stiffly at the table, struggling with the frustration that was becoming so familiar. *Damn him! I look up and he's watching me, he avoids me, he won't come near me or touch me, now he's sneaking up on me?* With any other man, there would have been a confrontation days ago. But she'd never had to work with a man quite so slippery as Thomas.

He rarely dematerialized in truth, but it would have been redundant given how adept he was at evading questions, sliding out of conversations, and just plain staying out of sight if he wanted to. The more she welcomed his company, the scarcer he seemed to make himself. He disappeared entirely for several hours every two or three nights anyway, for his forays, as he called them, to find animal blood. But given how much of the rest of the time they spent working together, the distance he succeeded in maintaining was impressive.

She jumped when he suddenly appeared in the doorway again, swinging around the jamb with one hand like an excited boy.

"There's a truck coming."

She hastily got up and followed him out the back entrance to hurry around to the front of the house. A small panel truck was pulling into the front yard, cautiously drawing up to the flats of bricks, which were heavily swathed in tarpaulins. After hours of kerosene lamplight, Diana had to shade her eyes against the headlights, wincing. The driver put on the parking brake, opened his door and jumped down. "Wow. I'm glad to see you," he said, wiping his forehead with his shirtsleeve. "I saw all those boarded windows and I thought I'd taken a wrong turn."

"Hello, Conor, I was going to call Maurice tomorrow."

Conor returned Diana's handclasp—he was another ex-member of the OSL. "I think I broke you a new driveway, there. I guess this is what the army would call camouflage."

"Right on the money. Of course, the locals know perfectly well there's something going on up here, but they're big on minding your own beeswax in Maine, thank goodness."

Thomas had moved around to one side to get out of the line of the truck's headlights. As he stepped up next to Diana, Conor started. Quickly, Diana said, "Conor, I'd like you to meet Thomas Morgan."

"Right, the guy whose name is on the bills." The two men shook hands, and Conor's eyes narrowed slightly, but then he smiled. "Well, let's get the stuff out. Ye gods, that traffic was brutal coming up here. Wish you'd warned me. I'd have taken the shortcut, through Canada." They all went around to the back of the truck, where Conor briskly unpadlocked the doors and swung them open. Six large wooden crates stood inside, and Conor pulled out the truck's ramp and climbed up into the interior. As he came forward rolling a dolly, he said, "Maurice said to tell you he's sorry for the delay, but we had a little trouble casting the bronze. I think you're damn lucky to get them this fast, but that's just me." With a grunt he hoisted the first crate and carefully walked it down the ramp, dolly almost horizontal. "Which way do we go?"

It took all three of them to get the crates around to the bulkhead and down the steps. Thomas signed Conor's shipping order, and he climbed back into the truck, grumbling about having to drive on to Bangor.

"You can stay here for the night, Conor, you must be bushed after driving all the way from Boston," Diana said earnestly. But Conor glanced uneasily at Thomas and forced a smile.

"Nah, nah, thanks loads, Diana, but I've got to pick up some supplies in Bangor and then hit the road early in the morning. Don't worry, the motel gets deducted from our taxes. Good luck with those things." He brutally slammed the truck's misaligned door. When he had performed an intricate and lengthy maneuver to turn around without hitting the bricks, and the sounds of crunching undergrowth had receded into the distance, Thomas finally spoke.

"Well. Tomorrow you can set up the appointment with our welder."

The following Saturday night, Diana pulled into Brent's station at eight o'clock sharp, and drew up by the office door, leaving the engine idling. The station's outside lights were turned off, and she could see Brent sitting at his desk. He half-turned and aimed a wave and a quick grin in her general direction, then went back to his paperwork. She watched pensively as he finished closing up for the night. He emerged from the dark office and locked the door behind him, then bounded to the passenger's side of the car in two steps, pulled open the door and tossed himself onto the seat.

"So, we ready to go?" His eyes were bright with anticipation.

"Don't you *ever* get tired, Brent?"

"Not till Labor Day. Can't afford it." But as if the word "tired" had set off a reflex, he yawned hugely.

She pulled onto Bridge Road a short way before the turnoff to Thomas' house. "We'll be meeting at the Schuller house. I want to warn you ahead of time, don't get all spooked when you see it. The place was boarded up when old man Schuller died, and we've left it like that."

"How come?"

"Security, and privacy. We don't want anyone barging in, or any kids getting curious about what we're up to. It's just as easy to leave the place looking deserted." The leaning fencepost with the ragged red bandana loomed up suddenly, and she stopped, backed up, and made the left turn into the undergrowth. Brent became very quiet as they broke through to the front dooryard and the headlights garishly framed the blank windowed, peeling façade. She parked the car and got out, and after a moment he followed.

"So, what are these?" he asked, widely skirting the tarpaulin-shrouded stacks of bricks as though he thought they might pounce on him.

"Plain old bricks. We'll explain what they're for. Come on, Brent, we only use the back entrance."

Golden kerosene lamplight spilled through the torn screen door, making an orange square on the cracked concrete step. Diana pulled open the door and went inside, ushering Brent quickly to the front room as he tried to peer into the darkened doorways they passed. Thomas was sitting at the metal folding table they had set up, reading one of his ledger books. He looked up, smiled and rose from his seat to meet them.

"Good evening, Mr. Crothers." He extended his hand to Brent, who stood staring like a marmot fascinated by a cobra. "It's a pleasure to meet you at last."

Brent blinked, glanced down, flushed and hastily gripped Thomas' hand and shook it. He opened his mouth and made a voiceless huffing sound, swallowed and tried again. "Hi...pleased to meet ya. I've heard...I mean, I...golly."

Diana could see that Thomas was enjoying himself. "I've met your aunt, I believe...Miss Margaret Crothers, isn't it?"

"Uh, yeah! Yeah, she's uh, mentioned you a couple of times."

"Charming lady. I can see that red hair runs in the family."

"Uh, yeah, we're Irish. My dad comes from...uh, well, never mind..."

Diana said, "Maybe we could show Brent the items he'll be working with."

"Oh, yeah, I'd like to see that."

Thomas shrugged. "We can start with that. They're down in the cellar. Would you take a lantern?"

Brent gingerly took a lantern from the table. As he turned to follow Thomas, Diana saw him crane his neck to stare at Thomas' ponytail, and then give his head a small shake as though he didn't quite credit his senses.

They filed down the steep cellar steps, Thomas leading the way. The side of the basement nearest the fireplace was now largely occupied by a low platform shrouded in white silk. Brent peered at the gleaming white fabric in puzzlement. "What's that?"

"A work in progress," Thomas answered smoothly. "But this is what you came to see, Brent." He reached up and hung his lantern from a long iron hook that descended from one of the floor beams, then walked to a set of uneven shapes, also covered with white silk, against the wall near the steps. He drew off the hissing cloth, carefully folding it to keep it from trailing on the floor, and Brent took in a long deep breath.

"Criminy..." he finally whispered, letting out his whole breath on the last syllable. "What are they?"

Diana walked up to stand beside Brent, fully understanding his reaction. She had been almost as awed when she and Thomas had opened the crates and pulled away the armfuls of crackling excelsior packing. Lined up against the wall on beds of silk-covered excelsior were six half-spheres in graduated sizes, ranging from nearly three feet in diameter to just over two. They were almost perfect, except for a slightly flattened bottom on each so that they would stand without rolling, and to guide their being fitted together. The largest pair, of cast iron, was rich black, their matte surface as smooth as fine charcoal. The bronze shell glowed with a rich sultry color, not yet touched by oxidation, holding the orange lamplight on its surface and giving it back to the room deepened and mystified. But it was the smallest of the spheres that commanded the eye—fiery copper, so bright it almost hurt to gaze at it. This was the heart of the athanor, the secret core where the power would be reflected back again and again into the glass vessel it cradled.

They all stood in silence, gazing at the six shells of metal. Finally Diana said softly, "Do you think you can weld these together, Brent?"

"Weld *these?* I don't know...I mean...they're just so..." his voice was almost reverent. "So...*perfect.*"

"But that will make it easier, won't it? They'll fit precisely. They've been specially cast."

He shook himself as though attempting to throw off a trance. "Oh, yeah...I mean, that always helps." His face took on an intently serious expression. "Can I...?" he said, gesturing to the closest iron shell, and Diana nodded. He stepped forward and knelt down by the shell, then reached out and ran a tentative finger along the edge, where the halves would be joined. "Like touching water, or...I didn't know you could make iron that smooth." He stood up. "These go inside each other?"

"That's right. There's a glass container that goes inside the copper first. Then you work from there. They'll need to be completely sealed, that's very important."

"And when they're all done, then what?"

"Well..." Diana turned to the platform. "The whole thing goes into this. It'll be a sort of...furnace." Brent frowned, puzzling over this, and Diana bent down quickly and lifted the silk so Brent could see the edge of the athanor's foundation.

"Oh, that's what the bricks are for. Man, these metal things are going to weigh a ton when they're all put together. How are you going to get 'em in there?"

"Oh, we've got block and tackle." And they had Thomas, who could lift the iron shells with one hand effortlessly.

"So what is all this for? I mean, it's incredible, but I just can't figure it out."

"Well..." she hesitated. "Let's go back upstairs and sit down, okay? There are a few more things about this job that I need to explain."

Thomas replaced the silk cover on the metal spheres and the three of them took the lanterns and returned to the front room. Brent sat on one side of the small table, looking nervously at Diana and Thomas. Diana had put considerable thought into how she would describe their procedures to Brent, and prayed that the approach wouldn't backfire. Now she studied his attentive face for a moment and took a deep breath. "Brent...I guess it's fairly obvious to you that these metal spheres are something very—special."

"I'll say," he said weakly. "That first day you stopped by the station, you said something about an art project?"

"That's true, in a way. That's how carefully we need each of them to be sealed—like you were making a sculpture. But that's only part of it. They're really a sort of...religious item."

"Religious?" Brent's brow furrowed. "You mean, holy, like something in a church?"

"Yes, exactly. Sacred, like something in a church."

"You mean, they've been blessed, by a priest or something?"

"Yes." Technically, it was true, given the qualifier, "or something."

"Man." Brent looked both awed and doubtful. "I don't know...I'm not sure I've got what it takes to work on something like that. I'm only...I don't even..." he trailed off, flustered.

"That doesn't make any difference, Brent. You're a good person, and that's all that counts. There's nothing special you need to do except, well, there are a couple of things that we're going to ask of you."

Brent swallowed. "Such as? Look, you know, I didn't even finish high school—"

"That's okay, Brent. We're hiring you for your skills, like the artisans who built the great cathedrals. They weren't saints, they were just doing the best work they knew how."

After a pause, Brent shrugged. "Okay, I guess that makes sense...so, what are the things you need me to do?"

"Two things, really. First, we're going to ask you to wear particular clothing while you do this."

"Uh, wait a sec...I got to wear heavy gear to do welding, you know."

"I know, but do you think you could wear all white? For instance, if we provided you with heavy white trousers, and a white sweatshirt, and white gloves, and so on? We'll take care of all the expenses, and the clothes will be ready for you. You'll just change into them when you get here."

Brent shook his head in bewilderment, but he said, "Sure...that sounds like it would work. Except I have to wear my helmet."

"The helmet's fine."

"Well, okay..."

"Your apparatus is portable, right?"

"Yeah, there are a couple of tanks. They go in the back of the truck."

"Good. So there's no problem there."

"I guess not. So, what's the second thing?"

"The second thing..." Diana hesitated, studying Brent's face carefully. "The second thing is that, for the time that you're welding, Thomas and I will be doing a sort of...ceremony. Probably we'll be upstairs here. Mostly you'll just be aware of us chanting."

"Chanting—you mean like monks or something do?"

"Just exactly like that. It will sound like that kind of chanting, almost like music. It won't be in English, at least most of it won't. You probably won't hear much of it through your helmet. And you really don't have to think about it. You'll focus on doing the best, the most perfect job welding that you possibly can. You won't need to pay any attention to us."

Brent leaned back in his chair, rubbing one hand over his close-cropped hair. "Okay....are you going to be wearing special clothes, too? Like a priest or, or whatever?"

"As a matter of fact—we are."

Brent looked from Diana to Thomas, obviously struggling to fit the scenarios in his mind into some kind of comprehensible context. "This is crazy. I never figured you for being religious or anything—I mean, no one's ever seen you in church..."

"Not conventional church," Thomas said.

"Trust me, he can be pious to a fault," Diana said in a more dry tone than she intended, and Thomas glanced at her with a raised eyebrow. Watching this, Brent blurted out a laugh, as if he couldn't suppress it.

"I'll take your word for it, but man, everyone always says you're—" he broke off, flushing to the hairline.

"A Communist?" Thomas said, amused, and Brent mumbled something. "Well, I'm not. And communism is a political ideology, not a religion, in any event."

"We're not asking you to help us do anything illegal or unethical, Brent, or for that matter, un-American. Look—what do you say? Do we have a deal?"

Brent, still flustered by his foot's close call with his mouth, took a few moments to answer. "A deal? Oh. Umm, I have no idea what to charge you for something like this. I'll have to think about it."

Thomas said, "May we make you an offer?"

"Sure. Shoot."

"We were thinking that thirty three dollars an hour would compensate you for all the inconvenience." He and Diana had agreed on this amount the night before, as much for the magical significance of the number as the generosity of the fee.

Brent gaped, his freckles suddenly standing out against his pale face. His mouth moved but no sound came out. "Thirty...thirty three *dollars?*" he finally choked. "An *hour?* What, are you nuts?" He seemed to realize that this was an ungracious response, but spluttered on, "No one pays that kind of money for welding! No one's ever...I never saw that kind of money in my life."

"You don't want it, then?" Thomas said, unperturbed.

"I'd feel like I was...I'd be cheating you. I can't take that."

"It's worth it to us. We are asking rather a lot of you, aren't we? Including..." his voice softened. "Including your confidentiality. You can't tell anyone about any of this, Brent. That's very important."

"Well, I wouldn't, anyway, but how'll I explain where the money came from?"

Diana said quickly, "Oh, you can say you've got a job, Brent, it's just the details we want kept private...I mean, you can see why."

Brent stared from one to the other of them, and finally his shoulders slumped. "Well...I mean, if you want to throw your money away like that..."

Thomas said, "It's worth it to us, Brent. And you deserve it. Don't undersell yourself. You must have aspirations beyond running a filling station."

"Well, sure, maybe someday...you must be pretty rich, huh?" he said as if confirming a long-held suspicion.

"Yes."

Brent looked reflective. Finally he began to grin, almost sheepishly. "Okay, you got yourselves a deal. Thirty three dollars an hour, huh? I'll have to tell my dad I won the Irish Sweepstakes or something." He put his hand out and Thomas, smiling oddly, shook hands. "I'll need to write up a contract."

"I understand. But don't include any of the specifics we've discussed here. Just the payment per hour and the fact that it's welding work."

"Right, I follow you." Brent glanced down at his hand with a grimace, and his forehead creased in a frown.

To distract him, Diana said, "We can talk more about how it will all work later, Brent. Think of it as a kind of theatre, in a way. All rituals and ceremonies are like that, really—look at weddings, they have rehearsals."

"Oh, yeah, I get that—I guess."

"Did you ever help serve at Mass, were you an altar boy?"

"No, nothing like that. But I was in the drama club in high school, did a couple of plays. *Midsummer Night's Dream*, we even did. Man, was my mom ever excited about that. I thought the guys would never quit ribbing me about it, though. I'm still getting it."

Thomas got up and walked around the table to adjust the wick of one of the lamps, which was smoking quite badly. There was a strong stink of kerosene exhaust in the air. "What role did you play?"

"Oh, I was Lysander. Kind of silly..."

"I'm sure you were excellent. I wish I could have seen you."

Brent shrugged self-consciously. "I only did it for laughs."

"It is a comedy, after all," Thomas said. "Doing it for laughs is highly appropriate." He walked back around the table toward his seat. When he passed behind Brent's chair, he stopped, reached his left hand around under Brent's chin, pulled his head sharply back and to the side, bent down and locked his mouth onto Brent's neck, over the vein. Brent half rose from his chair, reaching up with his right hand, and Thomas caught the hand in midair, with a smart slapping sound. As a dark line of blood snaked over Brent's throat to soak into his shirt collar, Brent's body sagged, whites showing beneath his eyelids, and he sank back down into the chair. Thomas released Brent's right hand and it drifted slowly down to hang limply by his side. He tugged Brent's head a bit further to the left and shifted his position slightly, and the trickle of blood that was escaping him stopped. Brent let out a long sigh, and whispered something under his breath.

Ten seconds all of this took, not an instant longer, and Diana sat rigid with shock in her chair, her fist jammed into her mouth to keep herself from crying out. *I didn't even see it coming,* she thought, as if that somehow made it worse. *I didn't even see it...* She wanted to look away, but she couldn't. Her hand hurt and finally she took her fist away from her mouth and saw deep tooth marks on the knuckles. Wincing, she straightened out her fingers and pushed her hands into her lap. Still Thomas held Brent motionless, drinking steadily, and Diana could feel herself beginning to shake. *This is ridiculous,* she thought, *pull yourself together! You'll have to take him home after this...* and she suddenly felt panicked. What would she say to him?

Thomas shifted again, and Brent shuddered violently and moaned. He took a deep breath, seeming to be recovering his faculties, and Diana watched in fascinated horror as Thomas took his mouth away from Brent's throat for a minute, licking his lips. Then he bent back down and painstakingly licked the blood off of Brent's skin, as methodically as a cat. He wiped the sticky little rivulet off of Brent's collarbone with his finger and sucked his finger clean. Slowly pulling himself upright in the chair, Brent dazedly raised his hand as if to push Thomas away but couldn't get his arm up quite far enough. When almost no blood was left, Thomas straightened up, putting his hands on Brent's shoulders. Where he had latched on there was a small patch of swollen, reddened skin that looked like it would darken into a contusion. In the center was a puckered bump like a tiny pinched mouth. Brent touched the blood soaked patch on his shirt and stared blankly at the red smear on his fingertips.

"Now, then, Brent, you should go home. Get some rest, and we'll see you in about three weeks. Agreed?"

After a long pause, Brent said, "Right. Three weeks. And, uh..." he looked down at his shaking fingers again.

"Don't worry about that, Brent. You'll be fine. Be sure to drink plenty of water tomorrow."

"Okay." Brent looked around the room as though he wasn't sure why he was there.

"You better take Brent back to his filling station, Diana. It's getting quite late, and he needs to get home." Thomas' voice was as calm and matter-of-fact as if they had simply concluded their conversation about the play.

Wordlessly, she rose from her chair, and Brent stood up and followed her, stumbling on the warped floor. They walked in mutually stunned silence to her car. On the drive back to the station, Diana glanced at Brent once or twice, and each time he was staring straight ahead, his face obviously pale even by the dim reflected illumination of the headlights.

When they pulled into the station, she asked, "Are you sure you don't want me to take you right home, Brent?"

"What?" he said slowly. "Uh, no. My truck's here. I'm okay."

"Are you sure you can drive?" she said helplessly, and he turned and looked at her. For a long minute they stared at each other in silence. Then Brent looked down at the dashboard, reaching up to touch the darkening spot on his throat.

"Is he...did he really..." He stopped, as though he wasn't sure how to even describe what had happened.

"Yes."

"But...but there's no such thing. I mean, I know there isn't. There can't be." He raised his head, his expression suddenly both distant and intense. "I can't tell anyone about any of this," he said slowly, with an odd inflection that didn't sound like his voice.

"No, you shouldn't. This is just between the three of us."

He nodded. "I can't tell anyone about any of this," he said again, with precisely the same tone and expression as before. Diana felt a chill clutch at the pit of her stomach. But then Brent gave his head a small shake and sighed. "No one would believe me, anyway," he added, sounding more like himself.

"Probably not."

"I mean, it's crazy. All that stuff about him, that people talk about. The food, and not being around in the daytime, and everything. It all makes sense. But who'd ever think of it? Not in a million years." His face twitched. After a moment he said, "I better get home. I've got a lot of work to get done tomorrow..."

"It's Sunday, Brent."

"Yeah, I get a lot done on Sundays." He opened the door of the car and got out. "Thanks for the ride back. I'll see ya later."

"Good night, Brent." She watched him walk unsteadily to his truck, and hoped he would get home without running off the road. After he was gone she sat in her car by the dark station for a long time, thinking about the glittering day two months earlier when she had pulled into this station for a bargain, and wished with all her heart that she had stopped someplace else.

ೞ 8 ೞ

Summer was already passing as August waned, the nights cooling to crispness under dark skies, only the crickets left to chirp their rhythmical chorus. Brick by brick the firebox and walls of the athanor rose from the cellar floor of the house. Thomas and Diana would devote one night to consecrating bricks, the next to ritually fitting them into place. The cellar stairs had begun to creak from their countless trips up and down, carrying one silk-cocooned brick at a time. By dawn, Diana's voice was hoarse from repeating the sing-song chants, and even Thomas appeared weary. Yet the firebox itself was completed, and the sloped outer and inner walls began to rise. The silicone sand arrived, four weeks past its promised delivery date.

"We don't have to consecrate this grain by grain, do we?" Thomas said as he brought the first heavy bag down the bulkhead steps, and she only rolled her eyes at him.

As the circular foundation slowly blossomed from the earthen floor like some sort of mineralized fungus, Diana could feel the mirrored network of etheric energy grow along with it. When she walked into the cellar with her magical awareness open, she felt as though she were wading through cool flowing water, filling the entire room with a slowly turning vortex. As they set each brick into position, it brought with it the tiniest increase in the invisible web, which already prickled her fingers like electricity when she touched the athanor's walls. From time to time she caught Thomas frowning down at the empty floor, as though, like a cat, he could see the magical energy directly. He picked his way across the cellar like a hiker crossing a rocky streambed. The magic had already begun to collect in the metal hemispheres, which sometimes hummed, almost imperceptibly, from a vibration that had no physical source.

Thomas became even more silent during these weeks, rarely speaking to her except when they completed and rehearsed the words for the final ritual. He corrected her pronunciation while she coached him on the placement of the cadence notes, and that was all. But these days, Diana felt almost relieved by his distance.

Ever since she had returned from taking Brent back to the station that night, Diana's feelings about Thomas had been both distracting and confused. She wanted him to be closer to her, yet when he happened to step too close, she had to restrain herself from recoiling. In each ritual they performed together, with its choreography of passing objects, moving and separating, Diana felt such an intensity of attraction, and such a depth of repulsion, that she had difficulty focusing on the magical workings. Outside of ritual space, she would catch herself thinking, for minutes at a time, about some tiny detail of Thomas' movements or body—the curve of his long fingers, the shadow his thick lashes cast on his cheek under the lamps. She had to force the images from her mind. For his part, Thomas was so psychically defended from her that his mental walls exceeded the brick ones they were building. Yet once or twice, she had turned or glanced up suddenly and had seen him quickly look away, as though he had been watching her. But of what, if anything, he was feeling, he said nothing at all.

And so the athanor took shape, until they were nearly at a stopping point, and would need to wait for the metal core. They awoke, spent the night doing their rituals, and slept. Thomas still needed to make an occasional foray, but he did so at longer and longer intervals—four days, then five. He never spoke about where he went, or how long he could wait until the next time. Despite her tangled emotions, Diana couldn't help feeling deeply impressed by his magical discipline.

The Thursday before Labor Day weekend, Diana arose in the mid-afternoon and drove over to Camden to see if Brent would be ready to begin welding the following week. No customers waited for service at the filling station, and Brent had once again propped the much-painted-over plywood sign against the southward pump. Diana pulled into the side of the graveled yard and parked. It seemed very quiet. She walked toward the open bay of the station, and Brent came to the entrance from the deep shadows inside and stood blinking at her. She hesitated, wondering if something was wrong.

"Hi," she said uncertainly, and he shaded his eyes with a hand and then smiled.

"Oh, hi, it's you. I can't see too well in the sun, when I've been in here for a while. Come on back."

She followed him into the dim bay, where only light from the doorway and a single grimy overhead bulb illuminated the interior. A boxy Ford sedan stood with its hood patiently open, like a resigned dental patient. Brent went to the front of the car and picked up a wrench that had been set on a rag spread on the car's fender. "I'm almost done here," he said. Diana watched him torque a bolt into place inside the car's engine.

Brent finished his work and turned to replace the wrench on a hook in a pegboard on the wall behind him. When he had tossed the rag into a canvas sack, lowered the car's hood, and washed his hands at a small chipped iron sink in the corner, all without speaking, Diana finally cleared her throat and said uneasily, "Are you all right?"

He studied the towel as it moved from one hand to the other. Finally he said, "Guess you'd know if I'm all right or not. That's what my mom keeps asking." He smoothed out the towel and hung it on a hook next to the sink. "I don't know what to say. I told her I thought I had the summer flu, or something." He suddenly looked up at her, and said softly, "Am I all right?"

At the expression in his blue eyes she had to catch her breath. Suddenly she remembered the way she'd felt when she'd woken alone in Thomas' house, too weak to move, and with nothing but her reason to combat the fear and confusion she felt. All Brent knew was that something from children's nightmares had just become part of his personal reality, and he was helpless to seek advice or defend himself. She didn't know how to respond, and floundering, asked him, "Well, how do you feel?"

"Now? Okay, I guess." He thought for a moment. "I get real thirsty sometimes. Keep having to come back here and drink water. And the light bugs me. But I..." he broke off, gulping in breaths of air as if he were sobbing. "It's like, it can't have happened, y'know? It can't have happened, but I keep dreaming about it, and then I wake up and I don't know...I don't know what..."

She glanced out at the empty yard and stepped closer to Brent. "We'd better talk about it, okay?"

He looked around furtively. "Not here...someone might come in..."

"But you can't go on just..." she paused, suspecting that there was some particular thing that was bothering him. "What is it, Brent? I mean, is there something that you really need to know?"

He glanced down, blinking rapidly, and spoke without looking at her. "Well, uh...do you think...ahh, this is stupid." He threw his head back, eyes closed, and sighed. "I got nothin' to go on, y'know? Movies, and, crap like that."

"Yes, but?"

"Well...you don't think...you don't think I could...you know..."

There was a pause, and Diana said cautiously, "...turn into a vampire?"

"Yeah," he said with a long sigh of relief.

It was certainly a valid question, and she pondered it darkly, one finger pressed absently to her mouth.

"You're not answering."

"I don't know," she finally said with a shrug. "But I don't think so...just from him drinking? No, I don't think so. I think it's a lot harder to do than that. He says it's never happened."

"Yeah? In how long?"

She gave him a sidelong look. "About...two hundred years."

He sat hard on the edge of the sink, as if his knees had given way. "Jesus jumping Christ," he whispered. "How can this be *happening?*" He rubbed his hands upwards over his face, wiping away the sweat that had gathered there. "I've been so scared...I couldn't even tell you. The way the sun hurts my eyes, and always being thirsty, and then the dreams...I thought, either I've gone right off the deep end, or else..."

"No, no. Believe me, Brent. You're not crazy. This is as real as it gets. But you're not changing into anything. Those same things happened to me, really. I don't know why, but...you don't want to know what you'd have to go through to be like Thomas. Brent, I'm sorry," Diana reached out and touched his arm helplessly. "I should have talked to you about it, I didn't even think...nor did Thomas, it was just—"

"Yeah, well, look. I feel better just talking to you about it, because y'know, the worst thing was, I kept thinking I must be crazy. At least I know it's real. I don't have to like it, but at least it's real. Because you know, if anything happens to me, my family...well, it'll be real hard on them."

Diana closed her eyes for a moment. "I understand." They both looked up as a car pulled in to the pumps. The driver honked his horn impatiently.

"Look," Brent said quickly, "don't you leave, okay?"

"Don't worry. I came on business. We need that job contract."

"Oh, right. I've got it. I'll be right back." He hurried out into the sun, flinching and shading his eyes with his hand, as the customer honked again.

It was just sunset when she got back to the stone house, and Thomas was already gone. Puzzled, Diana went to his study and put the job contract on his desk. He must have gone out on a foray. They always walked over to the Schuller house together unless he had gone out. She got some bread and peanut butter from the kitchen and walked down the road and through the woods to the house, munching, as the sky deepened to blue-green overhead. To her surprise, the screen door glowed with yellow lamplight. She went in, stepping carefully on the floorboards which now both creaked and wobbled, and stopped at the doorway of the ritual room. Thomas was there, preparing for the night's working. He glanced up at her briefly, then looked back down at the square of silk he was unfolding.

"Is everything all right?" he asked the silk.

"I thought you'd gone out."

"No, I want to finish these. We only need to do a few more and then we'll have to stop, at any rate. Where have you been?"

"I went over to see Brent."

"And how is he? Will he be ready to start work after the weekend?"

"Yes. He had the job contract all typed up, it's on your desk."

"Excellent." Diana leaned against the doorjamb, sucking peanut butter off her fingers. Abruptly, a mental picture came into her mind, Thomas sucking his fingertips clean of Brent's blood, and she hastily wiped her hands on her slacks. Thomas looked up at her, and his forehead creased slightly. "You look very tired."

She shrugged, avoiding his eyes. "You don't look so well yourself. How long has it been, a week?" He was even paler than usual, giving his face an almost ethereal cast.

"You needn't be concerned about that. I'm aware of my limits by now, believe me. The work is our first priority, don't you agree?"

She straightened, looking darkly at the heavy brocade draperies that concealed the peeling plaster walls. "Is it? I'm not sure right now."

Thomas set down the censer he'd been filling and frowned at her. "Diana—what is the matter? You seem upset, has something happened?"

She sighed, her shoulders slumping. "It's just that Brent is...well, he's not himself, Thomas. After all this time. He's so...quiet. As if he were still in shock."

Thomas stood still, studying her. "It's almost the end of the summer, and he's working very hard. I'm sure he's nearly worn out."

"Yes, but...it's more than that." Exasperated, she burst out, "Thomas, you know exactly what I'm talking about."

"Yes, I know what you're talking about. I'm sure he'll recover in time. I may have pushed him a little too hard, that's all. I've only tried to influence someone that way a few times, and I told you beforehand that my abilities lack subtlety. I'm sorry about that, but..." He paused, and when she didn't answer, he shrugged and leaned down to pick up the aspergillum. "Are you ready to begin? We may be able to finish tonight."

"Thomas...don't you understand? He had no idea what you'd just done to him! How was he supposed to cope? We didn't explain anything, we acted like it hadn't even happened! I just dropped him off at the station to go home, and for two weeks we left him to wonder whether he was losing his mind, or whether he would..." she stopped, unwilling to humiliate Brent by telling Thomas what he had feared. Thomas stared at her.

"Usually I don't need to explain," he said uncomfortably. "I had no idea that Brent was having such difficulties."

Diana took a breath, but so many emotions were welling up, with anger at the crest of them, that she couldn't continue the discussion. "I'm sorry, Thomas. I just can't work tonight."

She went out into the front room and leaned against the wall by the doorway, staring unseeing at the boarded windows. She felt overwhelmed by her frustration and utter helplessness in the face of Thomas' reserve. *He's not human, how can I work with someone like this?* Levoissier had not seemed this inscrutable to her. Despairing, she slid down to a sitting position and hugged her knees.

She heard Thomas walking down the hallway after another minute or so. He came in and went down on one knee a few feet away from her, studying her with an ambiguous expression. She raised her head and gave him a hard, cynical look. "At least I know how to get your undivided attention," she said with a sarcastic bite in her voice. "Go on strike. Take away the only thing you care about—the only use you have for me, and at least you'll look me in the eye for a moment." If she hadn't been so angry, she might have thought the expression on his face was hurt.

"Diana, I don't...I don't have any idea why you're saying this. Do you honestly believe I'm that calculating and unfeeling? Do you really trust me so little as that?"

"I want to trust you, Thomas, but...you remember that night when you promised you'd tell me anything I asked? There's so much I don't know, so much that you're still hiding—"

"Such as what?"

"Such as where you go at night, what you do, how you move around so quickly, just to start with..." She could see that guarded expression come back into his eyes, and she burst out, "Stop it! Stop throwing up those defenses like that! By all the gods, Thomas...for weeks and weeks, you've had such barriers up against me—it's like you weren't even here most of the time."

He looked shocked. "You know what I guard against."

"No! It's not that simple."

"Isn't it? I can't allow myself to be distracted. We have work to do."

"And I can't go on with that work under these conditions, Thomas." She leaned toward him, and he drew back. "I've been trying to tell you for two months what some of the side effects of all this might be, and you refuse to listen. You obviously know what you're doing magically. How can you be so blind?"

He looked down at the floor, and she saw his eyes traveling along the cracks and knots in the wood, tracing the path between the two of them.

"I am not blind. And when the work of preparing the athanor is finished, then I'll tell you all of these things that you want to know. There simply hasn't been time. I'm too aware of our deadline. I don't want to wait another year." He looked up at her with nothing guarded in his expression at all. "I'm too afraid to wait. That's why I've used you—yes, I will say it—and Brent, and why I've pushed you so hard. I don't dare wait any longer, Diana. It may be that you'll be rid of me at the end of it."

"I don't want to be rid of you."

He inclined his head. "God will make that decision." After a moment, his mouth quirked into a humorless smile. "I'm sorry, was that remark too pious?" But Diana was unabashed by his jab.

"It does sometimes sound as though you're evading responsibility. God, destiny, Providence—what about your own choices? You can't blame God for everything, you know. Eventually He'll file an objection, and He has a tendency to be sustained."

Thomas looked at her silently for a few moments. "What is it that you want from me?"

"I want you to open up to me. I want you to stop being so afraid of touching me, hurting me, letting me see what you're feeling. What is it that you're hiding? What great and horrible secrets could you possibly have, that you're so terrified I'll somehow perceive?" He hesitated, and she felt a surge of anger welling up again. "I'm not doing any further magical work with you until this is settled, Thomas."

For a moment, he looked slightly desperate, and then his face tensed with anger. "You made a vow."

"*After* you had promised to tell me everything. 'You need only ask,' those were your words, not, 'what I deem that you need to know'. You aren't upholding your side of the bargain. What am I getting from this, after all? This is all for you, we're doing this for you!"

He sat back, one closed hand pressed against his mouth, studying the floor before him intently. Finally he said, "You...want to know more about my forays, is that it?"

"Despite the way you've ducked around on that topic, I do think I've got the gist of it. There are a few puzzles, but they're not really critical. But there is one question you avoided that first night that I've never gotten around to asking again." She paused, as he waited warily. "How did you know my name, and why were you looking for me, and who told you such...flattering things about my capabilities? You claimed you still have contacts in the Order, but I'd never heard of you. Who told you about me, without letting me know about it?" Technically, that was against the rules of the OSL, although no one had ever been banished merely for gossiping to another initiate. Diana waited until the silence itself seemed to validate her point. "That's why you're keeping so distant. You're afraid that if you relax even for one moment, I'll see the answer to this. And then, I think, you believe that I'll pack up and leave. Which alone tells me something, doesn't it?"

He looked up sharply. "It's not only that."

"But it's partly that, isn't it?" She slammed her hands against the floor in exasperation. "Thomas, am I crazy here? Have you really not been aware of the *tension* between us these past few weeks?"

He looked away from her. "Yes, I've been aware of it."

"And you think this is a tenable situation?"

He looked squarely at her, at last, and Diana caught her breath, because in his eyes she saw the same combination of longing and reluctance that she now felt whenever she thought of him, but amplified. "You are...an *intense* distraction to me," he said slowly. "And yes, I know perfectly well how I've been making you feel. I think you suspect me of being considerably more obtuse than I am. I don't want to...to let my own temptation derail what we're doing." She kept on meeting his gaze with a level look, and after a moment he dropped his eyes. "Which is happening, in any event, obviously."

"Obviously." Diana looked down at the floor herself, saw nothing that would be holding his attention, and finally let out a long, resigned sigh. "There's only one way to really solve this, you know."

He looked up, genuinely puzzled. "And that is?"

She put her hands on the floor and deftly shifted, on hands and heels, to sit next to him. He pulled back, blinking, and she put a hand on his knee to stop him, making him gasp. He could have freed himself without even thinking, but instead he froze, like a startled animal.

"Stop resisting. It doesn't help the work, it's hindering it, and there's no reason for it." He opened his mouth to protest, and she cut him off. "You know you want to. You're starving. Go on, Thomas. Do you think I'm afraid of you? I'm not—not of that, anyway. You didn't lose control with Brent, did you? Go ahead—prove that you can trust yourself. Prove that I can trust you."

She let go of his leg and extended her hand toward him. He was watching her warily, but she could feel a subtle tension fill the space between them, and he wasn't hesitating nearly as much as she'd expected he might. Slowly he reached out and put his hand in hers. He was very cold, and his fingers curled around to the back of her hand. He closed his eyes for a moment, and she thought she could feel her pulse beating against his fingertips. She tightened her grip and he opened his eyes. He licked his upper lip slowly, and swallowed hard.

"You're...quite sure about this?"

"*Quite* sure. I want to feel exactly what it is that you do. I was in no state to analyze it the last time. I'm sure it's another of those intangibles you'll say you couldn't explain."

"Look up, then." He bent toward her without waiting for her to comply, and she looked up at the wavering shadows on the cracked plaster ceiling overhead. He took hold of her shoulders and pulled her toward him, his cool lips meeting the bare skin of her neck. She braced herself for a bite but it never came. Instead, there was a painful tug at her skin, and a sickening sense that she had simply been pulled open, like a hole torn into a piece of cloth. But the pain was instantly washed away by a flush of warmth, liquid and slippery, Thomas' mouth catching and holding it.

She opened her eyes, realizing she was pulling back against his hands, and let out her breath in a long sigh, her whole body relaxing as his arms slid around her. Erotic arousal tingled up and down her body in soft waves, and she abandoned herself to the pleasure of it. She could feel Thomas' intense relief from the strain of his self-denial, and the release he felt simply giving way to his terrible hunger. He must be drinking very fast, she thought vaguely, and it occurred to her that she should care about that, but she couldn't have resisted him now if she'd wanted to.

Far too soon, he shifted slightly, pulling a bit away from her. Then, where his mouth was, there was a cold thrill like a nerve pinched the wrong way, and she suddenly felt as though she had been dropped six inches onto the floor. She vaguely remembered feeling this on that first night, and she realized now that she had seen Brent react to it. It came as quite a shock, cutting off the flow of blood, the warm eroticism and her psychic connection to Thomas as sharply as a slamming door. She drew in a deep breath, aware now that her stomach was queasy and she was dizzy. Thomas drew his head back and looked into her face impassively for a moment, licking blood from his lips. Then he bent back down and carefully licked the blood off her skin, and she waited patiently for him to finish.

When he started to pull back from her, she caught his hands and held him where he was. He seemed surprised, and put his arms back around her. They remained sitting on the uneven floor like that for a long time, Diana leaning her forehead against Thomas' shoulder. It seemed she had been waiting for this for weeks. She could feel the magical energies around them spiraling to ground for a little while, taking with them all the tensions and defenses and emotions that had built up over the summer, and she clearly sensed that Thomas could perceive this as well. His relief at the change, for more than one reason, was palpable.

"Are you all right?" she heard him say, a bit cautiously, after several minutes had passed.

"You mean, do I feel able to get back to those beastly bricks?" Her tone was more amused than her words.

"If you think you can manage it."

"Give me a minute." She reluctantly pulled away from him and pushed back against the wall, trying to center herself and assess how shaky she was. "Maybe a half hour?"

He nodded, his eyes avid. She hadn't seen him this energized for some while, and he sat back on the floor and stretched his arms luxuriously. "Is some of your technical curiosity satisfied now?" His tone was wry but not unkind. "You're right—I couldn't explain it in words if I wanted to."

"Maybe a little. I think I could do without that bit at the end, though."

"No, you couldn't. Without that you'd bleed to death."

"Well, true."

"About young Crothers," Thomas said after a moment. "Perhaps I should speak to him."

Diana smiled, shaking her head. "I don't think that would help."

"You seemed to feel so guilty about his predicament, as though it was all your fault. If you had insisted on choosing another welder, I would have listened to you. But I thought your suggestion was ideal, for many reasons. I don't see what else we could have done. I would have had to exert the same influence on anyone we hired."

"You're right. I just never felt quite so...manipulative before. I always just paid any cowan that I needed to help me with a working."

"We are paying Brent. A small fortune."

"I know."

Watching him relax on the floor, as supple as a twenty-year-old, Diana was struck by how much his aspect had changed, not just physically but on other levels as well. She sensed that there would never be a more auspicious moment, and shot the question without warning or preface. "So, who told you? Who was your unimpeachable source, Thomas?"

Thomas paused only a moment, although he looked down when he spoke. "Levoissier."

Diana leaned her head back against the wall, closing her eyes. "I knew it." *Five years and five years…what can it mean?* "I've known it since Manchester. He's contrived this whole thing from the beginning, hasn't he?"

"That, I wouldn't know about." Thomas bridled a little. "But really, Diana—I've been amazed that you took so long to figure it out. Levoissier was your mentor. Wasn't it he who suggested that you study Welsh as a magical language? And when you tracked down the only alleged immortal whose records you could trace to the present day, and found that the trail led to a Welshman—didn't that ever strike you as a rather *astounding* coincidence?"

"A coincidence, yes, but…" she broke off, overwhelmed by her own stupidity.

"You see, I'm not the only one who can focus so closely on one goal that all distracting details are disregarded."

She couldn't repress a despairing groan. "I'll bet he even planted some of the information I found in the archives about you. I never told him what I was looking for, but he's been leaving a trail of bread crumbs for me, for five years! I can't believe it."

"If he did that, he certainly assisted you more than he ever did me. If it makes you feel any better, he didn't tell me much about you at all. The only thing he ever said, in a letter to me, was that he thought you and I could be of service to each other, and he told me your name. He never told me how to find you, and he did not indicate that he would send you to find me. Believe me when I say that my surprise when you showed up on my doorstep was unfeigned."

"Why didn't you say anything before now?"

"You refused to tell me the name of your mentor, remember? Besides…" he looked away uneasily. "One…doesn't talk casually about Levoissier."

She stared at Thomas' expression in disbelief. "You're afraid of him?"

He swallowed. "I wouldn't cross him, nor advise anyone else to do so."

"But…you're indestructible! What do you think—" but at his look, she broke off. "How long have you known him?"

"I wouldn't say I ever really knew him. I first met him in 1741."

This took a few moments to absorb. When Diana spoke again, her voice quavered a bit. "Did you ever work with him?"

"No. My contact with him has been quite limited, actually. When I returned to England in 1764, I was looking for him, but the Order told me that he had left the country some years earlier, as far as they or anyone else knew. I didn't encounter him again for over a century. I got the feeling, however, that he had been following my movements—how, and why, I don't know."

Diana swallowed hard. "Is he…do you know…is he a vampire, too?"

Thomas shook his head slowly. "I don't think so. I had no evidence for that, and he seemed very…*amused*…by me." Diana winced in sympathy at his bitter tone. "But you would be far more able to judge that than I would. He wasn't my mentor. I never slept with him." She looked up at him sharply, but he only smiled. "The extent of Levoissier's mentorship was very well known within the Order,

I'm afraid. You surely knew that would be involved, when he asked, didn't you?"

Diana sagged back against the wall. "Of course," she said after a moment. She glanced at Thomas. "You wouldn't have, anyway, would you?"

"When I was younger, no. But since..." he shrugged. "Another of those inexplicable changes I referred to. Suddenly the gender of my partners ceased to matter—at all."

"I guess it never mattered to me in the first place." She was tracing patterns on the floor with her finger, thinking now about Gregory, and what he'd said in Manchester. "I shouldn't tell you this, but...Levoissier mentored Gregory Fitzhughes. Before he took me on."

When she finally looked up, she saw Thomas sitting cross-legged with his chin propped on his hand, looking so deep in thought, she cut off what she was about to say rather than interrupt. After a moment he said in a somber tone, "Do you think *this* is a coincidence?"

"I have no idea. But Gregory and I are both using techniques we learned from Levoissier. The magical community is a rather small and rarefied one, after all, Thomas—and the Order is just a tiny part of it. There are going to be connections, it's inevitable. But I will say one thing. If I find out that Brent Crothers has ever met Levoissier—I'll be tempted to ground out our vow and give this whole endeavor up. That would just be too much."

Thomas said nothing to contest this statement, and she braced her hands on the wall behind her and carefully stood up. She only felt dizzy for a few moments, and she gave her head a shake to clear it. "Come on. I'm ready to start."

෴ 9 ෴

"I still can't believe you guys ripped out half of the floor."

"Well, you tell me how we could perform our ceremony upstairs and still know what you're doing in the basement."

"But the *floor*. S'pose one of you falls in?"

"Then you'd better duck. But I think that hole would be a bit hard to miss, don't you? We won't be working blindfolded up there. Now take a look at these and make sure they'll fit and everything." She handed Brent one of the large brown shopping bags that stood beside the little card table. He opened the crackling bag and drew out a pair of white duck pants, a white sweatshirt, and white socks.

"Ayeh, you got it right," he said, unfolding the pants and glancing at the label briefly. He reached into the bottom of the bag and took out a pair of heavy cream-colored leather gloves with gauntlet cuffs. "Hey...these are *nice*. Where'd you get these?"

"Bangor. They're not too small, are they?"

He fitted on the right glove and flexed his hand, turning the glove this way and that admiringly. "No, they're perfect. These must have cost..."

"Practically nothing, compared to our overall budget. Believe it or not, the pants were the hardest to find—white pants in September?"

Brent grinned. "Wouldn't know about that. Last time I wore white pants, they were diapers. You try wearing white and pumping gas."

"Good point."

He grew serious. "Now, I want to make sure I'm straight on what the deal is. The clothes will be up here in this little room, I'll change into them..."

"There are actually two sets—oh, and the shoes are here." She put a large shoebox on the table. "We'll keep them washed, and they'll be all ready for you to put on. If you can possibly avoid it, don't let them touch the floor when you change."

"Okay."

"Any more questions? You're all set up in the cellar, right?"

"It's all ready to go. No, I'm all set—no more questions, I mean. I'll just be a couple of minutes."

"Bring the lantern when you come down." She closed the bedroom door behind her and felt her way down the dark narrow stairs to the first floor. The front room seemed smaller and less empty with roughly a third of the warping floorboards pulled up, revealing the massive beams that had supported them. The gaping square hole filled the central part of one side of the room, with flooring left by the walls for walking. They'd pushed the folding table over to the floored side, and set up the altar and tools from the ritual room close to the edge of the breach. Below the shadowed beams, Brent's welding tanks could be seen gleaming dimly in the light of two hanging lanterns. On a stand directly under the gap the copper sphere appeared to float in midair, the glass vessel already enclosed between the two tightly fitted halves. In the lamplight the copper glowed red like dying coals.

Thomas was setting up the white-draped altar, carefully laying out the censer and aspergillum and small gold dish of salt with the precision of a maître d'hôtel placing the silver at the head table. He glanced up quickly as she entered the room, but without the furtiveness that had characterized that gesture all summer. "I gather he had no serious objections to anything."

"He'll be down in a moment. We'd better change."

Thomas followed her into the ritual room, where she opened a carved maple chest and handed him his robe, a simple garment of rust red silk with an attached hood and a twisted white cord that tied around the waist. Diana had aimed for a monkish effect rather than magical, in much the same way that she'd purchased church-like altar implements. She hoped this aesthetic would be less likely to spook Brent.

She and Thomas had been changing in and out of robes together for two months now, but Diana had felt oddly self-conscious doing so over the past week. This made her irritable with herself. A lifetime in the OSL had left her thoroughly accustomed to being naked in the company of other naked people, and she regarded modesty as prudish. She'd noticed that Thomas kept his back to her all of sudden as well, and he'd never been shy before, either. This awkwardness did make them dress faster, however, and they were finished and ready well before they heard Brent's eager footsteps on the stairs.

"You two look like a couple of those friars from that place up in Bangor," he said cheerfully when he saw them. "Are we just about ready to start?"

"We are if you are," Diana said. "Now you're clear about the bells, right? That's how we'll know when to start and stop. You're the one controlling that, Brent, because you've got the most painstaking job, and the most important one. When you start to get tired, we're done."

"I got it. I'm pretty sure I can get the copper piece finished tonight. Those other two—I'll have to see how it goes."

"Take your time. I know you're putting in a full day at the station before you come here. There's no cap on what we're paying you, you know."

"Hey, I wouldn't cut any corners." He'd stiffened his shoulders a little.

"I know. No offense meant. Now go on down, and we'll ring our bell when we're ready for you to start."

"And then you guys get to sing until I ring my bell." He grinned. "I hope your voices hold out."

"Me, too."

She stepped aside so that Brent could get to the hallway, but unexpectedly, he sat on the edge of the hole in the floor, legs dangling. "I'll just go down this way," he said, and hopped off into space, deftly caught the top of a beam, swung once and dropped two feet to land lightly on the dirt floor. He picked up his welding helmet. "Ready when you are."

Diana was still trying to catch her breath. "Brent—warn a person before you do that again, okay?"

"Sorry." It struck her that far from being spooked, Brent was enjoying the sheer novelty of this whole experience.

Thomas was walking clockwise around the room, lighting the candles that circled the gap in the floor, and extinguishing the kerosene lamps as he passed them. Diana stood at the altar speaking the consecration of the incense under her breath and completing the series of invoking pentagrams over the small pouch with one hand. She put a scoop of the powder on the hot charcoal and clapped down the lid of the censer. She went on to consecrate the salt. She heard Brent moving below her, getting his torch and supplies into place and making sure he could walk entirely around the sphere. His voice sounded a little hollow through her light trance when he called up, "Don't look straight at the torch, you guys know that, right?"

"We understand," Thomas said. She was just finishing the consecration of the water, as he went to the west side of the gap, facing her across it as she stood in front of the altar in the east. She picked up the small hammer and struck the bell that hung in a frame on the altar. Its tone was sweet, but so high pitched and clear in the quiet house that it hurt her ears for a moment.

She and Thomas began the rhythmical chant of the preliminary casting, as Diana picked up the censer and circumambulated the gap clockwise three times, leaving a hazy perimeter of smoke that spiraled in the candlelight. She and Thomas smoothly changed places and he took the water around, then they changed again so that Diana could circle with the salt. Finally, Thomas carried a twisted, three-wicked candle to complete the elemental quadrangle. Now they both could feel the circle forming, its boundary plaited from earth and air and fire and water and their unceasing voices, rising and falling, harmonizing and in unison.

They once again took up positions opposite one another and fell into the long spoken and sung chant that constituted the spell itself, sometimes a call and response, but more often in unison. The wavering melody was a minor keyed

Celtic lament that evoked such natural calls as the wind sighing in the chimney or water trickling from the eaves. The voices of the dead and the unborn echoed in the winding Welsh words. Diana, lost in the music of the chant, could feel the magical power thickening around them, pulling inward toward the center. She had to resist an impulse to step straight ahead toward Thomas. Perhaps Brent had not been so unrealistic to worry about someone falling into the gap.

She could sense, rather than see, Brent beginning his task below her. He put down his helmet mask, and she remembered just in time to avert her eyes from the depths at her feet. There was a blinding light, radiating upward from below in rays, or so it seemed to her. A sound like distant roaring mingled with the chant, which went on in her ears as though someone else were singing it. She looked up and saw Thomas standing with head back and eyes closed, rapt, yet somehow she knew that he also was fully aware of every move Brent made. Her nose filled with an acrid smell, and she had a sudden keen awareness of Brent's total focus on the work he was doing, the intensity of a skilled craftsman whose concentration blots everything else from his mind. She had not anticipated this, but it wound its own power into the magical circuit they were creating.

The light below blinked out. For several seconds it seemed very dark and the chant seemed to echo against a yawning silence. Then the light and the roaring resumed, and Diana felt a sudden burst of new strength. She didn't keep count of how many times this happened. The pauses were always short, but Diana was beginning to feel the strain in her voice and her stamina when one pause, longer than the rest, was finally punctuated with a single silvery chime. Brent had struck the bell that stood in the cellar, the twin of the one on the altar, and was quietly waiting for them to conclude.

The chant wound down, became a deep-pitched monotone and ceased. In its wake, the silence was absolute. No one moved, or even breathed, it seemed, for several moments. Finally Thomas moved to the north side and began banishing each elemental quarter, his voice oddly hollow. When he finished, Diana picked up a long hawthorn staff from next to the altar and walked around the circle perimeter counter-clockwise nine times, grounding out and releasing the energy with careful concentration. Her knees were shaking, which somewhat surprised her.

By the time she tucked the staff back under the edge of the altar cloth, she felt a bit more normal, and Thomas and Brent were relaxing as well. Brent took off his helmet and wiped his face with a sleeve. "Looks good," he said, but his expression was somewhat haunted. "The weld, I mean. It's real clean. Come down and see it."

Diana and Thomas took the stairs down to the basement, bringing two more lanterns with them. The copper sphere sat on the stand that Brent had constructed to hold it motionless, still radiating heat. Diana stood back and gazed at it, amazed, but Thomas carefully went around looking closely at every inch of the welded seam. The metal was discolored and very slightly warped around the sphere's equator, but otherwise Diana almost couldn't tell there had ever been a break. Thomas finally straightened up, shaking his head. "Brent—this is a superlative job."

"Well, thanks. I remembered what you said, about it being like art, and about the seal. Trouble is, the copper's so smooth and pure, there's no way not to leave a mark. But it's going to be inside the other two, anyway. I think that iron one is going to take longer than I thought, and—"

"Brent," Diana said with quiet amusement. "You're talking in your sleep. Let's go change so you can get home."

After changing back into street clothes, they sat at the folding table while Diana wrote the check for that night's work. Brent was sagging heavy-lidded in his chair, and Diana felt like doing the same. In fact, the next few weeks would be a slight break for her and Thomas. Brent's work load at the station required him to stagger his nights with them, and he could only weld for so long each night. As soon as the welding was complete, Diana and Thomas would be working as many hours per day as they possibly could to finish the athanor. She knew that the fear of not finishing in time was preying heavily on Thomas' thoughts.

"That was really something," Brent said, his voice a bit dreamy from fatigue. "I can't think when I've felt anything like that...except you know, sometimes I get to working on a job, and I just lose track of time and it feels like it wasn't me doing it. It felt like that, kind of."

"I know," Diana said. "I could sense that from you. You're a true artist, Brent."

He shrugged, grinning sheepishly. "Nah. It's pretty simple."

"So you're comfortable going on with this? We're all set for Thursday night, right?"

"Oh, yeah. No, I'm fine with it. What, did you think I'd be spooked by all the candles and robes and stuff?"

"Maybe just a little. You did seem to take a few minutes to get started at the beginning."

"Oh, well, I was listening to you two sing. That was really beautiful. We went to see some Irish singers once, and they sang something like that. Oh, thanks," he added as Diana handed him the check.

"Any questions or anything? When you come on Thursday, we'd like to get started right away."

Brent hesitated a moment. "Well...there's one thing I gotta ask—and you're really going to think this is nuts. Was there ever anyone else upstairs with you two?"

Diana stiffened, feeling a sudden chill. "Upstairs with us? No...like who?"

"I don't know, I just had this feeling there was someone else there. Kind of came and went, but I almost could see him. Tall guy, really thin, all this curly hair, like a girl almost. It was weird, I kept wanting to look over my shoulder or something."

Diana felt caught—should she tell Brent whose presence he was somehow picking up? Smiling, she said lightly, "you must have the second sight, Brent."

"Yeah, well, maybe so, maybe not," he said archly. "So that was someone you know?" Thomas was looking at her attentively, and something in his expression left no doubt that he also had sensed the person Brent described.

"That was the man who made the compound that's inside the copper sphere you were working on," Diana said.

"And he's connected to all this somehow?"

"Apparently." She leaned back in her chair, crossing her arms, and eyed Brent speculatively as he yawned. Evidently he was too tired, or by this time, too accustomed to the unusual, to be curious about what he'd seen.

"I gotta go. Same time on Thursday, right?"

"As early as you can make it," Diana said.

"I'll do my best." He got up, stretched, and left without a backward look.

Diana sat quietly, trying to take in all the events of the evening and the startling implications of the conversation they had just had. She heard Thomas begin to chuckle softly.

"Well, well. Our young filling station attendant is just full of surprises."

She could only shake her head wonderingly. "There are a lot of people out there with the gift, I know that. Many of them don't think much about it, especially if there's cultural support for it. The Irish tend to accept the supernatural pretty easily."

Thomas got up and began to pick up the candles that had marked their circle perimeter. "I think you must have detected his ability when you met him, on an unconscious level." His voice sounded almost smug. "It couldn't possibly be a coincidence. But it could mean more than that."

Diana had followed Thomas' lead and was at the altar packing up the ritual tools. "Be specific," she said over her shoulder, as she placed the smaller altar tools in their box.

"I only mean that we could assume that destiny is in our favor, that you should encounter Brent entirely at random, offer him this job and then discover that he actually has gifts. How likely would that be without some guiding hand behind it?"

"I don't know..." she said uneasily, folding the altar cloth with considerably more precision than she usually did, her fingers nervously twitching the linen edges into place. "Destiny can be a very mysterious thing."

"I'm not following you."

"This worries me, that's all. I don't like it."

Thomas stopped with an armful of candleholders and stared. "In God's name, why? What could possibly be more to our purpose?"

"Our purpose, yes. But what about Brent? What will this do to him?"

"What could it do? His part will be finished, and we'll release him ritually just to make sure. Diana—he's only assisting us, that's all."

"I hope you're right."

"He'll be fine." As she continued to frown unhappily at the floor, Thomas added, "...or is there something you're not telling me?"

The question hung in the air, but Diana didn't reply. In her mind was the uncomfortable thought, *It's not a coincidence, no, I'll grant you that...it's too much like a joke, a joke the faeries would play...* but she wasn't going to say that aloud. She didn't even want to think it. Thomas finally shrugged and took the candles into the ritual room.

"Can you finish clearing away here?" he said when he came back out.

"Yes." She felt slightly annoyed, because she was tired.

"Then I'll be back in a while." He went out, closing the screen door silently behind him.

The front room of the Schuller house lost all of its floor in the end, for this was the only way they could wrap enough chains around the beams for the block and tackle. The last night Brent came to work with them, he assisted them in moving the solid metal core into the base of the athanor. They fastened a heavy chain around the iron sphere, just short enough to circle below the sphere's widest point, and linked four chains to that. Despite Brent's knowledgeable prediction that they would need a truck or possibly a tractor to lift the metal core, Thomas worked the iron chains up through the pulleys, an inch at a time. He didn't quite make it look effortless, but neither did he appear to be straining himself. Brent stood holding one of the two guide ropes and gaping back and forth from the sphere, suspended silently in the rigid chains as though it were floating, and Thomas, who had hooked a knee around one of the support beams to keep from being pulled off the ground. Diana was afraid to take her eyes off the black iron core, as though her gaze was helping to hold it up.

They brought the hovering black globe directly over the bricks and slowly let it down, Diana drawing in hissing breaths with each downward slip, for if the sphere came down too hard it might damage the bricks. As the metal descended, she and Brent guided it with their bare hands, muttering directions to each other in order to center it as perfectly as they could, afraid to speak too loudly lest they break Thomas' concentration. Finally the sphere came to rest in its bed of bricks, and the chains sagged with a chinking noise like a whimper of relief. Thomas let go of the beam and sat down, somewhat suddenly.

"Wow." Brent stepped back to stare admiringly at the rounded black metal. "I'll tell ya—I didn't think you were ever going to get that thing in there. I wasn't going to say anything, but, man." He glanced around the sphere at Thomas. "You're not from the planet Krypton or something, are you?"

"From Wales, originally," Thomas said, so deadpan that Diana couldn't tell if he understood Brent's joke or not. All three of them were gazing at the black sphere as if mesmerized. She could still feel a tingling in her fingers from the touch of the metal.

Thomas stood up and stretched, at length. "Brent, I think this concludes our business with you. I'd like to thank you for all the time you've been putting in here the last few weeks. I hope you know how much we appreciate it."

"Well, you're welcome—don't take this the wrong way, but I've never been happier to finish a job."

"Oh, I understand. Neither have I. But our job is far from finished." He looked over at Diana, and she straightened up from pressing her face against the cool iron, feeling the pulsing currants of energy running through it.

"Yes, Thomas, I know. I'm just going to give Brent his last check."

She and Brent went up the cellar stairs—she had once challenged him to go back up the way he liked to go down, via beam, but he'd declined. They now had to clomp over sheets of plywood laid over the bare beams to get to the stairs to the second floor. When they got to the bedroom, she sat at the card table and calculated the hours, twice, and wrote out the check as Brent packed up a bag with his shoes and gloves.

"Seems a terrible waste, to burn those good clothes."

"You wouldn't want to keep them, Brent." They had done a ritual the night before to release him from the magical aspect of their working. Diana was by no means convinced it had changed anything, and she wished she hadn't promised him the shoes and gloves.

She walked out to Brent's truck with him, under a dark sky filled with the brittle, bright stars of early fall. The air was fragrant with the sweet smell of turning leaves, and their feet rustled though a carpet of yellow that made the ground pale in the starlight. Brent hesitated at the truck door. "You think I should've shook hands with him or something?" he said uncomfortably.

"It's okay. He didn't expect it."

"Should I shake your hand, then?"

"Sure." She gave his hand a firm shake, and noticed that he maintained the handclasp a few moments longer than was usual. He started to get into his truck, then paused.

"I'm kinda worried about you."

"Don't be. Don't even think about us, Brent. You catch up on your sleep."

☞ 10 ☜

She wouldn't have thought it possible to work like this, for day after day, week after week without once stopping. Thomas was like a driven thing, and although he never pressured her in any way, his urgency was infectious. They would start in mid-afternoon, setting up their tools and changing clothes, and then begin the now monotonous rhythm of consecrating the bricks and bringing them downstairs to be fitted into place. The sing-song chants filled Diana's thoughts, thrummed in her ears when she rested and echoed in her dreams.

As before, she and Thomas would spend a night consecrating, then a night building, but the tasks overlapped, and their night began with the sun still high and continued until mid-morning. It was always Diana who finally had to plead to stop each morning, just as she pleaded for breaks for eating and other necessities, and felt ashamed of her own human frailty. Thomas never grudged her, yet he would stop with the tension of a racehorse poised at the gate with every muscle bunched, waiting for the starting gun. Only when they took their midday break did he reluctantly and rapidly change out of his ritual robe and curl up to sleep on the cellar floor, without any apparent self-consciousness.

Diana also ceased going back to the stone house except to pick up the occasional food delivery from Thornton's grocery. She preferred not to sleep in the cellar—there were beetles—but she kept blankets in the ritual room. They didn't quite dispense with all niceties. The ritual robes had to be washed every day, and they usually washed at the same time, catch as catch can. When Thomas' beard started to annoy him too much he would scrape it off dry with a straight razor, a process which after two hundred years of practice he accomplished with alarming speed. Most of the time he looked fairly disreputable, however, and Diana suspected that both of them would have appeared like shipwrecked castaways to anyone from town.

The leaves fell outside, leaving the trees bare limbed and bristling against the brilliant skies. The athanor walls rose steadily, forming a graceful arch inward around the iron sphere, reaching toward their characteristic beehive shape. The vent for the firebox angled upward from near the base, giving the athanor a whimsical resemblance to an enormous teapot. They could already feel portents of midcoast Maine's harsh winter in the chill wind and biting air. Thomas began lighting a small fire in the cellar hearth, but this was for Diana's comfort, not his own. He was impervious to the cold, as he had told her, and most afternoons Diana awoke shivering on the ritual room floor, the fire having long since died out downstairs. But even the ritual room was always warmer than the little outhouse across the back yard.

They poured the first batch of silicone sand between the athanor's two walls on Samhain, which seemed like an emblematic date to do something a bit different. Unable to come up with a ritual for pouring sand, they settled for magically charging the sand to within an inch of its gritty life.

For the first time that afternoon, as Thomas went to open another bag of sand, Diana allowed herself to step back from the immediacy of their work and assess the magical energy as a whole. She closed her eyes and let tendrils of awareness stretch out around her into the room, caressing the earthen floor, the athanor, its metal core, the beams above. When Thomas came back with the sand, she placed a hand on his arm.

"Wait a minute. Feel this."

"I'm sorry?"

"Do you remember what the room felt like before Brent did the welding?"

"Yes…"

"Well, feel what it's like now."

He hesitated, impatience struggling with his realization that they should be paying attention to what they were doing. Then he straightened his back and became very still, his face relaxing into the unearthly quiet that she hadn't seen there for a long time. After a minute or so he blinked, and looked at her with consternation. "It's not there!"

"No," she said softly. "It's not. It's here. Feel." She stepped forward and placed her hands on the bricks of the athanor.

He followed her example, and caught a breath. The magical energy that had swirled around the room like a whirlpool had all drawn inward now, and it was far stronger than they expected so soon. Against their flat palms they could feel a dull throbbing, like the heartbeat of a growing embryo in a vast egg. In their desperate rush to lay each individual brick, they had completely failed to attend to the cumulative effect.

Thomas suddenly pulled away from the athanor and stood staring down at his open hands. He looked up at her with an expression of mixed incredulity, hope and desperation. "It's going to work, isn't it?"

"I hope so, Thomas…"

"Oh, no, it is—I can feel it…" and he reached out and grasped her hands tightly with both his own. "You've said yourself—the working depends on our absolute confidence. Well, I have absolute confidence now. I know this will work."

She looked at the athanor, seeing an illusion of rippling water before her vision, and blinked. Thomas was right. They couldn't possibly fail. The athanor wasn't even finished yet, and she was already almost in awe of it. She felt his hands tighten on hers, and when she looked back at him, he stepped forward, bent down, and kissed her on the lips. She was so startled that for a moment she didn't respond. His lips were cold, but they felt very soft. Her heart was racing, and there seemed to be a low sound all around her, like the humming of a beehive in late summer, dripping and oozing with honey. She finally remembered to open her mouth and return his kiss, and she reached her hands forward and slid them from his chest to his sides, feeling his lean body, aching at the touch of it. He broke off the kiss, slowly, and looked away from her, back at the athanor.

"God, can we finish it in time?"

"Six weeks? Oh, I think so."

"Only halfway done..."

"Two thirds. It gets smaller as we go up."

"Yes." The word was a long drawn-out sigh. She bent to help him with the sand.

The weeks of November went by. The iron sphere finally vanished beneath the hard yellow bricks. They built up and up, completing the high, solid packed crown that would hold and slowly radiate the heat from the core, so that the temperature in the center would remain constant. It was apparent now that they would, in fact, be finished in time, yet Thomas was not content. He arranged with a local contractor to cut and deliver seasoned firewood from his property, and Diana taught him the spell for splitting it into the size needed for the firebox. When they were not setting bricks, they were preparing and storing the wood. There had already been some light snowfalls, although this close to the coast, early snow melted away in a day or so. The copper pipe for the vent arrived, and here they ran into their first snag. They had neither the tools nor the expertise to cut the pipe.

"Do you suppose we could ask Brent back?" Thomas said after they had brought the pipe in through the bulkhead and spent a good hour considering their options. "He would have the correct tools, certainly."

"Thomas—"

"I know. But asking anyone else would mean...well, I don't want such a complication any more than you do. It's dangerous, if nothing else. Brent is a known quantity. And we can pay him for his time."

She sat beside him on the lowest step to the bulkhead, and put her head almost to her knees. "It's not fair to involve him further."

"I doubt it will take him more than half an hour to cut the pipe. Although it will be much easier to set the pipe into place with three people."

"You're right. I just wish we'd thought of it before."

"Can you go see him now?"

She plucked at her grimy shirt with distaste. "I better have a bath first. A real bath, I mean." The pump in the kitchen sink upstairs had never failed, but the water came out cold enough to numb her fingers now.

"You look fine. Don't be vain. I know whereof I speak."

"Thomas—I reek. The police will arrest me for vagrancy."

"You're exaggerating frightfully. Besides, there's no fire in the stove."

"Then I'm going to go start one! Thomas—please just relax. We are going to finish everything on time." At the bottom of the cellar stairs, however, she turned back. "You know, maybe you should try to get some sleep while I'm gone. You feel...stretched a bit thin." He leaned back on the bulkhead steps, sulking, and made one of his one-shouldered shrugs.

While waiting for the water to heat on the stove, she wandered through the two front parlors of the stone house, gazing moodily at the thick layer of dust on the floors and furniture which had been so carefully kept only a few months ago. She realized she was starving. She found a half jar of peanut butter in the kitchen and ate scoops of it neat, with a spoon. A thought suddenly struck her, and disturbed, she sat on a bench, casting her mind back over the weeks that had passed and wondering if she had been missing something.

Thomas had not been going out on any forays. Not once a week, not once in ten days...none, as far as she had noticed, at all.

Of course, she had been sleeping during the middle part of the days. He usually woke her by calling her from downstairs, so he could have slipped out while she slept. He had gone on forays very regularly while the welding was done. But think as she might, she couldn't remember his making a foray since... October. He couldn't possibly have abstained that long, could he? Could he store up blood, like a bear fattening up for hibernation? It certainly hadn't shown on him, if that were the case. An extra pound would be obvious on someone that lean—especially since she saw him naked so often.

She finally pushed aside her doubts. Thomas was certainly old enough to take care of himself. He must have been managing somehow. After all, she herself had barely left the Schuller house since October. Surely Thomas couldn't go without blood for weeks on end without appearing more emaciated.

She swept half a dozen dead spiders out of the big clawfoot bathtub before she filled it. The cistern was nearly full, but the water had grown a bit greenish from standing unused. They should be more diligent about keeping the stove going over here or the pipes were going to freeze. There was a thin layer of ice floating in the commode.

The car required considerable coaxing before it started, and when she was finally on the road toward Camden, she was still brooding over Thomas' apparent fast. What had he said would happen if he went too long? She couldn't quite remember. So much had occurred since then, and she had been light-headed from loss of blood and somewhat emotional at the time. What she did recall clearly was the look on his face when he'd mentioned it. She couldn't shake off her worried thoughts, and she didn't understand why. With each passing minute, she felt her anxiety level inch higher. *What's the matter with me?* Only fear of Thomas' utter exasperation prevented her from turning the car around and going back to Pepperell.

It was just past sunset when she arrived at the station, which appeared deserted with the bay door closed. Light shone from the window of Brent's office, but he had not yet turned on his outside floodlights. He heard her car pull up and emerged from the office, pulling on gloves. He stopped when he saw her, and slowly broke into a grin.

"Hey, come on in! How are things going up there, anyway?"

"Good," she said cheerfully as she took off her coat. Brent's crowded office was very warm, thanks to a small but energetic space heater. "We're going to finish on time. But we've run into a hitch, and that's why I've come to see you."

"Omigosh." Brent was staring at her blankly.

"What?"

"You look awful! Have you been sick? You musta lost twenty pounds."

She spread her hands and looked down at herself blankly. "Don't be silly, I didn't have twenty pounds to lose."

"That's what I'm sayin'."

She sighed as they sat down. "There's nothing wrong, Brent. We've been working eighteen hour days, and it's been hard to find time to eat, that's all. We're almost done. But we need your help."

"What can I do? Name it."

"We've got this big long pipe, like a stove pipe, only made out of copper. It needs to be cut and fitted, and we don't have the means to do that."

"A stove pipe? Oh, yeah, that's easy. I can do that."

"We'll pay you for your time."

"Forget it." His face, as he looked at her, was still drawn into a concerned frown. "You been having trouble finding time to sleep, too?"

She rubbed at her eyes, wishing he wouldn't remind her how tired she was. "It's almost done with, Brent. Can you come up tonight after you close? An hour at most, I promise."

After a moment's pause, Brent leaned back and shrugged. "Sure. I'll be there."

"Great." She got up and started to put on her coat, and he stood and clumsily helped her. "I'm sorry I can't stay longer, but Thomas just about has kittens if anything interrupts us. I have to get back and tell him you're coming tonight."

"You guys ease up on yourselves, okay? I read someplace that you go crazy if you don't get enough sleep."

"Oh, look who's talking, the man who puts in fourteen hours a day here all summer."

"Hey, I get my eight hours. I just don't do anything else."

"I think I can safely say that we won't go crazy from lack of sleep, Brent, no matter what—" she stopped suddenly, her hand on the doorknob, and Brent must have been alarmed by the look on her face, for his voice went up a note or two.

"What's wrong? You okay?"

"Fine," she said after a moment. "I just...thought of something I was trying to remember."

As she drove back to Pepperell, her stomach tightened into icy knots from a dread certainty she couldn't explain or dismiss. Thomas had seemed perfectly fine only a few hours ago—but that had been before the sun went down. *If I abstain too long, I lose my faculties...* Thomas was wholly unaccustomed to doing a working of this magnitude. He had no way to assess the additional strain it put on him. And she, oh so foolishly, had not taken the responsibility to keep an eye on his energy levels herself. *Partners look out for each other in a working, isn't that so?* She cursed herself, soundly, from an equal mixture of anger and fear.

The stone house was dark and silent when she arrived there and let herself in. The kitchen was warm and smelled of wood smoke from the damped stove. She lit a lamp and walked around the dusty rooms, sending out psychic feelers. The door to Thomas' study was open and the dust on the carpet was unmarred by footprints. But her feeling of cold apprehension sharpened suddenly, and she *knew* there was something drastically wrong—she could *feel* it. The lantern was dimming—it was running out of fuel. Leaving it behind, she walked rapidly to the Schuller house.

She stood in the back yard for a few minutes, trying to determine if Thomas was inside. She could sense some sort of presence, but she was uncertain what she felt. It certainly wasn't Thomas' consciousness—either waking or sleeping. With its boarded up windows and closed door, the small house was featureless and blank, giving her no clues. She braced herself and went inside.

There were no lamps lit, which was particularly dangerous with so much of the floor missing now. She couldn't remember Thomas ever failing to light the lamps for her, whether he had gone out or not. The presence she'd felt was stronger inside the house, but it was confused, unfocussed. She picked her way into the ritual room in the dark, dumped her coat, and groped for the box of kitchen matches they kept under the altar. She lit the lamp, and carrying it, went out into the hallway. Shadows wavered on the walls, reminding her of the very first time she had seen the house, almost six months ago. "Thomas...?" she ventured uneasily, but there was no response. She thought she saw something move at the periphery of her vision, and turned quickly, but there was nothing there.

She stepped out onto the plywood boards and hung the lamp out over the gap between the beams. Below her the cellar was inky black except for a mass of dying coals in the hearth. The lamp faintly illuminated the crown of the athanor and the long gleaming copper pipe. "Thomas, are you down there?" she called, wondering why she felt so sure he was here. He must have gone out, thinking she would be longer talking to Brent. She straightened up, sighing. She heard a floorboard creak at the top of the stairs, and caught her breath. Suddenly she remembered the way he had come in noiselessly and stood watching her while she cut silk and a burst of anger welled up to mask her fear. "Gods, Thomas, this isn't fair! Are you up there?" She went up the stairs, forcing herself to step firmly and rapidly.

She went down the narrow hallway, stopping and looking into each of the four tiny bedrooms opening off it. She stepped inside the last and largest room, looking around despairingly at the wallpaper, patches of black mildew obscuring its pattern of cabbage roses. One of the window panes was cracked, and she walked over to look at it, wondering how the window could get broken after it had been boarded over. She could see her reflection in the glass and was taken aback at how drawn she looked. As she peered at herself, she suddenly saw, reflected over her shoulder, Thomas standing directly behind her. She whirled around, stifling a shriek with her hand. Thomas didn't move, and after a moment she took her hand away from her mouth.

"Mother Goddess..." she whispered helplessly. Thomas inclined his head toward her slightly, as though she had introduced herself. His eyes fixed on her with a steady, intense gaze that didn't shift or waver. In his concentrated avidity he appeared to find her the most fascinating thing he had ever seen, yet there was no recognition in his eyes at all.

"I've been watching you," he said, in a tone that would have been conversational had it not been curiously flat. "Watching you go around with the light. Were you looking for me?" He smiled a little. She swallowed, hard.

"I was looking for...Thomas." His expression didn't change.

"Oh...." he breathed, rather than said.

"Aren't you Thomas?"

He blinked once, and took a step back from her. She could feel her legs begin to shake. She had seen that look before, on other faces, but those men had not been capable of single-handedly lifting hundreds of pounds of iron, nor had they been prone to drink blood. *Can I talk him back to rationality, or will I only provoke him?* She'd seen it go either way.

He let out a long sigh. "Don't be afraid of me. I can't hurt you."

"Why not?" *try to make him think, try to make him remember who I am...*

He tilted his head to one side and considered this. "I don't remember." He turned slowly, looking around at the walls of the room. A loud scratching sound suddenly came from within the wall—they heard noises like that constantly, since the Schuller house had mice, and squirrels nesting in the attic. Thomas froze, then sprang at the wall, for a moment a mere blur in the lamplight. He punched his fist through the lath and plaster as though it were paper and scrabbled desperately behind the wall, as plaster fell to the floor in chunks and crumbs. Finally he withdrew his arm and stared at his empty hand for a moment. He let out an incoherent sound of rage and beat at the wall, punching at the loose plaster until he'd opened a hole the size of a small window. Bits of plaster hung bouncing from shreds of wallpaper. Diana backed up against the window, too horrified to speak. Thomas stood staring at the damage he'd done, white dust powdering his drab clothing and tangled locks of his dark hair hanging loose around his face. Then he was gone. She thought he'd gone out the door, but she couldn't be sure. She hadn't heard a sound.

She clenched her fists until the pain of her nails cutting her palms forced her to move, and then she could walk. She went out of the bedroom and down the hall—he had gone downstairs, she could feel him, now that she knew what that presence was. On the plywood boards in the front room she leaned over the beams and called, "Thomas!" She saw something move behind the athanor, so quick it might have been a shadow from the lamp. For a moment she considered taking Brent's way down, but she didn't quite have the courage, and she went to the kitchen and down the long wooden stairs into the cellar. Thomas was against one wall, feeling along the stones carefully, sniffing at each gap. He looked around at her over his shoulder, and his blank expression and crouching posture reminded her of a dog about to charge. She walked halfway across the room toward him and reached up to hang the lantern from one of the hooks that descended from the beams. As she approached him, he straightened up slowly.

"Thomas, listen to me," she began helplessly, and saw him tilt his head slightly, his brows creasing. "You've waited too long...you need to go out, to..." she wasn't sure what to say, because she didn't know exactly what he did when he went out. He was looking at her with intense concentration, as though she was speaking a language he barely understood.

"Why?"

"Because you...because..." she was terrified that if she was too blunt, he would lose control entirely.

"I can't leave here. It's not possible."

He raised his head slightly, sniffing the air. Then he walked toward her, following his nose, and stepped behind her, lifting her hair in his hand and sniffing at it, then at the skin at the back of her neck. She stood still, her heart pounding. *He knows he doesn't dare leave the house like this...but he can't remember anything else...gods, what should I do?* Her skin prickled into gooseflesh as Thomas leaned toward her, drawing in deep breaths, like a dieter smelling a rich dessert when no one is watching. Suddenly he straightened up and looked over their heads. After a moment she heard something, too—a crunching sound, an engine being turned off, the thump of a truck door, footsteps. Thomas' head turned, following the steps as they progressed around the house, and she closed her eyes, not daring to make a sudden move, although she wanted to call out and warn Brent not to come in. The door opened and she heard him step in, pausing in the darkness.

"Hello...?" He walked down the hallway to the edge of the floorless front room, where he could see the light from the lantern and the athanor, half amber and half shadow. "Are you guys down there?" He sat on the edge of the floor, legs dangling down. Thomas let out a long sigh, almost a soft hiss.

"Brent—" Diana called, her voice quavering, about to tell him to leave the house and she would meet him outside, but at the sound of her voice he said, "Oh, you are down there." He hopped off into space, swung from a beam and dropped to the floor next to the athanor. He straightened up and turned to them and became very still, his eyes flicking rapidly between her face and Thomas'.

"What's going on?" he said, very quietly, and she felt Thomas shift, stepping out from behind her, moving with the gliding slowness of a stalking cat. Brent's face twitched, and he drew in a breath and looked straight at her. "Are you okay?" he whispered.

She was afraid that if she moved, so would Thomas. "Brent...maybe we need to...to go upstairs for a moment," *if we can...* she didn't add.

"Okay...okay...let's go upstairs, then," he said, and walked cautiously toward her, angling toward the stairs as he came, keeping his eyes on her face and not looking at Thomas. He reached out to her, his voice flat, carefully neutral, "we'll just go upstairs for a minute." She extended her hand, stepping toward him, but before they touched, Thomas moved. He went past her like a thought, grabbed Brent by the front of his khaki jacket, twisted him around and threw him up against the wall behind them. Brent, his brittle calm shattered, shouted in panic, "No, wait! No, no, let go!"

Diana felt as though she were moving through deep water. She turned and grabbed Thomas' arm and pulled with all her strength, and she must have caught him by surprise, because he stepped back toward her, his eyes wide. "Thomas, don't!" was the most inspired thing she could splutter out. He pulled free from her and clamped his hand onto her upper arm, yanked her towards him, and then flung her backward so she fell heavily to the dirt floor. There was no malice, not even anger, in his motion. He might have been brushing away a fly.

Brent twisted out of his jacket, leaving Thomas holding the empty coat in one hand, and sidestepped across the floor out of reach. He half crouched toward Diana, as she frantically tried to scramble to her feet. His face turned white in the lamplight, then scarlet patches showed on his cheeks. He swung to face Thomas and choked out, "You fucking bastard, is that all you're good for?" He charged forward and hit Thomas squarely on the cheekbone with a blow that, against any other opponent, would have been a knockout right cross. Diana flinched at the crack of bone against bone.

Thomas recoiled about as much as he might have from the brush of a leaf against his face. He blinked, reached forward, picked Brent up and threw him across the room, as if he were weightless. Brent's back connected solidly with the stone wall about six feet above the floor and he fell heavily to the ground with a hoarse grunt. By the time he was on the floor, Thomas was already standing over him. He dragged Brent away from the wall and tore open the neck of his shirt as Brent, stunned, flailed his arms in an effort to push Thomas away from him. Thomas' mouth was drawn into a snarl with no human expression in it.

But before he could straddle Brent's body and bend down, Diana had crossed the intervening floor, partly on all fours, and flung herself face up onto Brent's torso, her hands against Thomas' chest, frantically saying, "No, Thomas, no! *peidiwch, peidiwch a'i ladd, peidiwch! Rwyt ti eisiau gwaed, Thomas, cofiwch,*

cofiwch, doeddet ti ddim yn lladd erioed, o plis, Thomas..." and he pulled back, his face shocked. She couldn't think of the Welsh anymore, but she went on almost babbling, "you need blood, Thomas, you've gone too long, you don't want to kill him, you told me you'd never killed anyone, Mother of God, Thomas..." She ran out of breath and stopped, gasping. Thomas shuddered violently, and she saw lucidity return to his eyes like light rising in a lamp chimney when the wick is lit. He pulled away from her and Brent and crawled backward over the floor until he came to the stone wall and pressed himself up against it, his face distorted with horror.

"*Duw...*" he hissed, and then, "*Ah, Duw, fy helpiwch...*" and he pulled his knees up and covered his face with his forearms, his fists clenched.

Diana half-crawled to him as quickly as she could and touched his shoulder, and he cringed away from her, saying "*Naddo, ewch i fordd!*" But there was only one thing left to do at this point. She took his wrist and pulled his hand from his face, and he looked at her, too stunned, despite his words, to push her away.

"Here, Thomas, take it, now. In a few minutes your mind will be gone and you'll kill us both. You know that. Go on." She let go of his arm and extended her hand, palm up, before his face, pushing her sleeve back as she did so. He stared back at her numbly and then looked down at her wrist, the blue veins twining under the translucent skin. She saw him swallow, and then he grasped her arm with both his hands, brought her wrist to his mouth and clamped his teeth down on it like a picnicker biting into an ear of corn. She felt the flesh pulling open and gasped at the pain, which was worse than she expected. She couldn't stop herself from trying to pull away by pure reflex, but no human could have broken Thomas' grip by then. As her elbow bent, blood ran in shining dark ribbons over her arm and dripped onto the floor. She heard Brent make a sound between gulping and retching, but she didn't look at him. She clutched Thomas' shoulder with her left hand and rested her forehead on it, feeling her muscles slowly turning to water. Her left hand felt cold and clammy, and she thought, *I'm going into shock...this is not good...* and then she couldn't think about anything except trying to breathe as steadily and deeply as possible. It was so cold...she wished now she hadn't taken off her coat. She was shaking uncontrollably and there were none of the sensations she had experienced when Thomas had drunk her blood before, only his mouth sucking and pulling at her wrist and a terrible weakness.

He stopped finally, and there was a long silence, as all three of them, for very different reasons, were too stunned to move or speak. Brent huddled against the wall, his face so white that even in the amber lamp light his freckles stood out as dark specks on his skin. Diana, sick to her stomach as it was, leaned her forehead against Thomas' shoulder, trying not to go on imagining how differently this scenario might have ended. Her wrist kept on hurting, as though it were poisoned like a bee sting, and she cradled it in her other hand, hoping that there hadn't been any actual damage to the tendons. Thomas leaned his head back against the wall, his eyes closed. Finally, when Diana was so cold that she was shivering and she realized that Brent, still coatless, was hugging himself and shaking as well, she straightened up and gave Thomas' shoulder a small nudge. "Thomas, would you go build up the fire, we're freezing."

Thomas turned his head and looked at her blankly for a moment, then got up and went to the hearth, where he stirred up the coals and began adding pieces of dry wood from the pile nearby. While he was occupied, Diana moved over to Brent and peered at him anxiously. "Are you all right? You really hit that wall hard."

"Uh..." he flexed his shoulders and back a little, as if only now realizing that he might be injured. "No bones broken, I guess. I was lucky." *Lucky*, she thought bleakly, *I don't even want to think about how lucky you just were.*

He glanced uneasily at Thomas' bowed silhouette. "What about you? Christ, when I saw what you were doing, I nearly—"

"I'm used to it. No, really, Brent. I knew he wouldn't go too far." She reached over and touched his arm. "Come on, let's go over to the fire."

They joined Thomas at the hearth, but talking was too awkward. Diana's wrist stopped hurting as much and seemed to be fully functional. Once they were warmer, they ended up fitting the pipe after all, since Brent was there and by tacit agreement none of them wanted him to have to come back. The task was a simple one and they worked in near silence, broken only by monosyllabic directions once or twice.

When they finished, however, Diana insisted that they return to the stone house for a while, and the men reluctantly went along with her. Back in the brick-floored kitchen, Brent and Thomas sat stiffly at either end of a bench as Diana stuffed the stove with wood, opened the dampers wide and put on a kettle of water, as much for the comfort of it as anything else. She went around and sat at the table across from Thomas, who was staring unseeing at the stove. She leaned across the board and slapped his arm lightly, and he jumped.

"Turn around, we're having a meeting." He looked astounded, but immediately obeyed, and Brent, with the automatic conditioning provided by the United States public school system, came down and joined them, although he was careful not to sit too close to Thomas.

Diana met Thomas' eyes directly and he dropped his gaze, but didn't turn away. "Tell me how this happened. How did we get to this extreme?" He hesitated uncomfortably. "I'm sorry you're making me interrogate you, Thomas. All right. You've been fasting since October?"

He looked up, aghast. "Of course not! I couldn't...I couldn't possibly go that long."

"But you haven't been making your usual arrangements."

"No, I..." There was a long pause and then his shoulders, which had tightened defensively, suddenly relaxed and he straightened up and sighed in resignation. "My forays are time-consuming, depending on the circumstances and the season.

I have to be careful, and often I'll be out most of the night. Usually that isn't a problem. I just didn't want to be taking so much time from our work, not until the athanor construction was finished. So I was going out in the afternoons, after small animals—anything within the immediate vicinity of the house, every three or four days. But as time passed, as was inevitable, the animals became less numerous, and harder to find. I was decimating the local populations. The survivors grew more and more wary, and then many of them denned up for the winter. So I made do with whatever I could find and went for greater periods without. But I wasn't abstaining altogether. There have been many times in the past when I survived for longer on less. I honestly believed I would be able to manage until the Solstice, when I could go back to...my usual arrangements."

Diana still felt perplexed. "You seemed so...normal when I left. How could things change so fast? Was there some kind of trigger?"

"The sun went down," Thomas said quietly. "If things are going to...change, it occurs at sunset, or dawn, and very quickly. If I don't attend to those times closely...and I was in the cellar, I wasn't thinking clearly."

"But you didn't have any warning at all?" He looked up, his expression a bit hounded. "I'm not trying to blame you, Thomas, I just want to know how we can prevent this in the future. You didn't even have a suspicion? Nothing that we could watch for?"

He almost smiled. "What you saw *was* the warning. I still retained just enough conscience to know what I dared not do. That would have lasted perhaps another hour. Then..."

At the look in his eyes, Diana's mouth went dry. "It's happened before."

"Only once. And by the grace of God..." he looked straight up at her. "You were right, what you said to me. I'd have killed you. I wouldn't even have...I might have killed both of you before I knew what I was doing."

"I believe you," Brent whispered. Thomas rested his forehead on both hands, his eyes squeezed shut, and then he shuddered.

Diana swallowed hard. "There's no way of knowing what *would* have happened," she said as firmly as she could, "and no point in torturing ourselves with imagining it. It's over, and it's not going to happen again." Thomas sighed heavily, but he nodded, without looking up. "You just didn't realize how much the work was draining you. Under normal circumstances, I'm sure your judgment would have been correct, but Thomas—we've been working almost around the clock for weeks."

"You tried to warn me. I should have listened to you."

Diana forced a smile. "You're my witness, Brent, did you hear that?"

"I sure did. I don't have a clue what you're talking about, but sounds right to me. He should've listened to you."

"It would have helped if you'd been a little more forthcoming about your habits, but we've been all through that."

"Well, I haven't been." Diana and Thomas both looked at Brent in surprise, but he stiffened his shoulders and went on, "I'd kinda like to hear what these usual arrangements are you're talking about. Come on, I'm going to be black and blue for about a week. You owe me one."

Thomas took in a long breath, looking down at the tabletop uneasily. "Well, it's animals, mostly. There's a dairy farm up past Lincolnville, there are any number of horses on the Bay, there's a man back in the hills who keeps sheep and a few goats, there are some beef cattle, even pigs, although they're a last resort. I don't visit the same place more often than every three months or so. That's how I avoid even a rumor or suspicion."

"What about people? What about all those movies, don't vampires always go after girls, young ones, like—" he broke off, and Diana wondered whose name he'd stopped himself from mentioning. She knew he had sisters. "And then they don't remember anything, is that it?"

Thomas met Brent's intent stare directly, shaking his head. "No. It's not like that. I swear to you. There are...a few people, but not the way you think. Most of the ones who...who know me are, well, in the local phrase, they're not quite all there. It just works better that way. It's such a delicate relationship...I usually stay with the livestock."

Diana watched Brent's face as he pondered this information and reluctantly decided to believe it. "How do you keep dogs from going after you? I don't know anyone who keeps a lot of stock and doesn't have dogs."

"Ah, well," Thomas was clearly relieved to change the subject. "You'd be surprised how close I can get without the dogs detecting me. But there are several places where I've made friends with them. I take some bits of bread and cheese with me, and they actually wag their tails when I come in."

Brent let out a short laugh. "Unbelievable," he said, shaking his head.

When the kettle on the stove boiled, Diana made a pot of strong tea. She listened quietly as Brent asked Thomas questions, some of which Thomas answered forthrightly and some of which he fielded, although Brent didn't seem to care. As the heat from the stove slowly radiated out and up to the other rooms, the house seemed to be returning to life after months of dormancy. She realized she was sick to death of the crumbling, decaying Schuller house, sick of spending every moment there, sick of the smell of mildew, the cold and damp, the creaking outhouse, the blank boarded windows, the constant lamp-lit darkness. The Solstice was about two weeks away, and there was still much to be done, but never had she longed so desperately to make an end of something. At least when their working proper commenced, they would only need to go to the house for a short time each day.

It grew late and Brent abruptly realized he needed to leave, since the next day was a normal working day for him. They damped the stove and walked back to the Schuller house, where Brent climbed sleepily into his truck. Thomas nodded good-night and went around the house, but Diana lingered a moment by the open truck door.

"Are you sure you're going to be okay, Brent?"

"Oh, yeah. And, uh, hey..." Brent fidgeted awkwardly. "Thanks for saving my life, like you did. I don't know what that lingo was you were sayin' to him, but man, if you hadn't done that..." he swallowed hard. "Hey, it's over, let's just let it go, okay?"

She nodded, and stepped back so he could close the truck's door, then watched as he turned the truck around and left. She felt just a bit uneasy about how much Brent now knew, and whether any of tonight's events could possibly be included in Thomas' influence. But there was nothing that could be done about it now, at least no solution that she could live with. Pushing her disquiet aside, she headed into the house to see if Thomas was up to resuming the night's work.

11

By December 17th, the night of the New Moon, they had finished. The athanor was completed, consecrated and sealed, its technical workings tested and tempered, the flue checked and damped. Diana and Thomas burned or threw into the sea, at outgoing tide, their robes and every scrap of magical supplies and equipment they had been using. New supplies and equipment had been made or purchased, purified, consecrated and charged. There was actually very little needed, for the working they were about to commence was of a radically different nature than the construction of the athanor. It was a cumulative, gradual building of power whose progress would be almost imperceptible. On December 21st at 9:43 p.m., they would light the fire in the athanor that would be tended for the next eighteen months, and at midnight they would perform together, for the first time, the ritual that would be their daily mantra for more than a year to come.

For the next four days they were filled with a pitch of nervous energy. Thomas cleaned the stone house, obviously unhappy at its atmosphere of dusty neglect, and while he swept and shook out rugs, Diana went to the Schuller house to stay out of his way, and cleaned there. It was now full winter, with a few inches of crusty snow hiding the stacked floorboards and empty pallets in the front yard. She swept and dusted and organized the ritual room, got rid of all the oddments that had accumulated during the construction, and even scraped and swept the hard-packed cellar floor one more time. But finally there was nothing to do but wait, and mentally rehearse their lines, and meditate, and feel the suspense growing until the air seemed to crackle with it. Neither of them could sleep much, although Thomas made a dutiful effort and remained cloistered in his bedroom from dawn to dusk.

She admitted frankly to herself that she was genuinely afraid. The first working of the ritual, she felt, was like the sounding of a challenge, announcing their intention to storm the power of the dragon and win, at whatever cost. It occurred to her that such a challenge might have an instantaneous reply. She prepared herself for anything and tried not to let her imagination run away with her. Reason suggested that nothing dramatic would take place so soon, but reason often did not prevail in matters magical. One night she mentioned this possibility to Thomas, when they had briefly intersected in the kitchen to discuss their preparations, and he only shook his head.

"I've wondered that from the moment we laid the first brick of the athanor, but I've felt nothing in response all these months, and I wouldn't even speculate what might happen. We'll just have to meet it when it comes, if meeting be possible."

At least we have consensus, she thought resignedly. The athanor itself, she realized, must have been radiating enough magical energy to be perceived far beyond their immediate circle, but now that energy had drawn deeply inward, concentrating itself to a point. They could barely sense it pulsing at the heart of the metal core. It, like the two magicians, was waiting.

No matter how stressful the suspense was, getting to the end of it was worse. Early in the evening of the 21st, Diana was combing out her thick hair before the woodstove, hoping to dry it before she had to walk outside. She had taken her bath, and now Thomas was having his turn. It was suspiciously quiet behind the partly closed door, and he had told her to come roust him if he took too long. In his state of mind, any sensory distraction was far too welcome, and once in the water he could become so fascinated with the play of it on his skin and the feel of it as it cooled that he might forget to come out.

But long before she would have checked on him, he emerged from the small bathroom, dried and dressed, raking back his damp hair with his fingers. He came and sat near her on the bench, and for some time they didn't speak. She could feel the space between them filling with tendrils of connecting energy, tugging and pulling. There was nothing more to be said, after all the times in the past four days they had asked each other if everything was ready. The silence around them was palpable, and when the logs shifted in the stove, she jumped.

"I think we should leave," Thomas said, and she blinked, startled—was it that late? She looked at him and was astonished to see that his hair had nearly dried and he was tying it back with the usual narrow black ribbon. She put another log in the stove and closed the dampers.

"I'm ready," she lied, and he smiled, pushing his feet into shoes. She put on a coat, and they walked over to the Schuller house on the uneven trail beaten into the snow. It was a beautiful night—a perfect Solstice. Stars glittered overhead so brilliantly that the trees were clearly silhouetted against the sky, blue-white Sirius low in the south like a tiny moon. Diana paused at the squeaking screen door, looking back at the sky and the shadowy trees, and suddenly felt a dart of unfamiliar nostalgia. The OSL would be assembling tonight, in the cavernous ceremonial chamber, which would be decorated with ropes and wreaths of fresh greenery and fragrant with the scent of balsam. Strange, she hadn't thought of them at Equinox, or at Samhain. And Gregory, what was he doing tonight? Did he still observe the festivals, alone in his cold tottering house in Manchester with its patched windows and empty rooms? After a moment she realized that she was simply trying to put off what lay ahead. Thomas was standing in the dark hallway waiting for her, and she followed him into the ritual room.

The house was freezing cold, since the hearth downstairs had been extinguished and swept. They changed into their new robes, made of deep purple silk. Diana tried not to rush because of the cold. This was the first time they had put the robes on and she knew it was important to feel the material settle on their bodies and to absorb the energy of the new color. When she felt as prepared as she could be, she carefully knotted Thomas' purple cord for him, three knots, and stood still as he tied her cord in return. She led the way down to the cellar, feeling carefully in the inky blackness. For this ritual there would be no light, and in darkness this complete even Thomas could make out few inanimate objects. He could perceive her body by its heat, but to both of them, the athanor was detectable by the aura it gave off, not by sight.

Moving slowly, they separated and took up positions on either side of the athanor, Thomas at the north with the hearth at his back, she in the south. Then they waited, needing no timepiece, feeling the ancient symmetry ticking into place moment by moment, as the point of the true Solstice approached. Eyes open and gazing at nothing, Diana could faintly perceive other minds, dotted all over the globe like the stars they mirrored, raising power and sharing it on this sacred night. What she and Thomas were about to do would send a tremor through that web, and many of those who felt it would wonder what was disturbing them. But it was time now...

She raised her arms slowly, knowing that Thomas was following her, and they began a wordless, two-note chant, call and response, across the athanor. The notes changed and the pattern changed, and the sound grew steadily in the room, as though it were being caught and echoed back from all around them. She began to feel warmth growing around her, and the air seemed to be glowing pale yellow, slight enough to be a mere trick of the eyes. The chant went up a minor third and started its pattern over from the beginning, and now the glow was clearly not an illusion—she could see shapes against it, the mound of the athanor before her, a support beam standing on either side. The moment of the precise nodal point was fast approaching, only minutes away now, and the chant shifted up once more, taking up a faster rhythm. The glow was condensing, becoming redder, spiraling around the athanor counterclockwise, spinning faster, brightening, turning the color of flame. Their voices went on, and now there was a ball of flame over the athanor, dazzling her eyes, the heat from it reddening the skin of her face and the palms of her hands.

She had seen this done only once before. The wonder of it still amazed her, so that she almost forgot to sing, instead of just standing entranced by what was taking place. But she found her inner discipline and redoubled her voice, pushing her hands toward the fire as it grew smaller and brighter, even though her fingers were almost blistering from the heat. Thomas turned his face away from the light. There were red streaks on his cheek, but he was still chanting and his hands were still raised. The moment was coming now, time itself seeming to accelerate, and then it was here. For one panicked instant she was paralyzed by the sheer force of the conjunction between their working and the turning of the Solstice axis. Then she brought down both arms with all the force she could muster, barely aware of Thomas' arms falling in exact unison with her own. The miniature sun they had created shot downward, through the bricks, through the metal core, exploding from the firebox with a roar. The whole room filled with flame for one searing, terrifying moment. The flame vanished without leaving a trace of heat or light or smoke, only the crackle of burning wood from the firebox and a dull humming sound from the copper pipe. The athanor had been fired at last.

Diana stood dazed for a moment, her vision filled with the wildly dancing shimmer of after-images from the light. But the firebox door must be closed, and the dampers adjusted, or the core would get too hot. She could barely see, but she felt her way around to the north side, where Thomas stood backed up against the hearth, his hands over his eyes. She groped on the wall for the long iron hook hanging there and shut the metal door of the firebox, then eased the dampers on the copper pipe halfway closed. She could hear the fire settle inside and nudged the nearest damper closed a bit further. Yes...that was it. It would take some fine-tuning over the next few days, but it was almost perfect. She latched the firebox door with the end of the hook and turned to hang it back up, and only then did she realize that Thomas still had not moved.

"Are you all right?" She reached out and put her hands on his shoulders. She felt him lower his hands from his eyes, cautiously.

"I think so. For a few minutes I couldn't see, but it seems to be passing now." There was a catch in his voice, as if he had been deeply frightened.

"Let's go upstairs," she said, worried, and they moved carefully around the cellar and back to the steps. Thomas stumbled against a support beam once before he reached them. When they had gotten to the ritual room and she found matches and lit the lamp, she gasped in shock. Thomas' face was reddened and there were blisters on his hands. He blinked vaguely down at them.

"It's all right," he said calmly, although his voice sounded a bit hollow. "These will heal by midnight."

"We better put some cold water on them." They went across the hall to the kitchen, where the water from the sink pump was cold enough to douse any fire. Thomas gritted his teeth as he held his hands under the stream she pumped for him, but he looked relieved and dashed water onto his face as well.

"I knew about your having to stay out of the sun, but I didn't even think about the possibility that this could hurt you," she said as she worked the pump vigorously. He spat water into the sink and wiped his eyes.

"It occurred to me, but this is a slight price to pay. After all, what could we have done?"

"You could have protected yourself, somehow—"

"Oh, yes, I could have borrowed Brent's welding helmet. That would have made quite a picture. I don't think so." He was smiling with amusement at the thought.

"Well…how are your eyes?"

"Much better." He carefully wiped off his hands with the towel she'd found for him, and showed her his palms. "You see?"

She took hold of his hands, bending them toward her in amazement. The blisters had already flattened out to patches of shiny pink skin. "Incredible," she said finally. Even as she marveled at what she saw, she felt something shift. Her fingertips, sensitized by the heat of the firing, moved over the soft skin on the backs of his hands, dark hair making a nap like satin cloth. The shadows seemed to be enfolding them on all sides, with a secret and conspiratorial feeling, whispering of privacy and seclusion. She took in a breath, very carefully, as if she might be overheard. It was as if she stood just on the brink of something, and if she looked up and met Thomas' eyes, she would step past a threshold and complete something that only awaited one last motion. They still had another working to do, the most important of all. He had become very still, but now she felt him bend slightly toward her, and take in a breath as if he was about to speak. Without looking at him, she reached up and pressed two fingers to his lips. Then she raised his hand and kissed his palm, letting her mouth linger against the fire-warmed skin, brushing it with her tongue. He sucked in a shaking breath and touched her hair. She released him and walked out of the kitchen without speaking, leaving him standing by the sink looking at his empty hand.

She went and sat at the base of the stairs in the front room, feeling the warmth beginning to rise from the athanor below. Not since her initiation to Adeptus had she felt such a sense of some momentous thing about to happen. But apprehension mixed with it, as she foresaw a binding that could never be undone. This was no simple knot—there were strands leading into it from all directions, tangles and coils and counterknots, and all of it knitted into the clay and metal of the athanor in a way she couldn't see clearly. She was poignantly aware of every move Thomas made, even when he walked outside to stand in the back yard watching the stars.

As midnight grew near she stood up finally, stretching to ease the stiffness in her muscles. Thomas had come in and was in the ritual room, fitting candles into holders. He avoided looking at her when she came in, not from awkwardness but out of simple prudence. What they were constraining now must be directed into their magical working.

They went down the stairs and set the candles in the four quarters, and took their positions. They could feel true midnight, the actual mid-point between sunset and dawn, as it curved by them, the turning of the night's tide. Thomas, in the north, faced the hearth and raised his arms and called the quarter, then moved to the east, his voice mournfully sweet, as if he were singing a lament.

Diana took up almost on his ending note, calling south, and then west, and as one they pivoted to face inward once more and brought the circle out from the center, expanding to fill the room. The candle flames for a moment lay down flat, radiating outward as though a breath blew them. In unison they stepped backward a step, in unison reached hands toward the athanor, and in unison their voices joined at last in the words of the spell. The guttural syllables in rising and falling notes tingled up and down their spines, energized with the cadences whose secret had been passed down from a source known only to one living initiate of the Order. On and on the song went, wavering and spiraling, until it seemed that even the stones in the walls and the wood of the beams were listening. In the heart of the athanor the pattern they wove was caught for the first time, like the first crossing of the warp thread over a loom, setting the foundation for a complex tapestry that would grow one strand at a time.

Then it was done. The chant was finished, and for a moment Diana waited for something in the room to speak, to say *well done*, or *encore*, the feeling of being listened to was so great. But nothing came, and together she and Thomas sent the circle back into its center, taking with it the tiny increment of power they had raised, the first penny in the well. They banished the quarters, and extinguished the candles. As simply as that, it was begun.

They went upstairs in silence, and methodically changed and put away the candles and their robes, not speaking or looking at each other. Diana felt as though she were walking on thin strands of netted silk above the ground, which shifted and gave under her feet. When she stepped outside the door, the stars were too bright and too close. She could see the bare trees in such detail it almost seemed like daylight. She walked through the woods, the packed snow creaking underfoot. She heard no step behind her, but she knew he would follow soon.

She let herself into the kitchen of the stone house, where it was toasty warm and smelled of wood smoke and tea and soap. She put several logs into the stove, and sat watching the flames lick up around the dry wood eagerly, as if they had been waiting months for the moment when they could touch it at last. She didn't turn around when the door opened and a cold breeze blew over her, raising gooseflesh all down her back. She heard Thomas kick his shoes off by the door, and she waited, feeling the air in the room trembling like a live thing.

He came and sat by her on the bench, watching the flames in the stove. Diana closed the stove door, since this wood would have to last for a while. As she stood up, she reached over and put her hands on the back of Thomas' shoulders, feeling them tense and then relax, pressing her fingers along the curve and ridge of bone and muscle under his sweater. Through her hands she perceived the answer to her question, *yes, this is yours...* She bent down until her lips almost touched Thomas' cheek, and let only her breath reach further, warm against his skin. Then she drew away, trailing her fingers along his body. She turned and walked out of the kitchen, into the dark parlor beyond, not looking back.

She reached the stairs, and there was no sound behind her, and she climbed the narrow, twice-turned staircase with its treads each worn to a hollow like a cupped hand. In her own bedroom she lit a single candle, and she took off her clothes meditatively, folded them and placed them on the pine bureau, just as she did when she went to bed each morning. The bed was still rumpled and disheveled from her mostly sleepless day, but she wasn't tired now.

She didn't hear him, but she knew when he was there. She felt him behind her, and saw the shadow he cast in the candlelight. He put his hands on her shoulders, letting them slide down her arms. She closed her eyes, lost in the sensation, and then she turned around to face him. They melted against each other, and she wrapped her arms around his neck and met his open mouth with her own, feeling every inch of his skin against hers, soaking him up like a sponge. Their tongues danced and probed, as she wound her fingers in the long dark hair whose touch she had coveted since she first saw it. The kiss continued, neither of them wanting to stop, and Diana's hands moved down Thomas' body, taking in every curve, every brief tensing of muscle as he shifted, every line of bone in his spare frame, the smoothness of his skin which was more perfect than her own.

She had wanted this for so long, to simply explore his body, and he seemed more than agreeable. She pushed him, unresisting, back onto the bed, climbed up and snuggled down on top of him and went on kissing him until she tired of having to come up for air. Then she moved out to the farthest extremities, so as not to miss an inch of him with fingers and tongue, tasting, caressing, nibbling, even the soles of his slender feet and the webs of his thumbs. She worked her way inwards inexorably, but very slowly, for there was always some distraction, someplace to tickle and tease, and Thomas was not impatient. If he liked what she was doing he moved to accommodate her, and he never failed to move.

By the time she reached the softness of his belly, matching tongue strokes there with tickling fingers drawn up the insides of his thighs, he almost seemed to want her to stop, as if he had already had too much and needed a respite. He pushed himself up on his elbows and drew up one knee, abdominal muscles suddenly hard, and she looked up to see if this was a serious protest or not. With his long hair loose around his shoulders he looked very young, and his expression, like a bleary-eyed child's, was a little lost. She pulled back and bent down and trailed her tongue up his inner left thigh and didn't stop this time, but let it dip lovingly around the soft ruddy flesh nestled there and down the other thigh. He fell flat back on the mattress with a groan and she considered the argument settled. She wasn't going to tease him indefinitely. Her only frustration as she continued was that he refused to indicate any preference. He liked everything she did, and if she varied her approach, he liked it even more. When he climaxed she was taken by surprise, and had to pull back sharply to avoid biting him by accident, but he might have enjoyed that, too.

She sat up slowly, licking her lips, and pondering his odd metallic taste. He lay utterly still, one arm thrown over his eyes, wearing a look of complete abandonment, which was somewhat disconcerting when he didn't breathe.

But when she stretched out alongside him he took in a breath and smiled and put his arms around her. They began kissing slowly, his hands roving over her unhurriedly, and she was happy to let him do a bit more of the work now. For months she had been wondering how much finesse a self-professed rake with Thomas' years of experience would have mastered. She wasn't disappointed.

There was less of a pattern to his boldness. He moved here and there, lingering longer where he felt her react more strongly, but he also seemed absorbed in exploring every nook and cranny. His tongue was cool, like his skin, but the temperature difference added a special intensity to its tickling movements. When he finally got down to the point of reciprocating her favor, Diana couldn't stop herself from clutching at the bedclothes with both fingers and toes. She was amazed at long he managed to sustain the intensity. At last the point came when he could not tease her to any further extreme of tension, and her body suddenly released an explosion of pure energy, rushing outward from her loins to make her feet clench and her entire body shudder, sensation rolling back and forth like waves as she cried out helplessly. It was the nearest she had ever come to absolute ecstasy. For several moments she forgot who and where she was, almost lost awareness of her body itself.

It was several minutes before she recovered enough to stretch and move up on the bed a little, leaving a space. He came up and lay down next to her, and they held each other, not even kissing now, but intertwining limbs slowly, coiling hair around fingers, feeling the sensation of breath on skin. She pressed her body up against Thomas', and she clearly felt from him, for the first time, a restless urgency. He began to kiss her almost aggressively, tongue pushing deeply into her mouth. She broke off and he almost pursued her before he caught himself. But there was no need for patience. She slid her leg over his hip and reached down to guide him into her, being careful not to pinch in her own eagerness. She slid down onto him about halfway, then he could no longer resist and pushed her onto her back and thrust in hard. She saw a momentary look of surprise cross his face. She had known it was waiting, this sudden click, this final consummation of their months of work, binding them and their magic together.

She nudged him out of his immobility, and he moved cautiously, aware of how easily he could hurt her if he forgot his strength. Nevertheless he was tireless and unstinting, and the unceasing movement of his body against her and inside her became like an elemental force, the pulsing of waves which never feel mercy for the rocks they wear down. She had to breathe in rhythm with his thrusts, and she became intoxicated with sensation, feeling the muscles in his back and buttocks and shoulders knot and coil under her hands, gripping and hugging at his lean hips with her legs. He would vary the pace but never stop, and she felt herself building to yet another climax, this one not as intense as the first—but it scarcely could have been. Once again she shuddered at the waves of pleasure that rippled through her, clutching at him with all her strength, fingernails leaving red scores in his back. All too quickly, the blissful energy spiraled away and vanished, leaving her blinking up at the ceiling, her body soaked with sweat, Thomas nuzzling contentedly at her neck and ear. She wrapped her arms around him and drew him down to kiss him deeply, rocking in response to his slow pushes. He gradually increased to a quicker rhythm, and when he came to the end of it at last, she felt a tingle that went tickling over her body like little electric sparks and suddenly made her more awake.

The window slowly became visible as a pale gray rectangle, and the candle burned almost to the socket of its holder. It was growing close to dawn, and Thomas couldn't sleep here, the room was too light for him. With some reluctance they finally disentangled themselves and moved into Thomas' room, where the bed gave evidence that he had not had much rest the previous day either. But all that tension was gone now, channeled at last into the Intention it had been generated for. They piled unceremoniously into the bed, and Thomas almost immediately fell into the motionless, unbreathing quietude that for him served as sleep. Hour after hour he remained as still as a carved effigy on a tomb, then would startle her by suddenly shifting position like any other sleeper, only to fall once again into his enchantment. One thing was certain, he would never steal the covers. He used them mostly for the comfort they gave him.

Diana appreciated the covers, and she huddled down under them and nestled herself closely against Thomas. No matter how cool and still his body, it never felt dead. She could sense the vitality in it when she touched his skin, without understanding just what it was that gave this effect. But it was soothing, and she closed her eyes, drifting toward sleep. She thought of the athanor, silently nurturing in the Schuller house, and she saw the months before them, extending into the future and the unknowable end of their endeavor. The days would go back to a routine of domestic tasks, centered around their repeated ritual, the passes of the shuttle over the loom. Winter was settling in now. They would need to hire someone to plow the road for them...she yawned. *Maybe I can even go into town sometimes, get to know people...visit the library...*and with these thoughts she lost herself to sleep, as outside high gray clouds hid the rising sun. It would be snowing by dusk.

12

"Miss Chilton, I want to talk to you."

"Mrs. Wilkinson—I have an appointment at four." Diana tried not to sound exasperated, but she had had many conversations with the hostess of Holliston House Inn lately, and the topic was wearing a bit thin.

"I only need a minute of your time. Have you spoken to Mr. Morgan again about registering?"

"I mentioned that you asked me about it. You're going to turn me into a nag, Mrs. Wilkinson. You know how men feel about nags."

"Well, this is *very important*." Mrs. Wilkinson's thick hand, which looked as capable of running a lobster boat as an inn, rummaged in her huge patent leather handbag and emerged with a handful of mimeographed fliers, which she pushed at Diana in a way that brooked no refusal. Sighing, Diana took the fliers.

"Tell Mr. Morgan that we must have his vote at Town Meeting. Every good American citizen does his civic duty, Miss Chilton." She put a subtle but clear emphasis on the words "good American citizen"—the red tint that clouded the Hermit's reputation had only gotten deeper, and the Wilkinsons were among his few supporters in that regard. Diana had only escaped similar scrutiny by registering to vote and judiciously referring to her Mayflower pedigree, something she ordinarily detested doing.

"I know, Mrs. Wilkinson, and I'll be there, I promise. I do have to ask you, though—suppose Mr. Morgan comes in and votes *for* the name change?"

Mrs. Wilkinson squared her shoulders, already almost military in her impeccable tweed suit. "He told me himself he thinks it's a ridiculous idea." Diana had to smile; indeed, Thomas had laughed for almost a full minute when he had first heard the proposal.

"Well, it is. Although the sponsors do make some good points."

"Nonsense. Now you keep working on him, Miss Chilton. We girls can always wear our men down if we know our jobs." Mrs. Wilkinson's Blushing Rose lips curved into a simpering, conspiratorial smile. "Besides, dear—if you can get him into Town Hall, he just might feel like making an honest woman out of you."

Diana struggled not to laugh, as she'd heard this one a few times, as well. "Who knows, Mrs. Wilkinson? I'll ask him about Town Meeting again, I promise."

She sighed as she watched Mrs. Wilkinson head back up Main Street toward the Inn, striding as authoritatively as a woman her age could stride in a straight skirt and sharply clicking high heels. Being the gay divorcée from Boston living in Bohemian sin with the town eccentric lent Diana a reputation that she bore with some discomfort. It was true that no one had ever cut her dead, or pulled their children across the street when they spotted her, but she had not made many friends in this tiny town. Mingling in a more cosmopolitan venue was unhappily out of the question. The requirement that she and Thomas be at the Schuller house at some point every day for their ritual meant that Diana had not traveled even as far as Bangor for over a year. She was too worried that her car would break down or some other catastrophe would prevent her from getting back on time. She corresponded frequently with a few friends in Boston, and sometimes there was a letter from Gregory. But one surprising development had made the past year in Pepperell a little less lonely.

By the end of the first winter of their magical working, Diana had been cabin-fevered in the extreme. After the spring equinox, the timing of the daily ritual shifted from midnight to dawn, and Thomas generally went to bed immediately afterwards. Diana couldn't fault him for that, but this did lead to a drastic change in their level of intimacy, since the post-ritual sex was sharply curtailed. It was easier for her to get up at dawn than go to sleep with Thomas. When Thomas awoke, he often would go on a foray, and Diana, from equal necessity, went to bed early.

After three winter months of near seclusion, Diana had long stretches of restless hours alone and not nearly enough household or magical tasks to fill them. For the first time since she'd come to Maine, she found herself desperately missing Boston, and her work with Bread and Roses. She began taking long walks, then going into town to explore. She became a habitué of the coffee shop, and occasionally the local bar as long as it was either very full or very empty. To keep herself fruitfully occupied, she decided to try to improve her skills in alchemy, which had always been her weakest magical area. She ordered books and supplies, and set up a laboratory in the house she had used for her retreat to fill the glass vessel. She even considered building a small athanor, like Gregory's. But she could only concentrate on her self-directed lessons for so long before she yearned to be around other people.

One warm afternoon toward the end of April, Diana had felt particularly fidgety. The environs of the stone house were alive with courting birds and blossoming flowers, and the approach of Beltene left her torn between frustrated concupiscence and nostalgia. She found herself thinking too often about the night she'd spent with Gregory the previous July, but the memories evoked conflicted feelings. She decided to come into town and have lunch at the coffee shop. After she'd eaten, she drifted idly down Main Street, perusing the window displays in the shops. She was almost at the end of the street when an odd thought struck her: *Everybody seems to have the nicest hair all of a sudden.* Her own hair hung loose below her shoulders, and the best thing that could be said for it was that it was clean. There were now a dozen gray strands, the embryo of a white streak, on one side. She refused to pull them out, from a certain perverse defiance—she wanted to save them to show to Gregory.

At the south end of the street, the last commercial building was a blocky two-story red brick structure just wide enough for a single storefront on the ground level and an apartment above it. The generous plate glass window in front sported a gracefully painted name in gold and several different shades of pink: *Styles by Moira.* As she gazed at the swirling letters in fascination, Diana was startled by a voice that seemed to come out of thin air, since there was not another person in sight or earshot.

"Well, look who's here. The scarlet letter herself."

Startled, Diana glanced in several directions before she thought to step to the right and peer down into the shadowy alley. Squinting, she made out the figure of a thin woman with lean, rangy limbs, wearing a bright pink smock and holding a cigarette in one hand. She was standing in the partly open exit door at the back of the shop. The woman's expression was friendly and open, but Diana stiffened under her unabashed stare.

"Excuse me, have we met?"

The woman took a long drag on her cigarette and grinned cheerfully. "Let's just say you've been pointed out to me."

Diana looked back at the shop window, connecting it with the pink smock. There was a name in small gold script lettering at the bottom of the window—*how very Fifth Avenue,* she thought. "You must run the new beauty parlor. Moira Waterford, I presume?"

"The same." Moira switched her cigarette to her left hand and stepped forward, extending her right.

After a second's pause, Diana walked into the alley and shook Moira's hand, which had a very firm grip indeed. "Diana Chilton—but it sounds like you already knew that. Is that Waterford like the crystal?"

"Oh, puh-*leeze.*" Instead of releasing Diana's hand, Moira kept hold and turned it palm up, then palm down, studying it as though she were appraising a diamond. "Oh. My. *Gawd. What* have you done to your *hands?*"

A bit annoyed, Diana pulled away. "I work with chemicals, sometimes, that's all."

"Well, so do I, honey, but that's what rubber gloves are for."

"Yes, well..." Diana had no wish to elaborate on her specific work with chemicals. She didn't want any more fuel tossed on the fires of speculation regarding her activities with Thomas. But Moira expressed no further curiosity about Diana's hands. She had taken a step back and was now applying that sharp professional gaze to Diana's entire figure.

"You sure don't look like what I expected. Not from everything I've heard."

"Oh, really? And what, dare I ask, did you expect?"

Moira took another deep drag and waved a hand through smoke. "Oh, you know...skirt slit to here, blouse open to there, bosom out to Topeka, two pounds of mascara, three inch heels..."

"Oh, come on. That's how people describe me?"

"No, but...someone with your reputation, I didn't expect you to be so...plain."

Diana glanced down at her nondescript skirt and faded plaid shirt. These were her street clothes—at home she favored jeans or slacks and shapeless sweaters. "Someone with my reputation, I guess I usually try to dress down."

"No kidding."

"You really think I'm plain?"

Moira patted her shoulder reassuringly. "You'd probably polish up okay, but let's face it, honey—you're no Ava Gardner."

Diana looked steadily at Moira for a moment, seeing the teasing in her eyes, and then she laughed. "They say honesty is the prince of virtues, but not in a beautician. Maybe you've also heard—I've always had better things to do than sit under a dryer all day. I'm afraid I've got to run, I hope your business continues to flourish." She turned and walked to the mouth of the alley, as Moira took a last hasty puff of her cigarette and tossed it away.

"Oh, hey, wait a sec, don't be like that," she said, hurrying after Diana. "I was just—"

Diana rounded on her so suddenly that Moira came to a halt on tip-toes to avoid colliding with her. "You do have a rather strange way of encouraging new customers, I must say."

"I didn't mean...I've been wanting...oh hell. You did it again, Moira, tried to be funny and put your big fat foot right in your big fat mouth. Where it belongs. When am I going to learn?"

Diana folded her arms, somewhat mollified. "Honey—let's face it, you're no Fanny Bryce."

"Ain't it the truth. But look, let me make it up to you, how about it. Shampoo and cut, on the house, what d'you say?"

"Oh, I couldn't—for pete's sake. You have a living to earn, you don't have to do that."

"I had a cancellation this afternoon, I was looking at a goose egg anyway. Come on, I'll call it advertising, you just tell people where you got it."

"Well..." Diana hesitated, unconsciously fingering a lock of her undoubtedly overgrown hair.

"You're worried I can't read your style? Hey, I've got it down, kiddo—simple, wash'n'wear, no fuss. Fresh and natural look, right?"

Diana was impressed, in spite of her annoyance. Usually she had to argue with her hairdressers to convince them that she didn't want the latest expensive and high-maintenance fashion. "Yeah, that's exactly right."

"You just come on inside, then. Hell, I've been dying to meet you and here the first thing I do is foul it up. Give me a chance to do something right."

Diana allowed herself to be ushered up the steps and into the shop, which still smelled of fresh paint and new floor wax underneath the pungent odors of styling products. "Why on earth have you been dying to meet me?"

"Are you kidding? You sound like the only interesting person in this one-horse burg—well, you and that fella of yours. But I wasn't hoping that he'd walk in here. Sounds like he hasn't had a haircut since the Hoover administration."

Already swathed in a cape and settled in one of the shining new styling chairs, Diana bit her lip to suppress a smile. "Don't bet on it, Thomas might surprise you."

Moira started to comb Diana's hair straight back for the shampoo, and she paused, fingering the strands of gray. Diana quickly put her hand up to stop her from tugging one out. "Leave those alone."

"Sure, honey, whatever you say." Moira shrugged. "How come?"

Diana looked at her somber reflection in the mirror, feeling an icy echo of the chill that had gripped her at Gregory's words down in Manchester—*you're one of the ones the Sidhe will touch...* "I'm keeping them for good luck."

Recalling those words now, almost a year later, Diana had to repress a shiver again. The few white strands had companions, and made an authentic streak, but she refused to allow Moira to touch it up. Thomas said he envied her, and she didn't think he was being ironic.

Recalling the time, Diana hastened south on Main Street. It was too early in the year for the awnings to be out, and the sidewalks glared in the spring sunlight. The last snow banks had melted only a week or so ago, and the street gutters were still littered with the debris they left behind. Flattened cigarette packs, paper bags, food wrappers and newspapers in sodden layers lay against the curb or blew in spirals with the wind from passing cars. The streets would be swept before the vacation season, but that was some time away. Still, things were improving, even in Maine, as the post-war economy continued to boom. The second-hottest issue being laid before voters this spring was a proposal to build a new elementary school, and it looked likely to pass without much debate. New houses were popping up at a steady pace along the roads leading out of the center of town, and on weekends, it seemed there were children everywhere.

When she opened the beauty parlor door and went inside, she saw that Moira still had a customer. Sitting with a regal air of detachment in the further styling chair was a woman about her own age, who was condescending to accept the attentions of Moira herself and Moira's young assistant. Moira was deftly perfecting a permanent wave coif like a pastry chef touching up a wedding cake, while Carole, the high school age trainee, waved an impatient hand over a third coat of pink nail polish. Moira looked up with a half-apologetic expression. "Oh, Diana, honey, we'll be finished in just a few minutes, have a seat." Diana hesitated. Carole had pulled her knees together and hunched even lower over the customer's hand, refusing to look up, but Diana was used to that by now. What gave her pause was the reaction of the customer to hearing her name. Unable to turn her head due to Moira's rapid ministrations with comb and hair spray, she slid her heavily made-up eyes sideways to fix Diana with an intense gaze. The rigidity of her face and the narrowness of her look may have been due more to her position than her emotions, but Diana suddenly felt extremely uncomfortable.

"Thanks, but it's such a lovely day, I think I'll sit outside. I know I'm early," Diana glibly lied, and stepped back out onto the front steps. She wouldn't want Moira to lose a customer, especially one who appeared well-heeled. At this time of the year, there wasn't a business on the West Bay that could afford to spurn money. She ducked into the little alley separating the beauty parlor from the realty office next door and took out a new alchemy book she had just picked up at the post office.

She drew back a little when she heard the shop's front door open and close, followed by the sound of high heels on the concrete steps. The customer's perfectly sculpted silver-blond hair shimmered in the sun, and she carried her gloves in one hand to spare the new polish on her glittering nails. She had curves that made Marilyn Monroe look like a boy, but her outfit was unusual in a calculated way—a swirling five-gored skirt, a tight jacket that didn't match and a frothy, brilliantly multicolored scarf. As Diana rose to her feet, the shop door opened and closed again, and this time Carole passed the alleyway in a flash of pink skirt and lush honey blonde hair. She gave Diana a nervous sideways glance as she hurried by.

Shaking her head and sighing, Diana hefted her bag and went into the shop, where Moira was putting away bottles of styling products. "All right, spill it," Diana said cheerfully. "*Who* was *that?* The last time I saw a look like that, it was in the movies and the guy shot someone a second later."

Moira laughed out loud, and then swore as the cap she was replacing on a can of hair spray bounced out of her fingers and rolled across the floor. Diana scooped it up and handed it back to her. "Thanks, hon. That was Miss Catherine Jorgens, and I don't think she's packing a gun. She's..." Moira struck a pose, a long handled comb dangling between two fingers like a cigarette holder. "...an ah-*teest*." She almost dropped the comb, caught it and tossed it into a plastic bin on the counter.

"Take it easy, Moira, it's still early. An artiste? I guess that explains the get-up, not that I can talk. But she seemed turned out pretty nicely for sitting down on the beach painting the Bay, don't you think?"

"I'm not sure what she's painting or where, to tell you the truth. But she said she was having dinner with a gallery owner up in Bangor tonight, that's why she came in. She called at the last moment, big sob story, could I squeeze her in. There are plenty of other beauty shops, but—"

"But they don't have you. *You* are an artiste. And everyone knows it."

"Aw, cut it out," Moira said mildly. "But as for that look…I do feel honor-bound to warn you about Miss Jorgens. You better keep an eye on her."

"Oh? And why is that, pray tell?"

"Well—sounds to me like she's after your fella."

Diana had to think about this for a confused moment, and then she suddenly spluttered with laughter. "You mean *Thomas?* Oh, no, you're joking, you've got to be!"

"What's so funny about that? He's not bad-looking and he's rolling in dough. I can see some artistic type thinking he was a real catch. Sure, he's a pretty cold fish, but she probably sees that as a challenge."

"But how would she even know about him? Just from what she's heard around town since she got here?"

"I guess so. She doesn't know much, because she's been asking a lot of questions—and not just me. I've heard the other ladies talking about it, too."

Diana sobered a bit. "Well—has she met him?" She was sure she'd never seen Catherine Jorgens lurking around the stone house, but she still had only the vaguest notions of where Thomas went on his forays.

"It doesn't sound like it. I think she's been trying to avoid you."

"Ha. I wonder what she thinks she's got that Thomas would be so interested in."

"Well, she's got money from somewhere. And you saw her. I hate to break the news, but she doesn't need any peroxide. That platinum blonde 'do is the real McCoy, and as far as I can tell, so is everything else." Moira frowned in puzzlement at the quiet smile that crept onto Diana's face.

"Does she have blue eyes, by any chance?"

"Just like cornflowers. It's damned unfair, the way some girls get it all and the rest of us go begging."

Diana started laughing again. "You know—Thomas just might be interested in her, at that."

Moira put a hand on one hip, her mouth in a cynical quirk. "Now I would kill to know just what you think is so funny, but I know you're not going to tell me." Diana, smiling, just shook her head. "Okay, okay. I'm glad to see that you're not the jealous type, at least."

"You knew that anyway. But even if I was, I wouldn't be jealous of Miss Jorgens. She doesn't know what she's letting herself in for." Her smile faded as Moira turned away and started wiping down the counter below the mirror with short, sharp movements. "I wish I could explain everything to you, Moira. I really do."

"So you've said. I wish you felt you could trust me."

"I do trust you. It's just that—some of it isn't for me to tell, and even if I could, you—"

"—I wouldn't believe you, I know. Well, honey, try me sometime. I'm broad-minded, and I might already guess more than you think. It doesn't take an Einstein to figure out that there's something pretty damned unusual going on up at the Morgan place. I hear a lot, and I can add three and seven." She paused and flexed her shoulders, a hand pressed to her lower back. Watching her in the mirrors, Diana thought that the shadows under Moira's eyes seemed darker than usual, even for the end of a long day.

"Can I help with anything? You really look bushed."

"Oh, no, honey, I'm almost done here. I can get the rest in the morning. I've been on my feet for about ten hours straight, that's all."

They went to the Bay View in Camden, which was fairly quiet at this time of day. It got more lively as local businesses closed and the fishing boats came back in. "I'm flattered you're willing to go so far from home on my account," Moira said.

"Camden? Hey, if the A-bomb drops, I can walk from here."

"You mean even the A-bomb wouldn't stop you guys? You know, you're really going to have to tell me more about what you two are doing, one of these days." The waitress brought their drink order to the table, and Diana picked up her martini glass.

"One of these days, I will, maybe. But tonight we drink to you, *cherie.*"

"Oh, stop it." But she clinked her glass with Diana's.

"To Styles By Moira, congratulations on a great first year."

"To alimony, that paid the bills for the first six months."

"And to Pepperell's newest tradition, may you never close."

Moira hesitated a moment, and then smiled. "I'll drink to that." She did, then rummaged in her handbag and pulled out a cigarette and a book of matches. She struck a match after several tries, but seemed to be having difficulty lighting the cigarette. The match flame was trembling too hard to connect with the paper. After two tries she struck a second match and held the end of the cigarette with her fingers to steady it. Blowing out a great puff of blue smoke, she shook out the match and reached to drop it in the ashtray, but missed. Diana leaned back, watching all this with narrowed eyes. She picked up the burned match and put it in the ashtray as Moira smiled sheepishly. "Don't look so worried, kiddo, I've just been working too hard."

"Maybe I should get you a lighter. Pink, with 'Styles by Moira' inscribed on it."

"Aw, that would be sweet."

"You said something last month about hiring a part-time stylist to help you out, whatever happened to that?"

"I've got some feelers out. I'm not going to hire just anybody. Anyway, interviewing takes time, and I've been so busy."

"You went to Bangor a couple of times, though, didn't you?"

"Yeah, I had some dentist appointments." She picked up the menu from the table. "Come on, the waitress will be coming back, we'd better decide on our order."

They each had another drink with their appetizers, and Diana got a little morose. "You know, Moira...I guess I'm envying you a bit. Here you are, just starting out, nothing but great prospects ahead...and I'm not even thirty-five and I feel like I've been put out to pasture, like an old dray horse."

"I'm not getting you."

"I just got the quarterly report from Bread and Roses. You remember that tornado that hit Worcester last summer?"

"My god, yes."

"The sky hadn't even cleared up before Bread and Roses had people responding to that. They were there faster than the Red Cross. They got so much good publicity, they've practically been canonized in Massachusetts."

Moira looked at her blankly. "But—that's great, isn't it? That's what you'd have wanted them to do, right?"

"Sure—but now they're doing so fabulously well, they don't need any funding from the trust any more. They've doubled their services, and they're getting all their funding from private donors, the federal government and the state." Moira just shook her head, still uncomprehending, and Diana sighed. "I always kept my name off the masthead, I didn't want Bread and Roses to look like... like just an ego thing. But now...that's just it. The organization has taken off, and my name's not on it. They're flying without me."

"Be careful what you wish for."

Diana almost laughed. "Yeah."

"You sound like a housewife whose last kid has just left home."

Diana took a swig of her drink. "I do feel like that. I've been wondering a lot, lately—what the hell am I going to do with myself, when I'm finished here?"

"Finished here? You mean this thing you're doing with Mr. Morgan?"

Diana was silent for a few moments. "I don't know, Moira...with everything that happened last year, I'm just as glad I wasn't in Boston. I'd have been losing my mind. But even when I thought the world was going to hell and things were only getting worse, I still felt...like I had a purpose, somehow. Like I was standing up there with the front lines, and even if we were all doomed, we were fighting to the last. But now...I don't have any idea where I'm going. I just can't see the future anymore."

"I know the feeling," Moira said solemnly. Then she smiled and raised her glass. "But hey, kiddo, who does?"

Before they finished dinner, a dozen customers or friends of Moira's had stopped by the table to say hello, and everyone wished her congratulations when they heard about the one-year celebration. In addition, three men earnestly attempted to pick them up, and while the men were disappointed, they all bought a round of drinks. Moira, who was attractive enough with her curly red hair and wide green eyes, was always friendly in a polite way, but Diana had never seen her flirt with a local man, far less date. She had heard many stories about her friend's protracted and ugly divorce, although Moira had been a little vague about the exact reasons for the break-up.

By the time they shared a piece of chocolate cake, with a candle in it, for dessert, Diana's long-range vision was blurring. "Oh my god, was that five martinis? I can't drink like this any more, I'm too loaded to drive."

Moira's words were slurring. "Yeah, you're such a little thing, too."

"Little, hell, I used to drink Stephen under the table, he'd pass out every Beltene, but man oh man…it's been too long."

Moira, who had just taken a bite of cake, absent-mindedly chased it with the olive from her martini glass and choked. "What's a Beltene?" she said when she stopped coughing and was dabbing at her watering eyes with her napkin. Diana felt a sudden and sobering pang of alarm.

"Uhhh…"

"Isn't that something Irish? I've heard that word before, or something like it."

Before Diana could reply, the waitress appeared by their table. "How is everything, ladies? Can I get you something else?" Diana looked at Moira, who shook her head.

"Black coffee, and the check, please."

"Not going to be sick, are you?" Moira sounded as if this would be mildly entertaining to watch.

"Nah, but after I finish the coffee, let's walk around a bit until my head clears. I don't want to run off the road." There were places on Route 1 where that would be a very serious matter.

They walked, carefully, over to the open-air amphitheatre in the park in Camden center. It was just sunset, and somewhat nippy, but neither woman felt cold thanks to the bracing effects of so much blood-warming gin. There was no one else sitting in the park at the moment. Diana perched on the edge of one of the inset stone seats, her legs outstretched. Between the alcohol and the coffee, she felt as if her brain was trying to compress itself into her sinuses. She kept her eyes on the water, watching the play of light and the moving boats, because if she closed her eyes it felt like the ground underneath her was moving. "Oh, god," she said finally, "I am going to be so hung over tomorrow. Thomas is not going to be very happy with me."

"Well, tough." Moira had lit a cigarette—Diana hadn't paid attention to how long it took her to do it this time. She exhaled gustily. "He's not your lord and master."

"No, but he's my partner. We have an agreement." Diana couldn't keep her eyes open any longer. She closed them and immediately a cool breeze, smelling of salt water, caressed her flushed face. *Oh, that feels nice…*

"So, what kind of an agreement do you have?" Moira sounded as though she had moved a few feet away, but it was too much bother to look. "What is this, that you do every day, seven days a week? So what happens if you miss one, or you just start late? Hell, you couldn't sleep in?"

"I don't know." She wished Moira hadn't said the word *sleep*—now she had to yawn. "It is kind of arbitrary. But once we set up the pattern, we can't break it."

"Not ever?"

"Well, not till it's done."

"And when's that?"

Diana shrugged. "Soon, I guess."

"And your Thomas, he's never fouled up, not even once?"

"No. At least not since—" Diana stopped suddenly, blinking. Abruptly, a series of images had flashed into her mind, Thomas hammering a hole into the plaster wall with his fists, Brent's body flying across the cellar and crashing into the stone foundation, blood dripping onto the dirt floor...she looked down and saw that she was clutching at her right wrist with her other hand. *What have I been saying?* Adrenaline was more sobering than any amount of coffee. She swallowed hard. "No, he's very disciplined." Moira, she realized with relief, wasn't looking at her, but was pensively watching the Bay.

"So, what season is a Beltene? Isn't that some kind of a big holiday, or something like that?"

In the long silence that followed, Moira finally turned and looked at Diana, and they simply regarded each other, until finally Moira's cigarette burned down to her fingers, and she dropped it into the grass and ground it out with the toe of her shoe. *How many evasions can a friendship survive?* Diana thought. *Would it really be so bad to tell her? Plenty of cowans know about the Order, it's not so mysterious that its existence and history are a complete secret...I can trust Moira not to blab, can't I?* In a year, Moira had never shown her anything but loyalty—indeed, had gone out of her way to defend Diana's reputation. "It is a holiday, yes. In the spring. For the group I was raised in. I'm really not supposed to talk about it with outsiders..." Moira's eyes were riveted to Diana's face. Up behind them, several automobile horns suddenly blared out angrily from the main road, but Moira didn't even blink. "But I am allowed to make my own judgments about who I confide in, up to a point. I know you won't repeat any of this." Moira just nodded, rapt. Diana drew in a deep breath. "It all started back in a period of English history, in the 17th century, called the Restoration..."

The clock in the church tower in Camden center had chimed the quarter three times before Diana, interrupted with many questions from Moira, finished explaining what the Order of the Silver Light was, what its philosophies were and what its members did. Diana wasn't too drunk not to be judicious. "There's a very strict rule against revealing the actual names of any living members to an outsider, so don't ask." Moira, whose forehead had been creased in an intensely brooding frown for most of the time that she listened, only nodded. Diana wondered how much of this conversation Moira would recall when she sobered up, but she had a feeling that every word she said was cutting through the gin haze like a dash of ice water. "All of this probably sounds completely crazy to you, I imagine."

"What? No, no it doesn't, at all." At Diana's skeptical expression, she straightened up. "Look, honey, I've been around a bit. I've heard about things like this before. One of my uncles was a thirty-third degree Mason, and he lost a leg at Somme, in the first world war. Most nights, he'd drink to kill the pain, and once or twice, he got to talking to us kids about the Masons and the stuff they did. We knew he shouldn't have, but the stories were so wild, and it was so big a thrill, we wouldn't make him stop. So I know this kind of thing is out there. And it explains a lot about you that just didn't add up."

"Yes, well, the Freemasons...that's another story. We borrowed some stuff from them, though—and likewise. There's a lot of overlap among these groups."

"Yeah, what was the word you used, for an outsider? I remember he used that word once."

"Cowan. Yep, we stole that one from the Freemasons. It just means a non-initiate, that's all. Of course, you can make it sound like a scathing insult, if you want."

"I'll say." Moira shook her head. "I have to admit, though—orgies and everything? I mean, in the Twentieth Century?"

Diana laughed. "I don't know if I'd use *that* word, it makes it sound so lurid. The Order's philosophy is that human beings have this untamable, passionate side to them that has to be given some free rein, or it will burst out and cause havoc. Any civilized society must allow times and places for, for sanctioned license I think they call it, as a way of letting off steam. We used to have those, right up to the Middle Ages—the Saturnalia, Carnival, the Feast of Fools, everyone's heard of them. But ever since those old holidays stopped, after the Reformation, this irrational side of human nature has been repressed. Trouble is, it can't *be* repressed, so it keeps breaking through and making people do terrible things. That's why civilization is doomed to fall apart, at least, that's how the OSL sees it."

"Well, sure, it makes perfect sense the way *you* tell it. I'd just hate to be trying to explain all that to a judge."

"Us, too, that's why it's secret. Let's face it, just about everything that happens at a Beltene is still against the law in Massachusetts, from fornication on down. Hell, half of it is against the law for two married people to be doing in private."

"Which is bullshit," Moira said with surprising bitterness. "It's none of the government's business what people do in bed...or, wherever they are."

"I agree with you, but that argument won't work on a judge, either. And I don't see those laws changing any time soon, do you?"

Moira's expression became almost pleading. "Why don't you think so? With all the talk now about how natural sex is, my god, you can't pick up a magazine or a book without sex being all over it, and look at Kinsey, look at what's on the stage now...I think people are coming around, at least they're starting to."

Diana smiled down at the grass at her feet. "Maybe you're right, I'm too pessimistic. That happens, when you spend your whole life feeling like you have to hide a big piece of what you really are."

For some reason, these words appeared to particularly resonate with Moira, who sat back and took a deep drag on her cigarette—there was a little pile of butts at her feet now. "It must be different, though, being raised in such a free atmosphere, right from the get-go."

"I'm probably not the best judge of that. My parents were...more extreme in their attitudes than most. You see, they believed, quite fervently, that innocence was a myth created to keep children ignorant and subservient, and that all children should be exposed to the realities of life as soon as possible. They held that children were always brought up that way, until Rousseau and then the Victorians, and it was much healthier. They raised me according to those precepts, so..." Diana was quiet for a few moments. "The real irony is that I was so sheltered from the outside world, I couldn't appreciate how differently other people thought and felt until I was married and decided to start up Bread and Roses. I knew about society's rules because my parents were always telling me how bad they were, and I just assumed other people obeyed them under duress and couldn't wait to be freed from them. I got a real kick in the head when I first got out into the world thinking I was going to help people, let me tell you."

"By realities of life, you don't mean sex, do you?"

"Oh, yeah. I don't mean there was incest going on, but I'd seen it all by the time I was ten. But that wasn't unusual for the kids in the Order—still isn't. I was sleeping with Stephen when I was fourteen, and he wasn't the first."

"Oh, my god." Moira looked aghast. "How old was he?"

"Well, he was only sixteen, he was raised in the Order, too. We got married when I was eighteen. By then, it seemed like the only thing left to do. It wasn't as though I was going to go to college." She sighed heavily. "He was different then. Losing the babies...that was hard on him, too. And the war changed him."

"Was he wounded?"

"No, but he enlisted voluntarily, in the Navy. His family has a lot of pull in Washington, so he tended to be safer than he really wanted to be. Bread and Roses got War Department money, so I was busy with them—that's what really got us off the ground, the war. Which is rather a bitter irony, when you think about it." Diana yawned, but she was feeling much more grounded than she had been when they left the restaurant. The clock began to chime the hour. "Look at that, eight already. I think I can probably drive now. I should get back home. You've got to work tomorrow, yourself." It had gotten quite dark, and the breeze off the harbor was making both of them shiver. Diana stood up and stretched, and Moira ground out her last cigarette and followed her example.

"So, this thing you're doing up there, it's all about magic," Moira said as they started picking their way cautiously through the dark amphitheatre toward the street. "It makes a lot more sense now that you've explained that, anyway. But you can't tell me what you're doing it all for?"

"I can't say anything more about that without Thomas knowing, and being part of the conversation. That's not so strange, is it? He's bound the same way, he wouldn't talk about it, either."

She thought that Moira was about to ask something else, but they reached the sidewalk at that point and the taller woman cut off whatever she was starting to say. As they continued on to where Diana had parked her car, a young man emerged from a little alleyway that cut between two buildings toward the water, and paused at the sight of them. Diana stopped in amazement. "Brent! How are you?"

She hadn't seen Brent since the previous summer, and he looked much older to her. He seemed less gangling than she remembered, his shoulders broader and his jaw a bit heavier. She realized, after another moment, that he was dressed differently than she'd seen before, a corduroy jacket over a shirt and tie. He carried an old leather satchel by its handle, like a brief case, and it seemed to be quite full. He glanced around furtively for a moment, as though he was worried about being caught talking to them. "Hi, Miss Chilton...Miss Waterford. How are things?"

"Couldn't be better," Moira said cheerfully. "We've just been having a celebration dinner for the shop's first anniversary."

"Hey, congratulations." He looked inquisitively at Diana, who smiled.

"No news up our way—a little boring, actually. I've stopped at the station a few times, but there's always this young kid there—is that your cousin?"

"Oh, yeah. Cocky little son of a gun, isn't he? He's seventeen now and he thinks he owns the joint."

"He doesn't do a bad job, though. Looks a lot like you. But where have you been?"

"Oh, well..." he gave Moira an odd look. "I've been making plans, since I had that...extra job, you know. Actually, I've been getting my high school diploma."

"Good for you!" Diana was amazed.

"Yeah, I uh—I might be getting married. Not for another year or two, but, well...I'm thinking a lot about the future."

"Brent, that's wonderful. How old are you now, anyway, twenty-one?"

He nodded. He cleared his throat and said, "I'm sorry, but I've got to meet someone...it's, uh, tutoring."

"Don't let us keep you," Moira said expansively, and he mumbled good-byes and hurried on down the street.

When they were in the car a few minutes later, Diana sat with her hands on the steering wheel for a moment, shaking her head. "The stuff life throws at you."

"Nice kid, isn't he?"

Diana looked at Moira. "How do you know him? From the filling station?"

"Well, no, actually. Keep this mum, but—he's dating Carole."

Diana gaped at Moira so comically that Moira broke into a grin. "But she's—how did they—"

"He just told you, you idiot. I guess he had to sit in on some classes at the high school, and she met him then. But it's true love, all right, my god, you should have to sit there at the shop and listen to her carry on about him. He must be able to walk across the Bay when he misses the ferry."

"But she's only—"

"Nearly eighteen, she's graduating in June. And look who's talking."

Stung, Diana started the engine and pulled out onto the road. After a few moments of silence, Moira said quietly, "I didn't mean it that way."

"I know. Forget it." Diana's silence was only partly due to Moira's remark. She was considering the connections between Brent, and Carole, and the way Carole acted toward her, and wasn't sure she liked the implications. She also needed to concentrate hard to make sure the car stayed where it belonged on the road.

As they were passing Camden Hills State Park, Moira said, a little too casually, "There was one more thing...that I wanted to ask you. I'm just kind of curious."

"You know the rules, if I can't answer, I won't. Nothing personal."

"Actually, this is...pretty personal. I mean, it's not about your group, or Mr. Morgan."

Diana would have given Moira a curious look at this, but she had discovered that taking her eyes off the road was most inadvisable. "Go ahead."

"Okay...um. So. With all the...experience that you've had...have you ever been with another girl?"

"Sure." The white line on the road seemed to be a little too close to the car, and Diana leaned forward, peering.

"More than one?"

"You mean at the same time?" She slowed down and let the car drift a bit to the right—yes, that seemed better. *I should have had another cup of coffee...* Thomas would never forgive her if she killed herself in a car crash, so close to the end of their working.

Moira sounded a bit flustered. "I didn't mean...I wasn't talking about your, your Beltene things..."

"I wasn't, either." They were coming into Pepperell now, meaning there were street lights and mailboxes and sidewalks and many other helpful guideposts to assist in staying in the right lane. Diana relaxed with a sense of relief. She turned off of Main Street and very carefully drove the two short blocks to the duplex where Moira rented an apartment, and braked a little hard, bringing the car to a sudden stop. "Oops, sorry," she said as Moira caught herself on the dashboard with both hands. "What are we talking about, Moira? If you want to know everything I've done, in bed and out, I'll tell you! But we'll be here all night."

Moira stared at her for a moment, and she smiled weakly. "Nothing, I just... nothing. Thanks for dinner, that was sweet of you."

"Don't mention it."

Shaking her head, which was a mistake, Diana took the back way to School Street. She opened the driver's window all the way to let the reviving chilly night air blow onto her face. Her thoughts alternated between focusing intently on the road, and meandering with some puzzlement over Moira's questions. Just as she pulled up to the granite boulder and was about to make the turn, the shoe finally dropped. She sat in the idling car, staring blankly at the speedometer and wondering just how much of her brains had ended up in her sinuses, after all, and whether she should go back to Moira's house and talk to her some more. She had absolutely no idea what she would say, however. When she heard Thomas' amused voice just outside the car window, she jumped so badly, she lost contact with the clutch and the engine stalled.

"Are you pulling in? You're blocking the road, someone's going to come around that curve and rear-end you." She turned to stare at him and he walked up to the car, started to lean in to the window, and recoiled. "Good *Lord*. Did you really drink all that, or did you just pour a bottle of gin over your head?"

Without answering, she fumbled for the starter button. Thomas hopped into the passenger's seat before she had time to put the car into gear.

"Careful, you're putting your life into my hands."

"The risks between here and the house are fairly minimal." From his energy level, he'd had a very successful foray. "Did you have a nice evening?"

"Yes. Well, sort of. It turned out just a bit...strange." She looked up at his quizzical expression. "Don't worry, I'll tell you all about it. I'm going to have to."

☙ 13 ☎

Thomas was far more amused than annoyed by Diana's over-indulgence. "The best way to prevent a hangover is to stay awake," he said, and he found ways to keep her that way until it was time for their working. As soon as they finished the working, Diana collapsed into a sleep almost as deep as her partner's. She awoke late the following afternoon with a doleful headache and a severe case of self-consciousness about her conversation with Moira. It took several days for Diana to get back to a conventional schedule, and she spent most of that time in the house where her alchemical workshop was set up. When she fell asleep there, she tended to jolt awake from nightmares of which she could recall nothing but a sense of bone-chilling dread, and that was disturbing for a number of reasons. She told herself that she needed to talk to Moira, and that it was idiotic to avoid her, but somehow she just couldn't bring herself to go into town and initiate that discussion.

But she was avoiding Thomas, as well, and he'd noticed. The following weekend, he coaxed her into bed with him after the working—which itself was unusual. Never before had she required coaxing. Her mood dissolved in their post-coital laxness, and when Thomas finally asked her what her remark about her evening out had meant, she told him the whole story.

When she finished, he was silent for a while. Diana couldn't see his expression clearly in the room's dim light, but she finally said, "Are you mad at me for blabbing so much?"

"Mad at you?" He sounded puzzled, and it struck her that he'd been thinking about something completely different than she'd assumed. "Oh. Of course not. Who you choose to confide in about yourself, and to what degree, is entirely your prerogative. You didn't tell Moira about our working."

"I told her that there is one."

"I imagine she already knew that. You might be surprised how much is already known, or at least guessed, about what we're doing here. It's a small town, I knew from the start that there would be talk."

She had to concede this, recalling several things Moira had said the other night. "It's funny, though—no one has ever said a word to me, let alone asked a question."

"Well, they wouldn't."

"As long as we pay our taxes and don't cause any trouble…"

"Exactly. The only resentment I've ever felt here was from those who can't forgive me for not enlisting in the armed forces in 1942."

"But you served, stateside, up in Bangor—"

"Yes, but that doesn't really count, for some people. It earned me a few defenders, like the Wilkinsons, and I'm very appreciative of their support. But claiming you don't want to kill human beings doesn't make you popular in war time."

They'd talked about this before, and as always, Diana fidgeted under a sense that she was morally lacking compared to Thomas. There had been times during the war when she had fervently felt that she would have welcomed a chance to enlist for combat duty and kill as many Germans or Japanese as possible. That was exactly the impulse, she knew, that had filled military cemeteries across the country, and now the emotions she'd felt in those years seemed childish to her. "What were you thinking about then, if you aren't mad at me?"

"I was thinking about you and Moira, actually."

"Me and Moira? There is no me and Moira, Thomas—we're just friends."

"It sounds to me as though she'd like something more than that."

"Oh…Thomas, really! I may have completely misunderstood what she meant, in the first place…"

"No, I don't think so." She could hear his smile in his voice. "I realized what her proclivities were the first time I met her. You mean you really never guessed?"

"Guessed? I…Thomas, I wasn't looking for it. I'm not playing the field. I'm with you now." He didn't answer to this. In the silence that followed, Diana suddenly felt a cold chill in the pit of her stomach, and she pulled away from him and sat up. "Thomas? Am I being a complete fool here? Aren't I with you?"

"Of course you are." Somehow his tone was too deliberately assertive. "But…"

"*But?*" Now her heart was pounding. "Are you shoving me at Moira because you want me to back off from you, is that it?"

Now he sat up. "Diana, that's absurd. Why do you make it so difficult to talk about these things without getting so emotional?"

"These things? What things are we talking about?"

He pushed his hair back from his face with both hands wearily. "It's just that…sometimes I'm concerned about you. I know you're capable and independent and quite able to take care of yourself, but…I'd just like to think that you won't be left alone."

"Left alone?" Suddenly her mouth was dry, and she swallowed before she could continue. "Thomas, we don't know that will…we agreed that we had no idea what would happen."

"We did. But I said from the very first, even before you vowed to help me, that I was prepared not to survive this."

"You said you weren't seeking death, that you didn't want that."

"But I said I accepted the possibility. I assumed that you understood that. Diana—if we're to have any chance of success at all, our Intentions must be in alignment. Don't tell me that we've been acting at cross-purposes all these months."

"Now you're accusing me of sabotaging our working?" The minute she blurted out the words she knew she was being unfair, but she couldn't stop herself.

"I'm not accusing you of anything. Is your Intention the same as mine?"

"My Intention..." she struggled to keep her voice steady. "My Intention, I thought, has always been the same as yours: to break the dragon's hold over you. That is the objective you stated, that very first night. To break the dragon's hold. I wouldn't have considered it a success if we achieved that only at the expense of your life. That would have meant the dragon had the last laugh, after all."

"But I didn't see it that way."

"Well, I did. But my Intention has never wavered, Thomas. It has always been to defeat the dragon."

"To defeat the dragon and save me."

"No! I mean, there is no difference. I wasn't tying two things together like that, defeating the dragon *meant* saving you." He was silent again, and Diana wished the room had more light so she could make out his face. Suddenly she felt a surge of irrational anger. "This is a hell of a time to bring this up, Thomas!"

"Don't shout at me."

"Do you know something, something you're not telling me, about the outcome of our working?"

"I do not."

"It wouldn't be the first time that you'd—"

"I do *not*." He'd raised his own voice, and Diana pulled back from him, both angry and just a bit frightened. There was a tense silence before Thomas said, "Do *you?*"

It took a moment before Diana could choke out, "No! Of course not."

"I also could say that it wouldn't be the first time you'd kept things to yourself."

Diana took in a breath, but couldn't speak past her conflicting emotions—guilt that Thomas was right, fury that he would suspect her of undermining their efforts in any way, and beneath it all cold fear. In her mind was the unwelcome memory of her words to Moira about not knowing what she would do after the working was over. For the first time, she realized that no matter how lost she had felt when she considered life after their working, she had never fully confronted the fact that Thomas might not be part of that life. Her intellect had accepted it but her heart had simply denied it.

Finally she said, "I haven't felt...anything. In fact, it's been bothering me a bit—that there has been so little sense of, of culmination. We should be getting near the peak now, but I just..."

"Are you having any dreams?"

Something in his voice made her look at him sharply. "I've been having nightmares, but I can't remember any images, just the fear. Have you been..." she trailed off as he nodded.

"Almost every time I sleep. I keep dreaming that something is about to... engulf me."

"Engulf?"

"Like a great wave, or a wall of earth breaking off a mountainside, or even an avalanche, once. Thundering noise, and chaos, and I can't escape it—I awake just as I'm about to fall and be overwhelmed."

"Do you ever dream about the dragon?"

"No. And that's strange, as well. You remember that I told you how often I was seeing it, and dreaming of it, how I saw it whenever I drank from a human being. I haven't seen it once since we started the working. At first that was a relief. Lately I've come to see it as very ominous."

"Ominous of what?"

"I don't know."

This time their silence was less tense and more darkly thoughtful. "Dreams can have many meanings and many triggers, Thomas." Diana was trying to convince herself as well as him—she was finding the implications deeply unsettling. "This doesn't necessarily portend the outcome of the working. We may be approaching the peak, that's all."

"You may be right, yes."

"It needn't mean that you're going to die, whatever happens."

"It may not. But...I have put my affairs in order, just in case. I wanted to let you know that." Diana heaved a heavy sigh. "I think you know where my papers are, in my desk in the study."

"Yes."

"And I think..."

After a moment, Diana said, "What?"

"I think you should do the same."

"Me!" Her shock was genuine. "You think *I* might not—"

"We are about to confront an immeasurable power, Diana. As you said a few minutes ago, we have no idea what might happen. If we fail, I doubt that you will escape unscathed. I know you're aware of that."

"Yes, but..." she got off the bed and walked to the middle of the room, hugging herself tightly. "Somehow, making preparations...it's almost inviting failure, isn't it? On a practical level it would be the obvious thing to do, but magically—we shouldn't even be allowing the possibility of failure to enter our minds. I know *you're* aware of *that*."

"I suppose I was thinking more of you than of myself," he said after a moment.

"Well, thank you." She walked back to the bed and sat resignedly on the edge of it. "My affairs are pretty much in order, I guess. My will was changed after the divorce, and I tied up almost every other loose end when I came up here. Everything goes to the trust, mostly to Bread and Roses. It's not like I have any family." She turned, searching to make out Thomas' features against the light from the doorway behind him. "Thomas...every Equinox, and every Solstice, since we started, we've done an assessment of how we thought things were going, what our progress was, and how it seemed to be affecting us. You've never mentioned anything like this before."

"I've never felt anything like this before. This is all since the last Equinox."

"Then those dreams are something new?"

"Just the last two weeks. How long have you been having nightmares?"

"Just this week. I thought it was because of where I was sleeping, over in my workshop, or maybe because I'm worried about Moira. But now I don't know." In the still room, the cheerful bird song outside the curtained windows seemed to mock their gloomy mood. "It must be getting close to the peak. I don't know what else it could mean. I calculated eighteen months, but..." She punched at the mattress with her fist. "Why can't we *feel* anything? Day after day, the energy just purrs along, barely perceptible, like an idling engine. Shouldn't we be *feeling* something? All the time we were building the athanor, the welding, the night we fired it—cowans could have felt all that! What's wrong with us?"

"Maybe we're not looking for the right clues. Maybe the magic is completely different at culmination than during the process of forming it."

"I've never known it to be *this* different."

"It could be...that we're simply too close to the center of it to have enough perspective."

Reflecting on this, Diana fell back onto the bed, one forearm over her eyes. "Now there is a sobering idea."

"One which you yourself invoked quite strongly, right from the beginning."

"I know. But I thought we were being careful. I thought we were trying to keep our awareness as open as possible."

"So did I. But habit can be deadening." He slowly lay back against the pillows, his arms behind his head. "I'm afraid that I'm getting too sleepy for this to be a fruitful discussion much longer."

Diana got off the bed and groped for the chair where she'd left her clothes. "I'll let you get some rest."

"You're welcome to stay."

"No, I think...I think I'm going to do some work with all this. I'm not sure what, but...we've got to talk about this more tonight."

"We will." A moment later, she realized he was already asleep. She left the room as quietly as she could, fighting down her irrational resentment that he could sleep so peacefully when she was so upset.

That afternoon she went into town to see Moira. The shop was open on

Saturdays and usually quite busy—Moira took her days off on Sunday and Monday. Diana waited until fifteen minutes past closing time, but when she opened the door, she saw that a customer was still sitting under one of the dryers, leafing idly through a copy of *Redbook*, while another sat in the farther styling chair. To Diana's surprise, Carole was completing that woman's hairdo, spray can in one hand, teasing comb in the other and an expression of intense concentration on her face. Moira was leaning back against the counter with arms folded, watching her protégée closely.

Diana paused on the threshold as four pairs of eyes locked onto her. Carole's brow crinkled into deep frown lines and she spritzed the customer's right cheek with hair spray. The customer winced, and Moira hastily straightened up to intervene. Only then did she smile weakly at Diana for a moment. "Hey, kiddo, been a while. We're not quite through here…"

"Yes, I can see that…" Both customers' expressions were so avid, Diana could have sworn their ears had gotten physically larger. "I was just wondering… when you've got a moment, I wanted to talk to you about something. Nothing urgent," she added, trying to sound as casual as possible. The customers did not appear to be fooled. The woman under the dryer had hunched down a little to hear better, which made her look as though she were starting to melt.

Moira seemed completely absorbed with dabbing at the chair occupant's cheek with a damp towel. "If you don't mind waiting, I'll meet you at the coffee shop in an hour or so." Diana was silent, watching both Carole and Moira studiously not look at her, and finally Moira glanced up. "Okay, hon?"

"Sure. I'll just, uh…I'll be there in an hour, I've got errands."

As the door closed, Diana heard Carole say petulantly, "I don't *like* her…" She didn't catch Moira's reply.

The coffee shop was on Main, up past Holliston House, and Diana walked toward it slowly, even more dejected than before. At the intersection, she crossed Main and walked down to the boat ramps at the end of School Street, staring out over the Bay. The late afternoon sun glittered on the water, and the breeze today was free of the sulfurous smells from the paper mill effluent that sometimes stained the currents pink or yellow. For a moment, as she gazed toward Isleboro Island on the horizon, the water seemed to disappear, leaving the ocean floor exposed. A long silver line rose up behind the island, shining like glass. Diana recalled reading how tidal waves in the south Pacific sucked all the water away from the beach just before they struck the shore. Thomas' words that morning echoed in her mind: *like a great wave, thundering noise and chaos…* She staggered, and had to catch herself from falling. When she looked back up, her heart hammering, she saw only the peaceful surface of the Bay.

What the hell…? For the second time that day, a surge of irrational anger swept over her. *We're not going to fail, Thomas isn't going to die, it can't happen!* Realizing what she was doing, she took in a deep breath and forced those thoughts from her mind.

She'd been nursing an iced Coke for nearly thirty minutes before Moira startled her by dropping heavily into the booth's opposite seat. Diana had been lost in thought, and she'd stopped looking up every time the busy coffee shop's door opened.

"Sorry about that, kiddo. That last lady was a bit trickier than I expected."

"Looks like you're training Carole in styling now." Diana passed a menu over to Moira, but the taller woman set it aside and concentrated on lighting a cigarette. Diana saw that she was now bracing her elbows on the table and cupping her hands around the match and cigarette as though trying to light up in a stiff wind.

"Um, yeah." Moira exhaled a gust of smoke. "She's ready. She'll be graduating soon, and her folks don't have the money for beauty school. She's got real talent, though, and she loves the work. She's saving up for her wedding, and she wants to help hubby out with some extra pin money after that. A lot of housewives take jobs these days, at least until the babies start coming."

"I know. And you need the help. Too bad you couldn't find someone who can cover the shop for you solo sometimes."

Moira shrugged. "Hard to find someone you can trust. Hire just anyone, and next thing you know, they're skimming quarters from the till, or start their own place and take half your customers with them." She reached over to drop the match into the ashtray, and bumped the ashtray several inches across the tabletop.

"Moira...are you sure that you're okay? Is there something wrong?"

For a moment, something in Moira's eyes made Diana's stomach tighten. She'd seen that look on her doctor's face when she woke up in the hospital after losing the last baby. But then Moira smiled brightly. "Of course not, kiddo! What could be wrong at my age? I've just worked myself down to a nub, that's all. I can't run a going concern like this one by myself, who did I think I was, Superman? I've just got to figure out what to do about it—I hate cutting hours back at this point."

"You do seem busy."

"Busy, my god! We're booked solid all next week. The prom is next Saturday, and Carole's got her whole crowd coming in to get their hair and nails done."

"I trust she's going to be there to help."

"Are you kidding? She can't wait to show off. She's sharpening up her nail files right now."

Diana had to smile at the string of images this provoked. "You're scaring me, Moira. Reminds me of what Brent said about his cousin."

"It *is* scary. These teenagers are going to take over any day now, I'll telling you. It's like a revolution." Before Diana could reply, Moira picked up the menu. "But I'm *starved,* that's another thing. I never even got lunch."

"We can go to the Schooner, if you want."

"I'm not dressed for a place like that. I just want a burger—maybe two of them" She waved at the coffee shop's lone waitress, who returned a somewhat desperate look and raised one finger. "I'm buying tonight, okay?"

"Okay, big spender." Diana thoughtfully pushed the ashtray back to the center of the table with one finger. "But, Moira—"

"So where have you been all week? Thought you were avoiding me."

Diana hesitated, slightly frustrated. *One more change of subject that fast, and I'll have whiplash,* she thought. "I was. But not for the reason you probably think."

Moira leaned back and dragged deeply on her cigarette, her face a bit wary. "Okay...so how come?"

"I just felt like a big blabbermouth, that's all."

"You mean all that stuff you told me? What, did your Thomas give you a hard time?"

"No, he didn't. Although I just told him about it this morning."

Moira shrugged. "Then don't worry about it, hon. I won't say a word, you know that. I'm not even sure how much of it I remember, to tell you the truth."

"I remember every bit of it. That's why..." She expected another interruption, but Moira just took a drag of smoke and waited. "I can't tell you how stupid I feel about being so slow on the uptake on the way home. I mean about, um..."

"I know what you mean."

Diana wasn't sure quite what to say next, especially in the middle of the coffee shop. She and Moira looked at each other for a moment, then Moira half-smiled. "I guess I didn't plan to let that one slip just yet."

"According to Thomas, you shouldn't have had to. I feel like a dope. Like you said, it explains a whole lot about you that didn't add up."

Moira grinned for a half second. "Now you know the real reason I got divorced."

"Must be quite a story."

"I'll tell you sometime."

Diana looked away uncomfortably. "I just don't know what I can *do* about it, Moira. Things are so...complicated now. That probably sounds like a patent excuse, but—"

"Hey, I understand. It's not like you're available. Everyone in this town knows that."

"Yeah." For some reason, the thought gave her chills. *I might be available sooner than you think.* Her anger surged again, and when the waitress suddenly materialized by their table, pad at the ready, Diana started and almost knocked over her Coke glass.

"What are you so jittery about?" Moira said after the waitress had left.

Diana leaned her forehead on one hand, suddenly feeling exhausted. "I wish I knew, Moira. I haven't been sleeping much. I have bad dreams—or night terrors, I don't know what you'd call them. And now I'm seeing things, too."

"That sounds serious."

Diana just shook her head. "Let's talk about something else, okay? Tell me how Carole's doing with her styling lessons. I hope that poor lady isn't going to lose an eye."

Moira snorted, and they spent their meal talking about the shop and some of the local gossip Moira had been hearing. The mood was forced and both of them knew it, but it was a relief to evade heavier topics, even temporarily.

Diana found that her appetite was gone, and Moira was only up to one hamburger, after all. After they'd finished, they walked the few blocks to Pepperell's tiny library, where Diana had left her car. Moira declined a ride back to her apartment. As she was about to leave, Diana braced herself.

"Before you go, Moira, I have a question, okay?"

Moira turned back with a cautious expression. "Shoot."

Diana took a deep breath. "Just when exactly was your last dentist appointment in Bangor?"

There was a long silence. Moira looked over at the street, then up at the sky, then the street again, and finally back at Diana. The way she was rubbing two fingers together, Diana knew she would have killed to have a cigarette in her hand. "You see, you're no dope, far from it," Moira finally said.

"I have my moments. I'm not blind, Moira—and I know you're not training Carole just because she's finishing school."

"They've been running some tests, that's all."

"What kind of tests? What for?"

"The medical kind, and if they knew what for, they wouldn't have to test, would they?" Diana opened her mouth to reply, but Moira cut her off. "It's nothing for you to worry about, hon. The docs just feel that...well, they want to cover all their bases. You know how doctors are."

Diana sighed heavily, her shoulders sagging. "I'm sorry, Moira."

"Who says there's anything to be sorry about? It's probably nothing, they'll give me some pills and I'll be fine. People live with stuff like this every day."

With stuff like what? Diana wanted to ask, but she knew she was lucky to be getting this much information. "Gods, Moira...I wish I could do something. I know you need help with the shop, but...I can't even pin up my own hair, and I wouldn't have the first idea how to do a manicure."

Moira's laugh was a bit hollow. "I spotted that the first time I met you, hon. Some girls just don't have the knack. Don't feel bad about it. It's people like you who keep me in business."

"I'd come in and supervise Carole for you, but she can't stand the sight of me. She'd probably walk right out the door." As Moira nodded with a wry smile, Diana added, "Say, what *gives* with that, anyway?"

"I don't know, hon." Moira's response was so immediate and so weary, Diana felt sure she wasn't being evasive. "I've asked her and she just won't answer. I do know one thing, though—this all started after she'd been dating the Crothers kid for a while."

Diana had to swallow hard. "I was afraid of that."

"He did some work up there for you two, didn't he?"

"In '52, yeah. I hadn't even seen him for months before we ran into him in Camden."

"Well..." Moira waved a hand helplessly. "There you have it, that's all I know. Maybe you should ask Crothers."

The thought gave Diana a chill in the pit of her stomach. *Should I tell Thomas about this? Gods, I have to...* "Look, Moira, if there's anything I can do, anything at all, promise me you'll ask, okay?"

"I promise. Look, kiddo, I've got to get home and hit the sack, I'm beat. I'm glad you came by, though."

"Let me drop you off, Moira—"

"No, no, I can walk, thanks, hon." She was already striding toward the road with determination. Diana watched anxiously until Moira was across School Street and then got into her car with a feeling of deep unease.

When Thomas got up that evening, they talked more about their dreams and the working, as he'd promised, but there was little more to say. Thomas was fidgety and hungry and eager to go on a foray. Diana told him, with some misgivings, about the apparent connection between Carole's dislike of Diana and her engagement to Brent Crothers. Thomas pondered this news and then shrugged. "If Brent had been talking freely, there would have been repercussions long before now. There's nothing we can do at this point that wouldn't be ineffective, or backfire, or both. I'm inclined to just let things be, Diana." She agreed with a mixture of disquiet and relief. After Thomas left, Diana went to bed in her own room for the first time in days. As far as she could recall, she had no nightmares.

14

For the next two weeks, Diana tried so hard to think about their working from different perspectives, and to be aware of the energies, that she came perilously close to muffing her lines on several occasions. No matter how she tried to change the way she perceived things, she could detect no indication that the power was building or tensing to any kind of end point. She began to wonder if they had completely miscalculated their entire plan from the beginning. Was there no energy building at all? Was something draining it? Would they still be repeating the same steps fifty years from now, no closer to a culmination than ever? Finally she pushed her doubts aside. *There are still six weeks to go...and I calculated at least eighteen months, not eighteen months exactly...*

Wary of interfering with what little support Moira did have if she hung around the shop and spooked Carole, Diana stayed away from town. She saw Moira a couple of times for a late dinner, and heard that Carole was "a natural" and learning amazingly fast. Moira seemed to be doing better, as well, and looked more relaxed and less tired. Diana reflected that Carole's dedication must be taking a significant burden from her shoulders, and inwardly squirmed that she herself wasn't doing more to help. But all she could offer was money, and Moira wouldn't have accepted a dime.

Thomas seemed increasingly restless, sleeping for shorter periods of time than he usually did and staying out for hours on his forays. When Diana asked him if he was still having nightmares every day, he simply shook his head in resignation.

"Have they gotten worse?"

"Just the same, but...they seem to come more quickly after I fall asleep now." The strain was starting to show in his face, which gave Diana something else to worry about. The close call they'd had when Thomas almost lost control was seared into her memory. She realized that she had never considered that one effect of their working, whether it failed or not, might be a repeat of that incident. For that matter, what would happen if Thomas lost control and *never* recovered? How would you stop someone who could dematerialize and couldn't be killed?

She lectured herself that fears like this were typical magical traps, efforts by her shadow-self to test her Intention. *It must mean that we're approaching the peak, after all.* But she'd experienced such things many times before, and somehow, this just didn't feel the same. *But no two workings will feel exactly the same...and I've never had a vampire as a magical partner.*

One warm day in mid-May, Diana had been reading in her workshop nearly all afternoon. The black flies were out in force and the small house boasted no screens, so Diana had closed the windows. The room had grown close and stuffy, and the alchemical text she was studying was heavy going. She had been up before dawn for their ritual after an uncomfortable night. She put down the book to rest her eyes for a few minutes and almost immediately fell asleep.

She dreamed that she rose from the sagging armchair and left the house, walking along the path through the woods. The light was strange, bright but seeming to come from nowhere, as though the air was glowing. No sunbeams streamed though the tree trunks or dappled the forest floor. Earlier, the woods had been alive with bird song. Now, all she heard was her own soft footsteps on the pine needle covered path, and there was not a single insect in evidence, biting or otherwise.

It took the usual ten minutes or so for her to reach the edge of the cleared field where Thomas had built his circle of crushed stone, and she was feeling harried by the length of the walk, as if she was late for something extremely important. When she finally arrived, she stopped and stared. The field lay before her in the odd diffused light, but the stone house no longer stood on its farther side. Instead of the scruffy mixture of weeds and tall grass, the entire expanse was filled with dandelions, blooming so thickly that almost no foliage was visible between the furry round flowers. But in place of their typical vivid yellow hue, each dandelion was a pale tawny shade. Diana knew the color was familiar, but she couldn't remember where she'd seen it before.

As she hesitated on the edge of the field, she saw a child with light blonde hair and a white dress standing near the center of the design. The child bent over, poking around among the flowers. Diana felt a violent jolt of alarm, and hurried out into the field toward the child. Her heart was pounding and the flower stems kept tangling around her feet. She had to be careful not to break them or tread on the blossoms, and this slowed her down. The child straightened up, holding a little nosegay of dandelions that she had just picked. Diana gasped, and she started calling out without consciously realizing what she was saying.

"Little girl! Little girl! Don't pick those! It took us months to plant all of them, please don't pull them out..."

When Diana was about ten feet away, the child turned gracefully around to face her. Diana stopped running as sharply as though she had just come to the edge of a sheer cliff. She stared at the little girl, speechless, one hand to her throat. The child had the most beautiful face Diana had ever seen—the kind of beauty that she had only glimpsed for a fleeting instant, from the corner of her eye, half illusion and half real. Her flawless skin almost seemed to radiate light. Her simple white dress reached to the ground, Diana saw now, and her pale blond hair rippled in waves to her knees. But for all her unearthly beauty, Diana had never faced anything, not even the dragon, that filled her with so much fear.

The little girl looked at Diana for what seemed like an endlessly long time. Then the child's solemn mouth slowly curved into a sly smile and her emerald green eyes sparkled with mischief. Diana felt her whole body turn cold. The little girl raised her nosegay, and Diana saw that the dandelions had all gone to seed. Each one was a ball of delicate lace. The little girl parted her lips.

"Oh no, please, don't..." It seemed to take every ounce of strength Diana had to force those words out.

The little girl blew, a tiny, prim puff, and the flowers she held dissolved into floating seeds, dispersing into the air like ashes. A long gust of wind swept over the field, and the flowers, all of them now frail seed balls, bent and disappeared like wraiths. A blinding gray cloud flew into Diana's eyes, choked her mouth and nose and pattered against her skin like sleet. A low rumbling sound was building into a roar, and against that sound, Diana could hear the little girl laughing, but it was not the laughter of a child.

With a violent jerk, Diana awoke and half stood up from the sagging arm chair, gasping desperately for air. She fell back onto the groaning springs, coughing uncontrollably to rid her throat of feathery seeds that didn't exist. By the time she managed to stop, tears were running down her face. She bent over her knees, still almost paralyzed by the sense of pure, bone-numbing horror that she had experienced when she watch the little girl blow the dandelions into nothingness. The most obvious thing that the dream might symbolize was more than she could bear to consider. She squeezed her eyes shut, trying to force the raw fear from her mind. *You're being tested*, she thought urgently, *it's a test, that's all...what are you most afraid of? What always guards the final door?* It was many minutes before she stopped shaking, and her mental turmoil receded. She blinked down at the scuffed floorboards, wondering how the room could be so quiet and the birds outside so animated when something so terrible had just happened.

The alchemical text was on its face between her feet, its century-old pages bent and the spine cracking. She retrieved the book and got up shakily to put it on her work table. When she did so, another shock hit her. On the table she kept a spirit lamp with a metal ring over it for heating flasks. She had used several of the leftover, unconsecrated bricks from the athanor construction as a base under the lamp. Now she remembered where she had seen the odd tawny color of the dandelions in her dream.

She stood motionless, hugging the book to her chest like a shield, fighting with the panic that was welling up from the pit of her stomach. *It was only a dream, it was only...* but she could almost hear that mocking laughter. *I need to get out of here, go do something mindless and ordinary...* She had washed out their ritual robes that morning and hung them to dry on a line outside the Schuller house, and they needed to be pressed. She left her workshop and walked briskly through the woods, batting at the mosquitoes and black flies with a sense of relief. The late afternoon sun was angling through the trees and shimmering on the pine needles. She desperately drank in every normal, familiar detail, but the unnatural images of her dream overlaid the world before her eyes, giving her a queasy sense that she was seeing double. The feeling faded when she reached the field, weedy and tangled with blossoming wildflowers, the stone house warm and solid on the farther side and the clear blue sky arching overhead.

It took her another fifteen minutes to get to the Schuller house. Diana wasn't trying to be stealthy—making noise helped neutralize the lingering effects of the dream. When she came to the end of the well-traveled path to the house, however, she suddenly stopped, half embarrassed and half alarmed. Standing in the dooryard was a tall, lean man, his back to her, gazing up at the boarded windows. She had heard rumors in town about vagrants using some of the empty buildings in the area for shelter as they passed through. After a moment, she cleared her throat uneasily.

"Hello, can I help you?" The man started and turned around, and Diana gasped.

"Oh, hello there, Di, I didn't hear you."

"Mother Goddess...Gregory!" She managed not to run, but couldn't stop herself from wrapping him with a hard, unrestrained hug when she reached him. "I can't believe it, it's so good to see you."

"And likewise, love." He was hugging her back so hard it almost hurt, and he was in no rush to let go. Finally, they disengaged so Diana could step back and look up at his face.

"You pulled a fast one on me. You've cut your hair! That's why I didn't recognize you. And what's with the hat?"

"You don't like it?" He tugged at the brim of the steel gray fedora. "The first new clothes I've had in years, and all she does is laugh at me."

"It doesn't match the blue jeans, that's all."

"Ah, well." He gave an airy wave. "I can only do so much. It's to keep the sun out of my eyes, mostly. Even the cheaters aren't enough, sometimes." He patted the front pocket of his flannel shirt, where she now saw a pair of sunglasses.

"What on earth are you doing here, Gregory? Why didn't you write and let me know you were coming?"

"I didn't know myself, Di, things have been happening so fast."

"Have they? What things have—but wait. Let's go over to the main house where we won't get bitten to death."

"That sounds like a fine idea, love. I think we've lost all the blood we can spare." She stopped and stared at him, but his frown was genuinely puzzled. "What's that look for, then?" He smacked at a mosquito on his cheek and knocked his hat askew.

"Nothing."

Back in the brick-floored kitchen, Gregory drained three glasses of well water straight down, and cheerfully accepted her offer to make him a cheese sandwich.

"Sorry, we just don't keep meat around in warm weather." Thomas couldn't abide the smell, and Diana just went into town if she felt peckish for protein. Gregory didn't ask any questions about the peculiarities of their larder, however, and scarfed down his sandwich so hungrily, Diana made him two more without asking.

"You always seem to be feeding me, Di."

"You need a mother," Diana said as she sat down across from him at the long table.

He smiled slyly. "Or a wife."

Diana realized her cheeks were flushing, and felt irritated. "I'm in no hurry to get married again, and I never thought you were the marrying kind."

"Ah, but people change, though, don't they?"

"Are you proposing, Gregory?"

He simply took a bite of his sandwich and chewed at her blissfully. "You know, if I spent the rest of my days searching, I'd never find a better cheese sandwich than this," he said after he swallowed. "I'd stay for more, if I was a free man."

"What do you mean?" He took another long drink of water, and sat studying the tabletop. "Just how did you get here, anyway? I didn't see a car anywhere. Did someone give you a ride from town?"

"I walked from town, love. But I got rides the rest of the way, like this." He stuck out his thumb in an eloquent gesture.

"You *hitchhiked?* All the way from Manchester?"

"It's not that far, it only took three rides to do it. They wouldn't let me drive, Di, even if I could afford an old clunker, and they'd be right, I wouldn't want to be in a car that had me behind the wheel." He held up his hands, fingers splayed, so she could see the slight tremors, and she winced unhappily.

"But...why, Gregory? Why did you come all the way up here? What about your house, and your workshop, you've left everything behind? Don't tell me the city evicted you, after all."

"They were working up to it, I think. But you see..." he hesitated, as if framing his words carefully. "My brother-in-law lost his job, and they've got six little mouths to feed, and I felt selfish, not doing something to help. They've been building new houses all around the edges of the city, and a man has been offering me a lot of money for my property, for two years now. The house was falling down, Di, you saw it for yourself, it was hardly worth keeping. But it had enough land for three new houses and to spare, and no tax lien on it, thanks to you. I drove a hard bargain, but I got all I asked for. I gave most of it to my sister, though. She supported me long enough, it was the least I could do."

Diana thought Gregory's explanation sounded incomplete, and a little too pat. "So...you sold your house, and now you're just going to bum around the country? What happened to your belongings, and your shop?"

"In storage, mostly, I can pay for that now. I took down the athanor, though."

"You took it *down?* Mother Goddess, Gregory..."

He just shook his head. "It had to be done, love. I didn't have a choice."

"Why couldn't you move it, put it into storage with everything else? You spent three months building it! You moved it from your sister's, didn't you?"

He only shrugged, with a faintly apologetic smile, and devoted his full attention to the sandwich. Diana folded her arms, watching him eat and frowning dubiously. When he had eaten the last crust, and could no longer use the sandwich as an excuse not to reply, she said, "Gregory...I love you and I trust you with my life, but I know there's more to this than you're telling me. Come on, this isn't fair. What's going on?"

He sat back, with an uneasy smile. "I'm not sure how you'll take this, Di, that's all."

"*Gods,* Gregory, will you *stop* it? The last thing I need is any more suspense added to my day! Just cough it up and spit it out!"

"All right, all right! You're so touchy, love." He took a deep breath. "I've heard from *him,* finally, that's what it is. He wants me to come back."

"Him? You mean—" she dropped her voice to a hush without thinking. "Levoissier?" Gregory nodded solemnly. "But...you mean you're going?"

"Seven years, to the day—just like I expected."

"And you're *going?* Gods, Gregory, I can't believe it! After what he did to you, after what he did to *me,* he waves a finger and you drop everything and go running after him?"

"What did he do, Di? What did he do that was so terrible, after all? Sent us off to think a while, did he? Compared to him, we're mere babes, how can we know what he's seeing?"

"You talk about him like he's—you were the one who said he was merciless, remember?"

"The best teachers have to be, love. Maybe you'll see that, when you stop being so angry all the time."

She stared at him, too stunned to speak for a moment. "I am not...I am *not* angry all the time."

"You're at war with the world, Di, and you always have been. You think I don't understand? It'll be burned out of you, if you don't let it go. Why put yourself through that?"

Diana sat stiffly on the bench, but her silence came from the hard cold lump of fear that had just dropped into the pit of her stomach at the words, "be burned out of you." Gregory noisily drained his fourth glass of water.

"I can't stay long, Di. But where is your partner, this Thomas you talk about? I knocked on the door, when I first got here, but nobody answered. I could have sworn I felt someone inside."

"Oh, he's probably still asleep." Diana was so preoccupied she spoke without thinking and immediately felt a pang of chagrin.

"He sleeps all day?"

"Sometimes, yes, he, uh, keeps a strange schedule, he always did. It makes no difference to me, I actually have a workshop in another house, that's where I was before I saw you."

"You told me about that. How are the lessons going?" He nearly smirked, but he was one of the few people Diana could never resent for that. She just laughed ruefully.

"I'll never be you."

"But you have your talents, love."

"You think so?"

"It's not just me that thinks it. You've got the talent to get yourself into more trouble than all the angels could dream of."

For a moment they studied each other across the table. "Why *are* you here, Gregory?"

"I just wanted to see you, Di. I don't know when I'll get another chance, things being what they are. And I was nearly passing by, as it was, so, I took a side trip."

"Manchester to Boston, via Pepperell, Maine. That's quite a side trip." She spoke lightly, because the implications of his words were disturbing her. She was afraid to ask him why he wasn't sure when he'd see her again.

"Oh, not Boston. He left Boston right after you did, or so I heard. He's in Montréal."

"Montréal?"

"That's right. And I've got to be there by sunset, day after tomorrow."

"And you're hitching rides? You sold your house and you can't afford a bus ticket?"

"That's part of his test, Di—to get there on my own. I'll make it."

"Well, I hope so…for your sake, anyway, after you've given up everything for this." He'd given up less than she had, two years ago, she admitted to herself reluctantly. "Montréal…I had no idea."

"A lot of people have been leaving Boston, it seems. You started a fashion, Di."

"Who else? And how would you know? Have you been talking to people in the Order?"

"Not them so much, but…did you know those boys who had the foundry in Southie? I don't know if you ever met them, they made some of my equipment, and some parts for my athanor."

"You mean Maurice and Conor?"

"They're the ones. They've left. I wrote them to see if they wanted to buy some of my apparatus back, and the post office sent the letter on. Maurice wrote me back and said they'd closed their shop, and they're in Providence now."

Diana stared at Gregory open-mouthed. "But…they'd been there twenty years! What brought this on?"

"He didn't say."

"Are they opening a new foundry in Providence?"

"No, they're trading in rare metals, more than a year now. He said business is booming."

"I'm happy for them," Diana said faintly. *Over a year...they must have closed up right after...* "Who else?"

"He didn't mention names, but he said a lot of the Order has left the city, different places. They're colonizing the whole south of France, it sounds like."

"Yes, that's where my parents are." She sat staring down at the scarred tabletop, trying to absorb what Gregory had said. "Well, this is...a piece of news. I wonder why no one else has mentioned any of this to me."

Gregory got up from the table, stretching. "I've got to get back on the road, Di. I've got a walk before I can even start looking for rides."

"Let me drive you into town, Gregory, at the very least."

"Can't, love, much as I thank you. I can only take help from strangers, that's what he said."

"Son of a bitch," Diana muttered, and Gregory laughed.

"I'll tell him you said so."

"You *do* that."

She glanced past Gregory at the doorway into the west parlor, and Gregory, noticing this, turned to see Thomas standing there. He had the look of someone who had just gotten up after a bad night, and Diana felt a pang of unease. It was still some time until sunset, but lately, Thomas had been up much earlier than this. "Oh, Thomas, this is Gregory Fitzhughes, he's, ah...just passing through, it seems."

"A pleasant surprise." Thomas shook hands with Gregory, whose eyes narrowed slightly as he did.

"Pleased to meet you." Gregory stuffed both hands into his jeans pockets and stood awkwardly for a moment, as if he wasn't sure what to say next.

"Gregory was just leaving, Thomas, he seems to be running on a deadline."

"That's quite all right. In point of fact, I need to be leaving myself."

Diana hesitated, torn between an acute need to ask Thomas if he'd had any dreams during the day, and an urgent wish to get Gregory and his heightened perceptions out of the room as fast as possible without looking suspicious. But Gregory appeared anxious to depart, and he hastily trailed her to the door when she beckoned to him. "So long," he said over his shoulder, and Thomas, heading for the bathroom, only nodded.

"I'll see you later, Thomas, before our working, okay? Come on, Gregory, I'll walk part of the way with you. I promise I won't lift a finger to help you." She tried to sound humorous, but Gregory didn't even smile. They had walked around the house and half way down the gravel road to School Street before either of them spoke. Diana was wondering whether Thomas had really just gotten up, or whether he had been listening to their conversation from upstairs. The four bedrooms all had grates in the floor to allow heat from below to circulate to the rooms, and even a human could easily listen to voices in the kitchen. Gregory's expression seemed troubled.

"So that's him, is it?"

"That's him. I always thought the two of you might get along, actually. You have a lot in common." Gregory just nodded. Diana glanced up at him just in time to see him swallowing hard. She girded herself for awkward questions, but none came. To break the silence, she went on, "How did you find us, by the way? Did you ask directions in town, or did you just home in on your compound?"

Gregory grinned weakly. "The compound called to me, surely enough, but I wouldn't have needed that. I didn't have to ask directions. The energy's so strong, I could have ridden a boat on it, with the right kind of paddle."

"You can feel it?"

"I could feel it in Manchester by this past Brigid's Day, love. You're just too close to the center of it. That happens a lot, with something as big as this." His tone was blandly matter of fact, but Diana again had that sickening sense that an ice boulder had been dropped into her stomach from ten feet above.

"Thomas and I...have been wondering, why we couldn't feel the energy more clearly."

"Simple enough, you're in the eye of the storm you've made. All calm where you are, but around you...I could have gotten here blindfolded."

Diana sighed heavily. They had almost reached the road before she said, "Do you think cowans can feel it? People in town?"

"Feel it, probably not, but it must be affecting them. Someone might notice the leaves, though, and that could start a bit of a stir. Not sure what you can do about that, but—"

"The *leaves?* What are you talking about? What leaves?"

He turned and looked at her in genuine surprise. "You haven't noticed?"

Diana could only stare at him and shake her head, thinking numbly that her tolerance for unsettling news was just about at its limit for the day. Gregory straightened up and turned to peer back down the gravel road. "It's harder, at this time of day," he said finally, "but, look there. There's where your house is, where you're working, right?" He pointed west-northwest, in the direction of the Schuller house.

"Yes, that's about right, I think."

"And there's the sun, see, and that's south. Now, the leaves should follow the sun, or else they face south. But watch, now, when the breeze comes again."

They waited, as Diana hardly dared to take a breath, hoping that this was some delusion of Gregory's, and hating herself for even thinking that. Then a long breeze sighed through the young trees by the road and made the tall grass bend over. The leaves shimmered and flowed in the wind. Then, as one, they fell back to their original alignment—facing toward the Schuller house, every one of them. Not until they moved in the wind and then returned to a resting state could Diana see it.

"And look there, you see those little flowers?" she heard Gregory say, and as if in a trance, she followed his pointing hand and saw small daisy-like blossoms among the grass, that should have been turned toward the sinking sun. They all spread their petals west-northwest.

"It's like that all the way from town, at least, and all through the woods—everywhere I could see, for miles around. Some things are getting sickly, from not facing the sun enough, I'd guess. It's like a magnet tugging everything toward it—everything alive, at least."

Diana stared around at the trees and weeds, the entire world suddenly so changed to her eyes, that the surreal landscape of her dream was banal by comparison. "I can't believe I didn't see it."

"It doesn't jump in your face, after all. I looked for it because the magic was pulling me so hard, I wondered if it was pulling anything else, and sure enough. I don't know if cowans would notice it, but they might, if they have vegetable gardens and suchlike. And scientists would probably notice it. They'd be the ones who'd come looking to see what was causing it."

"The trees have only been leafed out for a couple of weeks," Diana said uneasily. "Maybe this is temporary."

"Oh, it is that, love."

Diana turned to look at the bend of School Street, curving down toward the town. "Do you think...this could be hurting anyone? Making them sick?"

"I don't know, Di. You haven't told me what you're raising the power for. It's not impossible, but you know that already."

"Oh, gods, Gregory...what should we do?"

"Do?"

She looked up at him, suddenly desperate, for the first time in two years, to ask another magician for some kind of advice. "We're having nightmares, when we can sleep at all. Something just feels...*wrong*. What should we do?"

He gave a short laugh, but he didn't seem amused. "You're asking *me*, love? You cook up something like this, the two of you, and you ask for my help? You're so far out of my league here, I wouldn't dare to say a word."

"But you have a different perspective, you can see what we can't—please, Gregory..." But he only shook his head slowly.

"You ride it out, Di. It's too late for anything else. That's the trouble with raising storms—you can't outrun them. To do their work, they have to overtake you at last, and only you can decide if it's worth that, when it's all over with."

Diana started to speak again, and stopped with a long, despairing sigh, her shoulders sagging. She knew he was right.

"I'd best go on alone from here. I'm glad I had a chance to see you, love. I hope all of this ends the way you want it to—whatever that is." He reached out and touched her hair, drawing the white streak between two fingers until it fell away and brushed her cheek. Diana managed to smile.

"You see, I told you. I'll get old." But he didn't smile back, and in his eyes she saw the same look that had been in Moira's eyes for a moment that day in the coffee shop.

"No, you won't," he said softly. Then, so suddenly that Diana had to stand up on her toes and almost lost her balance, he caught her face in both his hands, bent down and kissed her, hard. When he broke off he said huskily, "Good bye, Diana," and immediately turned away. She couldn't answer him. She stood still at the end of the drive, watching him walk toward town in long strides, until he had vanished from sight around the curve of the road.

The sun was sinking, and long shadows were shrouding the ground at the feet of the woods. Diana stood where Gregory had left her, pondering everything that had happened since that afternoon, and wondering what she should tell Thomas. She wanted to ask him if he had dreamed anything similar to her nightmare about the little girl and the dandelions, but she was afraid to hear his answer. Finally, she came to a decision.

I won't tell him anything. It's bad enough that I have so many doubts. One of us, at least, has to stay true to our Intention. If I share my fears with Thomas it will only make our success even more uncertain. I've got to be strong, and not lean on Thomas to make me feel better. I'm sure he has enough doubts of his own. This is all for him, he's the one with the most invested in the outcome...I can't do anything to shake his confidence, it wouldn't be fair.

She turned this resolution over in her mind, and it felt like the right thing to do. It was tempting to tell Thomas everything that she was so disquieted about and hear his calm, rational, determined response. But even if he was alarmed, what could either of them do? Just as Gregory said—they were long past the point at which they could have grounded the working and accepted the consequences. They *couldn't* stop now. They had to ride it out, no matter what happened.

Back to work, she thought, squaring her shoulders. *It can't be much longer now.* She turned and started toward the Schuller house, to get their ritual robes off the line before the dew fell.

༃ 15 ༄

Thomas didn't return for their dawn ritual until the sky was growing light, and he said nothing about Gregory. If he had overheard any of the conversation in the kitchen, he had no comments to make. Diana spent a good part of the morning pacing through Thomas' property, to see if Gregory's claim about the leaves was really true. Everywhere she looked, she found the same effect, as far as she went. The only greenery that didn't turn toward the Schuller house was the pine needles, even when that meant the plant was facing a hundred and eighty degrees from the sun. Finally she could walk no further and returned to her workshop, her feet sore and her mind deeply troubled.

During the next few weeks, Diana gave up on trying to feel the energy that Gregory had claimed was obvious in Manchester. If, as he said, she and Thomas were the eye of a storm, then that serene core probably moved with them, and they'd never be able to feel it. But she found herself almost obsessively looking for symptoms that the magic was doing some harm, everywhere she went. She wasn't sure whether to be frustrated or relieved that no such effects appeared evident. Pepperell's Town Meeting debated and defeated the vexing name change proposal with no more and no less sound and fury than anyone expected. Like General MacArthur, the proposal's defenders vowed to return, but that was inevitable. There was no more and no less petty crime or domestic strife reported in the local gossip than usual. Moira was putting in full days at the salon and Carole, now a high school graduate, was taking on styling customers unsupervised.

Half a dozen times, Diana started to tell Thomas about the leaves, and what Gregory had said, but stopped herself. She rarely saw Thomas outside of their brief rituals, in any event. He was getting up well before sunset, his eyes haunted and exhausted, and went out immediately, only returning when the stars were growing pale and the early morning bird chorus had begun. She didn't ask him if he was still having nightmares—the answer seemed obvious. Her dream, if it was a dream, about the little girl in the field of dandelions was never repeated, but Diana was still jolted awake, shaking and nauseated, every few nights by something she couldn't remember.

By the second week of June, Diana realized that she felt much more relaxed. *Whatever happens, happens,* she had been repeating to herself incessantly, like a mantra. It seemed to be sinking in at last. One afternoon, she read four chapters in her alchemical text with a degree of concentration she hadn't experienced in weeks. The tense cold knot in her stomach was dissolving, and by dusk she was ravenously hungry. Her appetite had been almost non-existent for so long, she hardly remembered what hunger pangs felt like. Back at the stone house, she lit the stove and was making a more elaborate meal for herself than she had for some time, when Thomas startled her by wandering into the kitchen from the parlor. She had assumed that he'd left the house that afternoon. It was now full dark outside, and that meant it was very late, so close to the Solstice.

"Did you just get up?"

He didn't appear nearly as worn as he had been looking, although he seemed a little groggy. He sat on one of the benches, rubbing his hands over his face and hair. "Yes, I did. This is the first time in weeks that I haven't been awakened by bad dreams."

"That's great—I hope."

There was a plate of homemade fudge sitting on the table with the other food Diana had put out—the Girl Scouts had been selling it at Town Meeting. Thomas picked up a chunk of the fudge and sat breathing in its fragrance with the look of a wine connoisseur sniffing a rare vintage. He finally took a small bite and sat motionless, eyes closed, completely focused on the taste. Diana, who had seen this before, wryly asked, "you're not going to go on one of your binges, are you?"

"No," he said after some time, and sighed deeply. "I think we've been worrying far too much. Whatever happens, will happen."

"Yes, that's what—" Diana broke off, suddenly feeling uneasy. "Worry is just a form of fear, and fear is always a trap."

"Exactly. I think we've just weathered some kind of test, Diana—the last one, perhaps." He took another bite of fudge and was silent for a few minutes, as Diana attended to her skillet on the stove. When she sat down to eat, Thomas remained at the table, and casually asked her how Moira was doing. It had been so long since they'd had an ordinary conversation, Diana felt a bit awkward. But Thomas kept on asking about everyday affairs in town, and further amazed her by helping her wash the cooking pans.

"Aren't you going out?"

"No, I don't need to. Aren't you going to bed?"

"Well, eventually, why? ...okay, silly question." He had wrapped his arms around her from behind, soapy hands and all, and was kissing the back of her neck and nuzzling at her hair. She had trouble stifling giggles, because it tickled. "Thomas, you just got up."

"I have nothing better to do."

She was curling her wet hands around his, and she turned around for what immediately became a long, deep, and uninhibited kiss. His mouth tasted like chocolate. She was amazed at how aroused she'd become, and how fast. Her knees were shaking, and the upstairs bedrooms seemed much too far away. As Thomas became more insistent, she broke off impatiently. "I am not making love to you on the edge of the sink, Thomas—no! Let's go upstairs."

They only made it as far as the west parlor, which had witnessed such goings-on before. It was Diana who couldn't bear to wait longer, pulling her very compliant partner down onto the antique braided rug, which was velvet soft from age. She was as ravenous for sex as she'd been earlier for food, and she had no idea where this sudden revived enthusiasm for life's pleasures came from. Thomas clearly was in perfect harmony with her on this, and it was quite a long time before they were both satiated enough to lie intertwined and completely relaxed. Only then did the abrupt change in their mood, and its possible significance, begin to sink in. Diana was reluctant to talk about it, or even think too deeply about it, because the sheer relief from all the fearful anticipation she'd felt was so great. Thomas broke their silence at last.

"It's peaking. It must be."

"I know." There was another long, reflective pause before Diana spoke again. "Do you think it will peak during our working? Or do you think it could happen at any time at all?"

"I don't think. It's reasonable to guess that one of the workings would be the final trigger, but..."

"But this isn't reason, it's magic."

"Precisely."

They were quiet for some time longer. The room was dark except for what little kerosene lamp light spilled through the door from the kitchen. Diana was looking up at the low ceiling of the parlor but she could only see shadows. It was strange to be free of the tension and anxiety of the past weeks. She tried thinking about the horrible imaginings that had tormented her—the dragon, Thomas dying, even something happening to her—but none of it seemed real. It was like trying to force a genuine wince with the memory of an ancient wound.

They got up when an unpleasant odor of hot metal warned them that the water kettle, which Diana had forgotten to refill, had boiled dry on the stove. Diana went to bed and slept so soundly that Thomas had to rouse her at dawn for their working. Like him, she had been waking up long before she needed to and felt slightly embarrassed, but at least they weren't late.

Their working felt different to Diana that morning. She couldn't identify quite what had changed, but she felt an uneasy detachment, as though she didn't really belong in the room. The athanor appeared smaller, somehow, and almost shabby. Over the past eighteen months, the tawny yellow bricks had become grayed with soot, and the bright copper chimney pipe had tarnished to dull green. The room itself had a tired feeling. There was a circle beaten into the dirt floor where their feet had trodden the same steps, hundreds of times, in the movements of their spell. Even her ritual robes didn't feel right on her body, and they weren't new. As she and Thomas were about to begin, a jaded thought crept into Diana's mind: *what are we doing this for, anyway? What is the point?* She forced the thought away.

When they completed the working, they both stood silently, facing the athanor in the darkness of the cellar, waiting. Nothing happened. Diana was taken aback by the disappointing sense of bland normality in the room. She could hear birds singing dimly from the woods outside, and the fragrance of the incense mingled with the smells of old wood, crumbling mortar, damp earth and mildew. Finally, after they had stood motionless for so long that Diana thought her legs would start cramping, they gave up and went upstairs to change.

Every successive morning was the same. They walked reluctantly to the Schuller house in the gray predawn, went through motions that seemed more empty each day, and then waited until it was obvious that waiting was futile. On the tenth day, as they hung up their robes in the changing room, both of them seeing the dejection in the other's face and posture, Diana said, "You were wrong, Thomas—*this* is the last test. It's one more trick to try to make us give up." She wasn't sure she believed it, but it was the only thing she could think of to ward off complete discouragement.

Thomas pondered her words. "You may be right," he said finally. She knew he didn't believe it, either.

But it was only a few more days until the Solstice. If nothing changed then, they would switch their ritual time from dawn to midday, and carry on.

Thomas went up to his room, and Diana settled in an armchair in the east parlor, by a window, to sew. She sewed their ritual robes by hand, and made them each a new set every quarter. The design was simple and involved little more than long straight seams and a lot of hemming, but it took several days to finish both sets. She never liked having to get up before dawn through the spring quarter, and after a couple of hours, the close needlework and her dispirited mood caught up with her. She leaned her head back on the chair, reminding herself that the last time she'd dozed off sitting up, she'd regretted it, but a moment later she was asleep.

"Is this a dream?" she asked Moira, as they walked together down School Street toward the boat ramps.

"Don't you know what day it is? You've got to keep a date book, kiddo."

"What for? How could I forget something that makes so much noise?"

"I don't hear any noise."

"Gods, what is that awful smell?" They'd stopped at the end of the concrete ramp, which was farther than they should have been able to walk. The Bay was no longer there. The water was gone, and Diana saw nothing but dry sea-floor between them and Isleboro Island. Mounds of seaweed glistened under a bronze-colored sky, and fish flopped sluggishly in the mud. Sea gulls filled the air, circling silently like buzzards, and Diana could hardly breathe for the overpowering stench. Moira gazed serenely out over the devastation.

"It's the end of the world, kiddo. You really did it."

"Where's the water?"

"Oh, it's coming back. You see—there it is."

Diana followed Moira's pointing hand and saw a long shining line rising up behind the island. As it grew higher, she saw that it was a great wave, dark below and sunlit above, about to pour over the entire island and crash down into the empty basin of the Bay. It rose and rose above the treetops, dwarfing the misty green island, rising taller than Mount Battie, the peak that overlooked Camden, and still growing. A deep roaring came from beneath her feet, a sound that had begun below the threshold of her hearing and was slowly rising in pitch. Diana's bones were vibrating with it. "Moira, we've got to run," she shouted, hardly able to hear herself over the din.

Moira's face rippled and she turned into a little girl with pale hair flowing down her back, who said, "Run away? After all the work you did to make this happen? Why would you run away?"

A stabbing pain in her right hand jolted Diana awake in the armchair. After a few moments of confusion she realized she had clenched her hands so hard in her sleep, she had run her needle into her palm. Wincing, she pulled the needle free, her dream driven from her mind by the shock. She was soaked with sweat and her heart was pounding. But as she rubbed at her hand, she became aware that she could still hear the deep, dull roar of her dream. It was distant, like the roar from a sea shell, but she knew she wasn't imagining it. The light from the window seemed oddly muted, and had a coppery tint. When she peered out, squinting at the sky, the sun appeared reddish, like it did at sunset on a hazy day, but it was close to noon now.

She stood up, the silk fabric in her lap falling unheeded to the floor. The sound was rising in pitch and volume—not quickly, but fast enough that she could sense the change. She could feel it in her bones, and vibrating in the center of her chest, the way she had in the dream. She walked through the entranceway and west parlor and into the kitchen, and was not surprised to find Thomas there. He was standing by the table, his head cocked slightly as though he was listening. He was fully dressed, and she wondered if he'd slept at all.

"Do you hear that?" he said as she entered the kitchen.

"Yes."

They stood motionless, listening to the sound as it slowly grew. The house seemed to be shaking with it, and just as Diana thought that must be an illusion, she realized that several small objects on the table, a spoon and some pencils, were moving. One of the pencils rolled off the edge and clattered to the floor, and the hanging lanterns were just beginning to swing.

Thomas watched the pencil fall and then turned toward Diana, but before he could speak, the entire room lurched once underneath their feet, as if the ground beneath them had heaved upward. Diana grabbed for the door frame next to her, stifling a shriek. The movement wasn't repeated, but Diana abruptly remembered something from long ago, her first night here when Thomas had drained her blood to show her the dragon. She recalled the feeling that they were on the back of something huge and alive, something of immeasurable power, something that was about to throw them off and devour them...

"We should go," Thomas said, and for a moment she didn't understand what he meant.

"Where?"

"The athanor...we have to get there..." He went to the back door and pulled it open, and Diana gasped. The air outside seemed to be filled with glowing golden mist. Thomas appeared undaunted. "Come on!"

She ran after him, and when she reached the door, he looked back at her and gripped her hand, as if he was about to say something. There was another lurching heave beneath them, stronger this time, and then they both were running, around the house and down the gravel road to the path through the woods, their ears filled with a throbbing hum that blotted out all other sound. Diana couldn't even hear their footsteps. *Am I dreaming?* she thought desperately. *This can't be happening, this can't be real...* But her hand still throbbed painfully from the needle jab, and she could feel blackberry brambles scratching her as she followed Thomas straight through the underbrush rather than run all the way to the head of the path. The bronze-colored sky above them seemed to be radiating heat and light, like a sheet of hot metal. *Do people in town see this? Where are we?*

As they approached the Schuller house, their steps slowed. The ground seemed to be softening and slipping under their feet, as if it was both mud and ice at once, although it looked the same as it always did. There was a pressure in the air, as if something was attempting to force them back. They pushed onward against it and finally broke into the back yard of the house. Here the pressure suddenly gave way, as if they had won through past some boundary, at least for a moment. Panting, Diana stood staring at the house, which wavered before her eyes as though she was looking through warped glass. Thomas' face was set, his eyes wide, and Diana thought that for all his insistence that he was prepared, he was terrified of going further. But then he stepped forward and she stayed close behind him. The deep sound was no longer rising in pitch but was even louder now, and the ground shook. She could see the leaves, without a breath of air to stir them, trembling as they hung limply from their stems.

They went up the steps and through the screen door. They were halfway down the hall when the house listed sideways like a ship rolling on rough seas. Both of them staggered against the wall as the beams of the house groaned in protest. Then the hall returned to its more or less level orientation. They picked their way over the warped boards, past the doorways into the changing room and the kitchen, because there was light ahead of them and there shouldn't have been. They came to the edge of the floorless front room, where the athanor was visible below the exposed beams. A golden aureole of light surrounded the entire beehive-shaped structure, like the one they had manifested the night they fired the athanor a year and a half ago. This light wasn't spinning, but it was intensifying, and they could feel the heat from where they stood.

The deep sound was a roar now, and Diana could barely hear herself think past it. She was so overwhelmed by what was happening, or seemed to be happening, that she had no idea what to do. *How could we ever have been so naïve as to think we could control this,* she thought helplessly, but that had never been part of their plan. All they had Intended to do was raise the power and release it—never in her wildest imaginings had she envisioned anything like this. She clung to the plaster wall with her fingers, expecting another heave of the floor that could toss her down into the basement. The light dazzled her now. She saw Thomas shielding his eyes from it, and remembered that he had been momentarily blinded during the firing. She caught his arm, pulling him back from the edge of the gap. He took one step back and then yanked free of her.

"I've got to get down there."

"Thomas, no! You can't!" He stepped forward blindly, covering his eyes with one arm and groping with the other, and she realized that he was going to jump down, the way Brent used to do. Horror-struck, she grabbed his arm and he shook her off impatiently. She looked down at the athanor, and gasped.

"Mother Goddess...this can't be happening...it's *melting*, Thomas!"

The bricks of the athanor were running like liquid wax, a wide pool growing on the floor around it. Even as she watched, the copper pipe sagged sideways and pulled loose from the top of the bricks, which now had the consistency of soft wet clay. The pipe fell clanging to the floor and the metal began to warp and curl like a burning tube of paper. The top of the iron sphere showed through the thick yellow liquid that now ran in gouts down the sides of the athanor, and it was glowing red hot. Thomas had stopped, staring down at this spectacle aghast.

The pitch of the sound in their ears suddenly began to rise, and Diana was sure she would be deafened by it. She felt something wet on her hand and looked to see viscous fluid running down the walls. Crumbs of plaster were falling on the floor and bouncing like hail stones, and she could feel the boards softening and bowing beneath her feet. She refused to believe the evidence of her senses, but this was no time to be analytical. Thomas' resolve was weakening, and he started to back away from the edge of the floor, looking down incredulously at his feet sinking into the wooden planks like they were mud.

"We've got to get out of here, Thomas..." She was shouting at the top of her lungs and still couldn't hear her own voice, but he looked at her, his face a mask of shock. They both turned and stumbled down the hall, shielding their heads from the mixture of sticky liquid and chunks of plaster and wood that cascaded down on them. The beams and studs were exposed now, bending and sagging as the house added its groans to the screeching roar. When they were nearly at the back door, Thomas suddenly doubled over, clutching at his abdomen, his face contorted with agony. Diana screamed his name and wrapped her arms around his upper body, dragging him physically through the doorway. *This can't be happening, it can't be...* the trees were whipping back and forth as though a gale was blowing, but she felt no wind.

As she swayed on the edge of the tiny porch, fighting to keep Thomas' dead weight from falling down the steps, all the noise suddenly stopped. Diana was sucked backwards and slammed up against the screen door, and then she was struck by a soundless concussion. It didn't feel like an explosion—it felt as though something picked her up and threw her twenty feet across the yard. She fell heavily to the ground, face down, and twisted around frantically looking for Thomas. He was lying next to her, his body almost convulsing, and from his lips came a sound she would not have believed a human throat could make. She reached toward him and realized that the entire Schuller house was swelling up, like an over-inflated balloon. Nails popped from the clapboards and the plywood boards on the windows split off in curling layers. She stared for one unbelieving second and then rolled over, covering her head with her hands, as a blast of boiling air raged over her. Tiny particles peppered her skin like hot sleet. She could sense a ring of pure power expanding outward, like a single ripple on a pond after a stone has been dropped into the water. She wanted to shout, "look out!" but she had no idea who she was trying to warn. As she struggled to get up on her hands and knees, a horrible pain suddenly wrenched her body. It felt as though a huge hand had gripped her entrails and ripped them out in one savage motion, but there was no blood and her clutching hands felt nothing but her own muscles, cramped to rigid hardness. Her diaphragm locked and she couldn't breathe, and then blackness overtook her.

≈ 16 ≤

When Diana awoke, she wasn't sure where she was. Every bone and muscle in her body ached and the exposed skin of her face and hands was stinging. At first she saw only a blur, and with some effort, she reached out and touched the ground in front of her face. That gave her eyes a visual anchor, and the world sprang into focus. Her confusion remained, however, for the ground was covered with a layer of loose particles, like fine gravel. She pushed herself up with her hands, and a rain of the same particles fell from her head and back, pattering softly. She was completely blanketed with them. She shook her head to get the stuff out of her hair. *What is this?* She looked up and around like a bewildered animal, and recognized the trees surrounding the back yard of the Schuller house. It seemed to be late afternoon. The sun shone bright and hot in a clear blue sky, birds were singing, and everything was calm and peaceful.

She sat up the rest of the way and turned around to look behind her. She stared, open mouthed, so far past emotion or amazement that her mind was simply numb, as she struggled to accept what she saw. The house was gone. No shell, no ashes, no identifiable wreckage, nothing remained but an empty hole in the earth. On the other side of the hole the stack of pallets from the brick supplier sat in the overgrown front yard. Finally she looked down at the layer of stuff on the ground, about an inch deep, and rubbed her hand over it. Plaster, wood, stone, glass…all that was left of the Schuller house, not a bit of it larger than a pea.

She became aware of an uneasy prickling feeling, as though she'd walked through a cobweb and was crawling with spiders. Then she heard a groan and something moved just beside her. She turned and saw Thomas slowly sitting up, the layer of particles that had disguised his shape falling off of his chest and shoulders. Diana jerked back from him and scrambled sideways so frantically that her feet kicked up little sprays of loose debris. He didn't look at her, and she had no idea what prompted her reflexive action. All she knew was that he had nearly touched her, and she had to get away from him. The sight of his dazed face and dusty hands evoked the most violent sense of pure revulsion that she could ever remember feeling. As he slowly climbed to his feet, and shook his head the same way she had, she pulled back further, as if the bits and pieces of house that flew from him might be scalding hot.

He walked unsteadily to the edge of the cellar hole of the house, his footsteps crunching loudly, and stood looking down for several minutes. Then he turned slowly, and his gaze rested for a moment on Diana. In his eyes was the coldest look of pure hatred she had ever seen. He glanced quickly away from her, as though he couldn't bear the sight of her face, and walked to the head of the path and into the woods, his stride much stronger and faster now. Diana wasn't the least bit intimidated by the look she'd seen—it matched her own mood perfectly. But she suddenly realized that he was going to get back to the house first, and if he did, she would be locked out. She jumped up and ran after him.

They were halfway down the gravel road before she caught up with him. She reached out to snatch at his sleeve, and he wheeled around and shoved her roughly away from him with one hand. She fell flat on the ground, her wind knocked out, furious because she wanted to shout at him and couldn't. Her chest was going to have a bruise from the force of his blow, but that only made her angrier. He continued toward the house, and as soon as she could, she got to her feet, running to cut him off before he could get inside. But he was too fast for her, and she reached the back door just as it slammed emphatically in her face. She heard the iron bolt shoot into place.

She stood frozen for an unbelieving moment, her mind so filled with pure rage that she couldn't think or move. The air around her seemed to be filled with a red haze. She grabbed the door handle, depressing the latch and shaking the door as hard as she could. Then she stepped back and howled at the top of her lungs.

"*Thomas!* Let me in! Let me in, you fucking son of a bitch! How dare you? How dare you?" Her voice shrilled and cracked, incapable of sustaining the volume and effort her anger placed on it. She sounded ridiculous to herself and this made her rage spike even higher. She flung herself at the door, kicking at the heavy oak planks and pounding with her fists. She could hear, or thought she could hear, her blows echoing inside the house, but the door didn't move. She kept on pounding until she realized that her fists were leaving splotches of blood on the door. Sobered for a few seconds, she backed away, flexing her sore hands. If she kept this up, she'd only break bones on the hard wood and stone. But that wasn't the only thing the house was made of.

She feverishly searched the ground, kicking with her feet and shoving long grass aside with her bleeding hands until she found several stones the size of baseballs. She was shaking with a fierce urgency—she had to get inside, it was already too late, gods only knew what Thomas was doing in there. Stumbling through the tall weeds to one side of the door, she drew a bead on the back window to Thomas' study and pitched a stone with all her strength. The resulting crash was very disappointing, as the stone neatly took out a single small pane of the window. She couldn't perceive any reaction from inside the house. *Maybe he's not in his study...*she half-ran, tripping, to the other side of the house and aimed the next stone at one of the kitchen windows. This time she took out two panes and could hear glass and the stone clattering onto the brick floor. Much better. She threw two more stones, destroying half the upper casement of the window.

"*Thomas! Answer me!* You let me in, or I'll break every goddamned window in—"

Thomas grabbed her from behind, spun her around and shoved her backwards until she slammed into the wall of the house. She had no idea whether he'd dematerialized or come around from the front door, she'd been so focused on aiming the last stone. His face was a mask of fury, but it didn't even occur to Diana to feel afraid of him. She wrenched and twisted to get out of his grasp.

"Let...*go* of me, you bastard! Don't *touch* me!"

He let go, jerking his hands back. From his expression, her revulsion at their physical proximity was matched by his own.

"Stop...destroying...my...*house,*" he hissed through clenched teeth.

"Let me in!"

"No!"

She turned, reaching for the frame of the shattered window, whether to open it or break it further she didn't know herself. He caught her shoulders and threw her back up against the wall.

"I need my *things!*" she shrieked, tears of helpless anger starting to fill her eyes.

"You're not setting foot inside my house, ever again. I want you off my property, now."

"You can't keep my things, that's stealing! I'll get the police!"

"I'll pack your damned things for you."

"The *hell* you will, don't you dare *touch* my things!"

"You're not going inside."

Her frustrated outrage choked every response that came into her mind. Her fury overrode her repulsion and she flew at him, flailing at his face and chest with her fists. He seemed startled, and took several steps backward before he managed to grab both her wrists. Twisting her arms frantically in his grip, Diana aimed hard kicks at his knees and calves, but she kept missing, and her light flat-soled shoes weren't capable of doing much damage even to a normal human. Abruptly, Thomas flung her down onto the ground, and she scrambled away from him, breathing hard as she fixed his eyes with a murderous glare. He was squinting, shoulders hunched, obviously inconvenienced as much by the bright Solstice sun as by anything she could do. Slowly, she got back to her feet, her legs shaking.

"If you think I want to stay here one more *second*, you couldn't be more wrong! But I'm not leaving without my clothes and gear—at least the stuff that didn't just get *blown up,* thanks to you!"

He stiffened. "Thanks to *me?* Where the *devil* do you think you get off saying that to me? This is all your fault!"

"*My* fault—"

"Of course it is! You *never* wanted us to succeed—"

"*What?*"

"You've been undermining this from the very beginning! You wanted me to stay enslaved, you were stupid enough to think you could spend eternity with me, like some kind of besotted little—"

"Oh, *fuck* you, Thomas, that is *bullshit!* I gave up my whole *life* to help you with this, and for *nothing!* I lost *everything,* all my friends, Gregory, my apartment, Bread and Roses, *everything!* Just for you, it was all for *you!* I got *nothing* out of this, and now you—"

"And whose fault is that, you stupid cow? What kind of a fool negotiates a one-sided deal? Even I don't believe you're that brainless. Don't pretend that you didn't expect anything from our bargain. You played me from the very first, you had your agenda, from the moment you came here."

"Agenda? *Agenda?*"

"I'll make note of the fact that your hearing is unaffected."

She gasped, and without thinking, reached down, scooped up the last stone where it had fallen and hurled it at his head. He dodged it easily. "All the *agenda* on earth couldn't help the fact that you're a spineless incompetent, Thomas! Just add this failure to your long list, I should have known better! You never felt the energies building, you couldn't even keep yourself under control! You manipulated me into helping you with this grand scheme, and you're just a rank amateur, a know-nothing, fiddling around and wasting my time, you, you *cowan!*"

He flinched, his mouth twisting, but recovered almost immediately. "And if you wasted two years of your life on a worthless scheme, what does that make you? You're the one who said you thought the plan was a good one and would work! You swore to me that we would succeed. I trusted you!"

"I *never* promised you a *thing,* Thomas! This working was your creation!"

"You did! You lied to me to keep me from doubting you! You withheld information from me, you did it deliberately!"

"I did not, what information?"

He swept his arm back in a violent arc. "You never told me about the leaves, the flowers! You never told me what that alchemist said!"

Suddenly her rage was replaced by icy dread. "Wha—how do you know about that?"

Thomas raised his chin, his face wearing an ugly smirk. "If you can't figure it out, I'm not about to enlighten you. You're the oblivious one, the world could come crashing down around your ears and you wouldn't notice. You can't even tell when some puppy-eyed Sapphist has an open crush on you, my god, you're the last person in town who didn't know—and you never noticed the leaves until someone took you by the hand and pointed them out. So who are you calling an amateur?"

"How did you know about that? Were you *eavesdropping* on me and Gregory?"

"As if I'd be interested. You, my dear, have a very big mouth. You have a thing or two to learn about discretion."

"So, am I indiscreet or am I withholding information?"

"You don't know when to do one and when the other."

"As opposed to you, who wouldn't tell me *anything* I needed to know—"

"God Almighty, not that again. I'm so tired of listening to your nagging, Diana, you're a scolding fishwife. No wonder your husband divorced you. Women like you always end up alone."

"Oh, is this domestic advice, coming from the ruthless rake who got himself run out of England?"

"Tell me again where your alchemist lover is now?"

"Tell me again how many magical workings you've blown now? This is what, the eighth, isn't it? You didn't tell me *that* before we started!"

"You knew what you were getting into."

"Maybe not, seeing as I'm so *oblivious*—"

"You are! I should never have trusted you."

"You never *did* trust me, Thomas, that's the problem. You were just using me, all along—you *said* so, remember? Rake, lawyer, *vampire*—you're a user on every possible level, people mean *nothing* to you! No wonder Levoissier sent me to you, you're just *like* him, he must be busting a gut right now..."

By this time, they both were staggering under the brutally accurate darts they'd aimed at each other. Like a bull in the arena with his shoulders full of picks, they were bloodied and weakening. Just as the bull cannot conceptualize his situation or the thousands of spectators cheering his imminent death, neither Diana nor Thomas had begun to understand the magnitude of what had just happened.

Diana's words trailed off, and Thomas had no retort. As they stood staring balefully at each other, Diana felt something shift for a moment. Suddenly, the entire scene took on a sheen of complete artifice. She had the sensation that she was standing on a stage, reciting words from a poorly written, histrionic melodrama while surrounded by painted canvas and plywood. The burning sun was an arc light, casting a spot on her and Thomas, its glare hiding onlookers who watched eagerly from beyond the visible set. She wasn't standing on the floor of this stage, but on the ceiling, or watching it in a fun-house mirror, or from the inside out. For a moment, she was overwhelmed with utter confusion. *What's happened? What am I doing? Why are Thomas and I yelling at each other?* She could see Thomas' face fallen into the same blank look of complete bewilderment that she felt. Then there was a loud snapping sound, and the entire sensation was gone. She didn't even remember it. The only thought in her mind was that Thomas had failed her, and she hated him with every fiber of her being. His expression was hard and cold.

"You'd better leave now," he said, and his tone was edged with menace.

"Not without my clothes and gear. I'm going in there, Thomas, like it or not. If you won't open the door, I'll climb through the window."

"No, you won't. I'll get them for you. Believe me, I don't want so much as a bobby pin of yours in my house."

"If you touch a thread of my clothes, I'll burn them."

"Go ahead. Burn them. That's your lookout. Do you think I care?"

"Let me—" but he was gone. This time he really did dematerialize.

She stood rigidly on the spot, her fists clenched at her sides. It seemed that every muscle in her body was hard and locked. Her stomach was roiling so much, she thought she'd never want to eat again—never had the expression "tied in knots" seemed so apt. The late afternoon peacefulness, filled with crickets chirping from the overgrown fields, was almost unbearable. She'd have preferred raucous city traffic or the noise of a construction site—or a battlefield, the bloodier the better. With each passing second, her anger expanded, but there was nothing to do but wait. She no longer had the wild energy to throw stones or beat on doors, and besides…it was so pointless. *I want you off my property,* Thomas said, but where would she go? She couldn't even remember what lay beyond the granite boulder by the road. All she could see when she tried to imagine it was a wall of blank white fog. Here there be dragons.

"Go around to the front," Thomas said, and she started—the back door hadn't opened. Maybe he'd nailed it shut, she thought. It wasn't like he needed a door. "Your car's there. I'll bring your things down that way." His voice was crisp, cool and businesslike. *You're fired. Nothing personal. Leave your keys on the desk, the security guard will escort you out.*

Wordlessly, she turned her back on him and walked around the west end of the house. By the time she got to the driveway, her suitcases, two bulging gunny sacks and a cardboard carton were already piled in front of the door, her purse perched on top like a cherry on a sundae. Thomas stood on the threshold and watched her as she stuffed the bags into the Chevy's trunk and put the box in the back seat.

"You'll need to get your books and equipment out of the other house. Once you leave here, you're not coming back."

She turned to glower at him. "I'll have to go around by the back road, then. I can't carry all that in one trip."

"Then do that. Don't try to move in and squat there, either. I'll know when you leave and I'll know if you come back, rest assured of that. I won't answer for the consequences if you do."

After a moment, she said flatly, "Ay-ay, sir," and gave him a mocking salute. The idea of trying to stay in either of Thomas' remaining houses hadn't even crossed her mind as a possibility. Without reacting to her sarcasm, Thomas stepped back inside the house and shut the door, shooting the bolt firmly. For a fleeting moment, Diana wondered what he was going to do now. Then she shrugged and started rummaging through her purse for her car keys. She took out her wallet and carefully went through it, even counting the change. As far as she could tell, nothing was missing.

She drove around via School Street and the private dirt road to the front of the small empty house where she'd set up her laboratory. The books and alchemical equipment almost filled the rest of the back seat, and she unceremoniously stuffed the rest of her possessions into the corners of the trunk. She'd bought a few pieces of second-hand furniture for the place, including the sagging armchair, but she didn't care about that. Thomas could do what he liked with it. She was glad now that she hadn't built a small athanor.

Once she was out on the road, her memory of the surrounding landscape returned, but her mind still felt blank. *What should I do now? Go home?* She felt a sudden, desperate longing to see Gregory, but the gods alone knew where he was now. The house in Manchester had probably been demolished at this point. She'd never been to Montréal, but the idea of driving there and wandering the streets until she spotted Gregory or Levoissier was suddenly the most attractive prospect she could imagine. But they might not even be there. Once Gregory had rendezvoused with Levoissier—and she had every confidence that he'd made it on time—they could have gone anywhere at all. Some intuition told her that chasing them would be useless.

Back to Boston, then? She couldn't face anyone in the Order after this. Maybe she could sneak into the city, bleach her hair with peroxide, put on an old housedress and apron and work as a cook in one of the Bread and Roses soup kitchens. At least then she'd be of use to someone. That seemed like the second most attractive prospect right now. Maybe she'd just wash her hands of magic. Maybe she didn't have any choice, for that matter. She wasn't sure she could do even the simplest spell now. She recoiled from the very notion.

These thoughts had occupied her mind for the drive back to Pepperell, and she turned onto Route 1 and started southeast toward Camden and the long trip home. There was no reason to stop for anything. As she passed the salon, she felt a brief pang—should she say good-bye to Moira? But she dismissed the thought instantly. How would she explain, what would she say? Moira was better off without her. Diana fidgeted as the traffic slowed, forcing her to pass the salon at a crawl. There were several cars parked in front of the building, which was odd, especially this late in the day. Moira should have closed hours ago. Even more peculiar, the door of the salon was standing open and there seemed to be a number of people inside. Diana wondered, idly, what was going on, but her curiosity vanished as soon as she was past the building.

But even as she focused ahead on the trip and her destination, a cloud of doubt rose in her mind. *Am I doing the right thing? Can I go back?* She had no idea why such an irrational thought occurred to her—why on earth could she not? What was stopping her? Couldn't she go anywhere she wanted? She certainly had enough money to travel to the ends of the earth. But she realized that she was driving more and more slowly as she approached the Camden town line, and she couldn't seem to force herself to press harder on the accelerator. The car behind her, a big lumpy Ford, was tailgating her impatiently.

As the sign for Camden came into view up ahead, Diana suddenly was clutched with panic. Her stomach turned to writhing worms of ice, she was shaking violently and she couldn't breathe. She slammed on the brake and heard tires squealing and a blare of horn behind her, but she couldn't look in the review mirror. Nothing hit her, anyway.

As she sat gasping for breath, white knuckles gripping the steering wheel, the Ford pulled around her and roared by, spraying gravel from its wheels. "Get off the road, ya stupid bitch," she heard the driver yell at her, but it barely registered. The Chevy had stalled, and after a few minutes she calmed down enough to start the engine. She was blocking the road, and it was a mystery why someone else hadn't pulled up behind her and honked. Indeed, the traffic did seem very light.

But she couldn't drive on. There was a disconnect between her intention and her muscles—she wanted to press her foot onto the gas pedal, but it wouldn't go down. Only when she finally decided to pull over onto the shoulder was she able to make the car move, and that was all she could do. The town line was about a hundred feet ahead of her. After sitting in the car for a few minutes, she put on the parking brake and got out, taking her purse, and started walking.

She was almost at the sign when she just stopped. There was no force field, no barrier, and no panic attack, this time—her feet simply stopped. She stood motionless, her eyes fixed ahead of her, willing herself as hard as she could to put one foot before the other and keep walking. But she was fixed as firmly to the earth as one of the trees rustling softly in the breeze off the water. She wanted to take another step, but her legs simply would not obey.

She stood there for nearly half an hour, as her shadow lengthened ahead of her and cars passed slowly in both directions. The wind had shifted to the northeast, and she kept getting whiffs of an unpleasant smell, like burning rubber and hot oil. At last she turned around and began to walk back to the Chevy, unable to believe that this could really be happening. She'd had dreams in which she tried to run and couldn't move her feet, but she'd never experienced such a thing in real life. *What's the matter with me? Am I trapped here? What if I tried to go to Bangor, to Belfast, to get on the ferry to Islesboro?* The growing suspicion that she was imprisoned here forever, in the same town with Thomas, filled her with cold horror. One day ago, she'd wanted nothing more than to spend eternity with Thomas, but now... *If that's the outcome of all this, then I've damned myself to hell.*

She'd just reached her car when a dark blue sedan coming from Pepperell passed her slowly and pulled over. The driver, a long-faced man with deep lines around his mouth, craned his head out of his window. "Are you okay, Miss? Trouble with the car?"

She hesitated for a moment, a flicker of hope kindling. *I can only take help from strangers, that's what he said*...She'd never seen this man or his car before, and concluded that he was passing through town from somewhere else. "Yes, it just—silly thing, it just died on me, and I've got an appointment in Camden. It's so far to walk..." She was relieved that he didn't jump out of his car, go raise the Chevy's hood and start tinkering with the engine, which about three quarters of the men in Pepperell would have done.

"Can I give you a lift?"

Something in her mind let off a klaxon of warning, but she ignored it. "Yes, please! That would be so kind of you..."

"Hop in."

She hurried over to the passenger's side and got into the car. Even as she shut the door, uncomfortable prickling sensations were needling her skin. When the man pulled back onto the road, her stomach lurched. She gripped the door handle, hyperventilating, as the car's speed increased. The sign came closer... closer...and Diana suddenly was overwhelmed with stark terror. She couldn't go further, she couldn't, she would die, crushed flat, rent limb from limb...*here there be dragons*...with the same blind, thoughtless reflex that would have made her jerk her hand away from a roaring flame, she opened the door of the moving car and dove out. She hit the ground with a bone-rattling jolt and rolled down into the gulley by the road, unable to stop her momentum as stones and brush scraped skin from her face and hands and tore her clothes. She heard the sedan screech to a halt and the driver's door slam.

"What the *hell?*" she heard the man say from the road above her, but he didn't try to scramble down into the gulley to help her up. He seemed afraid of her, and small wonder. Who knew what a crazy lady might do?

She was stunned from the impact of her body against the shoulder of the road and her pell-mell tumble into the gulley, but she struggled to collect herself, for his benefit. At least no bones seemed to be broken, for which she knew she was very lucky. "I'm sorry...I'm sorry..." she repeated helplessly.

"You jumped out of the car!"

"I know, I...look, you better just go on. Thanks for your help..." She managed to clamber to her feet, although she was shaking so hard, she couldn't stand up straight. She couldn't meet the man's eyes. Self interest trumped gallantry, and he adjusted his hat and turned away, muttering, "Jesus God Almighty."

After he was gone, Diana sank down to a crouch in the gulley, heedless of the biting insects and the stink of stagnant water and scattered garbage. Despair overcame her. *At least I can guess what will happen if I get on the ferry*, she thought. Of course, she could try to travel north, or west, but she didn't expect that she would be allowed to go in one direction and not another. Was this because of the spell backfiring, or would it have happened anyway? She gradually became aware of just how much her entire body hurt. She could see bruises on her arms, and she knew that by tomorrow she'd be black and blue from head to foot. Her clothes were grimy and covered in the dust and particles left from the Schuller house, and her reckless dive from the car had left her slacks and shirt with mud stains and rips. Her hair was snarled and full of dirt, and she could only imagine what her face looked like. She needed a place to clean up and rest, but where? It was the peak of the tourist season, she'd be lucky to find a vacant hotel room, cottage or house within a hundred miles. Out loud, she said, *"Why,* Mother Goddess? Why can't I leave? It's finished, it's *over!"*

Very clearly, and sounding very close, a voice said, "No, it's not. It's just beginning."

With a gasp, Diana stood up, looking around frantically, but there was not a soul in sight. "What does *that* mean?" she said, her voice shrill. "How can it not be over? What more could happen?" But the voice, its ageless tenor tones neither masculine nor feminine, did not speak again.

Diana finally drove back to Pepperell, because there was nothing else to do. She'd thought she would at least ask at the Holliston House Inn, perhaps offer to pay extra. Maybe the Wilkinsons would be able to make room for her somehow, with the credits she'd racked up voting against the name change that spring. But before she reached the Inn on the north side of the wharf, she passed Pepperell's bar, and abruptly she pulled into a parking space by the curb. Before she could walk across the street, she had to wait for a fire engine to trundle by, its slow speed and lack of siren indicating that it was returning from an emergency call rather than responding to one. She was startled to see that the fire engine was from Belfast, and wondered why it had been needed so far away.

As was typical at this time of day, the small watering hole was fairly full. Many of Pepperell's locals stopped off here on their way home from work. Diana paused inside the doorway, trying to interpret the strange atmosphere in the room. Not nearly as many faces looked up when she walked in as usual, and those that did displayed no curiosity about her appearance. There was a grim miasma in the air, which matched Diana's own mood but struck her as extremely ominous. No one here would be feeling desolated on her account, she was sure.

She pulled herself up onto one of the high bar stools. Marty, the bartender, did a second take when he glanced at her but kept his expression carefully neutral. "Ya been in some kinda accident, Miss Chilton?"

"Uh...yeah, something like that."

He shook his head somberly. "It's been one helluva day. What'll it be?"

His reply struck Diana as odd even through her preoccupied state of mind, but she wasn't going to puzzle it out dry. Usually she had some kind of cocktail, but today that wouldn't cut it.

"Scotch. A double, straight up."

When Marty set the glass in front of her, she picked it up and sniffed. The aroma made her nose wrinkle. Scotch tasted like candied rubbing alcohol, as far as she was concerned, but she didn't want it for the taste. She took a gulp of the intensely sweet liquid and closed her eyes, feeling her throat, then her stomach burning. As heat began to radiate outwards through her body, she tossed the rest of the glass back in one swallow. She felt like she'd just drunk liquid fire, and her eyes were watering, but it was wonderful. She put the glass down and tapped her finger on the bar next to it. "Another one, please."

"Take it easy, sister," said the man sitting next to her, but Marty just shrugged.

"I'll be pouring a lot of these tonight," he said resignedly as he put a second glass in front of Diana.

Diana paused, the glass halfway to her lips. A feeling of horrible premonition was creeping over her, and she heard herself say, without wanting to, "Why? What's happened?"

"You don't *know?*" asked the man next to her. Diana turned slowly and looked at him. She recognized him now—he was one of Pepperell's volunteer firemen. All along the bar behind him faces turned toward her, with the same haunted, empty look in their eyes that she had seen in some of the war veterans who came to Bread and Roses.

"I...don't," she said, forcing the words out, because she didn't want to know, but had to. The Scotch trembled in the glass she held.

"Yeah, well, looks like you had a few problems of your own," the fireman said, his eyes taking in Diana's disheveled clothes and hair. "Although I don't know where you coulda been, not to hear that place go up. Or see it, the smoke went up for a mile."

"Saw it from Brooklin, 'cross the Bay," someone at the end of the bar said.

"Place...go up? What place? Tell me! What place do you mean?"

"Why sister, that filling station t'other side of Camden blew up. Biggest ball of fire since Heero-sheema."

"Filling station? You mean the Texaco station, the Crothers station?"

"Ayeh, that's the one. Took out the station, the yard, and half the road, and that poor kid who worked the place went with it."

Diana made a hoarse sound. The glass thumped to the floor, but no one seemed to notice. "Kid...the teenager, the young kid?"

"No, it was the son, the one who ran the place, Brent I think his name was. Good fella, did a damn good job, smart as a whip. Don't know what his folks'll do now, he supported the whole clan of 'em."

"It's a damn shame, him about to get married and all," Marty said. "Poor little girl he was engaged to just about had a breakdown, my missus has been with her all day, up at that salon where she works—hey, hey, hey! Catch her, Lee—" The firefighter caught Diana just as she was about to slip off the bar stool onto the floor. She was only dimly aware of him through the sea of glittering white that was smothering her. To her mind had come the memory of the ring of power expanding from the Schuller house and the overwhelming impulse she'd felt to cry out a warning.

"I should have said something...I should have warned him..."

"Warned him? Sister, there was nothing you could have done." The fireman, seeming to welcome an opportunity to help someone not yet beyond all aid, was ushering her to a chair at one of the tables near the wall. "Crothers kept that place tight and clean as a Navy gunboat. No one knows what coulda happened. They're talkin' gas spill and cigarette, but it don't make any sense. Helluva thing. Helluva thing. You know him?"

She could only nod, her throat constricted past speech.

"I'm sorry. No easy way to break this kinda news. Maybe you should have some black coffee."

"Okay," she whispered. "But I want another Scotch with it."

She fumbled for her purse, but stopped when the fireman said, "It's on me."

She didn't cry. The shock was too enormous for that, like an injury so severe that the victim feels no pain because the very nerves are gone. She drank the coffee, obediently, like a child told to finish his milk, and then sat nursing her Scotch. She wanted the whole bottle, she wanted to drink herself senseless, she wanted to drink until she was violently, cathartically sick, but she couldn't do that here. Later on, she knew, she would do all of those things, and cry herself to exhaustion. But now, there was nothing left of her emotions but a black, bitterly cold void.

She must have sat there for hours, because it became completely dark outside the front windows. People came into the bar, stayed a time, left again. Diana finished her Scotch, finally, and ordered a third double. No one spoke to her, perhaps respecting her obvious grief. She caught snatches of conversation about the explosion, the resulting traffic jam earlier on Route 1, and how Carole was "holding up," but she found the words unbearable and tried not to listen. She'd have left, but she had nowhere to go. When a familiar voice suddenly cut through her haze of shock and alcohol, it was like sunlight pouring into a dank cellar.

"Oh, my god, what happened to you?" Moira collapsed into the chair opposite Diana's at the table.

Diana thought she had never been so glad to see anyone in her life. Finally her eyes filled with tears, but from sheer relief. "It's a long story," she said, smiling wanly. "I guess it was nothing compared to your day."

"Oh, god..." Moira buried her face in her hands. "Awful. Just awful. I take it you've heard?"

Diana nodded. "It's just...horrible. Poor Brent," she whispered. After a moment she said, "How's Carole?"

"Under sedation." Moira braced her elbows on the table to light a cigarette. "All afternoon, she's been..." She shook her head. "You know, in the old days they used to have a word, 'distracted,' for people in that state. Until today, I didn't really understand what it meant."

Diana just nodded. She knew exactly what Moira was talking about—she'd seen too much of it during the war. "Will she be all right?"

Moira leaned back and exhaled as though it took her last ounce of strength to do so. "I don't know."

"I guess you need a drink," Diana said, starting to get up to go to the bar, but paused when Moira gestured at her.

"You're right, I do, but that's not why I came in here. Actually, I was looking for you."

Diana felt a sudden deep qualm. "Me? Why?"

Moira took a long drag on her cigarette and sat studying Diana somberly as she exhaled. "I guess it can wait, all things considered. Can you get me a martini, hon?" Disquieted, Diana went to the bar for the order.

By the time Moira finished her drink, her lids were sagging and she appeared at risk of falling asleep at the table. "I'm sorry, kiddo, I've got to get home."

"No apologies needed, Moira. Come on. If I sit here any longer, Marty is going to charge me rent."

They left the bar, and Diana noticed that Moira was having trouble walking in a straight line. "I better give you a ride home, Moira."

"Oh, hon, I'll be *fine*."

"I'm serious. You're not going to make it. My car's right across the street." Moira didn't argue further, but followed Diana docilely. Diana realized, as they approached the Chevy, that she had forgotten that it now contained everything she owned. Before she could say anything, Moira had opened the passenger's side door and stared at the back seat piled high with books and boxes.

"Oh...my...god. What happened?"

Diana shrugged. "I left."

"You left or he kicked you out?"

"He kicked me out and I couldn't leave fast enough."

Moira swayed slightly, then fixed Diana with a hard stare, as if taking in the state of her clothing and hair for the first time. "He beat you?"

Diana wasn't sure how to answer this, and at her hesitation, Moira almost hissed.

"That son of a bitch."

"No, Moira, it...it wasn't like that. It's a very long story, and now...now isn't the time."

"You're leaving? You're not driving back to Boston tonight, are you?"

"I'm not driving back to Boston at all, at least not right away."

Moira's shoulders relaxed slightly. "Well...where are you going?"

Diana evaded her eyes. She'd lingered too long in the bar, and had missed her window to negotiate with the Wilkinsons or anyplace else within Pepperell's boundaries. "I...I haven't made any plans. I mean, it's still early..."

"Stay with me," Moira said flatly.

"Oh, Moira, I couldn't impose on you, not at a time like this—"

"A time like this is just when I'd rather not be alone. Come on, kiddo. I've got plenty of space, and what are friends for?"

"Well, I..."

"You got any better ideas?"

Diana shrugged weakly. "Camden Hills State Park?"

"They're full up, just like everyplace else."

Diana sighed. "Thanks, Moira," she said in a small voice. They both got into the car finally, and Diana fished in her purse for her keys.

"Weren't you even going to ask?" Moira said after a moment, sounding a bit hurt.

"Oh, Moira, please don't take it personally. I just didn't think, I thought I might just leave town, but I can't, and..." she was silent for a moment, staring unseeing at the quiet street. "It's just been...a helluva day."

ঈ 17 ৪

Brent's funeral was held on the Summer Solstice, a fact Diana was sure no one else appreciated the way she did. She wondered how they'd found enough of him to bury. There had been no visiting hours or wake, although the family had chosen a beautiful and costly casket. Services were held at the Long Funeral Home in Camden and then at the graveside in Mount View Cemetery. Diana had thought she wouldn't be able to attend. But now that she knew about the explosion, the boundaries of her new prison had expanded slightly. She could go as far as Camden center, or Lincolnville Beach in the other direction, but no further.

She wore a hat with a heavy veil, and sunglasses, and sat in the very last row of chairs in the funeral home chapel, hoping that Carole wouldn't spot her and make a scene. She had written a note to Brent's family and sent flowers, but doing so filled her with a crushing sense of hypocrisy and gall. *How dare a murderer offer condolences to the unsuspecting next of kin,* she thought bleakly. But her veil and sunglasses weren't merely a disguise. This was the first time since she'd arrived at Moira's apartment that she'd finally been able to stop crying.

That first night, as soon as she helped Moira make up the extra bedroom, she'd climbed under the mothball scented blankets, rolled up into a ball, and let herself go. She'd stayed that way for the next two days, refusing so much as coffee, not even wanting a bath or aspirin for her scores of scrapes, bruises and sore muscles. "Come on, honey, you've got to keep your strength up," Moira would say anxiously as she coaxed Diana to get up and have a meal, but Diana couldn't even think about eating. She only staggered into the bathroom a few times for two reasons, and one of them was to throw up. She couldn't shake the illusion that all of her internal organs had been removed, shuffled, and replaced aiming in the wrong directions.

When she dozed off, she dreamed about that, when she wasn't jolting awake from nightmares about explosions, or finding Gregory's lifeless body somewhere. That was the agonizing uncertainty that tore at her, waking and sleeping: who else had been impacted by the spell's violent failure? Who else had died? Was

Brent dead only because he'd been atop several thousand gallons of gasoline, or would the magic seek out the person and work through whatever it found? The other people, magical and cowan, who had been involved with their working—Gregory, Maurice, Conor—what had happened to them? Were they all dead? Even if she'd had a way to investigate, she couldn't bear to try.

Before Moira got home from work the day before the funeral, Diana crawled out of her cocoon, feeling, if not better, at least different. Enough of her self-respect was returning for her to react with dismay at her reflection in the bathroom mirror, and to feel chagrinned at how ungraciously she was reciprocating Moira's generosity. She bathed and changed clothes and put herself in order, very carefully because her entire body was now a mass of fully developed black and purple bruises, including an impressive shiner on her left eye that she hadn't even realized she'd incurred. She bustled around in Moira's kitchen, washing up dishes and rummaging through the refrigerator, determined to have supper on the table when Moira got home, and to eat something herself. She still didn't have a shred of appetite, but at least the food would stay down. Fortunately, the meal was almost ready before she discovered Moira's modest stock of liquor while she hunted for a serving dish.

She hadn't been fully sober since.

Thomas attended the funeral. He was dressed in a black suit that was several years old, but fit him like a glove and appeared almost new. He'd coiled his long hair into a tight knot and wore a natty hat and dark glasses, and he looked almost contemporary, if a little bit like one of the undertakers. Diana suspected that most of the funeral guests had no idea who he was. He never looked at her, not so much as a glance, although she knew he was aware of her presence. After the service was over, he did what Diana hadn't dared, and went through the receiving line offering his condolences to the Crothers and to Carole. Carole was veiled and couldn't stand without her father's arm tightly around her shoulders, and Moira was standing with her—apparently Carole had asked for her.

When Thomas had run the gantlet without causing havoc, Diana decided to risk it herself. She was the last guest in the line. She shook the hands of Brent's family, but couldn't meet their eyes. His cousin was white-faced and tight-lipped, his sisters awash in ceaseless tears. Mr. Crothers, Sr. was only slightly more drunk than Diana herself, smiling and nodding at each sympathetic murmur, while his wife clung to Diana's hand with her own limp, shaking fingers as though she forgot that she was supposed to let go. Carole didn't seem to recognize Diana, to her relief. Her pupils were enormously dilated from the medications she'd been given and Diana wondered if she even knew where she was.

The graveside ceremony was mercifully short, but at its conclusion, the casket was lowered and each guest stepped up to toss a clod of earth into the grave. Of all funeral customs, Diana had always found this one the most disheartening, but she supposed the finality of it was therapeutic in a way. The dead were dead, never to return, and there was no point in nurturing any hopes to the contrary.

At least, she certainly prayed this was true. Her nightmares had also brought back to her the long-ago conversation she'd had with Brent about whether he could turn as a result of Thomas' drinking. She hadn't believed so then, and she was almost certain there was no possibility of that happening now, but...what if she was wrong? She couldn't ask Thomas. And what if he didn't really know? Or the rules changed? *...I can never forget that the Good People are renowned for their tricks...*

There were far more mourners at the services than Diana had expected. Brent had been a well-known and popular figure in Camden. This made it easy for her to stay inconspicuous. As the crowd dispersed from the cemetery, Diana quietly slipped a distance away, among the trees and low shrubs, waiting until everyone else had left. Thomas was speaking to the priest, and Diana noticed that Catherine Jorgens was standing almost next to him, waiting with a proprietary attitude, like she belonged there. When Thomas turned to leave, he put his arm out and Catherine gave her shoulders a little flounce as she took it. *Well, when did this happen?* Diana thought sourly. She never did think to ask Thomas about Catherine—maybe he'd been seeing her long before now. Catherine, Diana suspected, wouldn't wear black if she was paid to, and might as well have had "look at me, I'm an artist" spray-painted on the back of her deep purple flamenco skirt. Her dark blue ruffled blouse had gold accents and Diana guessed that she'd designed it herself. She noted, with narrowed eyes, that it had a high tight collar, creating an almost Edwardian look and sufficient to cover any blemishes that might be marring her neck. But now that Diana thought about it, she'd never seen Catherine without a ruffled collar or flowing scarf or something of the sort.

"Quite a picture, eh?" Moira said, and Diana jumped.

"Moira, quit sneaking up on me like that, gods!"

"Sneaking up? Honey, these days a brass band could sneak up on you. You ready to go?"

"Yeah. I just need to stop at the liquor store first."

"No, you don't." Moira had to hurry to keep up with Diana's purposeful stride.

"I'm drinking you out of house and home. I can buy my own booze."

"Diana—you've got to stop this. It doesn't solve anything."

"Who said it did? It's a hell of a lot better than aspirin for all these bruises, though, that's for sure."

"It's a hell of way to fall down and get more bruises. Honey, you're not a wild kid anymore, you're old enough to know better. Come on..."

Diana scowled at her. "Aren't you a square, though. Tell you what, I'll give up booze when you give up cigarettes, how about that?"

"That's apples and oranges, kiddo. They don't arrest you for driving while smoking."

Diana shrugged. "I'll just be a few minutes, for pete's sake, Moira."

"Well, I'm not waiting for you. I'll go home without you, then."

"You can't, we came in my car." That silenced Moira, who didn't speak again for some time.

Out of deference to her friend, Diana tried not to drink too much in the house, or when Moira was present. But each day while Moira was at work, Diana would pour a dollop of gin into her morning orange juice and keep a glass by her hand as she stumbled through cleaning the house or cooking dinner. Moira finally threatened to pour the liquor down the sink, but retreated into stiff silence when Diana told her she sounded exactly like a husband. After that, however, Diana began spending her evenings at the bar. She drank until she could barely stand, drank until Marty cut her off and pushed her out of the door, drank until she couldn't think, couldn't feel, and couldn't remember, drank until she ignominiously vomited in the alley next to the building, and it wasn't enough. Worse still, her body began to get acclimated to the alcohol, so the effects were lessening no matter how much she drank.

She knew that she was only putting more of a burden on Moira, who was now covering the salon solo again. The only news Moira could get from Carole's family was that the girl remained "under a doctor's care," a euphemism understood by everyone to mean, "heavily tranquilized." The dark circles that had been fading under Moira's eyes returned with a vengeance, and she was falling into bed after dinner and sleeping for ten to twelve hour stretches. Business was good, but that seemed like a mixed blessing, under the circumstances.

About a week after the funeral, Diana was brushing her teeth in the bathroom and suddenly everything seemed to shift. She saw herself in the mirror with perfect clarity: her eyes red-rimmed, her skin blotchy, her cheeks sunken, her face looking ten years older than her age. Toothbrush forgotten, she stared in gape-mouthed shock. *What happened to me? Where am I? Where's Thomas?* It seemed that this had struck once before, this weird feeling that she was acting out some perverse and twisted role on a papier-mâché stage, but she couldn't remember when. As she blinked at her reflection in confusion, there was a loud snapping noise, and a smell of ozone in her nostrils, and her bewilderment was forgotten. *Thomas? Why am I thinking about him, I hate his guts!*

But after that, she tried to cut down on the drinking, at least during the day. It was much harder after the sun went down. Making her resolve even more challenging was the apparent budding romance between the Hermit of Pepperell Hills and the town's newest artist-in-residence, Catherine Jorgens. It, along with Diana's sudden departure from the Pepperell Hills property covered in bruises, was the talk of a shaken town desperately grateful for something juicy to gossip about. Moira tactfully bowdlerized any stories she mentioned hearing, but Diana overheard the unabridged versions every time she went out—in the bar, Thornton's grocery, even on the street, it was unavoidable. The looks she got ranged from smirks to sympathy, as Catherine's affectations fooled no one… except, it seemed, Thomas, who had never before been such a visible presence in town. The couple showed up nightly at eateries like the Lobster Pound or the Schooner, and frequently attended performances at the open-air amphitheatre in Camden. As far as Diana could tell, they never ventured further afield together, and Diana was fiercely curious as to whether Thomas had found that he, too, was prohibited from passing the boundaries of the middle West Bay area. When she saw them together, which she tried to avoid doing, even her cynical eyes noted that all the overt displays of affection came from Catherine, who practically preened in Thomas' presence. Her outfits grew gaudier and more "arty" by the day and she was one of Moira's best customers.

At the end of the Fourth of July holiday week, Diana was surprised to find Moira already home when she returned from getting groceries at about 4:00 p.m. A good proportion of Moira's current business consisted of summer people and tourists, and it was the height of the season. The traffic on Route 1 was brutal—locals went considerably out of their way to avoid it altogether. Moira was sitting at the kitchen table in a cloud of smoke, gazing into space with an expression so dismal, Diana felt a pang of alarm. She didn't look up when Diana came in.

"Hey, Moira—is everything okay? How come you're home?"

Moira gave her a wan smile. "Had a cancellation, kiddo, that's all."

"What, you didn't want to wait for walk-ins? You told me once that—" she stopped when Moira shook her head.

"I'm pretty beat, hon. I needed some time off more than a few bucks."

"Okay..." Frowning, Diana concentrated on putting away the groceries. She needed to start dinner, but Moira's dark mood disturbed her. She sensed that Moira needed to talk to her about something and didn't know how to broach the discussion. She stuffed the empty paper bags into the bag drawer and sat down at the table opposite her friend. "What's happened?" she asked flatly.

"Oh..." Moira studied the end of her cigarette, which was shaking. Her hands shook all the time now, Diana had noticed, some days worse than others. She was afraid to ask Moira about it. "Carole's in the hospital. Up in Bangor."

"The hospital? Why?"

"Well, apparently...apparently, she tried to hang herself a couple of days ago."

Diana sat frozen, her mouth open. "Mother Goddess..." she whispered after a moment. "*Why?* And how could she do something like that? I thought she was being sedated."

"They were trying to wean her off the stuff, I guess. She couldn't start to get back to a normal life when she was all doped up like that, could she?"

"It's way too soon, Moira, for someone in her condition..."

"I think money may have had something to do with it, too," Moira said bitterly. "She's at the state hospital right now because her folks can't afford a private sanitarium." Diana sat back in her chair with an anguished sigh. Moira went on, "And I'm sitting here kicking myself because she won't be coming back, and I don't know what I'll do without her. Aren't I a selfish bitch, though?"

"Moira, don't be silly! You're a saint, gods, look what you put up with from *me*."

Moira smiled wryly. "The things we do for love," she said lightly, and Diana felt her cheeks get hot.

"Yes, well...love's a mixed bag when it makes you attempt suicide because you can't live without your lover."

Moira's mouth twisted, as if she was choking back a sob. "As far as that goes...it's a bit more complicated than that, I guess."

"What do you mean?"

Moira seemed reluctant to continue. "Carole...talked to me a lot, you know," she said after a moment.

"So I gathered," Diana said uneasily.

"From what I hear, she wanted to talk to me last weekend, but her family wouldn't allow it."

"Why not? You were her mentor, her employer!"

"Well..." Moira bit her lip and looked up at Diana from under her brows. "Because of you, mostly. Because you're here now, and...well, your Thomas and Miss Jorgens aren't the only names that are being batted around in the local gossip. I don't think Carole knows, but her family sure knew how she feels about you."

"Oh." Diana fought back a sudden impulse to get up from her chair and go pull down the kitchen window shades.

"She left a note for me, but her parents destroyed it. I don't know if they read it first or not."

Diana could only shake her head in helpless frustration. "So...you don't really know why Carole's motives were more complicated than grief over Brent? That's just what you think?"

"Oh, I know, kiddo. That part's clear as glass. She blames herself for Brent's death. She thinks that it's all her fault. She said that day, if it hadn't been for her, he'd still be alive. That's why she'll never get over it."

Diana stared at Moira open-mouthed, too aghast to speak for a moment. "But that...that's...Mother Goddess, Moira. That's *insane!* How can she possibly think that?"

"I have to admit, it's hard to argue with her case, that is, if what she's saying is true. And this didn't just come up on the day of the explosion. I'd heard about it before."

"Heard about what?"

Moira waved her hands vaguely. "There was...there was some kind of warning. Or threat, something like that."

The sweltering, stuffy room suddenly felt like an icebox. Diana had to swallow hard before she could ask, "When?"

"A few weeks before it happened. Carole told me about it. He got some kind of letter—strange looking thing, according to Carole. Old fashioned parchment paper, funny handwriting. I didn't tell Carole this, but the first thing I thought of was your Thomas, and the stories you told me about that group of yours. The handwriting sounded a bit like his, you know how he writes, looks like the Declaration of Independence or something—"

"Yes, yes, I know." Just talking about Thomas raised Diana's irritation to dangerous levels. "But you don't think *he* sent this letter."

"Kiddo, I have no idea. I didn't see it. But the letter told Brent to stay away from his station for a week before and a week after the 21st of June." She tapped her cigarette into the ashtray, not looking at Diana. "Well, you can imagine—losing that kind of business, right when the season's getting into full gear."

Diana's mouth had gone dry. "He'd never do it," she whispered despairingly.

"Not so fast. He was going to."

"What?"

"According to Carole, he took this letter like absolute gospel. He was going to close the station for two weeks and leave town. He was dead serious about it."

"Then, why—"

"Carole talked him out of it."

"No," Diana said softly. She squeezed her eyes shut. 'Oh, no..."

"Her family's religious as all get-out, and Carole's a good church-going girl. She was very proud of herself when she told me about it. She told Brent that he was just being fooled by the devil, and she made him promise that he'd burn the letter and ignore everything it said. He wanted to talk to you about it, and she wouldn't let him. She made him swear on the Bible, she said, not to say a word. That's why he was there that day, and not his cousin. He promised Carole he would be."

Diana made a strangled sound, her hands pressed over her mouth.

"Then, the day it all happened, she—"

"Stop." Diana hadn't meant to shout, but she couldn't bear to hear another word. She stood up so sharply that her chair almost tipped over, and walked blindly across the room until she collided with the kitchen counter. *"That's why Gregory took down his athanor. That's* why Maurice and Conor moved to Providence. That's why...Mother Goddess...he *knew..."*

"You mean Thomas?"

"No!" Diana turned around sharply. "This letter, it came from Canada?"

"I don't know. The postmark was in French, she said."

"Montréal."

"Coulda been. What gives here? What do you know about this?"

Diana leaned back against the cabinet, her hands white-knuckled where they gripped the edges of the linoleum countertop. "She can't blame herself. She just can't. It's not her fault, not one single particle of it. Mother of all the gods..."

"How can you be so sure? I can see her point, at least—"

"No! There is no point!"

"Well, sorry, hon—"

"It's not her fault, it's *mine!* Mine and Thomas', Brent is dead because of *us!*

It's nobody's fault but ours!"

Moira stared open mouthed as Diana walked back to her chair and dropped into it, burying her face in her hands. "How do you figure?" she finally asked cautiously. Her cigarette had burned almost down to her fingers, and she sucked in a breath and hastily stubbed the butt out in the ashtray. Diana didn't move or look up. "That...magic...thing you two were doing?"

Diana finally whispered, "Too many secrets..."

"Never a good thing." She waited, as Diana bowed her shoulders, shuddering. "What happened to you that day, Diana?"

"I can't..."

"I think you should. Because one thing's for sure, it's still hitting you like a ton of bricks. You can either talk about it, or you can drink yourself to death, but it's going to be one or the other, the way you're going." Her voice softened. "Come on, hon. Don't you know yet you can trust me? Whatever you tell me, goes with me to my grave. And you've already told me plenty." Moira watched as Diana's hands slowly fell to her lap, but her head remained bowed. "Don't make me read it in a note."

Diana looked up sharply. "I'm not suicidal, Moira."

"Yeah? You couldn't prove it by me. Sure, maybe you haven't slit your wrists or anything, but I wouldn't leave you alone with a bottle of pills. There's more than one kind of suicide. How do you think my uncle went?"

"The Freemason?" Moira nodded solemnly, and Diana's shoulders sagged.

"The death certificate said cirrhosis, but we all knew."

Diana looked away, both chilled and frustrated that Moira didn't understand. "That's not the way it is, Moira, it's—I just feel...horrible. All...wrong inside. Like a skein of wool that's been played with by a cat, it feels like a mass of tangles, all snarled and knotted, nothing where it should be. Nothing feels right, nothing tastes right..."

"Should you see a doctor?"

"It's not medical, Moira, it's something else entirely. Gods...I want to tell you, I swear. I want to tell someone, so much. But I wouldn't even know where to start."

Moira pursed her lips thoughtfully and reached for the pack of cigarettes on the table. "Well, I can think of one place," she said, almost idly, as she struck a wooden match and braced her elbows on the tabletop to light the cigarette. When she finally succeeded, she blew out a gust of smoke and leaned back in her chair. "Why don't you start by telling me about the vampires. Oh, now don't give me *that* look," she added as Diana's jaw dropped. "Brent told Carole, who told me—"

"And who else?"

"No one else, as far as I know. She promised Brent she wouldn't talk about it, and she only told me after he was dead. She said no one else would believe her. Could be another reason why she's up at the state hospital now, though."

Diana pondered this darkly. "All right," she finally said. "You promise not to laugh?"

Moira raised her right hand, first three fingers up. "Scout's honor."

Diana took a deep breath. "Then I'll tell you everything."

18

As the weeks crawled by, Diana resigned herself to her situation. When Moira said that she was going to have to stop offering manicures at the salon because her hands were too unsteady to apply nail polish, Diana offered to take over the job. Manicures were a popular and lucrative segment of the business, and even if she could barely make a straight part in her own hair, she felt that she could handle tiny paint brushes and files. It proved trickier than she would have believed, to a humbling degree, but Moira was a patient teacher.

The privileged information they shared forged a unique bond between the two women. Diana had never felt quite the same way about anyone. Moira became part sister, part co-conspirator, as they both kept an eye and ear on Thomas and reported back to each other on what they'd heard from town gossip or rumor. Their relationship didn't remain on a fraternal basis, however—Diana no longer slept in the spare bedroom. She couldn't have called their affair torrid or passionate—neither of them was physically up to the challenge, with Moira needing so much sleep and Diana still waking up several times every night in a cold sweat. But Diana found a comfort in their intimacy that she could never have considered with a man in her present state. Despite this, and Moira's words to Diana about secrets, Moira said nothing about her health, and Diana didn't ask. She no longer wanted to know.

The Crothers packed up and moved away, to Chicago, Diana heard from a salon client. They'd received enormous insurance settlements for the filling station and for Brent, double indemnity for accidental death, according to the rumors. No one had known about any insurance policies before the checks arrived by certified mail. Diana, remembering Thomas talking so confidentially to the priest at Brent's interment, had fairly good idea where the money had come from. For her own part, she quietly contacted an attorney who arranged to set up a fund for Carole's continued care at an expensive private sanitarium near Portland. Although information about Carole's condition was restricted, Diana deduced that she wouldn't be leaving the facility any time in the foreseeable future.

Neither resignation nor amends brought resolution, however. The nauseating sensation of being turned inside out only worsened with time, so that Diana often found herself unconsciously twisting or leaning her body in various awkward ways when she was trying to work or read. The nightmares became more frequent, but at the same time less specific. Over and over again, she awoke gasping, the only image in her mind that of the Bay emptied of water, as she had seen in her visions repeatedly a few months ago. She kept thinking about the voice she'd heard, or hallucinated, out on Route 1 the day everything blew up. Increasingly, she felt a looming sense of disaster, as though there was another shoe yet to drop, another tidal wave still to come. But what that could possibly consist of, or do to her, she shrank from imagining. She stayed sober during the salon's business hours, for Moira's sake. But there were still many nights when she couldn't stay away from the bottle or the bar, and once she started, she couldn't stop.

It was her assistance in the salon that led, in mid-September, to the encounter she'd been desperately avoiding for three months.

By that time, Diana had attained a sufficient level of competence that she often was left a generous tip, and new customers were mentioning that a friend had recommended the salon's manicurist. Only a handful of seasonal clients asked what had happened to her predecessor, although Diana and Moira fielded questions about Carole and how she was doing on a daily basis. But there was one client who forbore to test Diana's new skills. Catherine Jorgens came in at least weekly to get her hair done, but she acquired her pristine manicures someplace else. It was obviously an establishment that excelled in removing paint and art media, Diana said cattily to Moira, because there was never a trace of pigment, dust or clay on Catherine's perfectly tended hands. Moira had just snorted at this.

On this particular afternoon, Diana had taken a break to run some errands, all the appointments having been for hair styling only. As she walked past the alleyway by the salon and climbed the steps to the door, she was deeply immersed in the quarterly report from Bread and Roses that had been in the mail. When she opened the door, she stopped short. Sitting in a styling chair, her hair half rolled in curlers for a permanent wave, was Catherine Jorgens. Diana usually made herself scarce during Catherine's appointments, but if she couldn't manage that, the two women made a point of ignoring each other. At this surprise confrontation, they locked eyes like a pair of territorial cats. Diana saw a range of expressions cross Catherine's carefully made-up face, from intense dislike to a sort of smug triumph. Her lip curled half in disgust, half in a smirk. Diana guessed that her own expression was no less eloquent. *At least I'm not worrying about cracking my pancake base,* she thought. Moira looked up with a bright, artificial smile, aware that Catherine was watching her in the mirror.

"Oh, Diana, hi! No calls for you this afternoon, hon, you can take the rest of the day if you want." It was obvious that Catherine's permanent would require at least another hour.

But Diana decided she had better make an effort to be nice, since Catherine spent a significant amount of money in Moira's salon. "Miss Jorgens, it's a pleasure to see you. How are things?"

"Very well, thank you," Catherine said in her throaty drawl. "In fact, I have some news that should interest you."

"Really?" She saw Moira's expression become wary, but she avoided looking at Diana.

Catherine extended her left hand dramatically. "Yes, we're getting married."

Diana stared blankly at the diamond solitaire on Catherine's third finger. It wasn't large enough to brag about, by a long shot. Thomas must have gotten it from the jewelers in Camden. "Well, congratulations," she said after a moment, trying not to sound sarcastic. Her actual responses to Catherine's announcement would not have been appropriate, given that the woman was Moira's customer, but it was hard not to collapse into one of the waiting area chairs laughing.

"Thank you."

"Have you set a date?"

"Yes, a week from this Thursday. September twenty-third."

Diana blinked. "I guess you don't waste any time. What's your rush?"

Catherine's mouth thinned. "There's no reason to wait. This isn't the Victorian age when girls had to be engaged for three years before their beaux could kiss their hands. Mr. Morgan thought—"

"Oh, it's Mr. Morgan's idea to marry you on—before the end of September, is it?" *On the Autumn Equinox,* she almost slipped and said. Catherine glared at her for interrupting.

"Yes," she said icily.

"Ah," Diana said, suspicion kindling in her mind. She closed the shop door behind her and walked around to the front of the styling chair. Moira studiously continued working as Catherine drew back a bit in the chair. "Rather a significant date, isn't it?"

"I don't know what you mean. It's the first day of fall, if you care about such nonsense."

"Yes, it is silly, isn't it? Just another fake holiday invented by calendar publishers. But hey, I guess it's lucky you're an artist. You already like the night life. No big lifestyle changes for you." Moira caught her breath.

"If I didn't, I'd learn to," Catherine said. "If a girl wants to keep her man, she has to make herself part of his life, for better or worse."

"Well, I admire your guts, anyway. It takes a lot of courage to marry someone as *unusual* as Mr. Morgan."

Catherine's eyes narrowed. "I don't know what you're talking about. There's nothing so unusual about my fiancé. He wants what every man does, a wife who'll stick by him and take care of him. Some girls understand that, and some just never seem to learn."

Diana studied Catherine somberly. *Can it be? Can she really not know—not a single clue?* "Miss Jorgens," she said slowly, "Has Mr. Morgan told you much about his past?"

"I haven't asked," Catherine said grandly. "I don't care about his past, I care about his future. If there was anything I needed to know, he'd tell me. I trust him implicitly."

"I see. How very...devoted of you."

"I'm not going to be taken in by petty, spiteful gossip. I know there are a lot of wild stories. These yokels just can't see what I do. They always hound and persecute people who are gifted."

"I guess they do, you're right. Well—" Diana tucked her mail under her arm. "Do give Mr. Morgan my best wishes, will you? Moira, I'll help you close after you finish up here. I'm just going to sit in the alley and finish reading this report."

She walked briskly into the back room, heading for the side door almost at a run. She heard Moira say frantically, "Diana—before you—never mind," but Diana had to get out of the salon before she did something unforgiveable. She shoved the heavy steel door open with her shoulder, slammed it shut behind her, turned, and found herself face to face with Thomas, so close to him that they almost collided. He must have been sitting or standing on the steps and been caught by surprise when she opened the door so suddenly.

Diana gasped and jumped down the three steps sideways, staggering on the rough dirt floor of the alley. It was sheer dumb luck that spared her from spraining an ankle. At the same time, Thomas recoiled in the other direction, so that he was backed against the railing facing the steps. They froze in place, staring at each other in mingled horror and revulsion. Diana could feel her heart racing, and her knees were weak, as if she'd barely avoided walking off a precipice. Under other circumstances, she was sure they would both have turned tail and fled, but each of them had a reason for staying here. After a few moments, Diana began to recover her equilibrium. Thomas straightened up, his shoulders rigid, and adjusted his tie. He always wore a suit now. At that simple gesture, Diana's skin crawled with irritation, and the rage which was never far below the surface flared. She was far too sober to handle this encounter politely.

"Well, Mr. Morgan," she said, her tone smoking with acid. "What an unexpected surprise. Aren't you the hen-pecked one, though. Stephen never stood around waiting while I got my hair done."

He flicked off that jibe. "I'm sure he didn't. Your ex-husband was no gentleman."

"I just heard that congratulations are in order."

"Thank you."

"I said they were in order, not that I offered them."

His icy expression didn't match the thin smile. "Charming, as I'd expect of you. Especially recently."

"Your very first wedding. What a milestone! I do hope you don't get cold feet...if you'll pardon the expression. Am I invited?"

"No."

"What a crushing cut. I'll never recover."

"Would you *want* to come?" he asked with unexpected seriousness. Diana's combative sarcasm was derailed by this, and suddenly her anger flared up even hotter than before. She walked up the steps so she was sharing the small landing with Thomas, who stiffened but restrained himself from stepping back.

"Let me ask you something, Thomas," she said very quietly. "Don't you think you should tell her?"

A spectrum of reactions crossed his face—surprise that she knew he hadn't, a thought of feigning ignorance, a note of fear, and finally cold anger. "That's none of your concern." His voice simmered with menace, but Diana was undaunted.

"Why are you doing this? You're making a spectacle of yourself, Thomas. You're the town laughing stock."

"On the contrary, that position is firmly held by you, my dear. You've become no less than the town drunkard."

"It's better than playing the fool for a gold-digger in front of the whole West Bay. Why, Thomas? You don't love her."

"She loves me."

"Oh, I doubt that."

He looked away. "It doesn't matter. I have to do this. I don't have a choice any longer. I have you to thank for that."

She stared at him incredulously. "Have to do this…Mother Goddess, Thomas. Are you actually going to—"

"That is a question you'd best not ask! And certainly not here, on an open public street."

"And you're not even going to tell her first?"

He appeared to be restraining himself with difficulty. "You would be wise, Diana, to abandon this line of questioning, and expunge any further interest in the matter from your mind, permanently. Our connection is finished, and has been for three months. Why don't you leave, go home to Boston? Or go back to your alchemist, there's nothing for you here."

"I wish I could, Thomas! Do you think I enjoy being trapped in this little backwater? Don't you think that I'd travel to the other side of the planet to get away from you, if I possibly could? I can't leave, Thomas. I physically can't leave. Can *you?*"

His expression was stunned. "That's…that's ridiculous," he said, but his weak voice made it obvious that he was lying.

"You can't, can you? I hope your bride will understand why you're honeymooning on Lincolnville Beach."

"I don't know why you'd—this is *my* curse. That's why I have to…"

"I really don't think it's that simple, Thomas."

"Of course it's not simple! But it has to be ended! You failed me, I'm in this position because of *you!* We *killed* a man, Diana!" She winced. "For the first time in my existence, I have a murder on my conscience. We've killed, we've destroyed lives! I have no choice left, I *have* to conclude the matter, as much as I loathe the idea. You've left me worse off than I was to begin with. Not a day goes by that I don't curse your name for it."

"Oh, my—no wonder things are going so well. And when you've 'concluded the matter,' do you think I'll be able to leave this godforsaken place at last?"

"By god, I hope so. Even if you don't, I will."

"Well, then, why don't you giddy-up and to get right to it? I can't imagine why you have to wait as long as the Equinox."

Thomas flinched and suddenly, he slapped her across the face—lightly, but reflexively. "How *dare* you speak so flippantly. You *know* what this means to me."

Her cheek stinging, Diana gave her head a shake and squared her shoulders defiantly. "Oh, stop whimpering about how awful it is, you coward. If you'd done it years ago, none of this would ever have happened. You curse *me,* you say, it's *my* fault, *I* left you worse off—bullshit! I just hope you enjoy the company of your intended, because you'll be together a long, long time, you and that little—" her mouth twisted. "*Saesnes.*"

His hand came up again, as if to backhand her this time, but froze. "You watch your mouth."

"Oh, go ahead, hit me again! Give me another black eye, everyone will just think I fell down outside the bar, like a dozen other nights. *That's* what you've done for *me,* Thomas, thank you *so* much."

He slowly lowered his hand, staring at her in frustration, as if so many responses were boiling up none of them could find voice. Finally he said, "We have nothing more to say to each other, Diana—ever. We're done." He pushed roughly past her, shuddering at the contact, and walked down the steps.

"If we're done, Thomas, then why can't I leave?"

He stopped and half turned to look back at her. "Maybe that's your punishment." He walked out of the alley and turned to go in the salon's front door and wait for Catherine inside.

Diana stood motionless at the head of the steps, her hands clenched at her sides, immobilized by a rage that seemed to have nothing to do with the conversation she'd just had. It seemed to pour over her in heavy, foul tasting waves, horrible and yet unstoppable. When the door beside her cracked open and she heard Moira's anxious voice, she had to take in a deep breath and force herself to answer.

"You okay, hon?"

Of course she'd be worried—she'd seen Thomas come inside alone and she knew what he was capable of. "I'm...fine, Moira, really. I'm upset, but I'm fine. You don't have to neglect your customer. I'll come in when you're ready to close."

Moira retreated, and Diana sank down on the top step, her folded arms on her knees and her head buried in them, shaking. She could hardly bear to think about what Thomas was considering—even though she didn't believe it. She couldn't. Her mind simply wouldn't fold itself around the possibility. *It's not right...something's just not right about this. It's...misdirection.* But to disguise what? It was like not being able to think of a certain word—or like wanting to take a step and being physically unable to. She knew there was something she was missing but no matter how hard she thought, it continued to elude her.

She calmed down enough to go on reading her mail, but her mind kept veering back toward what Thomas had said. *Can he be right? Is there something we're supposed to be doing? Something we* can *do?* It was hard to consider practical courses of action when the mere prospect of being in the same room with him made her shrink with utter revulsion, and he didn't even want to speak to her again.

When she heard the front door open and two pairs of feet descending the steps, she hastily rose and ducked inside the metal door, preferring not to see Catherine and Thomas stroll by the alley arm-in-arm. Moira had turned over the CLOSED sign on the door and was clearing up the paraphernalia and containers she'd used to finish Catherine's permanent. "I'm sorry, kiddo, I tried to warn you—"

"Oh, heavens, Moira, don't apologize! Yes, you did, and don't worry about it. It was inevitable that I'd run into Thomas eventually, I don't know how we've avoided each other for this long."

"I was just afraid he'd try something, that's all."

Diana snorted. "Oh, like what? He's not going to hurt me, Moira. He can't even stand to lay eyes on me, let alone anything more. I'm not in much danger from a man who couldn't bring himself to touch me on a bet."

Moira just shook her head, looking unconvinced. Diana got the dry mop and basin of cleaning supplies from the back room. "You cash out, Moira, and I'll finish cleaning up."

Moira went to the front counter and got the tray from the cash register. "He looks awful, though, doesn't he?"

"Who?"

"Mr. Morgan, your Thomas. I mean, I know that he's...well..."

"Dead?"

Moira looked exasperated. "You said yourself that it wasn't like the movies and books, that he's something different. I didn't really understand it, but..."

"Yeah, okay, sorry. He didn't look any different to me."

"No?" Moira studied her for a moment and then shrugged. Diana straightened up from wiping out the sink, one hand on her hip.

"What? What do you mean by 'awful,' then?"

Moira paused in the doorway to the back room, pursing her lips thoughtfully. "I guess it isn't something I can really put my finger on. He's always been pale and skinny. It's just...he seems so miserable. It just rolls off him, you can practically feel it. He walks in and the room gets ten degrees colder. You know that character in the funny pages with the little cloud over his head all the time?"

"Yes, but I thought I was playing that part these days."

"As hard as it is to believe, he seems even worse than you."

Diana sniffed. "You'll pardon me if I don't cry any big fat tears for him."

"I'm not asking you to. I'm just telling you what I see. He never used to be like that, when he was with you." She didn't see Diana's grimace. "I don't mean he was ever a barrel of laughs, but he was a serene kind of guy. He sure doesn't act like some kind of Romeo who can't wait to tie the knot, either. Oh my god, the way she carries on around him, it's crazy. Cooing and simpering, hanging off his arm, 'darling' this and 'sweetheart' that—and he stands there like a stick, she might as well be making love to a statue of General Grant. And she doesn't even see it." Moira sat down at her desk and started to sort out the receipts. "I'm really curious about something now, though."

"And that is?"

"Just what happens when a…uh, someone like him gets married? Does that mean, *married* married, or more like a Bride of Frankenstein kind of thing?"

Diana forced a laugh. "Moira—you're too much. I don't think it matters, anyway."

Moira craned her head to peer at Diana around the door jamb. "How come?"

"Because I don't think anyone's getting married. It's never going to happen."

"What, he bought that ring for a tax shelter?"

Diana stared at her reflection thoughtfully as she twisted the cleaning rag absently in her hands. "It's just a feeling I have."

❧ 19 ☙

As Diana had grimly anticipated, her confrontation with Thomas ratcheted her nightmares up several notches, in both intensity and frequency. That night she awoke several times, drenched in icy sweat, her mind filled with a jumble of images. Over and over in her tormented sleep, the athanor melted, tidal waves rose over the Bay, or she stood by an open grave—Gregory's, Moira's, even her parents,' who as far as she knew were blissfully happy in Provence. As she tried to calm herself and fall back to sleep, she was distracted by Moira's stillness in the bed next to her. Her lover slept so heavily, she barely moved, and her breathing was scarcely perceptible. It reminded Diana of Thomas' absolute stillness, and the similarity made her skin crawl. It was all she could do not to get out of bed and try to sleep somewhere else, but she couldn't bear to risk hurting Moira's feelings. She'd never understand. The lack of sleep began to wear on Diana, and the dark circles under her eyes grew even deeper.

By the weekend, she realized she was counting the days to the Autumn Equinox. She had no idea where Catherine—somehow she doubted Thomas was too involved in the decisions—planned their nuptials to be held, but it looked like it would be a much quieter affair than Diana would have believed Catherine willing to settle for. She would have thought someone so flamboyant would want a wedding for the books—but then, you wouldn't plan such an event all in a day, and time seemed to be of the essence. Neither Diana nor Moira heard from anyone who would be attending the ceremony or reception, but Moira did finally glean the information that the couple would exchange vows before a Justice of the Peace in Camden.

"Seems awfully low-key for our Miss Jorgens, doesn't it?" Moira said wryly.

"Maybe they're just doing the legal part now and throwing a big bash later. That happened a lot during the war."

"True, but I just wonder where the fire is. It's not like she could be expecting or anything—could she?"

"Not as far as I know."

On Tuesday the 21st Phyllis Poulin, one of their most gossipy regulars, strutted in for an appointment with a palpable air of self-importance. She could barely wait to be ensconced in the styling chair before she almost giggled, *"Well, my dears. There's bad news from the local art scene, I can certainly tell you."*

Taking her obvious cue, Moira said, "Really? What's happened?"

"Mr. Morgan has postponed! And *she* is just fit to be tied."

"Postponed?" Diana asked. "For how long?"

"Until the weekend." Phyllis sounded disgruntled that the short delay watered down the impact of her scoop. "But we all know what *that* means. On Thursday, he'll say wait until Tuesday. On Saturday, he'll say wait until next month. Oh, you don't have to be Einstein! He's coming to his senses, if you ask me."

Diana pondered this darkly as Phyllis prattled on to Moira. *Maybe he didn't pick the date for any particular reason, after all...maybe it was just the first day the J.P. was free.* But reasoning didn't alleviate the way her body had turned cold and a lump dropped into the pit of her stomach when Phyllis made her gleeful announcement. Diana's hands were shaking almost as badly as Moira's, and Phyllis had also requested a manicure. She caught Moira's eye in the mirror, and Moira raised her eyebrows eloquently. *You were right.*

That night, Diana slept more deeply than she had for weeks, not once awakening on sweat-soaked sheets while it was still dark. She was so unused to sleeping through the night that when she opened her eyes and saw light coming through the curtains, she felt disoriented, as if she'd lost a day or two somewhere. Then she became aware of an odd sound in the room. Even before she could identify it, she was hit by a shock of adrenaline. Heart pounding, she sat up, realizing even as she did so what she was hearing. Beside her in the bed, Moira was gasping for breath and struggling to talk. Her eyes were huge with panic.

"Moira...Moira, it's okay. It's okay, don't be afraid, I'm awake, I'm here..." helplessly, Diana stroked Moira's hair and face, then pulled back the covers, trying to understand what was wrong. "Relax, try to breathe..." A trickle of saliva was running from the right corner of Moira's mouth, and her right arm was rigid, the fingers clenched on the sheets. Her left hand came up and gripped Diana's hand painfully.

"Muh...muh..."

"Moira, I'm going to call an ambulance, I think you've had a stroke."

"*No!*"

"Honey, I'm going to get you help—"

"Muh...dress...boo..."

Diana stared at her. "Address book?"

"Dahsher...dahsher...beh..."

"Dah...doctor? Diana rolled out of bed and hurried around to Moira's bed stand, where her purse sat. She rummaged in the purse and pulled out a small address book. On the very first page, under "Emergency," she found "Dr. Bernstein," with home and office numbers in Bangor. "I've found it, Moira, I'm calling him. I'll be right back." Moira closed her eyes, sighing.

Trembling, Diana dialed the doctor's home number. Dr. Bernstein's groggy and irritable voice crisped instantly when she gave him Moira's name. After a short conversation, Diana returned to the bedroom almost at a run. Moira was breathing more easily and seemed to have relaxed. Her paralysis apparently hadn't been permanent, like a stroke, but some kind of a seizure or spell.

"Better...now...just a...just a...minute," she wheezed, as though she had just run a mile without stopping. Diana sat on the edge of the bed and took Moira's hand urgently.

"Moira...I just talked to the doctor, Dr. Bernstein. He wants to see you in his office right away. He may have to admit you to the hospital." Moira squeezed her eyes shut hard, but she nodded. A tear quivered under her eyelashes.

"Can you dress?...no, no, let's just get you into a robe and slippers..." Diane took Moira's bathrobe off the hook on the back of the door and fumbled with it, trying to untangle the belt and find the sleeves. The garment wouldn't cooperate, and she felt a sudden burst of rage. If it had been her own robe, she would have ripped the seams apart.

She helped Moira sit up and turn so her feet were on the floor, and knelt to put on Moira's slippers. Kneeling at her feet, with her head bowed, she finally said, "Moira...I...I can't take you, you know that. I can't drive to Bangor." Even as she spoke, she hated herself for it, but more than that, she hated Thomas. It was all Thomas' fault that she was trapped here, it was Thomas' fault that Moira would suffer...

"Call a...cab...honey..."

"You can't go all the way to Bangor, in a cab, like this! The cabbie probably wouldn't even take you." Diana helped Moira get her arms into the bathrobe sleeves.

"No...amblance..."

"*Why?*"

But Moira only shook her head. Diana put her arms around Moira, holding her tightly. She could feel the lean body shaking with tears and thought her heart would break.

"All right...all right, I'll try. I haven't...tested it for a while, maybe I can go further this time. If I have to stop, I'll call a cab, okay?"

Moira's left arm squeezed her harder. "Thang...you," she whispered.

Diana staggered to her car with Moira almost draped on her shoulders and got her into the front passenger's seat. She tucked a blanket carefully around her, and barely remembered to go back for both of their purses. She had no idea if Moira had any paperwork or medications that she should bring with her, and cursed herself now for not being more insistent about getting information from her friend against an event like this.

It was still very early. Traffic was just picking up on Route 1. It was going to be a perfect fall day, crisp and clear with a crystalline blue sky. Diana turned north on Route 1, her heart pounding. Holliston House Inn...the Schooner...

the short stretch of road between Pepperell and Lincolnville, with a steep bank down to the Bay on their right. Lincolnville Beach loomed ahead, empty and quiet, the Lobster Pound restaurant on its north end closed and the parking lot deserted. Diana's heart was hammering and her mouth was dry, but so far there was not a trace of the visceral, blinding panic that always struck her as she approached the allowed boundaries of her world since the athanor exploded. The car wasn't slowing down and her muscles seemed to be obeying her will. As she passed the Lobster Pound, she tried stepping harder on the accelerator. She overdid it—the car lunged ahead and almost veered off the road. Frantically, she corrected herself, slowing down a little, then speeding up again. The restaurant disappeared from her rear view mirror, and the open road lay ahead.

Despite her fear for Moira and her uncertainty as to how far she could really go, Diana felt such a heady sense of release, she almost started laughing. *I'm free!* she thought. *It's over, I can finally leave!* With every mile closer to Bangor, it seemed that chains and bindings were falling away. It wasn't until she reached the doctor's office that it occurred to her that if she was free, so was Thomas. Why this filled her with a sudden sense of dread, she had no idea. He wanted nothing more to do with her, and likewise, what did it matter where he went?

The doctor and his nurse both came out to the car and helped get Moira inside. They took her to an examining room and told Diana to stay in the waiting room. She sat in an uncomfortable hard wooden chair, flipping through dog-eared copies of *Reader's Digest* and *Harper's,* wondering what she was waiting for. After about an hour the doctor came out. His expression was not reassuring.

"Are you family, Miss, uh..."

"Chilton. Not really, I...I work with Miss Waterford."

"Um-hm. We've contacted Miss Waterford's sister, she's coming as soon as she can. I want to thank you for bringing Miss Waterford all the way up here."

"Of course. How is she?"

"I really can't divulge any information, but...I'm going to be admitting her to the hospital."

"For how long?"

A faintly pitying look tinged the doctor's face. "You do know," he said gently, "that she's a very sick girl."

"I don't...that is...I've been aware that something's wrong, but...she hates to talk about it."

"Yes. Well..." he looked away for a moment, as if hoping they might be interrupted. "If you'll leave your name, I'll ask Miss Waterford's sister to call you."

"All right," Diana said, because that was all she could say. "I'll leave my information with your nurse. May I see Miss Waterford before I leave?"

"I'm afraid not, we've given her a sedative."

Diana sighed. "Thank you, doctor," she said when she could trust her voice. "If Miss Waterford wakes up, and asks, tell her that I'll take care of everything at home for her, okay?"

"I'll do that."

On the drive home, Diana wallowed in self-recriminations. *I should have seen this coming...I did see this coming. I've known for months that she was getting worse, I knew it had to be serious*...but eventually she ran out of ammunition. It wouldn't have mattered if she had been more involved, it had been Moira who chose to withhold information, Moira who was in denial about her condition, whatever it was. She'd be in the same situation now regardless of Diana. At least she'd had a ride to the doctor's office.

When she got back to Pepperell, Diana went straight to the salon and called all the customers with pending appointments. That took most of the morning because she couldn't reach everyone on the first try. When she'd cleared the appointment book, she removed all the money from the till, turned down the thermostat, pulled all the blinds down and shut off all the lights. As she locked the front door, her eyes fell on the painted front window and she winced.

Back at Moira's apartment, she sat on the bed for a while, wondering what to do. Should she begin packing Moira's things, or was that jumping the gun? Would Moira's sister prefer to take care of the apartment, or would the family have more than enough on their minds? Diana wasn't even certain whether she could go on living here without Moira. She didn't want to, but the apartment phone number was the one she'd left with the nurse. *I've got to get out of here,* she thought finally. *I'll close up the apartment, pack my own things and find somewhere to stay in Bangor.* That way, she'd be close to the hospital, and she could give the new phone number to the doctor's office.

It took her the rest of the day to clean the apartment. She stripped the bed and did all of Moira's laundry, stacking everything neatly on the bare mattress. She emptied the refrigerator of perishable food, throwing most of it away. If she was going to be moving to a hotel, she wouldn't be doing any cooking. She made up a deposit of all the money from the store till and a strongbox Moira kept on the high shelf in her closet, and put together all of Moira's personal, business and legal paperwork, without snooping through it. That was for Moira's family to deal with.

What puzzled her, as she worked, was how tranquil she felt. The sense of release she'd experienced when she passed the Lobster Pound with no panic or paralysis remained with her, suffusing her consciousness with a sort of glow. But it was more than that. She walked to the bank with the deposit, and found herself appreciating the beauty of the sunlight and bright day with almost poignant pleasure, when she'd barely noticed the weather for the last three months. She wasn't at all hungry, and just ate some leftovers as she cleaned the kitchen. But she also didn't feel the tiniest desire to have a drink. The rational part of her mind wondered what might be behind this change, but Diana didn't want to question it. It was too enormous a relief to be free, even temporarily, from the unremitting emotional pain she'd suffered for so many weeks. *Maybe this crisis has just burned out the fuses finally,* she thought wryly—or she was in shock and the pain would start later, perhaps when she saw Moira in the hospital.

But something plucked at her memory as she paused in the shabby front yard to bask for a moment in the warm sunlight. She had a fleeting vision—a dark, warm room, kerosene lamplight, a shadowed ceiling overhead, a voice murmuring, "it's peaking...it must be." As she puzzled over this mental scrap, suddenly she realized who was with her and what they had been doing, and her stomach turned over in a violent lurch as she shuddered in disgust. With a choked sound she cut off all further thoughts. It wasn't difficult to do. For three months, she had worked so hard to block every possible memory of her time with Thomas, now she couldn't recall the events leading up to that disastrous day if she wanted to. Still plagued by a sense of déjà vu, she cautiously probed the edges of her memory, troubled by a sense that there was something very important that she could not bring into focus. But the recollection would not gel, and finally she shrugged and gave up. The soothing blanket of serenity, like a muffling layer of thick cotton wool, settled over her once more.

It was after dark when she finally began putting together her own belongings and loading them into her car. Half her clothes and almost everything else had been stashed in the apartment's basement storeroom where they'd rested undisturbed since she moved in, and Diana put those in the car as is. Her suitcases were under the bed in the spare room, and now Diana got them out to begin packing.

As she started to stuff lingerie into the suitcase side pockets, she realized that one of the long elasticized pouches was almost full. Puzzled, because she was sure she'd thoroughly emptied the suitcases in June, she pulled a rather large bundle from the pocket, and recognized a bulky roll of the deep purple silk she'd used to make their robes. A needle, with thick silk thread still in place, neatly tacked the fabric. For a moment, Diana recalled standing up in the east parlor of the stone house, eerie bronze light shining through the window as her lapful of half-sewn silk fell to the floor. *Why didn't I see this when I unpacked?* But the silk bundle enclosed something thin and hard. Gingerly, as though the cloth was a soiled diaper, Diana unrolled the bundle, and a long slender knife clattered to the bottom of the suitcase.

Thomas, as he'd promised, had shown it to her once. Forged of an unknown metal that contained no iron or steel, the blade's two edges remained undimmed by oxygen and as keen as though freshly honed. The handle and haft, made of silver that never tarnished, glittered with tiny but perfect inset jewels in every color of the rainbow. The metal was worked in an elaborate curling pattern that repeated as engravings on the blade. It almost looked like some sort of script, but its meaning remained cryptic. Diana had only seen similar figures in one other design: the symbols in Thomas' stone mandala which she couldn't identify. She knew instinctively that the knife was immeasurably old, but nothing blemished its surface except tiny bits of dried blood encrusted among the jewels and incised crevices of the metal.

She stared at the knife, rigid with shock. She felt an impulse to dive for cover, as though a grenade with a freshly pulled pin had been tossed through the window. *How did this get here?* She was dead certain that the bundle had not been in the suitcase when she'd dumped it out to wash her clothes.

"Thomas," she hissed aloud. "You worthless son of a bitch." He had to have snuck into the house and put the knife there. This was another way of threatening her, reminding her yet again that he blamed her for the predicament he'd only brought on himself. In a fury almost as blinding as the one in which she'd beat her hands bloody against Thomas' back door, she hurled the knife across the room with all her strength, heedless of Moira's security deposit. The knife left a deep scar in the flowered wallpaper, bounced off the wall and spun across the floor.

As it came to rest, the whole building shuddered, as though it had shifted on its foundations. Diana had to sidestep to catch her balance, and stood rigid, her heart hammering, for a moment wondering if the house was about to melt or explode. But she heard no sound except the distant noises of a peaceful neighborhood evening outside the window. She must have imagined the movement. She kicked the knife over to the edge of the room and started packing, yanking clothes off hangers and out of drawers impatiently. *I am leaving, Thomas!* she thought furiously. *You're not going to bait me, I am gone from here!*

By the time she finished packing, it was too late to drive to Bangor and find a hotel room. Diana decided to spend one more night in the spare room and leave early the next morning. She wondered how Moira was doing in the hospital and whether her sister had arrived—Moira had spoken so little about her family, Diana couldn't recall where her siblings lived.

Shortly before 11:00 p.m., she was putting an extra blanket on the spare room bed when the apartment's buzzer startled her. *What the hell?* Either the police or someone about Moira, she couldn't imagine who else would be ringing the doorbell this late. But when Diana hurried to the door and yanked it open, she had to exercise considerable self-control not to instantly slam it shut.

"Miss Jorgens. Isn't this a little late to come calling?"

"Yes, it is, and I'm very sorry," Catherine said, her voice quavering. "But you must know I would never bother you unless it was an emergency. I hope I didn't get you and Miss Waterford out of bed."

"Miss Waterford isn't here."

"She isn't?"

"She's out of town. So if you're looking for a quick touch-up, Miss Jorgens, I'm afraid that—"

"No, no, no! It's you I need to see. *Please...*"

Catherine's voice held a note of panic that dampened Diana's hostility. After all, Catherine was a victim of Thomas as well, in a sense. She grudgingly stepped back from the door. "You can come in for a minute. I was just getting ready for bed."

When Catherine was inside the kitchen, Diana studied her with a frown.

Catherine's hair, usually almost shellacked with hair spray, hung in stiff tangles. Her lipstick badly needed refreshing and beneath her red-rimmed eyes, mascara smeared her cheekbones. It would seem that she was taking her wedding postponement rather hard. Diana gestured to one of the kitchen chairs. "Have a seat."

"Thank you..." Catherine hobbled to the chair, and Diana saw with amazement that one of her heels was broken. *Did she run here? From how far?* Her flowing cobalt blue skirt sported a long rent near the hem and an assortment of burrs. Tantalized in spite of herself, Diana sat down in the seat facing her unexpected visitor.

"How can I help you, Miss Jorgens?"

Catherine hesitated. "I know you don't have any reason to like me, Miss Chilton, but...but...we have something in common. At least—I don't know where else to turn. It's about Mr. Morgan."

Diana kept her expression carefully neutral. "What about Mr. Morgan?"

"I just can't understand how he's acting. I think he's in very serious trouble."

"What makes you think that?"

"He postponed our wedding date, the date he wanted! And now he won't even speak to me."

"Did you have a fight about the postponement?"

"No! I was disappointed, of course, but I never said a word! I told him over and over that whatever he wanted was fine with me, that it was his decision! But tonight, he—" her eyes started to well with tears. "He stood me up!" she blurted in a strangled voice. Either her feelings or her pride were so clearly wounded to the bone, Diana couldn't suppress a twinge of sympathy. "We were going to meet at the Schooner, and he never showed up."

Diana had to admit, that didn't sound like Thomas. "Maybe something came up. He doesn't have a phone."

"I know, so I drove up there to see if everything was all right. He wouldn't even answer the door! There were lights inside, and I knocked and knocked. Then I went around to the back, and I could see him through the window of his library, so I knocked on the glass, and then he came to the front door."

"You walked around the house in the dark and spied through his windows?"

"I was *worried* about him, worried *sick!*" She rubbed her calf absently with her hand. "I broke one of my heels trying to get through all those weeds."

"So...you said he wasn't speaking to you, but he came to the door."

"Yes, he—" Catherine's voice squeaked and she stopped, pressing her hand to her mouth for a few moments. Then she cleared her throat and went on, "I asked him if he was all right, I said we were supposed to meet for dinner, and he said...he said..." She squeezed her eyes shut, and two tears trickled over her cheeks. "He said, 'Go away.' Just, 'go away,' and then he shut the door." She gulped back a sob, her shoulders shaking.

Diana sat back, pondering this. There was a tight, cold knot in the pit of her stomach. She had a vertiginous sense that somehow the room was tilting, as if she and Catherine were sitting at a table glued to one of the walls. *Something's not right...Thomas is a creep, and there's nothing surprising about his dumping Catherine...but this doesn't feel right...* "Miss Jorgens...what was Mr. Morgan doing, when you looked through his window?"

Catherine sniffed. "He was standing by his desk, looking at some papers spread all over it. They looked like diagrams and sketches, I don't know, I'd never seen them before—what?"

Diana had stood up abruptly and taken a few steps away from the table. "I thought he'd burned all of those," she said to the air. She looked back at Catherine, who was staring at her blankly. "I did try to tell you that Mr. Morgan is a very unusual man."

"He's never acted like this before."

"You haven't known him very long. Forgive me, but I think your engagement was unrealistically short." Catherine's expression turned sullen, and Diana sat back down with a sigh. "Just what do you expect me to do, Miss Jorgens? I'm not his mother."

"No, but—you *know* him. You've known him longer than I have. Could you talk to him? At least, at least get some sort of explanation, anything! If I did something wrong, if he needs help, if there's anything I can do..." her voice was edging on hysteria. She reached over and clutched one of Diana's hands. Diana restrained herself from wrenching her fingers out of Catherine's damp grip with difficulty. *"Please.* I don't have anybody else to ask."

"You want me to talk to him now, tonight?"

"No, no, not tonight, although...this is when he's up and around. But..." Catherine seemed flustered by the question.

"There are at least two small problems with your request, Miss Jorgens. In June, Mr. Morgan told me in no uncertain terms that I was never to set foot on his property again. And the last time I saw him, which was only about ten days ago, he made it very clear that he never wanted to speak to me again."

"But that's not true!"

"What's not true? Are you calling me a liar?"

"No, I—he may have said that ten days ago, but it's not true now."

"What do you mean?"

"He told me, just this past Monday, that he needed to talk to you soon but he didn't know how to manage it after everything that had happened."

"And what did you say?" Catherine's eyes shifted uneasily, and Diana said, "Never mind."

There was a silence in the kitchen then, punctuated only by Catherine's sniffles. Diana wondered where Catherine's purse was. She got up and found some paper napkins in one of the partially packed boxes on the counter and proffered them. Catherine blew her nose daintily and daubed at her eyes.

"Miss Jorgens—uh, Catherine. I'll see what I can do. I'd suggest that you go home and try to get some rest. You look about done in, and there's nothing more you can do tonight."

"You'll talk to him?"

"I said, I'll see what I can do. Frankly, it's a bit unconventional for a fiancée to ask the ex- to intervene on her behalf. But I suppose nothing about this situation is conventional, so...no promises, though."

"Thank you," Catherine whispered.

"Thank me later, if there's any reason for it. To be perfectly honest, I don't expect to have any more luck than you just did. Now forgive me, but it is getting very late."

Catherine rose reluctantly. Her eyes wandered around the kitchen, taking in the boxes on the counters and the open cabinet doors. "Is Miss Waterford moving away?"

"We've just found a bigger place, that's all. Good night, Catherine."

She ushered Catherine out the door firmly, closed it and leaned against it until she heard her visitor's car start and its engine fade into the distance.

She stayed there for a long time, her skin crawling and her stomach cramping with anxious tension, and she didn't know why. The whole room still felt off-kilter, and any moment she dreaded another one of the inexplicable shifts she'd felt earlier. Catherine's story kept running through her mind. She didn't want to believe it. She wanted to think that it was all a trick, that Thomas had sent Catherine to the house to fool her into coming to Pepperell Hills—although for what purpose, she couldn't imagine. Besides, she didn't think Catherine was that good an actress. Her distress had seemed most genuine. *I should forget about it, it's not my problem. Tomorrow morning I'm moving up to Bangor, and that's the last this miserable little dump of a town will ever see of me.* But she couldn't bring herself to brush off Catherine's request and go to bed. She was exhausted from the events of the day, but she knew she wouldn't be able to sleep.

"Oh, the hell with it," she finally said aloud. As Catherine said, this was when Thomas was up and around. It wouldn't make any sense to go in the morning, so this was her last chance. She strode into the spare room, got her purse and a sweater, and retrieved the knife from the floor. At least she'd return that to Thomas, and let him know what she thought of his transparent attempt to intimidate her. It would be nearly midnight when she got there, he might have gone out on a foray by now. Even if he was home, he probably wouldn't answer the door, and if he did, he would likely just order her off his property again. But at least she could say that she'd made one more good faith effort.

She'd forgotten how long the drive back into the hills was. Despite her defiant attitude, her uneasiness grew as she approached the turnoff. When she pulled up by the big boulder, looming out of the darkness like a crouching animal, her knees were shaking. Thomas had said he wouldn't answer for the consequences if he caught her on his land...but surely he wouldn't do anything truly desperate.

As she got out of the car in front of the stone house, she suddenly thought of the night more than two years ago when she'd met Thomas for the first time. *It should be raining*, she thought, looking up at the starry autumn sky. She took a step forward, and that was when everything changed.

She froze motionless, unable to breathe for a moment. It was like the day the athanor blew up, when she'd tried to walk past the town line and her legs simply wouldn't move. Except now, she was moving even though she didn't want to. The house in front of her looked artificial, as though it was a painted façade, a *trompe-l'oeil* reproduction of stone and lichen carefully applied to some insubstantial surface. She had no control over what happened. She was a performer, acting out a script in a language she didn't understand, obediently parroting words fed to her line by line. Some part of her rational mind was frantically trying to make her turn back, get into her car and leave, as fast as possible, but she couldn't. She kept walking forward, and just as she reached the door, Thomas opened it. Of course, he'd have heard her car, but she didn't think that was why he'd come to the door. He silently stepped back and she walked into the house. *You can hang your wet coat on one of those pegs*, echoed in her mind from long past, and she automatically took her sweater off and hung it up. She followed Thomas into his study because that's what she was supposed to do.

They turned and faced each other in the middle of the room, like a pair of dancers, the way they'd turned to face each other as they called the quarters in each of their hundreds of rituals. Thomas' face no longer held the hard, bitter coldness he had worn the last time they'd met. His eyes looked confused and his expression was blank, which was exactly how Diana felt. *Ad lib*, the script seemed to say here. She struggled to form words.

"Catherine...came to see me tonight."

He didn't react. After a pause, he said, "Yes, she was here earlier."

"She's very worried about you."

"She needn't be. It's almost over now."

The mutual repulsion that had pushed them so violently apart every time they encountered each other had reversed. Diana couldn't remember now why she had felt so revolted by the very thought of touching Thomas. It didn't make any sense. But neither did the slowly increasing pull drawing her forward now.

She reached into her purse and took out the knife, extending it towards him. "I found this."

He looked down at it and raised his eyebrows. He stepped forward. As if connected to him by a pulley, so did she, although a dim sense of panic was beginning to rise in the back of her throat. He slowly reached out and took the knife from her, then set it on the back of the armchair next to him.

"Catherine told me that you needed to talk to me?"

His expression shifted, and for a moment she saw sheer terror in his eyes—then it was swallowed by a look of such intense yearning, her heart skipped a beat. "No. I said that I needed to meet with you."

How had they gotten less than an arm's length apart? She tried to pull back but instead she moved forward, and she couldn't look away from his eyes. She wanted to turn her head aside but her muscles wouldn't do as she willed. She couldn't even close her eyelids. Thomas reached forward and placed his hands on her shoulders, very gently, as though she might dissolve if he touched her too hard. A tingling thrill of energy ran through her body from his hands, but it was ominous, not pleasant, like the first little pang of warning from a deadly poison. She reached up and put both her hands over his, her fingers sliding over the cool softness of his skin.

Suddenly there was a tremendous shock. For a moment, the world turned white and a deafening sound seemed to roar in her ears. When Diana's vision cleared, so did her mind—for the first time in three months. She looked at Thomas and she was absolutely and utterly *aware*—of the look and smell of the room, the soft crackling of the fire in the grate, the touch of his hands. She knew, from the expression in Thomas' eyes, that they were sharing this experience, that they both, in that instant, were like initiates whose blindfolds have been flicked away so they might see the final Mystery at last. In that burst of clarity, Diana knew why she was here and what their magical working had come down to. She knew they were poised at the cusp of true midnight, and she knew exactly what had to be done to untwist the Moebius strip of their spell and bring it to its final conclusion. She held that knowledge for one unbreathing, incredulous second, and then she turned to bolt from the room. Between her sudden move and his stunned immobility, Thomas didn't react for a moment, and she almost got to the door before he caught her.

He wrenched her towards him, and she turned and struck out blindly at his face, before he got hold of her free hand. Then she was twisting and struggling desperately to escape his grip, not kicking at him because she didn't want to hurt him, she only wanted to get away. He swept her feet out from under her with his ankle and they were both on the floor, Thomas pinning Diana down. She found her voice and shrieked, "Thomas, no! No, let me go, don't do this—" but even as she protested she knew it was pointless. Thomas had no power to stop himself. Despite her terror she could feel the tremendous inevitability of this moment. *Run away?* echoed the voice of the little girl in her dream, *After all the work you did to make this happen? Why would you run away?* She had her hands braced against Thomas' shoulders, and he gripped her wrists and forced her arms down, as her feet thudded against the carpet, trying to find a purchase so she could throw him off.

"Stop it," he said, "this is the final thing, the ending of it! This is the only thing that will end it, the only thing that will release us both, please, Diana—"

"No! No, Thomas, I don't want this, I never wanted this—"

He'd let go of her hands and taken hold of her shoulder and her jaw, and her groping fingers found a book she'd pulled off the shelves as Thomas dragged her back into the room. She gripped it two-handed and hit Thomas over the head with it. He reared back, startled, and then clenched his right fist and struck

Diana in the face. Her vision burst into a spray of sparkling light for a moment, and while she was stunned by the blow, he grabbed her jaw again, twisted her head sideways, and clamped his mouth onto her throat. She felt that sickening, tearing cloth sensation and then blood running down the back of her neck and soaking into the carpet as he drank like a dying man at a desert oasis. By the time she had recovered from his blow, the paralyzing effect of his drinking was draining the resistance from her muscles.

*Here there be dragons...*and it was there, it had been waiting for her from the very beginning of their endeavor, perhaps from the beginning of her search for Thomas Morgan seven years ago. She didn't need to be at the point of death to see it, nor for it to take her. She and Thomas had willfully and painstakingly dismantled all the natural barriers that held it apart from the world of breath and blood. The room before Diana's eyes had faded back into a shadowy haze, and all she could see was the dragon, blindingly bright, throwing off showers of fire as though Fourth of July sparklers had been woven into the skin and scales of a living thing. She shrank from its unimaginable power, but escape was impossible. It grew and coiled, loop after endless loop rising up above her, focusing itself to a point, drawing a bead on her like an archer drawing his bow. Nothing was holding it back. Thomas, after decades of keeping the dragon in restraint, had conceded to its demands and released it, by conscious choice, to work its will on her. She sensed its primordial, utterly unhuman consciousness fixed on her, and the emotion that radiated from it was pure, triumphant joy. For an endless moment it hung above her, anticipating its feast, and then it shot downwards and exploded into her body.

If she had thought Thomas' descriptions somewhat hyperbolic, she knew now she'd been wrong. No words were strong enough to convey the intensity of the pain she felt. It was as though every cell, every molecule of her physical self was being consumed by a flame so intense, the stars were cold by comparison. She had been granted the ability to experience each and every particle of her very essence die in agony and be recreated on the dragon's forge. She would never be the same again, and not just on an individual level. The dragon's touch would cut her off from the human race and remove her from the wheel of life and death, forever. For the first time, Diana understood what this meant, understood it to the core of her being. For the first time, she comprehended what it meant to feel *spiritual* agony. She'd heard that this was what a soul felt when it incarnated in a physical body, but if that was true, souls mercifully had no memory of the transition.

The dragon withdrew, rising up again, and the pain decreased to an almost bearable level. The room around her came back into view, distorted and shadowed. Thomas was there, but she couldn't see him clearly. She felt the dragon flex and arch, and then it dove down again and pain once more exploded through her, even more intense than before. The worst part was that she couldn't scream. Even if she'd been able to breathe, she couldn't have screamed loud or long enough, but to be in agony and suffocating at once was double the torment.

After endless minutes, years of minutes, the dragon withdrew a second time, further back. The pain receded almost completely, but Diana knew, instinctively, that the only reason for the greater relief was to enable an even deeper and more powerful onslaught. She knew it would kill her, finally, but she had no idea how many attacks she could survive before her body's organic life gave way to the transformation taking place. She couldn't endure it. She would go mad, and awaken raving, a thing that could not be destroyed and would wreak havoc, a demon unleashed on the world. She could see the fireplace next to her and one of the armchairs, a wall of bookcases and the dim ceiling overhead, rippling as though they were at the bottom of a running brook. Then Thomas bent over her, his lips moving, although she couldn't hear his voice. His face was stricken—she had never seen anyone look at her like that. She could move, for a few more moments, and she reached up and clutched at the front of his jacket. Her voice was a harsh croak.

"Thomas...Thomas, please stop it. Don't let it devour me, Thomas, do something...kill me, anything..." He pulled back, his eyes desperate. She could feel the dragon expanding, its coils twisting up and up, and panic overwhelmed her. With her last strength she forced out the words, "Gods, Thomas, *please stop it!*" Still straddling her body, he straightened up and snatched the knife from the back of the chair where he'd set it, bent down and slashed it across her throat in one sweep of his arm. She felt the drag of the metal through her flesh but no pain. A spray of warmth soaked her face and she heard the fire hiss, and then the room, the dragon, Thomas and everything else was gone.

≈ 20 ≈

When Diana opened her eyes, all she could see was white. For a long time, she remained still and looked at it, with no curiosity about what she was seeing, and no particular desire to move. She had the odd impression that she was being reassembled. Bits and pieces were clicking neatly into place, and until everything was connected, she didn't want to think, or attempt to interfere. Emotionless, neither patient nor impatient, she watched the field of white before her, as reality slowly phased back into existence.

She grew aware of her body. She felt pressure against the back of her head, and her shoulders, back, hips, calves and heels, so she was stretched out flat on something…something soft. She didn't smell anything. Her hands were folded across her abdomen. She was wearing clothing, but her feet were bare.

As sensory impressions accrued more quickly, she started to feel a vague urgency. She'd been sleeping a long time, she needed to wake up. She had left many things unattended to, many loose ends, and she didn't even know where she was. She squeezed her eyes shut and opened them, blinking several times, and with this first conscious movement, her bodily control snapped into place. She flexed her hands and feet, and realized she was lying, uncovered, on a bed. The blur of white that she was staring at cleared and resolved into the white plaster ceiling and wall of a room. Abruptly, Diana sat up. Her muscles moved so fluidly, movement required no exertion at all.

Looking around, she recognized her surroundings: a bedroom in Thomas' stone house, but not the same one she'd occupied for two years. This was one of the two front rooms, with windows facing north and west—Thomas' room was on the east side. She'd recalled the windows being fitted with splitting green window shades and faded calico curtains, like her old room and the one next to it. Only Thomas' room had heavy, lined full-length drapes. But Diana saw that the windows in this room were now covered with blankets, nailed over the entire window frames. Light still seeped through and around the woven wool. She puzzled over this—was Thomas sleeping in this room for some reason? And why did the room still seem so bright? She could have read a newspaper without straining her eyes.

She thought of standing up and she was standing. For a moment, she was startled by this, but nothing magical had occurred. Her body moved with such perfectly coordinated strength and grace, that as soon as she thought of doing something, it was done. She felt so light, and so unburdened by her physical form, that she would have imagined she was floating if it hadn't been for her feet. She could distinctly feel the finest details in the grain of the wood floor beneath them. It was rather distracting, in fact. She stood still for some seconds shifting her weight—for she did have weight—and curling her toes in order to experience the sensation of the wood against her bare soles. Every inch of her skin was equally hyper-sensitized, making her acutely aware of the least brush of fabric or draft of air.

She wondered if she was dreaming, but all of this was merely strange, not illogical. Maybe she was on some kind of drug. She'd taken some fairly strong mind-altering substances as part of her work with the Order, but none of them had felt anything like this. Walking carefully, she went to the door of the room and opened it. The hallway outside seemed very bright, although the only light came from the bottom cracks of the bedroom doors. Diana went down the hall, her bare feet soundless on the worn floorboards, and pushed open the door to her old room. Immediately, she recoiled. The room was flooded with blinding, dazzling light, the window an unbearably bright rectangle that pierced her eyes with pain the second she glanced at it. She stepped back and pulled the door shut, blinking as tears trickled down her cheeks. It was the pain that brought everything back to her at last, that and what the light reminded her of—or perhaps her memory was simply the final puzzle piece.

She retreated to the front bedroom, shut the door and leaned against it, sliding down to sit hugging her knees as her memory relentlessly played back the events that had brought her to this pass. She sat like that for a long time, somberly thinking over all the details of the working, the disastrous outcome, the three months afterwards and the final resolution. Now, she could see with perfect clarity, as though she was observing another person, how her mind had been twisted and blocked, her perception blinded, her emotions turned inside out. She didn't even want to think of the dragon and what it had done, but as for the very last memory of all…she probed at her neck with shaking fingers, and felt a thin, ridged scar. Unlike Thomas', it ran almost straight across, and was low enough that clothing would conceal it. She realized now what the warm wet spray that had soaked her face had been, and had to admire Thomas' courage. It must have made quite a mess.

Thinking of that, she looked down at herself now. Thomas must have cleaned her and changed her clothes, because she wasn't wearing the same clothing. She was dressed in a skirt and blouse that were hers, but seemed looser than she remembered, and she had nothing on underneath them. She registered this without judgment—it couldn't have been easy for Thomas to wash and dress her lifeless body. It would have been difficult for anyone, but she recalled his saying he had a horror of the dead. He couldn't stay in a house with a corpse in it, he'd told her. For the first time, she wondered where he was now.

A corpse...*I suppose I must be like Thomas now*, she thought. She was cautious about assuming. Thomas had never released the dragon before, and consistency was not an outstanding characteristic of the Fair Folk. If she was like Thomas, she wasn't an animated corpse, but... *if we're not dead, what are we?* She realized that not once since she'd awakened had she taken a breath. She tried now, drawing in a breath consciously and releasing it. It was as effortless as everything else her body did, but she had to do it deliberately. With no discomfort, she was as oblivious to not breathing as she usually had to been to her respiration while she was alive. It was going to take some practice, however, to talk naturally without gasping. With the breath came smells, heady and pungent: old wood, dust, traces of fragrance left from soap and shampoo, dry grass and leaves from outside, and much more, a complex tapestry of aromas from one inhalation of undisturbed indoor air. This was also going to take a lot of practice to get used to. Recalling how Thomas reacted when he ate something, she resolved to hold off on trying out her sense of taste for a while.

She felt her wrists for a pulse with no success. Her hands were completely white. Her fingernails were the same color as her skin, with no pink flush. In all the time she'd been with Thomas, she had never noticed that detail about his hands. *How much else was right in front of my face without my even seeing it, while I complained to Thomas that he wasn't telling me enough?* She heaved a sigh, letting her head lean back against the door.

She reflected that she should be much more emotional. She didn't feel numb, or depressed, or in shock. She simply felt...peaceful. Moira's words came back to her: *he was a serene kind of guy*. What she'd thought of as distant or cool, now struck her differently. Part of her calmness was physical—it was hard to feel emotionally agitated when she was experiencing such a profound sense of well-being. She didn't have the slightest twinge of pain or discomfort anywhere, her muscles were completely relaxed, and as for fatigue, she had never felt so rested and alert. All of the torturous illusion that she'd been twisted, crumpled and tangled inside, so that she'd imagined herself contorted and hobbling like one of Lon Chaney's movie characters, had completely vanished. The pure relief from that alone was soothing.

But there was more than that. Uneasily, Diana recalled Gregory telling her that she was angry all the time. She hadn't wanted to believe him then, but now she realized that he had been right—about that, and many other things she hadn't wanted to hear. She cast her mind back over the years of her life, and saw a woman who raged and battled against every obstacle she encountered, the way she had mindlessly flung herself at Thomas' bolted back door, when it might have been more fruitful to look for a way over, under or around. That hadn't been a complete waste—after all, Bread and Roses had been born out of that fury, and the same passion had driven her magical accomplishments. But now...all of that was gone. She remembered, vividly, how she had once felt but the emotions themselves didn't even echo. *It'll be burned out of you, if you don't let it go*...damn Gregory, anyway. He was going to be so smug when he heard about this.

But she wasn't sure she had the full explanation. After all, Thomas had his passions, he was far from a Buddha. Somehow, she felt that she was *waiting* for something. She certainly didn't feel free to even wander around the house, let alone go outside. The light was far too bright, she'd need a white cane or a guide dog. She wondered what time it was. She'd just have to be patient until sunset. That thought made a little ping in her mind, and she tried to sort out what it reminded her of. Something about...things changing at sunset. But she couldn't quite nail down the context. She went over what she remembered of Thomas' story about his first awakening, but he'd omitted a lot of details that now she wished she knew. Why had she woken up while it was still daylight? Had he?

As she painstakingly reconstructed Thomas' words that night, his admission about drinking his horse's blood came to her mind. Suddenly, her cogitations stopped cold, and before she knew she'd moved, she had stood up and taken two steps into the room. *Will I need to drink blood?* She felt like an idiot for not having asked this immediately, when the answer was so obvious. For the first time, she had a physical sensation unpleasant enough to impel her to take action to stop it—hunger cramps, almost painful. Her mouth was watering, and with a shock, she realized that she knew how to do whatever it was Thomas did to get blood. It was like an instinct, as automatic and certain as swallowing or blinking. She knew how to—Thomas never spoke of it, but "open" was descriptive—and how to close the breach to prevent her victim from bleeding to death. She was salivating so much now, she kept swallowing repeatedly, and she was licking her lips unconsciously. But there was no horse on Thomas' property, or any other livestock, and she couldn't go out now. She would need Thomas' help for this one. She knew how careful he was to avoid detection or suspicion.

Her reaction slowly subsided. *Where is Thomas, anyway?* She left the bedroom and checked his room. He wasn't there, but the bed was rumpled and the wardrobe full of his clothes, so she felt sure he planned to return. She went to the top of the staircase and peered down, listening, and sniffing, for any sign of movement on the first floor. There were a lot of intriguing smells down there, but nothing that suggested she wasn't alone in the house. She took in a breath and tried speaking for the first time.

"Thomas?" Her voice was a little hoarse, and much louder in her own ears than she remembered it being, but otherwise she sounded quite normal. She cleared her throat and called more confidently, "Thomas?" She heard the name echo dimly in the empty rooms, but that was her only reply. Her shoulders sagged. *Well, I guess I just have to wait for him.* He'd be back. She was absolutely certain of it. He just didn't expect her to awaken so early. Wherever he was, he was probably still sleeping, himself.

With a guilty qualm, she wondered how Moira was doing. Had she recovered from her seizure, would the doctors be able to help her? She was in the hospital, she was being cared for, but she must be puzzled that Diana wasn't there. Maybe she was still being sedated. Diana hoped that Moira's sister hadn't tried to get in touch with her today. As soon as she possibly could, she'd have to get to Bangor and find out what was going on and what she could do to help. But she had to solve her present problems before she'd be of any use to Moira. She was sure that Thomas would do everything he could to support her in this crisis.

As the time crawled by, she grew more restless. The light dimmed behind the tacked blankets, and finally she ventured a look outside. The sun had sunk below the tree line to the west, and the landscape around the house was in shadow. The sky was still bright. It must have been glorious, like the day before, cloudless and sunny. Diana had to squint and half-cover her eyes with one hand to survey the scene, but she wasn't blinded and immobilized like she had been earlier. She decided it was safe to go downstairs, and did so. She'd barely been aware of the house the night before, with the magical trap closing its jaws before she entered. Thomas hadn't made any major changes to the property over the past three months. She walked around the rooms sniffing at everything, and touching any object or surface that looked like it would feel interesting. The door to Thomas' study was ajar, so she could see that he wasn't in there, but she had no desire to go inside. She could smell stale blood in the air that drafted from the open door and it made the hair on her arms stand up.

Wandering became pacing. It wasn't that she was impatient, but physically she couldn't sit still. Her stomach cramps were hitting at shorter intervals, and she was forcing herself not to think about blood, or even food and water. She had no desire for ordinary food, but the minute she contemplated eating, she thought next about drinking, and then...she wondered what would happen if she didn't get blood soon, but she firmly excluded that speculation from her mind, as well. It was too alarming to pursue.

She was sitting on one of the kitchen benches, hugging her knees to her chest against the cramps, when she felt an odd sensation. It was as though she had been holding up a heavy burden—like Atlas with his globe—without being aware of it, and the weight had been gently lifted off her shoulders. She straightened up, blinking, stretched luxuriously, and sighed. *Oh, that feels* so *much better.* She looked around the kitchen. *Why am I just sitting here? I need to go out!*

She got up and walked to the door, but stopped with her hand on the bolt. *But I can't go out.*

Why not?

No, no, I can't go outside. That would not be a good thing.

You need to go on a foray, you can't wait much longer. It's not safe.

No, I've got to stay here.

After a few moments, she let go of the bolt and started toward the bench.

She stopped halfway there, turned around and went back to the door. This time she shot the bolt but froze with her hand on the door latch. The internal dialogue repeated. She couldn't remember why she shouldn't go out and she couldn't remember what she was waiting for. It didn't even occur to her to try to remember who she was. All she could think about was her complaining stomach, which now was sending painful twinges out into her limbs and making her fingers twitch. Her mouth was no longer watering, it was bone dry. Her lips felt parched and licking them only made her tongue even drier. The third time she went to the door, she depressed the thumb latch and swung the door open.

The cool evening air gusted in past her, and she sucked in a deep breath, filling her lungs with intoxicating smells. There was blood out there—close by, but very faint and elusive, mice and shrews and other small creatures, hot and vital, their hearts thrumming with energy. She stepped outside, so immersed in the information her senses were collecting that she didn't bother to close the door behind her, didn't remember that the door even existed. It was late dusk, the sky overhead deepening and filling with stars, the very last glow of sunset making silhouettes of the trees in the west. She stood on the beaten path to the door, her bare feet soaking in the sensation of dry grass and soft dust, her face upturned as she sniffed and sniffed, turning this way and that. Small creatures would be hard to catch, and not very profitable for the effort. No, she needed something…something…her mind had regressed beyond verbalizing, although it was still, in its way, thinking logically. Visual images flicked by, as though she was searching the pages of a book. Yes. Barn. Up at the end of the ingress road, past the boundaries of Thomas' property. One of the farmers in Lincolnville used it, he pastured heifers there in the summer. It was isolated. No dogs, no people nearby. He stored hay there, too.

She was already walking even as she thought this, around the house, past her car out to the ingress road, turning left. She had a single-minded fixity of purpose that exceeded even the most disciplined focus she'd achieved from years of magical training. There was not one extraneous or distracting thought in her mind. Her awareness was open for any closer opportunity that might appear, and she was keenly alert for anyone who might see her, because she knew she couldn't allow that. But the woods were empty of anything larger than a woodchuck, at least close enough to be worth chasing. She could see them, occasionally, like fuzzy balls of light dashing into the underbrush or up trees, claws loud on bark and stone. If they were close enough, she could hear their hearts beating.

The stars were brilliant in the sky by the time the barn loomed into sight on the far side of the shadowed meadow. There was a long drive leading to the structure from Bridge Road, but the meadow was entirely surrounded by trees, making the barn a secluded spot. To Diana's eyes, it wasn't dark at all, but the landscape didn't seem illuminated by an outside source—instead, it appeared to be faintly glowing on its own, so that details and textures had an artificial, flat look. Her eyes fixed on the barn, Diana unthinkingly hopped over the fence, which was four feet high, and walked slowly toward the building. She could already smell a rich, deep fragrance on the light breeze. There were unquestionably larger animals here. She'd have to be careful about approaching them so they wouldn't get spooked. She slowed her steps, with effort, unaware that she was moving so quietly, a dog wouldn't have heard her.

When she reached the barn, however, she paused in puzzlement. It was very quiet inside, and the smells of manure and mud seemed stale and old. The maddening rich blood scent was strong, but it seemed to be coming from above her. There couldn't be livestock up in the rafters. The large main door of the barn was chained and padlocked. Diana walked around the building and came to a smaller door. It also had a padlock, but on closer inspection, she saw that the hasp had been pried off the door and cleverly tacked up to create the illusion that the door was secure. It wasn't even latched. She carefully pulled the door open just far enough to slip inside. She could feel that the hinges wanted to creak and lifted the knob upwards to silence them.

It was much darker inside the barn, and she had to let her eyes adjust for a few seconds before the beams and stalls and a small tractor resolved as contrasting shapes of gray fog. There were no large animals, just mice skittering through little tunnels in the dirty hay on the floor. But, oh, the *smell*...now her mouth was watering again. Forgotten, the door swung shut behind her, creaking, and thumped lightly on the jamb. She heard something move above her, and looked up. Something was up in the loft, something that smelled pungently delicious. She spotted the ladder and started to climb up.

The ladder creaked once, and a gravelly man's voice barked, "Hey! Who's down theah?" After a series of scrambles and thuds as the voice's owner slipped and skidded on the loose hay, a sharp scratching noise was followed by a flare of light. Diana froze on the ladder, shocked. She hadn't expected a human being. For a moment, she almost quailed, but she took another breath and the warm smell, like a restaurant kitchen, washed over her consciousness like the rush of a drug. She climbed the rest of the way up the ladder.

The loft's occupant was thin, dressed in filthy jeans that barely clung to his hips and bagged around his bony legs and posterior, matched by a grimy flannel shirt and a rank, too-small denim jacket, one sleeve half detached at the shoulder seam. His sallow face was mostly obscured by a short ratty beard, over which red-rimmed eyes squinted at her in the light of the kerosene lantern he'd just lit. He relaxed slightly when he saw her, although his body was still tense. He had a crowbar in his right hand, but his arm was by his side.

"Hey, girlie, ya should warn a guy, ya know? I mighta done sumpin desperate." Diana stepped over the top of the ladder and hunkered down easily, studying him. His mouth crooked into an ingratiating smile, revealing gaps where he was missing teeth. "This bahn yours? Hey, ya wouldn't begrudge a vet a place to lay his poor old head, wouldja? No room at the inn and all that?" He laughed wheezily. A khaki duffle bag, looking mostly empty, was rolled up in the straw, and a bottle peeked out from under it. He reeked of whisky, and even more from lack of bathing. But all Diana could smell was his blood, tinged with an exciting whiff of fear and adrenaline. His heart was beating very fast and kept skipping.

"Ya all alone?" He craned his neck to peer down into the lower level, although to him, it was pitch dark. "'Lo...! Anyone theah?" Diana just watched him silently. Later on, she would recall these words, but now, they had no meaning for her at all. They were just noises, and all she was listening for was the opening to make her move.

"Guess not. Whatja want, honey, come to keep a lonely guy comp'ny? Cold night, ain't it?" His smile became a leer. He looked so ridiculous, Diana smiled back at him, and his leer broadened to a grin. He shoved the crowbar underneath the duffle and hung the lantern from a nail that stuck out from one of the wall studs. "Come on over heah, honey. Don't be shy. Wassa matta, can't ya talk? 'S okay, girl like you don't need to say nothin', I get the pictcha. Come on, honey...'as right..." She half rose and walked slowly towards him, crouching like a stalking cat. Doubt clouded the man's face, and he glanced at her bare feet, his brows creasing. "You okay, baby? Why'ncha say sumpin?"

Diana hunkered down again directly in front of where the man crouched on one knee. The tricky part, she knew, was getting a good grip on him so he couldn't get away. She smiled again, because that had worked well the first time, and he giggled nervously. "Yeah, okay, I get it, s'okay..." She put her hands on his shoulders and bent towards him. He tried to meet her mouth with his own, but she ducked down toward the side of his neck and he bumped his nose against her cheek bone. "Hey," he said, and tried to push her back. She jerked her head up and tightened her grip on his shoulders, and his eyes widened.

"Hey, that hurts, cut it out—" His road-bred wariness had snapped to full alert now. Diana might not look threatening, but she was far too strong, and he was canny enough not to trust the situation. He put his hands together and brought his arms up sharply in front of him. Startled, Diana let go of him and jerked back, and he scrambled toward the head of the ladder, babbling. "Look, I'm gettin' outta heah, okay? See, honey, I'm leavin', sorry for all the trouble..."

Diana stared at him as he passed her and then sprang after him, snarling impatiently. He glanced back at her face and blanched. "Hey, hey, hey!" he shouted, and flung himself at the top rung of the ladder in blind panic. He tried to heave his leg around and over, missed the lower rung with his foot and lost his grip with a panicked yelp. Diana reached the ladder just as he started free fall, grabbed hold of the ladder sidebar, reached down and deftly caught the man in midair by the back waistband of his jeans, left handed. He seemed to weigh almost nothing. He swung suspended in space, arms and legs splayed and eyes bulging, his breath forced out of him. Diana braced herself, tightened her grip and swung him back up onto the loft floor—or that's what she meant to do. She misjudged the amount of effort it would take and the man's inertial mass. As he soared up over her head and through the air in a graceful arc, she stared after him in open-mouthed surprise. He crashed into the back wall of the loft, barely missing the lantern, and crumpled to the hay, wailing in pain.

Diana reached the wall a second after he did and pounced on top of him, tearing his shirt open. His right arm was limp, but he flailed at her with his left, his feet kicking up loose hay. "Lemme alone, lemme alone, I wasn't going ta hurtcha, lemme go—" She put her hand over his mouth to shut him up, but she couldn't stop the muffled squeals and his body heaved underneath her. No matter. She had him now. She twisted his head to the side, leaned down and locked her mouth onto his sour-tasting skin. His pulse hammered against her lips. She focused her attention and *opened,* the way her instinct told her to—but far too much. Blood burst into her mouth, hard pumping spurts that she couldn't swallow fast enough or contain. She gulped huge mouthfuls as fast as she could, but the thick red stuff was everywhere, soaking the man's shirt, her own shirt and skirt, and the straw around them. Splatters dimmed the kerosene lantern.

She'd never felt such a rush of absolute euphoria, or tasted anything so delicious. Her stomach cramps instantly stopped. The man's alcohol-laced, anemic blood was like the ambrosia of the gods, every swallow sending heat all through her body, to the tips of her fingers and toes. She hadn't realized until then how cold she was. She couldn't get enough of it, and so much was getting wasted. She hadn't meant to waste a drop. But the flow was already slackening sharply, and the man's heartbeat was a fluttery whisper. His body was shuddering underneath her, and she felt a sudden alarm go off in her mind: *stop, stop, enough, you need to close now...* But it was too late. He'd lost too much blood too fast, and his heart had arrested. Even as she pulled back, blood dripping from her mouth and chin, his heartbeat stopped, and a long, rasping breath sighed out of his gaping mouth. His half open eyes stared past her at the cobwebbed rafters overhead.

Diana sat straddling his chest, staring numbly down at his face, suddenly and mercilessly lucid. *Mother Goddess, what have I done?* It wasn't that she didn't remember how she had gotten here or what had happened. Every detail was etched into her consciousness, including her state of mind between the time the sun went down and this awful moment. She didn't want to believe it, but her new senses were ruthlessly feeding her every grisly detail of the brutal reality. She was crouching on the body of a dead human being, and she had killed him. He had done absolutely nothing to deserve it. She had stalked him, attacked him, and slaughtered him while he struggled and begged for his life. The smell of blood almost overwhelmed her if she took in a breath—she was drenched with it. Back in the kitchen, she'd asked herself what would happen if she didn't get blood, but in her worst nightmares, she hadn't imagined this.

*Thomas will never forgive me...*but that didn't matter. He was the only one who could help her now. She bowed her head, tears welling from her eyes. *I'm sorry, I'm sorry, whoever you are, I didn't mean for this to happen...*It was true. As hungry as she'd been, never had she wanted or intended to kill anything. After all, Thomas never had. She knew it wasn't necessary. She'd just wanted the cramps in her stomach to stop. A few long swallows would have been enough.

She turned out the lantern, thankful that in all the chaos, the barn hadn't been set on fire. It might be one way of destroying the evidence, but it would attract far too much attention to Thomas' property. She carefully set the jerry-rigged door latch the way she'd found it. She trotted across the meadow, vaulted the fence without breaking stride and continued down the ingress road at a jog, more anxious about someone spotting her than eager to confront Thomas with what she'd done. She hoped that Thomas was back at the house by now, but this whole misadventure had taken less than an hour. Dread over his probable reaction mingled with bitter defensiveness in her mind—he owed her, after all, not only for her current predicament but for the extremely close call when he'd lost control before the athanor was fired. He couldn't justify condemning her for this. She kept repeating that silently, but beneath her bravado she was writhing with remorse.

When the stone house came into view, she felt relief and apprehension simultaneously. Lights showed in the first floor windows. She slowed down, walking as silently as she possibly could, feeling a qualm that had nothing to do with the dead tramp in the barn. This was the first time she'd seen Thomas since their spell had been grounded. She had no illusions that things between them would simply go back to the way they had been before June. Too much had happened between them for that. But she didn't know what to expect.

As she walked around to the back of the house, through the windows she saw Thomas in the kitchen. He sat at the long table, his chin resting on his clenched hands, his expression one of worry and guilt. She tried the door latch. The door wasn't bolted, and she pushed it open and stepped in. Thomas leapt to his feet when he heard the door, and as she entered, he stood frozen in place, staring at her. His look of relief and joy almost instantly melted into one of aghast horror. She self-consciously held one hand up to her throat, trying to hide some of the blood with her arm, but the gesture was a futile one under the circumstances.

"Oh, my god..." Thomas said softly. "What have you done? Where have you been?"

She couldn't meet his shocked eyes and looked down at her gore-soaked clothes. "I...I just went..." Unable to suppress her guilt in the glare of his appalled look, she was choking up too much to talk, stinging tears already sliding down her cheeks.

"Where did you go? Did anybody see you?" She shook her head mutely, and he looked behind her and said frantically, "Shut the *door!*" as if they had neighbors who might be spying on them. Suddenly angry, because it was easier to be angry than endure the other things she was feeling, she turned around, slammed the door and bolted it.

"What *happened?*"

"What do you think? You weren't here, Thomas! I woke up and you weren't here!"

"That's...I didn't know...I had no idea you'd wake up, Diana. I couldn't wait here all that time, there were critical issues I had to attend to."

"Critical issues! By all the gods, Thomas, what could have been more critical? You knew I'd wake up the next night!"

"Next night?" His expression softened for a moment. "Diana—it's been three days."

She gaped at him, stunned. "Three days? But—"

"I was starting to despair that you'd awaken at all. And in the meantime—"

"Three days! But, Moira, the apartment, gods, Thomas, I have to go to Bangor!"

"I'll get to all that in a moment. Right now, we obviously have a crisis on our hands. You've got to tell me what happened."

"*I killed someone!* That's what happened!"

"*What?* You mean a human being? Who, where?"

"I don't know who he was, some vagrant! He'd broken into that old barn on Bridge Road, the one that...that..." she choked back a sob. "There are cows there sometimes, that's why I went there."

"Did anyone see you?"

"I don't know! I wasn't in my right mind, Thomas, you should have been here! I didn't know what I was doing, I *opened* too much, I couldn't stop it...oh, gods, Thomas..." she buried her face in her hands, unable to continue. Thomas turned away and started pacing back and forth.

"You shouldn't have left the house, Diana, you should have waited for me."

"That doesn't matter now, Thomas—"

"But a murder, practically in our back yard, do you know how much trouble this could cause? How could you do such a thing?" He came to a halt directly in front of her. "Stop it, Diana, stop crying! You can't blame me for this. You lived with me for two years, you should have known better!"

She stared at him incredulously. "Known better?" She thought of the hours she'd spent that afternoon trying to recollect things he'd said, and her frustration over all the enormous gaps he'd left in her knowledge. "How could I have known better, Thomas? How could anything have prepared me for this? A man is dead, and all you can think about is how much trouble it will cause you, and whether anyone saw me?"

"That's not what I—"

"And you say I can't blame you?"

"Blame *me?* In two hundred years I never caused one single human death, and you've started a body count on your very first night! How is that my fault?"

The emotion in his eyes and voice was fear, not anger, but Diana couldn't bear his recriminations—they parroted her own guilt too perfectly. Before she could stop herself, she blurted, "damn you to hell, Thomas!" then hauled back and punched him in the face. For the second time tonight, she underestimated her new strength. She felt bone give under her hand. He reeled back, staggering, crashed into the kitchen table and barely stopped himself from falling to the floor. As he recovered his footing, Diana, appalled, took a step towards him, and he flinched violently. He took several steps back from her, both hands cradling his face tightly, his eyes wide with shock.

"Thomas...? I'm sorry, I didn't think...I didn't know I could..."

Without moving his hands, he said in a husky whisper, "You broge muh shaw."

That put an end to their conversation for the moment. Diana wondered if there was anything else she could do to foul things up more thoroughly tonight. "Mother Goddess," she choked as she sank down to sit in a miserable huddle on the brick floor. "I should never have woken up."

"Don' say tha,'" Thomas hissed urgently. He stood absolutely still for several minutes, his hands tight against his lower face as if he had applied epoxy to the break and was waiting for it to set. Finally he lowered his hands, wincing as he cautiously worked his mouth a little. He went over to the table and sat down on the bench, facing Diana where she sat on the floor, head bowed to her knees.

"Come over here and sit down, before I give you some ashes from the stove to put on your head," he said gently, still slurring his consonants a bit. She looked up at him blankly, then got up and joined him at the table.

"So...where is the poor bastard?"

"In the barn, up in the loft."

"You think he was a tramp, someone who won't be missed?"

She nodded. "He'd broken in, or someone had. People talk about tramps using vacant buildings around here, I thought it was just paranoid rumors."

"No, I've seen them sometimes. They travel along the coast between Bangor and Boston."

"That farmer doesn't keep his cows up there anymore?"

He shook his head. "I'm surprised that you remembered that, in...in the state of mind you were in. He moves them in late summer, you didn't know." He looked down. "I'm...sorry I wasn't here. I would have been back before sunset, but...I was delayed."

"How do you go out on a day like this?" she burst out suddenly. "I couldn't even look out the window."

"We'll talk about that. It will take some time for your senses to balance out." He rubbed his eyes tiredly. "Diana, we've got to go to the barn and take care of things. We don't want anyone to discover the body. You'd better clean up first just in case we have the desperately bad luck to meet someone."

She spread her hands helplessly. "I don't have clothes to change into."

"You have all your clothes. Some were in your car—that's where I found those—and I've got your suitcases now."

She'd completely forgotten about the belongings packed in her car. "You got my suitcases? From the apartment? How did you know they were there?"

"I didn't, but…Moira's sister has been here."

"Oh, gods…"

"She drove down here looking for you when you didn't answer the phone. She's hired a moving company to pack up the apartment and salon. She asked me if you wanted to take over the apartment lease. I didn't know what to say, I told her I'd give you the message."

"She's closing everything up? Thomas, is Moira—"

"She's not deceased, apparently, but her sister wouldn't give me any details." He got up from the table. "You'd better start cleaning up. I'm going to put together some tools."

Diana sighed. "This will take hours. I hope no one sees us."

"Oh, it won't take that long. You're going to be amazed at how fast you can dig a grave now."

෴ 21 ೲ

Thomas was right—the two of them, with spades, a mattock and their enhanced strength and speed were able to dig a grave six feet deep with amazing alacrity. For someone who'd never committed a murder, Thomas was thorough and efficient about disposing of a body, calmly thinking of details that would never have occurred to Diana. At his insistence, they stripped the pathetic corpse naked and stuffed all his clothes into the duffle, along with the bloody straw. Diana scrubbed down the blood that had soaked through, cringing at how widely it had splattered. The stains wouldn't come out of the wood surfaces, but Thomas told her they were unlikely to rouse any suspicions. "If anyone does come up here and find blood stains, they'll just think an owl or a cat caught something."

As they shoveled the dirt back into the grave, Diana whispered a prayer to Persephone for her victim. Under other circumstances, he could have been one of the aimless drifters who stopped at Bread and Roses' soup kitchens for a hot meal—in fact, for all she knew, he had done that, in the course of his wanderings. They'd dug the grave in the meadow, and once the thick top layer of turf and long grass had been replaced, and the excess soil scattered to the winds, there was no sign that the ground had ever been disturbed. Before they left the meadow, Thomas repaired the hasp so the barn door was secure. "Not that it will take long for the next determined tramp to break in," he said resignedly. He hunted around and found chalked marks near the road and barn, signs that tramps left for each other, he said. He rubbed them out.

They burned the duffle, along with all their own bloodied and dirt-soiled clothing, in the large firepit where they'd made a bonfire from debris cleaned out of the Schuller house two years ago. The few metal bits mingled with all the nails and scraps already there. Diana was humbled to see how completely a human being could be erased from existence. Was there still anyone out in the world who cared about him, thought of him, wondered what had become of him? They would never know his fate. She hadn't even known his name.

After they had completely finished their grim tasks, cleaned and put away the tools, and washed off the grime and dirt from the digging and burning, they found themselves sitting in awkward silence at the kitchen table. It seemed impossible to simply carry on without talking about everything that had happened since the day the working had peaked, but neither of them knew where to begin. Even if they rationalized that their mutual antagonism had been magically forced, they couldn't simply forget their feelings, or the things that had been said and done. Diana knew, as surely as if she could read his mind, that Thomas would never again be able to look at her without recalling his violence against her three nights ago, and the fact that he had deliberately released the dragon and let it take her. That act alone would stand between them forever. Except for her hitting him, they hadn't touched each other once since she'd awoken. Diana felt fairly certain that they never would.

She recalled their months of intimacy with sadness, but as she reflected on it, she wondered how much of it had ever been genuine. Before that moonlit night in June of 1952, when she'd taken Thomas' hand and vowed to complete the magical working with him, she hadn't felt any special attraction to him. She'd wanted his knowledge, nothing more. As for Thomas' natural tastes—well, she certainly wasn't a blonde. Their bond, and their passion, had been spun and woven out of their combined magic, and when the spell dissolved into the infinite cosmos like dust, it took their connection with it. *One more thing,* Diana thought bleakly, *that I should have anticipated, and was totally blind to. That would have happened even if the working had been successful. I just didn't want to admit it.*

When Thomas finally interrupted her deep brooding, Diana started—it felt inappropriate, like someone laughing during a memorial service.

"I was...very glad to see you walk through that door tonight. I apologize if my subsequent behavior was ungracious."

She smiled weakly and shrugged. "Perfectly understandable. I apologize for hitting you. Do our bones really heal that fast?"

"Smaller ones, that don't take a lot of stress, will knit in a few minutes. They'll take a day or so to fully heal. Apology accepted, I fully deserved it. But when I arrived here and found the door standing open and you gone, I almost panicked. I'd tried to get back before sunset, but—"

"I'd been awake for hours by then. What happened? Did you just not want to be in the house with me?"

He looked down, shame-faced. "A weakness for which I make no excuses. But...I was seldom far away. I checked on you regularly. Unfortunately, I had to go into town, in order to forestall visits from anyone who would ask questions about your car being here. And I needed to conclude matters with...with Catherine."

"Catherine." Diana sighed. "So what happened there? Did you break off your engagement?"

"It was the only decent thing to do. She...took it very hard. That's what delayed me this afternoon. Then there was Moira's sister, and all her questions about you and the apartment. I couldn't think of any reasonable explanations for your disappearing."

Diana made a despairing sound. "I've *got* to get up to Bangor tomorrow."

Thomas shook his head. "You can't drive by yourself yet, Diana."

"I'll go after dark, visiting hours are—"

"It's not just the obstacles presented by bright light. Those can be managed. It's not *safe* for you to drive just yet. I don't mean safe for you, it wouldn't be safe for other people on the road."

She stared at him blankly. "I don't understand. I can't drive anymore?"

"You'll be able to drive. You'll need some time to adjust to your physical abilities, so you don't over-control the car." Diana, thinking of the tramp soaring over her head, and the way she'd broken Thomas' jaw, nodded soberly. "But that's not all. You're...you're still changing."

"I am? Mother of all the gods, Thomas, what *else* could possibly happen?"

"You're forgetting something rather dramatic," he said quietly. When she still looked blank, he prompted, "'clothes and all?'"

She pressed her hands to her mouth, staring at him incredulously. "I can dematerialize?"

"You *will* dematerialize. Until that ability makes itself known, and you've learned to control it—well, you don't want to be behind the wheel of a car."

She imagined that, and gulped. "But how can you be sure? Maybe I won't be exactly like you—maybe I'll pop out with some other weird talent."

"I'd prefer to err on the side of caution. You may be right, but I still doubt you'd want to be on the open road when something else unexpected kicks in. So far, however, your experiences are duplicating mine exactly."

" But...what am I going to do? Call a cab?"

"I'll drive you, if you trust me with your car. Oh, I can drive," he added at her surprised look. "I have other ways of moving around, as you've realized from the beginning. I know you were frustrated that I wouldn't tell you about it. Your curiosity will soon be satisfied. But I've been able to drive since automobiles were invented. I've always thought it wise to master the fastest available forms of escape."

"Do you have a license?"

He smiled wryly. "I'll drive *carefully*." She rolled her eyes. "If it's sunny tomorrow, I have dark glasses you can use. They're triple-lensed."

"I didn't even think about dark glasses today." She looked at Thomas sadly. "I'm afraid Moira isn't your biggest fan, after the last three months."

"I can imagine she wouldn't be. Her sister doesn't have a high opinion of me, either. I'll stay out of sight, she needn't know I'm there."

"Well, thank you, Thomas. This...means a lot to me." Now that the effects of the magical working were gone, Diana honestly didn't know how to sort out her feelings about Moira, but she knew she had to see her.

"It's the least I can do. What actually happened, by the way? Her sister was rather tight-lipped. She made it sound like you dumped Moira at the hospital and fled, but I can't imagine—"

"Oh, for pete's sake." She sighed. "It's a long story."

He spread his hands. "The first of many. I knew she was ill, I could perceive that much—but I didn't know just what was wrong."

By habit, Diana took in a deep breath, and began to tell Thomas about waking up to find Moira having an attack, and taking her to the doctor's office in Bangor. From there she had to back and fill and talk about what happened when she tried to cross the boundaries imposed on her by their backfired working. For the rest of the night, they traded stories, painfully and cautiously confessing what they had experienced during the past three months, sometimes retracting hard words that had been spoken.

"I did overhear what Mr. Fitzhughes said to you that day," Thomas admitted, when Diana asked him again how he'd known that she didn't tell him about the leaves. "But not because I was deliberately eavesdropping. I heard most of your conversation in the kitchen through the grating, and I was heading out on a foray when I passed you talking by the road."

"Why didn't you ask me about it?"

He just shook his head. "I honestly don't know. When you didn't tell me what he'd said and showed you...I think I didn't want to believe it, quite frankly. I wasn't telling you everything about my nightmares. I just didn't want to confront the increasing likelihood that everything was going to go wrong and we'd fail. I didn't want to shake your confidence and faith in our working."

Diana closed her eyes for moment. "That's exactly how I felt."

They were silent for a time before Thomas asked, "Have you heard anything from Mr. Fitzhughes?"

"Nothing. Not a word. But..." There was one topic they had yet to broach, it was so painful for them both. Diana braced herself. "Let me tell you about Brent and Carole."

He flinched. "There's more, besides the obvious?"

"A *lot* more."

They were both sagging with fatigue by the time the sky was light outside. Without discussion, they each retired to their separate rooms. Thomas gallantly carried Diana's suitcases upstairs for her, but Diana wasn't sure what to do about all the things in her car. She supposed she should bring them inside, but she wasn't yet certain about moving back into the stone house. She went and got the quilt and pillows from her old room, because she liked them. After she'd curled up under the covers, like Thomas needing them only for comfort, not warmth, she unconsciously hugged a pillow to her chest the way a child hugs a teddy bear. She stared blearily at the light growing behind the blankets over the windows until she fell asleep, if sleep was what it could be called. Her last thoughts were about Gregory.

Before they left for Bangor in the late afternoon, Diana worked up the courage to look at herself in the spotted, age-filmed mirror over the bathroom sink. Thomas' appearance had prepared her for some of the changes, and she told herself that she only looked so startlingly rejuvenated because she'd been so haggard and worn a few days earlier. But she knew something else was disturbingly different. She stared into the glass for some minutes before she finally realized that the white streak in her hair was gone.

Thomas drove a car with the same unassuming competence he displayed in everything he did. Diana wore a wide-brimmed hat and the triple-lensed dark glasses and was still barely able to see for the glare. When they arrived at the hospital, Thomas discreetly settled in a lounge near the vending machines, while Diana found the wing where Moira's room was located. She checked in at the nurses' station, where she was relieved to learn that Moira had no other visitors at the moment. Clutching a paper-wrapped bouquet of gladiola sprays from the apartment yard, Diana walked apprehensively down the hall to Moira's room. Moira had roommates, but Diana didn't plan to discuss anything sensitive. She avoided taking a breath, since the odors of antiseptic, blood, human waste, inadequately bathed bodies and illness was nearly unbearable to her enhanced sense of smell.

She hesitated in the doorway of the room. The curtains screening the beds were partially pulled. One of the roommates was immersed in a book and the other was snoring. Moira appeared to be asleep. She looked terrible, but Diana wondered if that was really new, or if she had been as blind to Moira's suffering as she had been to everything else. Dark smudges lay under Moira's eyes and her closed eyelids looked bruised. Her haggard face appeared ten years older than it had a week ago and her tall body seemed shrunken, somehow, under the thin hospital blanket. Diana slunk into the room and took a plastic vase from the shelf under the wide window. She put the glads into it and set them on Moira's bedside table, then sat in the creaking straight-backed chair by the bed. Moira stirred at the sounds she made.

"Um...Muriel?"

"It's me, Moira. It's Diana."

Moira's eyes flickered open and she slowly turned and stared groggily at Diana, squinting to focus. Her whole face curved into a slow smile, like dawn breaking through fog. "Baby...oh, thank god. I've been so worried." Her voice was a throaty whisper. Her pupils were dilated, so Diana guessed that her affect wasn't entirely due to her illness, which was reassuring in a perverse way.

"I know, Moira. I'm so sorry." She clasped Moira's fingers, gently, because there were band-aids over the veins on the backs of her hands.

"When Muriel said...you weren't answering the phones anywhere...I was afraid that...that maybe..." Her lip was trembling.

"That I'd been done in? Not a chance." Diana forced herself to smile. "I had a personal crisis, very unexpected, I had to leave the state. The doctor wouldn't give me any information."

"S'okay, I understand. Happens. I'm so glad you got here in time."

Diana's mouth felt dry, but she tried to keep her voice light. "In time for what? Your prognosis can't be that bad."

Moira smiled. "Dumb doctors, what do they know?"

"Not much. What do they say?"

Moira was silent for a moment. "Muriel's taking me back to Philadelphia with her. There's a nice place down there where they'll look after me. Docs say I'll be home for Christmas."

Diana felt her throat constrict. She just nodded.

"We're leaving tomorrow. That's why I'm glad you made it, kiddo. Can't wait, we've got a nurse traveling with us."

"That's good—about the nurse, I mean. And I'm glad your family is coming through for you, Moira."

"Wasn't my family who cut those ties, hon. But it doesn't matter now. Time to let bygones be bygones." Her face creased in a frown. "Your hand's so cold."

"I've been worried, too."

There was a silence, as Moira stared into space. Finally she said, "Kiddo... what we had...it was great, but things change, y'know?"

"I know, Moira. We both needed someone for a while, and we were there for each other. We were just lucky, that's all."

Moira turned and smiled at her again, the understanding smile of a loving parent. "Sure were."

"You don't need me to...to come down to Philly with you?"

Moira closed her eyes, shaking with a whispery chuckle. "Oh, honey. My family would have ten fits apiece. They already figured out that we're more than just friends. If Muriel walks in before you leave, there'll be an explosion."

"I gave the nurses my real name. She'll have to yell at them."

Moira chuckled again. "She will. 'Course, they're used to it."

"I can see the family resemblance." Moira's chuckle almost became a real laugh, until she started coughing. "Oh, damn, now I've done it," Diana said patting Moira's shoulder helplessly.

"Nah, nah, not you," Moira wheezed when she got herself under control. "These damn tubes they had in me reamed me out. I'm better now than I was, can you believe it?"

"I brought some of the glads you planted, by the way." Diana gestured at the vase, and Moira craned her head back to look.

"Oh, you're so sweet! Those must be the last of them."

"Just about."

"I heard what you did, hon, cancelling all the appointments and depositing the money and all. I can't thank you enough."

"You don't need to thank me at all, Moira. I owe you, so much."

"Baloney. You do not. Did you want the apartment?"

"I don't think so. I'm going to make other plans. I'll keep the post office box, though. You think you can get away with writing?"

"I'll sure try. I'll bribe some cute orderly to smuggle the letters out in his pants."

"Now you behave."

They talked for a few more minutes about town trivia, a few of the more outrageous reactions Diana had gotten when she called clients, and similar banter. Finally Moira glanced uneasily at the door.

"You better make tracks, kiddo. Muriel was only out running some errands, she's been here almost all the time, day and night. She's really been a brick. But if she sees you..."

"I'm going to have to talk to her...but not here, no." Diana got up, leaned over and kissed Moira's forehead. "Good-bye, Moira. I hope your trip to Philly goes well."

She had to duck into the ladies' room on that floor to compose herself before she went downstairs. It took longer than she'd expected, and finally she had to consciously visualize one of her most infuriating fights with Stephen to work up enough anger to stiffen her backbone. When she got downstairs, she was not surprised to see a tall red-haired woman, looking much like Moira but fifty pounds heavier and stylishly dressed, talking to Thomas. Her green eyes were blazing, and Thomas was responding with such unctuous charm, he was almost oozing onto the hospital floor. He nodded towards Diana as she approached, and Muriel turned, scowling.

"Well, it's about time! Mr. Morgan here says that you were called out of town." *I don't believe that story for a minute,* her expression said.

"Yes," Diana said crisply. "I'm sorry I missed your calls. Moira is a dear friend, but this was family. Family comes first, you know. I'd left Moira in good hands."

She could see that she'd landed a perfect sucker-punch. Muriel bridled and cleared her throat. Diana deduced that she'd been simmering a planned confrontation with her sister's Lesbian lover for three days and the pot had just been knocked off the stove. Thomas was suppressing a smile.

"Well. Of course. I hope everything is all right. With your family, I mean."

"No, but that's nothing you need to worry about. Moira says you're taking her down to Philadelphia?"

"That's correct. She'll be cared for by the best doctors in the world. We're sparing no expense. Are you interested in taking over her lease?"

"Thank you, no. Is there anything more I can do to help you close up the shop or the apartment?"

"It's all done. The movers left this morning. Thank you for offering."

Diana found the dark glasses to be a nuisance on the way home—she kept having to lift them up to wipe away the accumulated tears. Thomas respectfully kept his eyes on the road and pretended that she wasn't there. She'd pulled herself together by the time they got to Pepperell.

☙ 22 ☙

Diana unpacked the Chevy and moved back into the stone house. The night of talking had cleared the air between her and Thomas, although their relationship remained one of mutual, almost professional respect and little more. Without their magical working to fill her time, Diana wasn't sure what to do with herself. But adjusting to her new state of being and Thomas' lessons in how to handle her abilities and go on forays did require time and energy.

For all her curiosity about Thomas' forays during the past two years, now she was learning far more than she wanted to know. Thomas patiently taught her the way to approach domestic animals, methods of detecting, stalking and catching the more elusive wild ones, how to *open* just the right amount, and *close* when she felt the signal that she had drunk as much as her victim could comfortably tolerate. That, indeed, was one of the most difficult lessons, because the signals were subtle and Diana never wanted to stop. Smaller animals, obviously, could not survive this treatment, and Thomas made her practice her technique so she was as swift and humane as possible. He also advised her to conceal the bodies, because humans of a naturalist bent tended to notice dead wildlife and would easily become suspicious. Diana hated killing things, but Thomas pointed out that she had never been squeamish about eating meat when she was alive, and she had to concede to that argument. She told herself that it was much better for a few woodchucks or rabbits to succumb than for her to risk another human death like the tramp's.

Accustoming herself to the enhancements in her senses and physical abilities took more time and conscious effort than she would have expected. Thomas encouraged her to seek out complex sensory situations because she needed to recalibrate her experience of the material world. The first time she walked down Main Street on a Saturday evening, she was almost overwhelmed, flinching back from the curb when a car passed yards away, distracted by the babble of conversations she clearly overheard from almost every building, trying not to breathe in because the smells of human bodies and blood, cooking, car exhaust, trash, even the buildings themselves were so intense. She had long been aware of Thomas' tendency to become completely immersed in tactile sensation, especially. Now she understood exactly why. More than once she was jerked back to awareness by some noise or movement to realize that she had been standing motionless for ten or fifteen minutes, completely focused on the sensation of a leaf brushing repeatedly over her hand or a breeze caressing her face. Increased strength meant that she broke quite a few things before she learned to gauge herself correctly, and increased speed would have made her even more destructive had it not been for her greater agility. Nevertheless, there were days when it seemed to Diana that all she did was send things flying with one hand and catch them in mid-air with the other.

Thomas evaded teaching her about one of her new talents, however. Diana knew instinctively, the way she'd known how to *open* and *close,* that she could now blot out memory and "influence" human minds the way Thomas did. As apprehensive as she felt about drinking again from a human, the temptation to try out this skill was strong. Although she had no worries that she might try and fail, she knew that she'd have to practice and fine-tune the memory blotting the same way that she had to practice everything else. But Thomas never even hinted that he thought she should or could attempt a human victim, and Diana didn't want to ask him about it.

She was kept fully involved with absorbing and processing all of this, and she'd forgotten Thomas' warning that there might be more changes in store.

Four nights after she'd awakened, Diana was sitting at the kitchen table writing a journal entry. She'd been debating whether to resume the alchemical studies she'd abandoned so precipitously last June, and was catching up with some of her notes. She got up to go find a book, took a step toward the parlor door, and her foot never contacted the floor. It disappeared—along with everything else. With no warning whatsoever, her body literally dissolved, with a sickening, vertiginous sensation that Diana could not compare to any experience she had ever had in her life. Suddenly she had a consciousness with no form, perception with no structure, and no sense of up or down. Lacking any physical boundaries, it seemed to her that she was about to irrecoverably dissipate into the atmosphere like a drop of dye splashed into the ocean. Panicked, her mind tried to make her limbs flail, but she had no limbs to obey. She couldn't make any noise, because she didn't have lungs to inhale air or vocal cords to speak. She could see, very clearly in fact, and she could hear, but other senses were mute. If she directed her vision to the space she should have been occupying, there was nothing there.

Before she could react further to this event, she solidified—and that was exactly what it felt like, as though she had condensed and flash frozen within about one second. But somehow, she was now about a foot off the floor. With a teeth-rattling drop, her feet hit the bricks and she staggered into the table.

"Thomas!" she shouted desperately. She heard him shove back the desk chair in his study.

"What is it?" Alarmed by her tone, he was hurrying toward the kitchen.

Diana was standing frozen, her muscles rigid, as if she could hold herself together by tensing up, and she was hanging onto the edge of the table with both hands. Just as Thomas appeared in the doorway, she felt a shift, her hands fell through the table, and she was once more floating bodiless in space. Thomas stopped in the doorway, holding up his hands as if he was trying to calm a belligerent debater.

"All right, just...stay calm. You need to take control of it. It's like magic, don't try to move your body. You need to Intend it. Just...imagine yourself standing on the floor, like—"

She solidified, this time only a few inches off the brick, and gave a little yelp as she dropped. Thomas let out a sigh, rubbing a hand back over his hair. He looked rather shaken.

"Very good, now, can you dematerialize consciously?"

"I don't *want* to!"

"You've got to practice, a lot, or you'll be at its mercy."

"I have to practice *now?*"

"Unless you want to spend the rest of the night puffing in and out of existence, yes."

"Mother Goddess..."

"I told you this would happen."

"How do I—" she broke off. She'd had too many years of magical training not to understand what Thomas was saying about Intending. Reluctantly, she closed her eyes, recalled the ghastly feeling of ceasing to exist and Intended that it happen. The response was instantaneous, but now she felt much less like she would simply expand into nothingness. She could perceive that she did have a sort of form in this state—it was simply drastically unlike her material body. She focused on solidifying with her feet on the floor, and succeeded.

"Now, do that again," Thomas said firmly. With a resigned sigh, she did.

After some hours, Diana felt that she had the process under control, but Thomas shook his head when she said so.

"You'll never have it totally under control. But I need to show you something else. Try dematerializing only partially, about half way."

"What? Is that possible?" Then she blinked in amazement as Thomas half faded out, his form wavering and transparent like the cinematic cliché of a ghost.

"Like this," he said, his voice sounding faint and distant.

She tried twice before she managed to stop dematerializing at the midway point. It was a very uncomfortable sensation, as though she was a rubber band stretched to its limit, and took concentration to maintain. She was also visible this way, her form fading and rippling and distorted as though seen through running water, and this made her feel self-conscious, vulnerable and faintly silly. Exasperated, she solidified, but Thomas stayed as he was.

"Okay, that's a cute parlor trick, but what good is it? What if I'm seen, the jig's up, isn't it?"

"Or someone will be drinking heavily for the rest of the night," Thomas said, solidifying. "What this is good for, is traveling."

"Ohhhh..."

"You can't get far, or move fast, fully dematerialized. You have to partially materialize to cover ground in the physical world. With practice, which I recommend, you'll be able to move very fast, and move long distances."

Diana looked down at her clothes, which had been appearing and disappearing with her. "Carrying things, even?"

"Inanimate objects. Living things won't dematerialize with you. You can try carrying them in an emergency, but the risk of dropping or injuring them is very high." He grimaced slightly, and Diana decided not to ask—her imagination was making gruesome suggestions without any help.

"And I can talk like this, I can make sounds."

"Yes, but usually you won't want to. The last thing you'll want is to be detected by humans."

"But if you and I are out together—"

He hesitated.

"Well, of course. I've never had a companion who could do this."

He looked so uneasy, Diana said, "You don't want one."

"It's not that, but...I hate the idea of having a witness, even another ghostly one. I just feel...ridiculous when I do this. I use it only when and for as long as absolutely necessary. I've never been able to get away from the fear that someday I won't be able to materialize again."

Diana pondered this darkly. "If it hasn't happened in two hundred years, chances are you're just being paranoid," she said finally.

"Chances are, yes, but it does inhibit me from taking undue risks."

"We can just go through walls and things?"

"I have yet to encounter an effective physical barrier. I have run into magical barriers that were quite effective, though. But usually those won't stop you if you solidify."

"Didn't you once say something about, dematerializing to avoid something harmful?"

He nodded. "If you're actually struck by a bullet, for example, or anything else that would cause extreme injury—an axe, or—"

"I follow you, yes. I'll just go poof?"

"Exactly."

"Even if I'm sleeping?"

"Yes. Of course, the disadvantage there is that you can't stop it from happening, it's a reflex. If there are witnesses, you'll be instantly exposed as...well, as something clearly very unlike a human. I'd rather not have to deal with the consequences of that."

"No wonder we're invincible," Diana said. She meant to be humorous, but Thomas looked away from her, his expression troubled.

"Let's sit down for a minute."

A bit apprehensive, Diana sat down opposite him at the table and waited while he seemed to struggle with some ambivalence about speaking.

"You know," he said finally, "that your essential nature has fundamentally changed. You know that you can't be killed or destroyed now—even if you reach a point where you'd wish that."

"I understand..."

"This, your ability to dematerialize, is the most elementary indication of what you are now. You're not real, not in the way you once were."

"Thomas—that doesn't make any logical sense. Of course we're real. We're just different." But he shook his head.

"We have stepped outside the rules and laws of the natural world. We don't occupy it in the same way that ordinary humans do. We're interlopers, in a way—we've been artificially created, like...are you familiar with jewelry making techniques?"

"Not really, I knew people in the Order who make jewelry."

"Do you know the technique of casting soft metal known as lost wax?"

Diana suddenly felt cold. "Yes..."

"The artist models his design out of wax and makes a mold around it. When the hot metal is poured in, it melts the wax and replaces it. That's what the dragon does to us. Whatever we once were was the mold for what we are now. But the original is gone."

"But, our memories, our personalities—"

"All reproduced perfectly."

"What about—what about our souls?"

"I couldn't say about that. What would you think?"

Diana stared down at the table, stunned. "I don't...*feel*...soulless."

"And how would that feel? In Faery lore, Diana, *longaevi* have no immortal souls."

Her mouth felt very dry. "I don't believe it," she whispered.

"That's your prerogative. I don't know for certain. All I can tell you is what I think."

After a long silence, Diana looked up to see Thomas apparently deep in thought. Then he got up from the table. "Go on practicing, if you like." He went back to his study.

As the weeks went by, fall peaked and passed, the leaves brightening the ground almost like snow while the trees bristled against the crisp skies. Diana and Thomas stopped going on forays together, since it was safer and more practical for them to split up and hunt as far apart as possible. Both livestock and wildlife were increasingly difficult to find or access, but Thomas still said nothing to Diana about the human alternatives that he had admitted he fell back on regularly. They spent so much time on forays, they saw very little of each other, but this no longer bothered Diana the way it did when they were partners. She was getting used to her heightened state of being, and had learned how to evaluate sensory impressions naturally and handle everyday tasks and interactions without damaging breakables or giving herself away to other people. She also became much more comfortable about dematerializing to travel than Thomas was, fascinated by the potential of this ability. She used it to roam long distances away from Pepperell, and frequently returned to the house after dawn, when Thomas was already asleep.

It never occurred to her that she and Thomas were avoiding each other, because she felt no conscious aversion either towards or from him. But they largely kept to themselves when they were both at home. They seemed to have little to talk about beyond Diana's vampire lessons and occasional household concerns. With each passing day, the gap between them grew a little wider. Diana longed to hear from Gregory or Moira, but no letters or news came from either of them. She did get a couple of brief, cheery notes from friends in Boston. One of them asked if she was thinking of attending the Order's Samhain ritual, a large and festive event drawing members to the Motherhouse from considerable distances. Diana considered it, but quailed at the thought of being around magically trained people. Would they perceive that she was now something inhuman? She remembered the looks that came over both Gregory's and Conor's faces when they met Thomas. Diana didn't think she could risk it and unhappily sent her regrets. She wished now that she hadn't cut her ties with Bread and Roses so completely. No magical working limited her decisions now, but she still couldn't pick up the threads of her old life.

Perhaps it was her increasing sense of singularity, and the loneliness it brought, that impelled Diana to ask Thomas something she'd never stopped wondering about since his brief comment two years earlier.

"You once said…there were no other vampires exactly like us, but there were other vampires. Can you tell me more about them now, or do you still feel you have to, how did you put it, respect their confidentiality?"

He thought about this for a while.

"I suppose you should know something about them. But I don't feel that I should say too much. After all, you wouldn't want me to gossip to them about you, would you?"

"I'd hardly call it gossip."

"You looked aghast at the idea that another initiate in the Order had been talking to me about you, as I recall."

"Well…" she couldn't argue with his point. "Generally speaking, then. How are they different? If they're not *exactly* like us, in what ways *are* they like us?"

"In most ways, we're the same, but they can be destroyed, for one thing. And they have different abilities."

"Different, how?"

"It varies from one to another. But they can't dematerialize—at least, not the ones that I've met."

"But they can do things we can't?"

"Some of them can influence matter directly in a way that we can't do. I once met one—" Thomas smiled wryly "—who could open locks by willing it. He was the most accomplished thief I've ever met. I doubt there's anything on earth that he couldn't steal, if he took a fancy to it."

"Good gods."

"I believe he's a reformed character now."

"Where are these other vampires?"

Thomas shrugged. "It's been several decades since I was in contact with any of them. We all have to keep moving around, remember. I know some in Europe and some here in America. Most of us have places we prefer and keep returning to, and there are certainly parts of the world where we exist much more comfortably and safely than others. But our fortunes can take us anywhere, even more than humans, which is saying a great deal."

"Could you...could you tell me any of their names?"

But Thomas shook his head somberly. "That would be a violation of etiquette, to the extent that there is any. I don't mean that we have rules or laws. We're rare and scattered, and we have no organization or hierarchy. But there is a sort of gentleman's agreement among us. We respect each other's territory, we don't reveal each other's identities. Mavericks among us don't last long. In any event, we all change our names constantly, so knowing what they called themselves a decade or a century ago wouldn't help you much."

"Could you introduce me, then?"

"I could, but as I said, I'm not presently in touch with any of the others. There are several who have deep roots in the northeastern United States, but I know they've moved on since I last encountered them."

"Can we sense them somehow?"

"You'll recognize them instantly if you meet them, because you'll perceive that they don't have body heat or a heartbeat, any more than we do, and they'll smell like us, which is to say, they don't have any smell at all. But we don't have anything like long-range radar to alert us to their presence. Some of them could be living in the next town over and we wouldn't necessarily be aware of each other."

"Except for the territory-respecting part."

"I was speaking hypothetically. There are too few of us to make crowding a problem."

Diana slumped dejectedly, but Thomas just smiled. "I wouldn't feel too hopeless. I suspect that you'll meet some of them eventually. We tend to cross paths much more often than chance would dictate. They'll identify you just as easily as you will them, and they'll want to find out who you are. You'll just have to be patient."

"If you do happen to run into any of them, Thomas, you have my unqualified permission in advance to let them know how to reach me."

"I'll remember that." He hesitated a moment. "I believe...that they stay much more aware of each other than I have of them. After I left New York, I withdrew from that small society as much as I did from the mortal world. That was my choice, not theirs, and I regret that it now leaves you at a disadvantage."

"Well, at least I've got you."

He looked down uneasily. "As far as that goes."

"I don't know what I'd have done if I'd had to figure this out all by myself, the way you did."

He smiled faintly. "You underestimate yourself, Diana."

"Now that's the first time anyone's said *that* to me."

One morning in early November, Diana returned to the stone house after a night spent aimlessly roaming down the coast. When she materialized inside the bolted kitchen door, she was instantly on alert, without immediately knowing why. She stood very still, trying to analyze what seemed so wrong. It was very quiet, and nothing smelled different. But there was…a certain quality, a residue of something magic, as though the whole house had been touched by an otherworldly power. After the athanor blew up, Diana had felt magically neutralized, but that illusion corrected itself along with everything else when the dragon took her. Still, she had been somewhat wary of magic since that night, and did not want it invading her life uninvited. Had Thomas been doing some kind of working? It was possible, but this didn't feel like him. For some reason, Diana thought of the dream she'd had on the day of Gregory's visit, the little girl in the field of dandelions, with her preternatural beauty and her pale rippling hair. At the memory, Diana's skin prickled all over, and she tensed, as though anticipating an attack.

Gradually she relaxed. Whatever she was sensing, it was over and done with. But the house still felt changed in a more ordinary way…emptier. With a growing suspicion, she started looking carefully around the rooms on the first floor. The kitchen and parlors appeared the same as ever, but Thomas's study was much tidier than it had been the last time she'd seen it. She avoided that room and didn't step past its threshold unless it was absolutely necessary, but Thomas spent much of his time there and the room usually conveyed that impression. Now the desk was clear, the hearth cold, and the shelves neat and dusted.

Frowning, she went upstairs. Thomas was not in his room, and his bed had not been disturbed. The wardrobe still contained clothing, but Diana thought it didn't look as full as she remembered. She couldn't be sure about that, however.

When she went into her own room, there was a folded piece of paper on her pillow. She stopped dead at the sight of it, although she wasn't surprised. Sitting down on the edge of the bed, she very slowly picked up the paper and turned it over in her hands. There was nothing written on the outside of the paper. Reluctantly, she unfolded the sheet. It was a piece of the crisp off-white linen stationery that Thomas used, and on it, in Thomas' angular, old-fashioned script, were a few terse lines.

Diana—
I have been called away unexpectedly. I hope that I will have an opportunity to explain everything to you soon. Presently I cannot commit anything more to paper. You are fully entrusted to make any necessary decisions regarding the property in my absence. You know where to find my papers.
Thomas

She read the note over several times, wondering what she was missing. Who could have called Thomas away, and so urgently that he couldn't even wait for her to return home and hear his explanation in person? Why couldn't he put any more details in writing? She was used to this sort of mystification from Levoissier, but it was out of character for Thomas. Finally she refolded the paper and put it on the nightstand. *I suppose I shouldn't be surprised. He's been pulling away for weeks, and anyway, he's mentioned a number of times that we can't stay in one place for too long. He's been here for almost twenty years, and he was very visible when he was seeing Catherine. Maybe he feels over-exposed now.* But her speculations felt like straw-grasping, and begged the question of the unsettling magical aura that she could still detect in the house. Finally she gave up and went downstairs to wash up and make sure the house was secured for the day.

23

When she awoke that evening, Thomas had not returned, and as the days passed and early winter began to bite down, she heard no word from him. She now had the whole area to herself for her forays, but this only made her more restless than before.

One night she found herself wandering along the main street of a tiny inland town, one of several whose chief economic base relied on the stinking paper mill on the nearby river. The mill operated twenty-four hours a day, and so did the local bars, apparently. But it was now around one in the morning, and the bars were almost empty. They filled up around the shift changes. Diana was hungry enough that her fingers hurt as well as her stomach—she had hunted for two days without success, although that might have been partly because she was so bored with animals. She wandered into two of the bars, had a drink in each, played a game of pinball with two local men who either took their pinball very seriously or were very depressed, and gave up on the bars as a loss. As she strolled down the main street past the last commercial storefronts, wanting to get well away from any lights and buildings before she dematerialized, she became aware that she was being followed. One of the men who had been sitting in the bar she'd just left was trailing her.

She watched him sauntering after her for a minute. He didn't appear threatening. She wondered if he thought she was a prostitute. She wasn't dressed to entice, but nice girls didn't generally hang around strange bars in the middle of the night in mill towns. She did recall making eye contact with this man a couple of times—which meant he'd been staring at her—but she didn't think she'd given him a come-on. But then, come-ons were often born in the eye of the beholder. She folded her arms and adopted a casual pose as the man approached.

He stopped about six feet away from her, swaying a little. He was quite drunk, and a crooked grin was stuck to his face like an off-kilter band-aid. "Hi ya," he said.

"Hi. Pretty cold night." Neither cold nor heat affected her at all, and she was only wearing a light jacket. She reminded herself idly that she was going to have to dress more warmly or it would look suspicious.

"Ayeh, 'tis." The man's breath smoked in the air. "I got a place over theah, if you want ta warm up."

Diana smiled brightly at him, thinking, *No, it can't really be this easy, can it? What's the going rate these days?* She had to suppress a giggle. "Yes, I'm freezing, let's go to your place." He jerked his head back the way they'd come, and she walked up next to him and threaded her arm through his. He seemed delighted.

"You got anything to drink up there, soldier?" He was wearing an army-issued khaki coat.

"I might."

His place was a room on the back of the third floor above a storefront. Diana had deduced that he worked in the paper mill, by his smell, although he was certainly cleaner and better fed than the tramp had been. A narrow wrought iron bed with a disheveled tangle of grayed sheets and old blankets stood on one side. The rest of the furnishings consisted of a card table, a straight-backed chair and a small dresser, next to a sink attached to the wall. A steam radiator pumped enough heat to make the small space almost summery. The man shucked off his coat and tossed it over the back of the chair.

"Make yourself comf'table, honey." He went to the bureau and took out a bottle of bourbon, pouring generous shots into two juice glasses that obviously hadn't seen hot water or dish soap since he'd moved in. He handed her one of the glasses and took a large swig of his own. Diana took a sip, to be polite, then set the glass down and shrugged her jacket off, slowly. Her host's eyes widened as he followed the jacket downward. It couldn't be her looks—Diana's figure was boyish and anything but buxom. Obviously he wasn't too picky. *That makes two of us*, she thought with amusement.

Indeed, the whole situation both amused and excited her more than she could have believed. She was amazed to realize that she *wanted* him. Not until tonight had she even considered what sex might be like with her enhanced senses and body. Now she almost couldn't wait to pounce on this unwitting gigolo, not just for blood, although that was definitely on the menu, but for a simple rut. She hoped he wasn't too drunk to perform.

She began unbuttoning her blouse and he put down his glass, his hand shaking.

"Ya in a hurry, baby?" He didn't mean it as a protest, if his leer was any clue. She just smiled and dropped the blouse on top of her jacket. He stepped forward and grabbed her shoulders, rather roughly, and started kissing her, or more accurately, slobbering onto her chin. His hands roved clumsily everywhere he could reach, groping and pinching. When he got too involved in trying to unhook her bra, she broke off and pulled back, towing him after her by his belt buckle. She was very careful to keep her strength under control, remembering how easily the tramp had been spooked by that.

"Take a load off," she said, pushing him back against the foot of the bed.

The rusty springs groaned and squealed as he dropped down on the end of the mattress. She gave him a shove backwards and climbed up to straddle him. She flexed her arms out of her bra straps and pulled the whole garment off over her head, then stretched out over the man, who began probing and fingering her breasts as though he was trying to find spare change. Somewhat awkwardly, she hoisted her skirt and got her underwear off, making a mental note not to bother wearing any in the future.

He wasn't having any more luck with his own belt and fly than he had with her bra hooks, so she took care of that. He wasn't as hard as he might have been sober, but it would do. She tucked him in and slid down onto him, richly enjoying the loud groans he made. It was a good thing the bathroom was between the two back bedrooms. She herself was enjoying the sensations so much, she almost forgot that he was a part of the situation, despite how hard his fingers dug into her thighs and buttocks as she moved. He came rather quickly, and when he did she felt a wave of energy burst through her body, and suddenly the room seemed lighter. She sat back, blinking in amazement at this. Her partner was breathing so heavily he wheezed, and this finally caught her attention. She looked down at him anxiously, hoping he wasn't having a coronary, but she could hear his heart pounding and it didn't sound impaired.

She shifted forward and bent down to kiss his mouth and cheek, and he smiled, his eyes still closed. She pushed his face to the side and went on kissing down past his ear. When she found the pulse point on his neck, she locked on and *opened*. Blood filled her mouth, sparkling and hot, warming her more with the first swallow than all the radiators in the world could have done.

"Hey!" He jerked in surprise, his hands suddenly grabbing at her shoulders and his knees coming up against her behind, but he didn't have a chance of shaking her off. In a few seconds, his muscles sagged and his arms and legs fell limply onto the rumpled blankets. Far more practiced now than when she'd attacked the tramp, Diana stayed acutely aware of what she was doing despite the euphoria that she never experienced to this intensity from non-human blood. As soon as she felt the first warning signal from his body, she paused, focused her concentration, and made her virgin attempt at memory-blanking

Oops. The man's whole body spasmed, and he was rendered instantly and frighteningly unconscious. *Too much.* She hastily *closed* and licked the blood off his skin so it wouldn't make a mess. Nervously, she put her fingers against his temples and tuned in. He wouldn't recall any of this encounter, or following her, or seeing her in the bar, or what he had for dinner. She sat up, sighing. Too much was better than too little, but she didn't want him to complain to anyone else about his lost time and attract attention to the mark on his neck.

She put her clothes back on, and took the rest of his off, tossing them on the chair back with his coat, then tucked him into bed. She put away the bottle and rinsed out the glasses. When she'd double-checked to make sure she hadn't forgotten anything evidential, she turned out the lights, dematerialized and left the locked room by the crack under the door, letting herself blend and soar with the chill wind that tossed the tree branches outside. It had been a long time since she'd had such a glorious night.

It was hard to go back to animals after that. She found, however, that the ease of her encounter with the paper mill worker had been serendipitous. It was no simple matter to identify, approach and pick up likely prospects in such a way that she could blot herself completely out of their memories, and usually sex wasn't part of the deal. Sometimes, when she was back in the stone house washing up before going to bed, she wondered what Thomas would think, and where her self-respect had gone. What would she have thought, in life, of a friend who had taken to whoring herself for alcohol or drugs? That's what it amounted to. But she brushed off these thoughts. *There's no comparison. I'm just doing what I have to do. I have a responsibility to make sure that I don't go insane from blood starvation and murder anyone else. I'm protecting these people, not preying on them.* If she thought that earnestly enough, it was quite convincing. She didn't like to look at herself in mirrors on those mornings, though.

As the Solstice approached, Diana started going into town every day to check her post box. The sun had set before the post office closed at this time of year, but she'd have gone at high noon if she'd needed to. She took her car on those occasions to avoid provoking questions from the locals, since she knew she still provided a rich vein of gossip in Pepperell. She was hoping for a note from Gregory, or news from Thomas. Her parents sent her a postcard from Rome, but that was the only piece of personal mail she received. Even her friends in the Order seemed to have given up on her. She kept watching for a letter from Moira, but she suspected that, kidding about orderlies notwithstanding, Moira's family would have confiscated any letter Moira wrote. Even more grimly, Diana strongly suspected that Moira was not capable of writing or reading letters by now. Without hearing from her, Diana had no idea what hospital or nursing home she might be in.

She had just gotten back home from one of these errands when she was startled to hear a car pulling up to the front of the house. She'd never heard a car drive up to the house before, and to her sensitized ears, it sounded like a Mack truck—with a plow blade on the front. Her first thought was that it might be Thomas, although she hadn't expected him to arrive in a car. A knock at the front door made this theory unlikely, however, and she hurried to answer it.

When she pulled open the door, she could only stare blankly at the visitor, a stocky man wearing a black cashmere coat and expensive shoes, neither items very practical for the Maine countryside.

"Miss Diana Chilton?"

"Yes...?"

"My name is Harold Winston, I'm an attorney. I'm here on behalf of Mr. Thomas Morgan."

"Thomas...?" She gaped at Mr. Winston in confusion. "Is Thomas...all right?"

"As far as I know. He asked me to come see you in person. I've got some papers for you to look over and sign. If this is a convenient time, that is."

"Oh! Uh, yes, please, come in." She ushered Mr. Winston into the kitchen, where she kept the stove going so the pipes wouldn't freeze. He shivered at the chill in the front parlors, but didn't comment. In the kitchen, he put a calfskin briefcase on the table and unsnapped the clasps, drawing out a folder of legal paperwork.

"What...what is this all about, Mr. Winston?"

"You don't know?"

"I haven't heard from Mr. Morgan for quite a while."

"He's been out of the country. He's asked me to arrange a meeting between the two of you, if you're willing."

Why is Thomas sending an attorney to set up a meeting? Diana thought in utter bewilderment. With a short laugh, she asked, "Is he suing me?"

"Oh, no, no, no!" Mr. Winston said hastily, trying to sound jocular. "Quite the contrary. He's signing the deed of this property over to you. All I need is your signature on a few things and then I'll file the paperwork. The taxes will be paid by escrow for the next five years. Of course, if you have some objections...I'm sorry, I didn't realize this would come as a shock to you."

"A shock" was putting it mildly. Diana was speechless for a few moments. Finally she said, "No, I...have no objections. I'm happy to...I mean, where do I sign? We don't need a notary?"

"Not for this." Mr. Winston seemed relieved to be getting to the business at hand and took a fountain pen from the briefcase. "Now, you can read these over if you wish..."

When Diana had examined the paperwork and signed where Mr. Winston indicated, and he'd replaced the folder in his briefcase, she asked, "Now, what is this about a meeting?"

"Oh, yes. As I said, Mr. Morgan is presently out of the country, but he'd like to meet you on December 27th, if that's convenient for you. If it's not, we can—"

"That will be fine. Where? And what time?"

"Well..." Mr. Winston hesitated, looking a bit apologetic. "Are you familiar with St. Thomas' Episcopal Church in Camden?"

"Of course, everyone is."

"Mr. Morgan has asked if you can meet him in the church at 5:30 p.m."

"In the church? Well, I...of course I can, it just seems..."

"He didn't explain his choice of venue, I'm afraid. That's what he asked."

"Is the church open then?"

"The church is open until 6:00 p.m. daily, and on Mondays they have a chapel service."

"Well...fine, I'll be there."

Mr. Winston removed a small silver case from one of his breast pockets and took an embossed business card from it. He wrote the date and time on the back of the card and gave it to her. "Call at any time if you have questions."

"Thanks, but I'm saving all my questions for Mr. Morgan."

She spent the next week in an agony of suspense. On the night of the Solstice, she walked out to the center of Thomas' stone mandala, where the wild rose bush stuck withered brambles out of the shallow crusted snow. The stars overhead seemed unnaturally bright and large. Diana didn't feel up to performing a ritual, far less having any kind of celebration. No one had asked her to come to the Order's Solstice rites this year—perhaps after her regrets at Samhain, people assumed she wasn't interested. Memories flowed through her mind, scalding her like hot spilled wax: the ritual chamber in the Motherhouse bedecked with fragrant greenery, the night two years ago when she and Thomas had fired the athanor and begun their spell. After a long time, she knelt down and dug into the snow with her fingers. She found a piece of jade almost the size of a penny and tucked it into her pocket.

On Monday the 27th, she dressed with care, put a scarf over her hair, and drove to Camden. She arrived at 5:20 p.m., and waited until services were over and congregation members were leaving the building, which was famous for its stained glass windows. When she went inside, there were still about a half dozen people in the sanctuary. She looked around, wondering if Thomas was here yet. She started when she spotted a man in a dark double-breasted suit who had a similar build as Thomas, but as soon as she looked more closely, she saw that he was mortal, his body glowing faintly in the subdued light. Sighing, Diana scanned the church, but everyone here was human—warm, alive and fragile. The combined thrum of their heartbeats hummed in her ears.

The last stragglers left the church, and the priest, who had been talking to a congregant up in the nave, retired to the vestry to change. It was past 5:30—soon the sexton would be locking up the building. Was Thomas coming? She walked out of the sanctuary into the portico, where the man in the double-breasted suit was standing with his back to her, examining a bulletin board. She was almost at the doors when she heard Thomas' voice.

"Hello, Diana."

She jerked around, thinking for a moment that he must be partly dematerialized, although his voice sounded close. She looked in confusion at the only other person in sight, the man by the bulletin board, who had turned around, and then realization crashed over her like a tub of ice water.

"Thomas..." She couldn't believe what she was seeing, with her vampiric eyes. It had to be a trick. "You're...you're..."

He put a finger over his lips, glancing at the doors to the sanctuary.

"But...but...*how?* What did you do?"

"Let's go sit down."

They went back inside the sanctuary and sat at the far corner of the last row of pews. Diana was so stunned, she doubted she would be able to do anything but stammer. "You cut your hair," she said finally.

He smiled. "I usually wore my hair in the current mode, before I moved up here. I decided it was high time I rejoined the twentieth century."

She could only shake her head helplessly. It wasn't merely his hair, or his being human. He looked older, and his skin no longer had the flawless, almost translucent appearance that Diana's now did. She could see wrinkles crinkling the corners of his eyes, and gray frosted the hair at his temples. He looked like a man of about forty, the age he had been when..."What did you do?" she whispered.

He looked down, but only for a second. "I made a bargain."

"With the—with *them?*"

He nodded.

"They came for you," Diana said slowly, remembering the disquieting aftereffects of a powerful magical presence in the house the day Thomas left. "*She* came for you."

He nodded, his eyes haunted. "Once I had...done what she wanted, she came to ask me...what I wanted."

"To die?"

"To be free of the dragon. That's all I asked."

"But...I don't understand! Why, why did we go through all that, why did you fight so hard to free yourself magically, if all you had to do was—" she stopped, her mouth hardening. "You always knew, didn't you? You always knew that if you only asked, bent your stiff neck and asked, that they'd free you! This was never about your getting free, this was about winning, on your terms, all along!"

"No, Diana. Don't you think I would have asked if I could? You don't simply whistle up the Teg like a sheep dog. I tried to communicate with them, for over a century, by any means I could think of. Nothing I did evoked a response. I started the magical workings because I saw no other hope. I thought that if I wasn't able to succeed on my own, I might at least provoke the Teg into speaking with me. But I had begun to seriously doubt that they even existed. I didn't ask for your help simply to get the Teg's attention, I swear to you. My intentions were sincere from the moment I started searching for you."

She'd already realized that her reaction had been unfair—she was still in shock from the revelation of Thomas' achievement. "I'm sorry. I know. I wish I could say the same."

"I would say so, Diana. You never dissembled to me."

"My intentions may have been sincere, but they weren't pure, that's the trouble. I couldn't see that—until it was too late." She sagged against the back of the pew, looking at him bleakly. "So now you're mortal. And middle-aged. All you have left is—"

"The rest of my life—the life I was given at my birth. With enough time, perhaps, to make up for the mistakes I made in my youth, to have some of the things I was too stupid to want then."

"It seems so...so pointless. After everything you've seen, and done, you're just going to age and die like—"

"Like a normal man, which is more than I deserve." His voice softened. "Diana—I have had so much. I've seen so many things, wondrous things. Think of it—I lived to know you. I can't fairly ask for more. I never wanted to be immortal. I'm not afraid of death. My soul is immortal."

She looked at him sharply, blinking through her tears. "Is there a price?"

"There's always a price," he said quietly. "I could have said no."

She sighed deeply, and they were silent for a few moments. "And what about me? I'm still—" she broke off.

"That is between you and the Lady, Diana. I don't think your situation is at all like mine. Certainly, the motives that brought you to this pass were far more honorable."

She shook her head despairingly. "I don't know why you say that, Thomas. I finally did figure out what you meant when you said I didn't want immortality, that I wanted something else."

"And you don't think you have it? I'll say once more: you underestimate yourself." Diana couldn't suppress a single humorless laugh.

"You're living in Europe?"

"In Paris, for the moment. In fact, I need to catch a plane out of Boston this evening."

"What about your things at the house? Your clothes, your library? You have some books that are priceless, Thomas."

"I'm sure they're priceless to someone. I don't need them. They're yours, if you wish to keep them. Perhaps you can give the clothing to Bread and Roses. I'm leaving my past behind, Diana. I'm making a completely fresh start."

"Is that part of the price?"

"No. It just seems like...the right thing to do."

She nodded somberly, the implications sinking in like cold rain into snow. He didn't have to spell out that she was included in that past. The growing gap between them had finally become an abyss. She could probably get in touch with him if she wanted to—she had his attorney's card, after all. But she knew that she never would.

The sexton began going through the first rows of pews, checking for forgotten items and placing prayer books back in their brackets. Diana and Thomas rose and filed out of the pew to the door. In the parking lot, they paused between their cars.

"Thank you for giving me your property in Pepperell, Thomas. That was extremely generous of you."

"I thought you might need someplace to call home. I know what helping me cost you, Diana—I'm aware of just how much you've lost. Your organization, your apartment in Boston, your friends, your life...it seemed like the least I could do."

She couldn't face the expression in his eyes and looked away self-consciously. "You don't owe me a thing, really. I'm not exactly destitute."

"I know. But you're wrong. I owe you a debt that...well, there's no point in belaboring it. But I have a very strange feeling that someday I'll be able to repay you in truth. I can't explain what form that recompense will take, or why I feel so sure of it, but—that is what I think."

She smiled wryly, and finally forced herself to look at him again. "Well, I... wish you the best, Thomas. May you have a happy life."

"And I wish the same for you, with all my heart."

She shook her head. "You know, a couple of years ago, Gregory warned me that this would happen. I didn't believe him. I honestly didn't think that we could possibly fail."

Thomas looked at her with genuine surprise. "Fail? You still think we failed? On the contrary, our working was a complete success. After all, haven't we both gotten what we really wanted?"

When she got back to the stone house, she went into Thomas' study and methodically went through the desk drawers and shelves, removing the few things that she thought she might need. When she was done, she closed the door tightly, then went outside and closed and barred the shutters on the windows. She couldn't imagine anything that would compel her to enter that room again.

She didn't go out for the next two days. The cheerful holiday decorations everywhere were too jarring, and she dreaded the imminent New Year's celebrations. But finally she grew stir-crazy, and drove into town to check her post box. Along with a couple of advertizing circulars was a small envelope with a Philadelphia postmark and no return address. She stood looking at it for a while, then stuffed it into her coat pocket, tossed the circulars into the trash bin and went back to the stone house—no longer the Morgan place, she thought, it was her property now, every inch. That hadn't sunk in yet. She'd never owned a piece of property, not really. Bread and Roses owned several million dollars' worth, but it was held by the trust. She'd never wanted anything for herself.

In the kitchen, by the stove, she pulled the envelope out of her pocket and tore it open. Inside was a single half-sheet of plain paper.

Dear Miss Chilton,
I promised my sister Moira that I would let you know that she passed away on December 22nd. The family had a private funeral on the 26th. Thank you for all your help.
Muriel Waterford Bergeron

She couldn't pretend it was a shock. Those dumb doctors had called it exactly.

Diana sat brooding for a long time, watching the fire dying in the stove. She thought about what Thomas had said, and the things she had done since he left. *So, what do I do with myself now? Hole up alone here like Thomas, become the next crazy Hermit of Pepperell Hills? Listen to the lichen growing on the walls and wait for the Teg to tap me on the shoulder? I'm nothing but a predator now. Well, maybe I should act like one.*

She got up from the table and went upstairs to change into heavy jeans, a flannel shirt and a jacket. She put out the fire in the stove, drained the pipes, bolted the doors, and dematerialized to leave the house. Then she headed northwest, towards the woods beyond Penobscot Bay.

·

24

In the second week of February, she learned that she had become a part of local folklore.

She didn't leave civilization—or human habitation, at least—very far behind. Predators have to go where their prey is, after all, and she wasn't interested in chasing down moose, bear and bobcat up in the north country. She stalked the densely thicketed second-growth woods that surrounded and separated the communities near the coast, spending a lot of time in trees where she could watch over a wide expanse of terrain for isolated people on foot or large domestic animals. The snow in the woods was deep, but she rarely was on the ground. She spent a fair amount of her waking time dematerialized for more than one reason. She'd quickly discovered that even though she didn't feel the cold, her body could freeze in the bitter temperatures of Maine's winter. She needed to sleep away from direct sunlight, because just a couple of hours of sun on her bare skin resulted in third degree burns. They healed without scarring, but they were excruciatingly painful while they did. For these reasons, Diana found a number of secure sleeping spaces among which she circulated: attics, barn lofts, root cellars, places that stayed at least above the thirty-two degree mark.

She dumped the jacket because it constrained her movements, and she never bothered with boots or shoes. They were just a nuisance in the trees. Her clothes, hair and skin rapidly collected pine pitch, and she began rubbing it on deliberately, along with dirt and moss, as a way of camouflaging her shape and smell. She had no idea what she looked like, but she couldn't have cared less. The whole point was to look like nothing at all. One day a boy walking below her outside of Searstown unexpectedly glanced directly up at her, where she was stretched along a thick branch about fifteen feet above him. He didn't even see her.

She spent a lot of her time that way—not moving, not thinking, not remembering, keeping her mind empty and blank, filling her awareness with sensory impressions, focusing on nothing but the present. The past and the future were irrelevant. She discovered a profound peace in that state. She'd often heard people in the Order talk about "being at one with Nature." Diana felt as though she was literally merging with the natural world, so much a part of it that the boundaries between herself and the earth were unclear even when she was fully materialized.

But then there was the hunting, which required a bit more engagement. Most of it involved tremendous amounts of patience, which she certainly had, but she needed to observe, consider, follow trails, interpret clues. People did not spend a lot of time outside, alone, in Maine during the deep winter. Diana also had no intentions of leaving an unconscious victim in the snow to die of exposure. She drank from domestic animals when she could get inside barns and sheds without creating a disturbance, which often wasn't easy. She could calm dogs and most other mammals, but cats could perceive her dematerialized form somehow and went into full aggression mode, puffing their tails and hissing, and they upset everything else. Chickens and geese were even worse, raising such a din of squawking and noise that their humans usually came to investigate, often with a shotgun. Diana could take advantage of that by simply dropping onto the person from above, but she didn't dare unless she knew for certain that the human lived alone, which was rarely the case.

The fact that inexplicable nighttime disruptions were accompanied by animals, and occasionally a person, being found weakened and groggy with strange puckered, blackened wounds created a bit of a stir in the region, and stories started to circulate. Diana was disregarding all of Thomas' careful teaching and example on the wisdom of staying unnoticed. She could no longer appreciate the value of rational calculation in meeting her needs. When, inevitably, she was seen, the embers of rumor exploded into a bonfire.

She'd gotten a bit careless, because it was almost impossible for her to be unaware of a living creature due to its body heat. She would reconnoiter carefully from the air before she alighted and materialized, and even the tiniest creatures showed up as a dull glow to her vision. She had spotted a shed behind a rambling old house. The shed had some kind of large, warm animals inside, the house appeared dark and still, and the yard between the two of them was an empty expanse of trampled snow and mud. Diana drifted down and solidified on the frozen ground so she could use her sense of smell.

With no warning, the snowbank next to her exploded. The homeowners had a dog, a shaggy and very large Husky/German Shepherd mix that had denned up underneath the snow for the night like a sled dog in the Yukon. She hadn't been able to see its body heat or hear its quiet breathing through the thick packed layers. Startled, she leaped aside and knocked the yelping dog halfway across the yard with one sweep of her hand. It hit the end of its chain, fell heavily to the ground and scrambled frantically on the ice to regain its feet. Suddenly the yard was full of dazzling light as floodlights on the shed and back porch switched on and the back door was flung violently open. Momentarily blinded, Diana whirled around, half crouching, as a man dressed only in a torn white undershirt and dungarees burst out onto the porch, holding a gun. She instantly dematerialized, but it was too late.

"Jesus God, what the hell was that!" There was a shrill woman's voice shrieking something, and the dog leaped at the spot where Diana was now hovering invisibly about four feet off the ground, all its teeth bared and its snarl almost a roar.

"Don't shoot, don't shoot, you'll hit Maxie!" a boy's voice screamed.

"Did you *see* that? What *was* that thing?"

To move with any speed, Diana had to partially solidify, and she didn't dare do that in the glare of the floodlights. She had to drift slowly upward about thirty feet before she could risk becoming visible enough to move. The dog was howling, a wild atavistic bay unlike ordinary barking, as it stood on its hind legs below her jumping up and pawing at the air. Its behavior even unnerved Diana, while its human family were semi-hysterical. "Leave it Maxie, leave it, come here boy—" was the last thing she heard before she shot to the north as fast as she could, considerably shaken. She saw a police car, blue lights flashing, on the road below traveling in the direction of the place she'd just left, but she didn't hang around to see if it was responding or just a coincidence.

That had been ten days ago, and since then, hunting had gotten much harder. Dogs were being left outside, people weren't walking anywhere alone, lights were being left on inside and out of outbuildings. Diana thought it all seemed a little histrionic—after all, she wasn't *hurting* anyone. This was what she needed to do to *prevent* herself from doing real harm. They just couldn't understand how dangerous it was for her to get this hungry.

When she awoke that evening, she could feel that the weather had changed. It wasn't nearly as cold as those clear, still nights when arctic air flowed down from Canada and pooled under high pressure, sinking the mercury as far as thirty below. But it was well below freezing, and the wind had a fierce bite. There was something big coming, a major storm, the kind that only hit once in a few years, even a few decades. She could smell it bearing down, like the dust and sweat of a distant army.

She'd bunked down in the upper loft of a barn, which she used because it had an attached greenhouse that warmed the building, but there was no livestock here. It looked and smelled like the owners reared poultry, veal calves and pigs for market, buying them in the spring and selling them all off in the fall rather than go to the expense of keeping them over the winter. That was a common backyard farmers' practice that contributed to Diana's privation now. But she wasn't alone in the barn tonight. She could hear a radio playing, and two boys were talking. From what she could infer, they'd been assigned to spend the weekend day cleaning up downstairs, and now were smoking cigarettes and relaxing. Diana remained quiet, listening.

"...and residents are urged to stay off the roads. Repeat, stay off the roads unless you have an emergency. Forecasters are predicting a major winter storm over the area during the next twenty-four hours," she heard the radio announcer say.

"Ah, *jeez*," one of the boys said. "I'm gonna be shovelin' snow 'til *Easter*."

"Why'ncha dad get a plow blade on his truck, anyway?"

"He's got one, it's called his son," the first boy said tragically.

"It's good for ya, you'll getcha muscles that way."

"Yeah, yeah, easy for *you* to say. When's your mom pickin' you up?"

"She said five."

"That's now."

"I know, she's comin'. Probably had to wait for the old man to get home, he went over ta Bangor. Hey..."

"Yeah?"

"Aincha scared to be here all alone? You wanna come back with us?"

"You kiddin'? My folks'll pitch a fit."

"Yeah, but...you know all that stuff the guys were sayin'."

"Like *what?*" The first boy's voice dripped with contempt.

"No, listen, I heard it straight from Danny!" the visiting boy's voice had risen excitedly. "He saw it!"

"That's such a pile of crap."

"It was in his *yard!* It just about killed Maxie, tried to strangle him with his chain."

"Crap," the first said in a sing-song jeer. "Crap, crap, crap."

"Is not. You can ask Danny's dad, and his mom, they filed a police report and ever'thing. Eight feet tall, they said, and all covered with moss, or hair, and just one eye glaring out. It was after Maxie, it was going to tear him apart! Then when they turned the lights on, it flew straight up in the air, and Danny's dad, he shot at it, and the bullets went straight through."

The first boy hooted a loud fake laugh. "You are so full of crap, and so is Danny. And his old man is crazy, last year he shot up his own car."

"He thought it was a deer, come on, anyone could do that."

"Too bad the bullets didn't go right through that time. Car's still got holes in it."

"Yeah, well..." the visiting boy muttered. He obviously had a high level of loyalty to Danny. Diana started when a car horn honked from outside.

"That's your mom," the first boy said helpfully. His visitor got up slowly. Diana cautiously peered down over the edge of the loft and saw the boys both getting up, one of them grinding a cigarette into the dirt floor with the toe of his boot. Smoke tickled Diana's nose.

"Are you sure you don't wanna come? When are your folks gettin' home?"

"I dunno, an hour maybe. Nothing is going to get me in my own house, fer pete's sake. Now go on, your mommy's waiting for you."

The visitor broke into a trot as he crossed the yard. Diana moved to the wall of the loft and peered out through the crack between two boards. The first boy taunted from the open door downstairs, "Run, sissy, run! Look out, it's coming for ya, run to your mommy! It's going to getcha!" The visiting boy didn't speed up, but he didn't look back, either. He seemed genuinely scared to be crossing the open ground—it was a fair distance between the barn behind the house and the road out front where an old Ford pick-up truck was waiting.

Diana waited until the truck had pulled away and was out of sight, then dematerialized and ghosted down to the first floor. The first boy had turned off the radio and was down on one knee, facing the wall, putting tools into a wooden crate. Diana solidified directly behind him. He had that utterly delicious smell that only younger people had, rich and delicate at the same time, and her mouth was watering. There was no reason to hesitate and certainly no reason to let him see her. She stepped up behind him, put her hand over his mouth, yanked his head back and clamped onto his neck. His arms waved wildly and when she *opened,* he squealed, but within seconds his muscles had gone limp, stopping his struggles. All he could do was emit gasping whimpers in blind panic. She blanked out his memory then, so he would lose consciousness, and drank past the first signal, and the second one, because it felt too wonderful to stop. She really couldn't let herself go so long without drinking.

She finally forced herself to *close* and let the boy down to the ground. When she looked at his face, a shock ran over her, and she froze motionless. He was younger than she'd estimated—not more than thirteen, tall and gangly for his age. She'd assumed the boys were high school students. His face was dead white and clammy. She'd drunk too much.

She stared down at him, her mind unbearably clear and lucid for the first time in weeks. *Is this what I've come down to? Now I'm attacking children? I have become a monster.* She stood there, too appalled at herself to move, until the boys' words came back to her mind and she realized that she either had to clear out before his parents returned, or be caught. It was far too cold to leave the boy in the barn unconscious, especially if he was in shock. She hauled him up onto her shoulder, legs and arms dangling, and walked across the back yard to his house. The door was unlocked, and she took him inside and carefully arranged him on the shabby couch in the living room. She locked the door, dematerialized to leave via the keyhole, and took to the air, traveling crossways to the wind that had turned northeast.

She went on for a long time, her mind in turmoil, and finally stopped in a part of the woods some miles from any roads or trails. It wasn't deep wilderness here. The trees were widely spaced, having been logged over in the past, and she was at the crest of a steep bank. A small stream, not quite frozen over, ran along its foot. Nothing shielded her from the wind on this hilltop. When she solidified, she had to lean forward a little to balance.

What am I doing? This is no solution. I can't be killed, I can't be stopped, I can't stop myself! If I don't drink, I'll lose my mind and people will die. More people will die, she amended grimly. There was no peaceful union with Nature for her. Thomas was right—she didn't belong to the natural world at all any more. She didn't belong anywhere—but she couldn't leave. There was no power that could hinder or destroy her now.

She thought about the story that the visiting boy had told, and clearly believed—Danny, she deduced, had been the one screaming at his father not to shoot Maxie that disastrous night ten days ago. *Eight feet tall, covered with hair, one glaring eye?* Diana looked down at her pitch-blackened skin and her shirt hanging in tatters. Her hair, matted with pitch and full of twigs and bits of bark, blew around her face in snarled dreadlocks. As for what her face itself must look like...no wonder Danny's family had been hysterical. *This is what I want?*

The snow had started falling, but it wasn't falling straight down. Carried on the relentless wind, the tiny hard flakes peppered Diana's face in a stinging blast. Her fingers were stiffening. She'd have to get out of the wind, or they'd freeze, and be useless until she got somewhere warm enough to thaw them out. If she stood here long enough, she might just freeze solid, like Lot's wife turned to the pillar of salt.

The thought struck her like an inspiration. Maybe that would stop her, render her harmless, at least for a little while. Was it possible? Was the storm strong enough to overcome the power of the dragon, even temporarily? Or would she just dematerialize before she froze too far? She turned into the wind, and it seemed that she could hear a hissing, caressing voice: *Stay. Rest. Embrace me, my love. I'll hold you fast. I'll be your conscience. Sleep with me until spring...*

She moved to the northeast side of one of the big trees, the unobstructed force of the wind pinning her against the trunk, leaned back against it and slowly sank to her knees in the old snow that was already a foot deep at its base. She spread her arms out to the wind. She couldn't move her hands at all now. With numbed lips she spoke three words.

"Yes. Show me."

Her consciousness sank down into a state deeper than her daytime sleep. Her body stiffened and froze to the tree, and the snow, more than two feet of it in this single storm, covered her completely, disguising her form, sheltering her from the sunlight, hiding her from the world.

❧ 25 ☙

Spring came slowly to the woods, and last to north-facing slopes. Snowmelt had swollen the little stream to twice its summer breadth. Stones that usually stood dry and clear stared up bewildered at leaves, branches and other flotsam sailing over their submerged heads. The early April sun was flexing its muscles, and the air had softened. Just beginning to open, the leaves in the thickets filled the air with a lemony fragrance. The trees were still bare, but swelling buds made their clean silhouettes look furred. Everything was wet and dripping, and the ground under the leaves and pine needles was soggy mud.

It was the chickadees that awoke her, or at least, finally brought her to the point of opening her eyes. The tree had sheltered her from the direct rays of the sun, and she had mostly thawed out, although she was still stuck to the trunk. She stared blearily down at the rushing stream below and the long angled beams of sunlight, catching the new foliage and making it glow. Bird song filled the air. She was caught between two conflicting feelings. The first was summarized by her thought, *Mother Goddess, it's beautiful here.* The second thought, like the shadow of an ugly building falling across a sunlit garden, sighed, *Why am I still here? Why did I have to wake up?*

After a while, she peeled herself loose from the tree and stood up. Except for being stiff in its thickest parts from the cold, her body felt perfectly fine, and she wasn't particularly hungry. Her mind was tranquil and clear. But the cloud of dejection became denser, like choking smoke. *I'm a blot on this lovely world. I can't go back. Maybe I'll just stay here forever.* She sank back down onto her knees. *I wanted to be immortal? I wish I'd never been born.*

She was quite unprepared for the solid impact to her posterior that came out of nowhere. If she hadn't been in an isolated tract of woods miles away from anything human, she would have identified it as a booted foot, connecting mercilessly and painfully with her gluteus maximus. "Ow!" she howled out loud. She was flung forward over the crest of the slope onto all fours, and her hands sank into mud and sodden leaves up to her elbows. Before she could pull them free, she got another boot in the rear, hard enough to flip her over in a somersault. Then she was rolling down the slope, flailing, too stunned to try to dematerialize, blow after hard painful blow landing unerringly on her rump no matter which way she tumbled.

She landed in the middle of the stream, which was deep enough that she was completely submerged. To her added shock, she could *feel* the coldness of the water, which was about one degree above freezing. She should have been impervious to it, but the icy water jolted her almost as much as it would have done in life. The current grabbed her and dragged her along the stream bed, scraping skin off and banging her hard against boulders, and it *hurt*. She finally got to a wider, shallower section, got her footing, and stood up, choking and spluttering. She splashed frantically out of the stream on the far side, her feet sinking into the soft ground, and then the blows started hitting her again. But no one was in sight, in any direction.

"Ow! Stop it, stop it! Let me alone, damn it!" She grabbed a tree, turned around and planted her backside tightly against it. She could have sworn she heard laughter all around her, but it didn't sound like voices from living throats. It could have been an illusion created by the running stream and the wind.

Then she heard a deep-timbered woman's voice say, in a tone of the utmost exasperation and contempt, "Then *wake up*."

"I am awake, okay? I'm awake! What the hell do you want?"

"We have had *quite* enough of this."

"We?" Diana felt a sudden burst of self-righteous petulance. "What do you know about what I'm going through? Who are you to judge? Where do you get off—" Something invisible, and much stronger than she was, grabbed her by the back of her shirt and the waistband of her pants, marched her forward, bent her double and dunked her head into the stream. She couldn't drown, but as before, the water she shouldn't have felt was so cold it seemed to burn her face to the bones. She desperately kicked backwards and tried to reach the unseen hands, but she couldn't find anything solid. Then she was yanked back upright, gasping, water running off her in gouts.

"How many cold baths will it take to cure you of all that self-pity? We can do this all day," the voice said with cutting scorn.

"Self-pity..." Was that what it was? Immediately, she heard a mocking imitation of her own voice, with the whiniest, most childish inflection imaginable, repeating back to her, "Why am I still here? Why did I have to wake up? I'm a blot on this lovely world. I can't go back. Maybe I'll just stay here forever. I wish I'd never been born." The speakers—for it seemed to be a group of voices in perfect unison, not just one—had difficulty keeping a straight face during this speech, by the sound. The final word dissolved into whoops of derisive laughter. But it wasn't the laughter that made Diana cringe.

Grasping for her last shred of pride, she said, "What do you want? Who *are* you?"

The woman's voice laughed. "Oh, Diana. You know who I am."

Suddenly Diana went rigid, struck by a deeper chill than any stream or snowstorm could have inflicted. "Your Ladyship..." she whispered.

"*Now* you're awake."

Diana swayed on the bank, all the past three years, and especially the last six months, vividly clear in her mind. She didn't see the sequence of events but the entire timeline all at once, in one whole, and she shriveled in shame at her own actions.

"Now, *stop* that," the Lady said impatiently.

"But, but...I *killed* people, your Ladyship!"

"Then make amends, or make peace with yourself. Do you think you're the only person on earth with blood on your hands?"

"I have to hurt things just to exist! If I don't, I'll turn into some kind of monster—" she broke off as the invisible crowd of hecklers erupted into shrieks of glee.

"You make a very unimpressive monster, little ragamuffin." The Lady's amusement was searing. "All living things exist at the expense of others. That's the curse of Middle-earth, the responsibility all of you share. You're no different now than you were before."

"But I'm not a living thing! I'm a fake, a counterfeit, I'm not real!"

"You're not real? Then does it matter if you die?" The Lady's voice had sunk to a soft hiss, seductive and threatening at once. Diana couldn't answer. "Do you wish it to end here, Diana? Shall I end it, are you so hopeless and miserable as that? Is there nothing in this world worth staying here for?"

Diana could feel herself shaking. Her muscles were getting weak, and the light seemed to be dimming around her. If she died now...she'd never see Gregory again. She'd never get a chance to tell Levoissier exactly what she thought of him. Her parents would never know what happened to her. Thomas's property would go to rack and ruin. She'd never see Bread and Roses grow and evolve. She'd never find out what Thomas meant when he said someday, he would repay her... her knees gave way and she sank down, feeling vitality ebbing from her body.

"No! No, please, I don't want to die! Please..." Her strength flowed back in a warm rush, and the world brightened again.

"You are different from humans in one respect. If you want your existence to continue, you'll have to appreciate it. You wanted power, Diana. You were willing to exchange everything you had for it. You need to remember why."

"I didn't want...*personal* power. That was never—"

"There is no other kind."

"But what can I do, all alone? Even Thomas said, from the very beginning, what can one man do, what can anyone do isolated from the world—"

"You'll have to find those answers. Do you think your destiny has nothing to do with anything else but you? For twenty years, you've dreamed of changing the world. Now the world is about to change, in ways you've never imagined. There will be violence. There will be blood. But this is what you've been waiting for. Stop wasting your time, Diana. You have the gifts you asked for. Start using them."

Slowly Diana pushed her sopping hair back from her face, at last finding the balance point she had been seeking without even knowing it. That tranquility she had felt for the first few hours after she had awakened in September—*that* was her natural state. To save herself from becoming a monster, she would have to nurture that serenity in herself. Maybe that was how Thomas had done it. He couldn't teach her that because he hadn't even been aware of it himself.

"You see? It's not so hard, is it?"

Diana just nodded. "I guess it's time for me to go home."

"Long past, I would say. The woods will carry on perfectly well without you. Go back to your house and make yourself presentable. Spirits of gum turpentine will take that pitch off."

"Thank you for the tip. May I wait until sunset?"

"You may, but no longer."

Something shifted, and Diana suddenly realized that she was alone in the woods. The Teg may have withdrawn, but she knew they were watching, and always would be.

But, no—she wasn't alone. She was surrounded by living things, trees sucking up the moisture of the melting snow as their sap flowed to the tips of every budding branch, hundreds of thousands of birds, small animals in every hole and cranny, everything she could see or touch was bursting with life. She'd missed the Equinox, but Beltene was coming, and it was time to let her regrets and guilt burn away for good, *time to let bygones be bygones,* as Moira had said. Suddenly she felt impatient for darkness to fall so she could get moving. She wanted to check her mail, find a radio, buy a newspaper. *I will build an athanor and set up an alchemy lab,* she thought. *And I'll get in touch with the Board of Bread and Roses, maybe resume an advisory position...the world is changing? What can that mean?* She raised her head and sniffed deeply, as if that would give her a clue. The stone house, Thomas' gift to her, would need a lot of cleaning when she got back. She could hardly wait.

Acknowledgments

The Longer the Fall has been slowly evolving for fifteen years. Over that stretch of time, many people contributed invaluable assistance, feedback, support, information and encouragement. I'd particularly like to thank the members of Vampyres List, without whom this story would never have been written. I owe them a huge debt for their inspiration, feedback, and the self-esteem boost they gave me by voting my rough draft Best Long Fiction posted to the list in 1995. I virtually display my virtual Golden Fang Award with pride.

I'm deeply appreciative to the dozens of people on the West Penobscot Bay of Maine who assisted me in my research, in person and over the phone. Many thanks to The Camden-Rockport-Lincolnville Chamber of Commerce, the Owl and Turtle Bookshop, the Town Clerks of Lincolnville, Camden and Rockport, the First Universalist Church of Rockland, and Eaton's in Camden and the Lobster Pound Restaurant, both of whom showed me photos of their buildings as they existed in the 1950s. Special thanks to Heather Bilodeau, Archives Director of the Walsh History Center in the Camden Public Library, who called me back long distance to answer my questions.

My love and gratitude goes out to my family, including my mom, who passed away in 2006, and my dad, who both kept on encouraging me to write and put up with a semi-sane and often frustrated and raving creative spirit. I'm indebted to my sister and brother-in-law for reading and critiquing the galleys of my books, offering insightful feedback and giving me their unflagging support.

Warmest thanks as well to my friends and colleagues in the writing community, online and off, including the members of Broad Universe and New England Horror Writers.

Finally, I'm deeply grateful to all the fans and readers of The Vampires of New England Series, and all the friendly people who come to my public readings and charitably listen to works in various stages of development performed aloud. I've grown from a dreamer to a storyteller and author because of all of you. I hope I never let you down.

Inanna Arthen
January, 2010

More Books by Inanna Arthen...

The Vampires of New England Series, Book 1
Mortal Touch
All I need to do is touch you...

Regan Calloway got more notoriety than she could handle seven years ago when she used her gift of psychic touch to help catch a brutal child murderer. When a string of bizarre assaults strikes the mill town of Sheridan, Massachusetts, Dr. Hiram Clauson persuades Regan to use her abilities to help him interview the victims. As the investigations take an unsettling turn, Regan's lifelong friend, Veronica Standish, begs her to try to find out more about a new man in town, Jonathan Vaughn.

Regan and Jonathan's first meeting triggers an escalating series of disasters, for Jonathan Vaughn is one of the rare and scattered group of men and women known as vampires only to those few people whom they trust. In the chaos that follows, Regan struggles to hold on to everything she thought she could never bear to lose. As friends and associates turn into ruthless adversaries, and allies appear from unexpected places, Regan is forced to make choices she never dreamed she would have to face.

Paperback, $16.95	ISBN: 978-0-9793028-0-0
Hardcover, $28.99	ISBN: 978-0-9793028-3-1

Print editions available from By Light Unseen Media, Amazon.com, or your favorite bookstore. E-book editions available for the Amazon Kindle and multiple formats via Smashwords and Scribd.

and coming in 2011...

The Vampires of New England Series, Book 3
All the Shadows of the Rainbow

http://vampiresofnewengland.com